Don't miss th rted

THE DRAGONS
OF DORCASTLE

PILLARS OF REALITY ❖ BOOK 1

JACK
CAMPBELL

FOR NEWS ABOUT JABBERWOCKY BOOKS AND AUTHORS

6

Job Number: 5

ISBN Number: 9781625675064

Due Date: Tue 27. October 2020

PO#: 26549

Title: Explorer of the Endless Sea (9781625675064)

Type: POD

Qty: 21

Trim Size: 5.5 8.5

Paper Stock: 50# Natural

Cover Stock:

BW Pages: 310

Color Pages: 0

Laminate: NONE

Finishing: Perfect Bound

Number of Pages: 310

Spine Bulk Fraction: 0.625

Production Notes:

N/A

Job Number: 5

ISBN Number: 9781625675064

Due Date: Tue 27, October 2020

PO#: 26549

Title: Explorer of the Endless Sea (9781625675064)

Type: POD

Qty: 21

Paper Stock: 50# Natural

BW Pages: 310

Laminate: NONE

Number of Pages: 310

Spine Bulk Fraction: 0.625

Production Notes:

N/A

Trim Size: 5.5 8.5

Cover Stock:

Color Pages: 0

Finishing: Perfect Bound

EXPLORER OF THE ENDLESS SEA

PRAISE FOR THE PILLARS OF REALITY SERIES

"Campbell has created an interesting world… [he] has created his characters in such a meticulous way, I could not help but develop my own feelings for both of them. I have already gotten the second book and will be listening with anticipation."

—Audio Book Reviewer

"I loved *The Hidden Masters of Marandur*…The intense battle and action scenes are one of the places where Campbell's writing really shines. There are a lot of urban and epic fantasy novels that make me cringe when I read their battles, but Campbell's years of military experience help him write realistic battles."

—All Things Urban Fantasy

"I highly recommend this to fantasy lovers, especially if you enjoy reading about young protagonists coming into their own and fighting against a stronger force than themselves. The world building has been strengthened even further giving the reader more history. Along with the characters flight from their pursuers and search for knowledge allowing us to see more of the continent the pace is constant and had me finding excuses to continue the book."

—Not Yet Read

"*The Dragons of Dorcastle*… is the perfect mix of steampunk and fantasy… it has set the bar to high."

—The Arched Doorway

"Quite a bit of fun and I really enjoyed it… An excellent sequel and well worth the read!"

—Game Industry

"The Pillars of Reality series continues in *The Assassins of Altis* to be a great action filled adventure… So many exciting things happen that I can hardly wait for the next book to be released."

—Not Yet Read

"The Pillars of Reality is a series that gets better and better with each new book… *The Assassins of Altis* is a great addition to a great series and one I recommend to fantasy fans, especially if you like your fantasy with a touch of sci-fi."

—Bookaholic Cat

"Seriously, get this book (and the first two). This one went straight to my favorites shelf."

—Reanne Reads

"[Jack Campbell] took my expectations and completely blew them out of the water, proving yet again that he can seamlessly combine steampunk and epic fantasy into a truly fantastic story… I am looking forward to seeing just where Campbell goes with the story next, I'm not sure how I'm going to manage the wait for the next book in the series."

—The Arched Doorway

"When my audiobook was delivered around midnight, I sat down and told myself I would listen for an hour or so before I went to sleep. I finished it in almost 12 straight hours, I don't think I've ever listened to an audiobook like that before. I can say with complete honesty that *The Servants of The Storm* by Jack Campbell is one of the best books I've ever had the pleasure to listen to."

—Arched Doorway

PRAISE FOR THE LOST FLEET SERIES

"It's the thrilling saga of a nearly-crushed force battling its way home from deep within enemy territory, laced with deadpan satire about modern warfare and neoliberal economics. Like Xenophon's Anabasis – with spaceships."

—The Guardian (UK)

"Black Jack is an excellent character, and this series is the best military SF I've read in some time."

—Wired Magazine

"If you're a fan of character, action, and conflict in a Military SF setting, you would probably be more than pleased by Campbell's offering."

—Tor.com

"...a fun, quick read, full of action, compelling characters, and deeper issues. Exactly the type of story which attracts readers to military SF in the first place."

—SF Signal

"Rousing military-SF action... it should please many fans of old-fashioned hard SF. And it may be a good starting point for media SF fans looking to expand their SF reading beyond tie-in novels."

—SciFi.com

"Fascinating stuff... this is military SF where the military and SF parts are both done right."

—SFX Magazine

EXPLORER OF THE ENDLESS SEA

EMPRESS OF THE ENDLESS SEA
BOOK II

JACK CAMPBELL

JABberwocky Literary Agency, Inc.

To
Selena "The Dread Pirate" Rosen, a great writer,
and perhaps the kindest person I've ever known.

For S, as always

ACKNOWLEDGMENTS

I remain indebted to my agents, Joshua Bilmes and Eddie Schneider, for their long standing support, ever-inspired suggestions and assistance, as well as to Susan Velazquez, Adriana Funke, and Lisa Rodgers for their work on foreign sales and print editions. Many thanks to Betsy Mitchell for her excellent editing. Thanks also to Catherine Asaro, Robert Chase, Kelly Dwyer, Carolyn Ives Gilman, J.G. (Huck) Huckenpohler, Simcha Kuritzky, Michael LaViolette, Aly Parsons, Bud Sparhawk, Mary G. Thompson, and Constance A. Warner for their suggestions, comments and recommendations. And, of course, thank you to Steve Feldberg for his strong support.

ACKNOWLEDGMENTS

CHAPTER ONE

*E*very sail set, the *Sun Queen* rolled over the top of a vast swell and plunged into the trough beyond, an explosion of white spray erupting as her bow cleaved the dark waters of the Sea of Bakre. Jules of Landfall, high on the mainmast, grasped a stay line, hearing the wind singing in the rigging and feeling the tension in the rope as if the *Queen* were a racehorse trembling with the excitement of the chase. Ships might be made of wood and metal and rope, she thought, but they were nonetheless living things, and like all living things they craved the lack of confinement that only the open sea could offer. And with the *Queen* running on a broad reach with a brisk breeze coming from aft and off her port quarter, she had sea room to spare and the wind to urge her on.

Jules raised one hand to shield her eyes as she gazed at another ship visible a ways to starboard and ahead of the *Sun Queen*. From this high up on the mainmast, she had a good view of the other ship, its hull and masts easily visible as the distance between the two ships continued to shrink. The *Queen's* prey this day had begun running once catching sight of the other ship, but he wasn't as fast and he had the deadly rocks of the southern coast on his other side, preventing him from fleeing that way.

Trapped.

She felt a moment of sympathy for the captain and the crew of the other ship, penned in by the savage reefs of the south to one side and the oncoming danger of a pirate ship on the other. Jules knew how it felt to be trapped, to be caged. She'd grown up in a harsh Legion Orphanage, a ward of the Emperor whose generosity toward the orphans of those who'd died in his service was grudging and minimal. She'd escaped the walls surrounding the orphanage by earning a chance at an officer's commission in the Emperor's legions, only to learn that the Imperial officer corps was another prison whose cells were formed of rules and regulations and demands, as well as social expectations that the spawn of an orphanage could never meet.

The whole world of Dematr was a cage, of course. The iron hand of the Emperor ruled over the entire area to the east of the great land-locked sea, forbidding cliffs walled off much of the coasts to the north and south, and the land to the west, according to every map, was a nightmare of unexplored, hidden reefs with desert wastelands beyond. And ruling over the Emperor and every other common man and woman were the Mechanics Guild and the Mage Guild, the two Great Guilds who controlled the lives of every common person, and did what they wanted to anyone. The Great Guilds weren't above the law; they *were* the law.

And then the final, biggest trap of all. The prophecy spoken by a Mage as he stared at her. *The day will come when a daughter of your line will unite Mechanics, Mages, and the common folk to overthrow the Great Guilds and free the world.* The prophecy that had tried to turn her into nothing but a vessel for some future outcome, robbed of any meaning regarding who she was.

But also a way out of those cages someday—for everyone who might be alive when the prophecy came to pass. But not for her. So rather than wait for an event likely to occur long after she was gone, Jules had resolved to start breaking out of some of the cages. Some of those who had already tried to stop her had not lived long enough to regret their mistake.

Since the prophecy, she'd come to realize that the people of Dematr accepted their cages as facts of life. Things had always been like, and always would be. But if the prophecy was true (and Mage prophecies were supposedly always true) things would change. But that would require men and women who believed they could break out of their cages, who were willing to do things no one else had ever done.

Jules felt the wind at her back and the rolling of the ship, smelled the salt-laden air, and knew no cage could ever hold her. Not while the sea was open to her. Unforgiving though the sea might be, jealous of her secrets and eager to punish those who took her too lightly, her waters also offered the only freedom to be found on this world.

Turning her head to look back to the west, Jules felt a familiar urge, a desire to seek out those uncharted and allegedly deadly waters, to see what really lay there.

Someday.

Because someone would have to show the world that every cage could be broken. And, from the looks of things, that someone would have to be her.

She glanced upward before heading down the rigging, seeing her new banner flapping in the wind. Two crossed swords, one a straight Imperial blade and the other a curved pirate's cutlass. The two halves of her, united into a single outward force even as they struggled for balance inside.

Stepping off the ratline she'd balanced on, Jules hand-over-handed down a shroud to the deck, her calloused hands barely noticing the stings of the hemp fibers sticking out of the rope. She dropped the last lance to the deck, the Imperial officer boots she still wore thumping onto the wooden planks. Running up the short ladder onto the quarterdeck, Jules gestured toward the other ship. "I didn't see anyone on deck except for the sailor at the helm. He's holding course and keeping all sail on."

"He doesn't have much choice," First Mate Ang replied. Large, with a sturdiness that could be reassuring to friends and intimidating to everyone else, he didn't seem pleased by what should be good news.

Jules nodded to the sailor at the helm. "Keep her on this heading." Sound calm, she reminded herself. Give clear orders. Don't let excitement or worry mess with your head. Pay attention to the mood of your own people. Lessons for an Imperial officer that had proven to be useful to a pirate captain.

Turning to Ang, she gave him a questioning look. "What's the matter?"

Ang made a face that shifted through a few expressions before settling into a frown. "Cap'n, it just seems too easy. Most of the Emperor's ships are trying to catch you, and the Mechanics and the Mages are trying to kill you. Nothing should be easy."

"He's right there," Liv agreed. The older woman leaned on the starboard rail of the quarterdeck, looking toward their quarry. "There're no other masts visible?"

"No," Jules said. "I scanned the whole horizon. If he has hidden help, they're well beyond him."

"Not to his starboard. They'd be grazing the reefs there."

"They'd be *in* the reefs," Ang said. "He's steering closer to shore than I'd be comfortable with in these waters."

"We are chasing him," Jules said, leaning on the railing beside Liv.

"Ripping his hull open on those rocks wouldn't help him get away," Ang said. "He's too close to them."

"Maybe there's a stupid owner aboard demanding it," Liv said, frowning as well. "Or maybe their captain knows these waters well enough to think he can dare waters like that, maybe even lure us onto one of the reefs?"

"Maybe," Jules said. She glanced up at the sails, all drawing well. Unless the wind shifted, there'd be no need to adjust the sails. But she worried over Ang's concerns. Ang had been at sea a lot longer than she had. His instincts were worth listening to.

She gazed toward the fleeing ship again, asking herself a question that had grown familiar in the last few months. What would Mak do? The *Sun Queen*'s former captain had been the only authority figure Jules had met in her life who had tried to teach her instead of trying to break her. But he'd had far too short a time to work with her, and at times like this Jules felt the ache of how much she still had to learn. The crew of the *Sun Queen* had voted her captain despite her being only twenty-one years of age, but more than once Jules had wished she had as much confidence in herself as her crew did. "Ang, Liv, what do you think Captain Mak would be thinking right now?"

"Mak?" Liv shook her head. "You got to think for yourself, Captain, not worry about what Mak would've done."

"She's right to ask," Ang protested. "Mak could out-sail anybody, and he could smell trouble a hundred lances off. I'm thinking now of what he used to say when something looked easy. If it looks easy, he'd tell me, that likely means there's something you don't know about it."

"That's no Imperial galley," Liv said. "And there's no help lurking nearby or we'd see it. He's just a cargo ship, and by the way he's riding he's got a good load aboard. We need the money that cargo'll bring," she added meaningfully.

Jules nodded, her eyes on the waves where they washed against the other ship's hull. Heavily laden, probably with salt out of the Imperial mines. With the Emperor's warships scouring the waters off the Imperial coast for any sign of Jules, it had seemed prudent to seek safer waters for a while. But there were lean pickings this far west, so the *Sun Queen* hadn't found many ships to prey on in recent days. Even the pirate of the prophecy had to worry about such mundane things as having enough money to keep the ship in repair, buy food and water and rum, and keep the crew happy. "But he's out here alone. No Imperial warships in sight even though they've been prowling this coast looking for us. What are we not seeing? I think we need to get closer and find out."

"How much closer?" Ang said.

"We're upwind of him, and we're faster. If we have to open the distance quickly, we can do that. We'll get close enough to look him over, see if there're any signs of a trap, before we go alongside. I got enough of a look at his deck to be sure he doesn't have a ballista mounted, so he can't hurt us if we're out of crossbow range." She'd trained on crossbows under the far from gentle guidance of Imperial centurions, and knew how far they could fire and have a good chance of a hit. "Fifty lances. No hand-held crossbow will have decent accuracy at that range. Take us in to about fifty lances from him and hold us there."

Ang nodded. "Aye, Cap'n."

"Liv," Jules said, "get the boarding party armed."

As Liv ran off to see to the task of arming most of the crew, Jules went back down the ladder and into the stern cabin. The captain's cabin. She still thought of it as Mak's, but it belonged to her now.

She didn't require much preparation, strapping on a belt from which a cutlass hung on one hip. On the other hip was an oddly-shaped leather sheath for a weapon the Mechanics called a revolver. She drew out the strange weapon, looking at it and wondering again at how it could have been made. The Mechanics guarded the secrets of their technology with deadly and highly efficient means, leaving even smiths among the commons unable to guess the methods by which the metal of the revolver had been made and shaped.

"You going to carry that?" Liv asked from the doorway.

"I need it," Jules said. "You never know when I might run into another Mage." She settled the weapon carefully back into the holster.

"If you run into any Mechanics, they'll kill you just for having that. How many commons do you think have ever held one of those? Let alone shot one?"

"I might be the first," Jules said. "The Mechanics thought they'd use me to kill Mages."

"They were right," Liv said. "I don't know how many other commons have ever killed a Mage. Maybe none."

"Then it's about time someone started." Jules felt in her pocket, pulling out the two objects kept safe in there. "Do you know about these? The Mechanics call them cartridges. They're what the revolver shoots, like the bolts for a crossbow. But a cartridge can only be used once, then it's empty and useless."

"How many of them have you got?"

"Eight left of the eleven I had after the Mechanics gave me more that last time."

Liv shook her head. "That'd be the time they realized that they hadn't been actually using you, that you'd been using them?"

Jules' grin at the memory felt tense. "Good thing I didn't snap and speak my mind until after they'd given me more cartridges. But... all's well, right? I got away after."

"With Mechanics shooting and a Mage dragon breathing down your neck," Liv scoffed. "They say nobody else has ever been that close to a dragon's jaws and lived to tell of it."

"But I did live, didn't I?" Looking down at the weapon again, Jules glanced at Liv. "I should teach you and Ang how to use this. Just in case something happens to me."

"*No*," Liv said. "I'll not touch that thing. Not just because the Mechanics Guild demands the death of any common who meddles with their devices—and why should I invite as much attention from them as you have to deal with—but because I have no use for something that kills by means I don't understand. It could do me in, couldn't it?"

"I don't think so," Jules said. "The Mechanics told me if I tried to use it against one of them it would explode and kill me." She raised the weapon, smiling again. "Someday I'm going to try it anyway."

"Save it for Mages," Liv said. "Jules, sometimes you scare even me."

Jules shrugged and put the revolver back into the sheath the Mechanics called a holster. "Maybe you don't need a Mechanic weapon to kill Mages. Liv, I killed two Mages on this ship, and I did it using a cutlass."

"Yeah, *you* could do that. But... Jules, you're different than the rest of us."

"Am I?"

Liv sighed and raised her eyes upward like an aggravated parent. "I know you don't like being reminded of the prophecy—"

"Do you think I ever forget it? For even a moment?" Jules turned her head to look through the cabin's small stern windows at the sea, though what she saw wasn't the restless waters but a memory seared into her mind. "I can still see as clear as day the eyes of that Mage as he stared at me. Ever since then my life hasn't belonged to me."

"And you've been so careful with it," Liv grumbled sarcastically. "You shouldn't be running any risks. Not until—"

"That's enough of that, Liv." Jules grasped the dagger in a sheath at the small of her back, checking to be sure it could be drawn easily. "I won't spend my life in hiding. I'm going to do things that that daughter of my line will hear about and know she has to match, whenever she shows up. Mak thought it might be hundreds of years."

"You'd better hope that daughter doesn't inherit your stubbornness," Liv said.

"She'll probably need it." Jules kept her eyes on the waves behind the *Sun Queen*, feeling the now-familiar frustration. "How can anyone ever do that? Mechanics and Mages hate each other, and to them commons like you and me might as well be cattle or horses. But this daughter of my line is going to unite some of them, get them to work together, to free everyone? It's impossible."

"If a Mage prophesized it, it has to come true," Liv insisted. "That's why the Mages, and the Mechanics, want you dead before you start that line. And that's why for the first time the commons have hope."

"And that's why half the men in the world seem to think they'd be doing me a great favor by getting me pregnant so they could claim credit for the things that daughter of my line will do," Jules said.

"If you keep slitting the throats of those that proposition you, they may start being a little less eager to ask."

Jules laughed. "There's that to hope for! I didn't have nearly as many men bothering me for a while after I knifed that jerk Vlad. Let's go see if we're close enough to give that other ship a good look over."

Out on deck again, Jules paused to gauge the distance, nodding in approval. "I'm going up again!" she called to Ang, and grabbed the rigging to swing herself up onto the lowest ratlines.

She went all the way up to the highest top, where one of the crew was stationed to keep watch. "See anyone else, Kyl?"

Kyl shook his head. "Maybe a masthead way off to port, but barely showing. That way."

Jules gazed in the direction Kyl indicated, studying the horizon where a tiny dot might or might not be appearing and vanishing as the Sun Queen rolled and pitched to the motion of the sea. "Yeah. Keep an eye out."

One foot on the top, one hand grasping a stay line, Jules leaned out to starboard, gazing down toward the ship they were pursuing. Both ships were heading east, the nearby coast to the south of them, open water ahead for many thousands of lances, as well as to the north and back to the west. But with the *Sun Queen* upwind of her prey the other ship couldn't break north or come about to try tacking west. East was the only path open to him, and as the *Sun Queen* closed in he wouldn't be able to avoid capture much longer.

In contrast to the crowded deck of the *Sun Queen*, the only sailor visible on the other ship was the one at the helm, both arms spread to grasp the wheel, his or her face averted from the *Sun Queen*, perhaps gazing at the water to the starboard of the other ship.

Jules gasped as she raised her own gaze to those waters. Just on the other side of that ship, she saw patches of water of varying shades, eddies and currents that spoke of sudden shallows, and here and there the flash of white spray against the jagged fangs of some reefs that extended above the water. "Blazes, he's close."

Kyl nodded. "That scared of us, you think?"

"Have you seen any others on deck or in the rigging?"

"No, Captain. Just that one."

"Maybe some sort of illness?" Jules wondered. "Is the rest of the crew sick or dead? But his sails are all set and trimmed. One sailor couldn't do all that." She leaned out a little more, trying to see all of the deck of the other ship. A strip of the deck concealed behind the bulkhead still escaped her gaze, but not many could be hiding there and still be unseen from this angle. Raising her eyes, Jules looked past the other ship, seeing a few thousand lances to the south the light brown of patches of land and the gray-green of the salt marshes beyond. Nothing could be seen besides that, though, not a surprise on a stretch of land known as the Bleak Coast. "Keep an eye out for anyone else coming this way," she reminded Kyl, before once again hand-over-handing her way down to the deck.

"He's close enough to those reefs to his starboard to shave on them," Jules told Ang. "But there's nobody else visible above deck."

"He could have fifty legionaries ready below decks," Ang pointed out.

"The hatches are battened down. Legionaries, or anyone else, would have to come up the ladders one by one." An odd situation, but not one that posed any obvious danger. And breaking off the pursuit, leaving the other ship to escape, would baffle her own crew and perhaps leave them questioning her nerve. Still, an odd situation.

Most of the *Sun Queen*'s crew were at this moment on the main deck, lining the rail facing the other ship, weapons in their hands and dreams of profit in their heads. Jules blew out an exasperated breath and made a decision. "Ang, bring us in to about five lances off his side so I can hail him. Liv, get the crossbows loaded and tell those carrying them to be prepared to shoot at anyone who pops up over that bulwark."

She walked to stand by the quarterdeck railing facing the other ship as Ang directed the helm to bring the *Sun Queen* closer to her prey, holding her balance easily by shifting her weight on both legs as the deck tilted in response to the push of the rudder. The sailor at the helm spun the wheel again, steadying out on a parallel course only about five lances away from the other ship. After overtaking the other craft, the *Sun Queen* was now almost even with it, so that Jules was looking across the gap at the sailor at the helm, who still had his gaze firmly fixed in the other direction. Cupping her hands around her mouth, Jules bellowed across the remaining distance. "Ahoy the other ship! Surrender yourself and no one will be harmed, on the word of Captain Jules of Landfall."

The helmsman didn't react at all.

A rogue wave churned up by the nearby reefs and the water trapped between the hulls of the two ships slapped the side of the *Sun Queen*, spray flying to wet one side of Jules' shirt and pants as she leaned out, further aggravating her.

"Ahoy!" Jules called again. "My patience is limited and you're out of sea room! Surrender now or bear the consequences!" To emphasize her words, she drew her cutlass and brandished it over her head.

The reaction from the other ship shocked her as the sailor at the helm suddenly twisted his body to put the rudder over. A command to Ang to swing the *Sun Queen* away to avoid a collision froze on her lips as Jules realized the other ship had turned not toward the *Queen* in an attempt to ram but toward shore, into the reefs.

"He's out of his mind!" Ang shouted.

"Hold our course!" Jules called back, wondering how much longer it would be before the inevitable happened, staring as the other ship opened the distance between them as it wove a desperate path toward land between the shoal waters and reefs.

"He's trying to reach the shore!" Liv called. At the same time the fleeing ship heeled over as one side scraped a series of rocks rising like jagged teeth just above the surface, before lurching free to stagger onward.

"He won't make it," Ang said.

The merchant ship, heavily laden, navigated the deadly underwater maze of obstacles like an old ox trying to avoid stepping into rabbit holes. "Whoever's at the helm knows what they're doing," Jules said. "How much farther do you think he'll get?"

"He shouldn't have gotten that far," Ang said.

The other ship tried to turn hard, the bow coming around too slowly and the hull continuing forward. The next moment the ship shuddered as it struck a submerged reef, the hull rising out of the water as it ran up on the rocks. Jerked to a sudden halt, with the wind still pushing the sails, the mainmast shattered. Jules winced as the sound of the wooden mast snapping carried clearly across the water, followed by a discordant series of sharp notes as rigging and stay lines parted under the strain. The mainmast toppled forward, slamming into the foremast in a welter of tortured wood and ripping canvas, bringing down the foremast as well in a tangle of splintered lumber, lines, and torn sails falling across the bow of the doomed ship.

Perhaps twenty lances distant now, the *Sun Queen* sailed past the wreck, her crew stunned into momentary silence.

Ang broke the hushed silence. "If we launch our boats we might be able to salvage some of the cargo. And take off any survivors."

Jules shook herself out of her shock at the watching the death of the other ship. "Good idea. Bring her about and see how close we can safely get before we launch the boats."

"Aye, Cap'n." Ang raised his voice to a shout. "On deck! Let go the braces! Slack windward sails and braces! Haul lee braces and sails! Helm, bring her about to port!"

The sailors who'd been gathered at the railing in anticipation of boarding the other ship raced to grab the lines, slacking one side and hauling in on the other side so the sails would be set to tack against the wind as the *Sun Queen* swung about to where the wreck of their prey rested on the reef. The ship's speed dropped off sharply as the wind beat against the front of the sails before the *Queen* settled onto the new tack.

"Ready the boats," Jules ordered, her eyes on the deadly waters between the *Sun Queen* and the wreck.

Liv yelled up to the quarterdeck. "I can't see anyone on that ship! Where the blazes are they?"

Jules frowned, studying the wreck where it shuddered as waves slapped into it. Those waves would in time pound the wreck to splinters. The crew should be scurrying about, trying to launch their own boats. But no one could be seen moving on the other ship, even the sailor at the helm no longer visible.

"Leave it," Ang advised, his face shadowed with worry. "There's something wrong about that ship."

"I won't argue that," Jules said. The need to try to salvage some of the cargo and save any members of the wrecked crew warred with her concern at the oddness of the situation.

Her next words died unspoken as Jules saw three figures rise into sight on the wreck from where they had been concealed behind the upper bulwark of the other ship.

Not sailors.

Mages.

Male or female couldn't be told since the figures' Mage robes concealed their shapes and the hoods of the robes their heads and faces. But there was no mistaking what they were.

If a Mage can see you, they can kill you, the old saying went.

She couldn't see the eyes of any of the Mages, but Jules could feel their gazes on her. Feel it as if the eyes of the Mages were daggers already pressing at her throat.

Her thoughts flew in a whirl that felt slow but took only seconds. The distance was too great to have any chance of hitting any of the Mages with a shot from the revolver, even if she could get it out in time. Her crew, unnerved by the sudden appearance of three Mages, stood frozen, those who still held crossbows as unmoving as the others. That's what commons did upon sight of a Mage. Run if you could, and if you couldn't flee then freeze and hope the Mage would take no notice of you. It was widely known, after all, that no common weapon like a crossbow could kill a Mage. Trying would only bring their wrath upon you.

"Ang!" Jules shouted. "Hard to starboard!" Her cutlass still in one hand swung up in an instinctive gesture, as if that weapon's blade could parry a Mage's spell the way it could the slash of a sword.

A brilliant flash of light filled her eyes, and her thoughts vanished into darkness.

CHAPTER TWO

"Jules! Jules! Captain!"

Faces loomed over her, close and frightened. Jules struggled to focus on them. "What the blazes?" she tried to say, but the words came out in a hoarse whisper.

Liv bent very close, her eyes staring into Jules'. "Can you think? Are you all right?"

"I…" Jules clenched her teeth as she suddenly became aware of a stripe of pain running down her body, as if someone had carefully poured acid along her arm, down her torso, and down one leg to her foot. At the same time, she realized she could smell smoke. "What's burning?" she managed to gasp despite the pain.

"You are." Liv stepped back, and someone splashed a bucket of seawater over Jules.

Jules fought back a scream as the cold salt water hit the burn.

Healer Keli came into her view, eyeing her. "Give her another, and get me some rum."

By the time Jules got her eyes clear of the stinging salt water, Keli was leaning over her with a bottle. "Have a drink."

She swallowed, the rum burning its way down her throat. Keli knelt and carefully poured a stream of the liquor down her body. Jules raised her head enough to see a strange pattern running down her arm and side, as if the outline of a many-branched fern had been seared into her flesh. The shirt on that side, and her pants as well, were ripped as if something had torn through them from the inside. "What the blazes happened?" she got out between clenched teeth as the burns blazed in response to the alcohol.

"It was lightning," Liv said. "They say Mages can call it down from the sky, but it seemed to me it came straight from that other ship and hit you. We heard the crash of thunder at the same moment it struck. You went flying and landed on your back in a puff of white smoke."

"What happened to my clothes?"

"No idea, girl. They were like that when you hit the deck. The lightning must've caused it."

"Look at this," another sailor, Marta, spoke up. "Your cutlass."

Jules felt a strange crawling in her gut as she stared at the warped and blackened metal of the cutlass blade.

"Back where I grew up," Marta said, "they put metal posts on top of buildings to draw the lightning away from the wood. Looks like your cutlass did the same."

Jules squinted at her arm, seeing that the line of fern-like patterns ran from where her hand had gripped the cutlass, the marks on her resembling a thick trunk about two of her fingers wide, the strange fern marks branching out just as if they were growing from that main scar. "The lightning went down my side instead of into me?"

"You're protected," Liv said.

To her own surprise, Jules managed a derisive snort at the words. "That side of me was wet with spray. My clothes that ripped open were wet. Maybe that made a difference." She tried to struggle to her feet, but Keli held her down long enough to gaze into her eyes again.

"She seems to be all right," he finally said.

"*You* won't be if you don't get your paws off me!" Jules growled, shoving aside the healer's hand.

"Yeah, she's fine," Liv commented.

Jules made it to her feet, seeing that the *Sun Queen* was on a beam reach now, the wind from the east coming straight on against her port side as the ship sailed nearly due north away from the coast and the Mage-haunted wreck. She staggered to the stern rail, glaring at the small shape that was all that could be seen of the wreck from this distance. The heat of her burns faded into nothing and cold filled her as she thought of getting revenge on those Mages.

"Leave it," Ang said, standing beside her. "They're marooned on the Bleak Coast. Let thirst and hunger and the sun's heat be their end, if such things can harm Mages."

"What about the crew of that ship?" Healer Keli asked. "They're marooned as well, and we all know they were forced to serve the Mages in this."

"They were putting their boat in the water after we turned away," Ang said. He raised his head and called to the lookout far above. "Kyle! Did they get their boat in the water?"

The answer came down faintly. "Aye! I saw four sailors get in, and then the three Mages."

Jules stared toward the wreck before yelling upwards. "Kyle! Are you certain all three Mages got into the boat?"

"Aye, Captain. It came out into clear water, and they hoisted a sail and headed east. I can just make it out still."

"The rats left the sinking ship," Liv muttered. "Heading back to Landfall, no doubt."

"Were there only four sailors aboard that ship?" Jules asked.

"Four couldn't have handled a ship that big," Ang said.

"Why'd the Mages just leave?" Keli said. "And not chase us in that boat?"

"A longboat couldn't have caught us," Ang said, then frowned. "Unless Mages can make a boat move very swiftly, as Mechanics can."

"Yes," Keli said. "And only the one attack, against the captain."

"Ask a Mage," Liv said. "Why do they do anything?"

Jules inhaled sharply. "They think they killed me."

Keli thought about that, and nodded. "Like as not. That lightning should've done it, too. I never heard of anyone surviving a Mage attack like that. I met a healer once who talked about flowers left over from lightning striking a body. What's on you must be what he meant."

"Mages couldn't even kill the Captain with lightning," Gord said, sounding half-proud and half-amazed.

The silence that followed his words aggravated Jules as much as the pain of her injuries. "Lay off that nonsense. That lightning should've done more damage, but it didn't. It was weak."

"Why would it be weak?" Ang asked doubtfully.

"Ask a Mage!" Jules looked toward the wreck again. "As soon as we're certain that boat the Mages took can't see us, we're coming about again. If there's anyone left on that ship, they need rescuing."

This time no one argued.

"I need to get a new shirt and pants," Jules said, feeling the shredded fabric flap against her side and causing new flares of pain.

* * *

The sun had sunk far in the afternoon sky by the time the *Sun Queen* made it back to the vicinity of the crippled ship. Ang adjusted the sails so the ship would drift slowly past the wreck while Liv supervised getting the longboat into the water.

But when Jules moved to climb down into the boat, Liv stopped her with a stubborn expression. "I know appealing to your sense of self-preservation would be a waste of time, so I'll mention what anyone else would've thought of before this. Those Mages think you're dead, Jules. They'll tell their Guild that, and all the Mages will stop hunting you until they learn you're still alive. So wouldn't it be wise for the sake of this ship and her crew, as well as your own life, to keep the Mages in the dark for as long as you may? Which means not showing yourself right away!"

"There aren't any Mages left on that wreck," Jules said, glowering at Liv.

"Is that what you say? Because we see none? And how many Mages did we see when we were approaching that ship the first time?"

Mak had told her more than once that being captain meant knowing when *not* to insist on doing what you wanted. Knowing that Liv was right, Jules bit her lip, stepping back. "All right. You command the longboat. See if there's any chance of getting anything off the wreck, but not at any risk to the boat."

"If you didn't want to risk the boat, you wouldn't be sending us into that field of reefs," Liv scoffed. "Don't worry, Captain. I've been sailing the Sea of Bakre longer than you've been breathing the air of this world."

"I'll still worry about you, Liv," Jules said. "Don't take any foolish chances."

"I won't. I'm not you," Liv said with a grin before heading down into the boat with the other sailors who'd row it to the wreck.

Mak had also told Jules that sometimes responsibility meant sending someone else to do a risky job, and that she'd find that harder than doing the job herself. As in so much else, Mak had been right. Jules tried to distract herself by helping Ang keep the *Sun Queen* near the wreck without getting too close to the reefs, but still found her gaze frequently straying to the longboat as it navigated the reefs to reach the wreck without suffering damage or running aground.

Cori had relieved Kyle on lookout during the afternoon. "They're alongside!" she finally called down from the maintop. "I see people on the wreck! No sign of trouble!"

Jules squinted toward the wreck, wishing she knew more of what was going on there. "Mechanics and Mages are supposed to have mysterious means of quickly passing messages over long distances," she grumbled to Keli the healer, who was standing beside her on the quarterdeck. "I wish I had something like that."

"And what good would that do?" Keli asked. "Isn't Liv busy enough without having to deal with your questions? What would you tell her to do that she doesn't have sense enough to do on her own? Being able to talk over a distance like that would be a mighty nuisance, if you ask me."

"What about a healing problem?" Jules asked. "Suppose you had a special problem with someone on the crew and didn't know what to do. Wouldn't it be nice to be able to ask another healer for advice?"

Keli shrugged. "I suppose. Have you ever heard the one about how many people does it take to save a patient?"

"No, I haven't."

"It takes two," Keli said, "one healer, and one big, mean bodyguard to keep any other healers from telling the first healer that they're doing it all wrong."

Jules laughed despite the tension inside her. "All right. But suppose one of the survivors on that wreck is badly hurt? Wouldn't it be nice if Liv could talk to you about what to do?"

Keli shook his head. "I teach everyone on the crew what to do if someone gets hurt. How to stop bleeding and such. Liv and those with her know those things. If one of the survivors is hurt so badly that those measures can't save them, then it's doubtful that anything I could do by calling out advice could save them either. There's only so much a healer can do to treat the ills that befall people." He paused, his expression growing wistful. "They do say the Mechanics have devices that can save people who wouldn't have a chance of surviving with what common folk healers know. But they reserve those devices for other Mechanics. And Mages can do anything, supposedly. I wouldn't mind being able to save those I can't save with what tools I have and what skills I've learned. But the Mechanics won't share, and who'd dare ask a Mage? If that daughter of your line overthrows the Great Guilds, do you think she'll force them to share what they know?"

"I hope so," Jules said, squinting again to see more as distant figures clambered down into the longboat, passing along burdens of some kind. "But that worries me, too."

"Why is that?"

Jules tapped the revolver at her hip. "Suppose the Emperor could equip his legions with Mechanic weapons like this instead of swords and crossbows? You've seen the Mechanic ships, all metal with big weapons mounted on them. What if the Emperor had ships like that? What hope would the commons have to be free of the Emperor's control? Maybe we'd just be trading one set of overlords for another."

"I thought the prophecy said your daughter would free the world," Keli said.

"Yes," Jules said. "It does."

"Then there must be a way to do it, even if the Emperor gets his hands on such weapons." He leaned on the railing, giving out a long sigh. "To you, that Mechanic weapon seems amazing. To me, it's just another way of tearing holes in a person. We've both seen what swords, or a crossbow bolt, can do to a body. None of it's pretty. All of it's awful."

Jules glanced at him. "Why do you help me, Keli? Why are you a pirate? Hurting people is often what we do."

He shrugged again. "A healer depends for work on people getting hurt, and we're never short of work no matter where we are. I guess it matters to me *why* it happens. I don't want an Emperor, or Mechanics or Mages, telling me what I can and can't do. Not as long as I'm helping instead of hurting. Out here on the water I have a voice in what happens. I get to vote for who's to be captain, and on what the ship'll do next. As to why *this* ship, well, there was Mak. And now there's you. I could do worse."

"I'll never be half the captain that Mak was," Jules said, her gaze shifting from the sun dropping steadily lower to where the longboat was still alongside the wreck, bobbing up and down as swells rolled by, sailors in the boat using oars to try to keep the boat from slamming into the side of the wreck.

"Mak thought otherwise," Keli said, standing straight and shading his eyes with one hand. "Looks like they're casting off."

"Finally," Jules breathed. "Ang! They're starting back!"

After that what remained was the longboat's cautious exit from the reefs, as the sun reached the horizon and sank beneath it, the sky dimming through twilight and the countless stars coming into view above. But brilliant as the fields of stars were, they didn't cast nearly enough light for the longboat to safely navigate. Jules breathed a sigh of relief when the longboat finally cleared the reefs and the sailors aboard drove their oar strokes straight for the *Sun Queen*.

With darkness falling, lanterns were lit and hung from spars to guide the longboat and illuminate the area when the boat reached the ship.

Liv came up the ladder from the boat first. "There were ten more aboard."

"Any hurt?" Keli asked.

"Just some bumps and bruises. They were confined below when the masts came down so they didn't get caught in any of that." Liv made a face. "We took off their bags with their personal possessions, the ship's strongbox, and a few slabs of salt. It was too rough to risk taking more."

"I won't second guess you on that," Jules said, though she understood Liv's disappointment. The full cargo of salt on that wreck would've turned a tidy profit for the *Sun Queen*.

The rescued sailors were coming up the ladder as the crew of the *Sun Queen* hastened to bring the longboat back aboard. Liv gestured one over to Jules. "Here's our captain."

The man stared at Jules as if at a ghost. "She's alive?"

"Nah," Liv said. "She's been dead for years. We just prop her up when we want to impress people."

"Very funny," Jules said.

Gathering his wits, the sailor offered a rough salute. "First Officer Daki of Sandurin off the…" He faltered, looking back through the gloom to where the wreck was only a darker smudge in the night. "I was off the *Merry Runner*."

"Marta," Jules called, "get these other survivors down below and give them some food and a spot to hang their hammocks. Daki, I'd like to speak with you."

Her cabin wasn't large, so a single lantern sufficed to light it. She glanced at the former first officer of the *Merry Runner*, seeing the tension in him, the nervous twitches, like those of a dog that had been mistreated for too long. Jules knew that look from her childhood in the legion orphanage, where the guards or the supervisors could single out a boy or girl for any reason or no reason at all and make their life a misery. What had worked for those fellow orphans would probably work with this man. Jules put a hunk of cheese and a biscuit on the table, then filled a mug with a mix of rum and water. She gestured Daki to one seat before taking another.

Daki sat down, hesitated, then took a big bite of the cheese, chewing quickly. Jules waited, saying nothing, watching him calm down as he ate and absorbed the quiet normality of her cabin. The former first officer of the *Merry Runner* was somewhere in his middle years, that area between young and old that was hard to narrow down, especially in someone whose face had borne many days of sun and wind and salt water spray. He was missing the thumb on his right hand, a long-healed scar where it had been, the result of either an accident or an old fight.

"What happened?" Jules finally asked.

Daki flinched and closed his eyes as if trying to block out the memory. "We were at the loading pier for salt. You know where that is? West of here, where there's a passage through the reefs. Nothing there, really. Just the desert as far as you can see, and a few storehouses where the salt that Imperial convicts mine inland is brought to wait for a ship. We were loading it, no problems, when they showed up." He shuddered.

"The Mages told you to take them?"

"Not in words. They just walked aboard. Who'd dare to stop them or question them? And the one who seemed to be in charge pointed out to sea and east." Daki took a quick drink, breathing heavily before he could speak again. "We put off and headed out, of course. What else could we do?"

"You had a large cargo aboard," Jules said.

"Yeah, we were mostly loaded. So, we headed east along the coast. If our captain tried to get too far away from the coast those Mages would point him back closer in, so that's where we stayed."

"Where's your captain?"

Daki grimaced. "They took him and three others when they left the wreck they'd made of the *Merry*. They headed east again, so I guess they want to get back to Imperial lands. Of course they needed some sailors to do the work of getting them there."

He didn't look happy at the idea. Jules knew why. If that captain and his three sailors were lucky, the Mages would reach their destination and simply walk away without a word, leaving the sailors destitute but alive. But sometimes Mages got rid of commons when they were no longer needed, killing them with the same lack of concern as someone stepping on an ant in their path. "At least that gave the rest of you a chance," Jules said.

"We didn't think so," Daki said. "The waves will make short work of the *Merry* where she's hung up, and then we'd have to try to make it to a shore where food and water are both lacking. I got the others tearing up deck planks and working on a raft even though we all knew it'd probably be wrecked on the rocks before we got far from the *Merry*. Had to try, though, right? But we thought we were done for until we realized your ship was coming back. Even then... some pirates are pretty awful, you know. But Fran, she said she was sure it was your ship, Captain Jules, and we'd be all right."

"Fran must be a smart sailor," Jules said, pouring more water and rum into Daki's mug. "So, the Mages insisted you sail east and stay close to the coast."

"Not in words," Daki said. "Just pointing and those awful dead faces they have. We never knew if—" He paused, wide eyes staring at Jules. "One afternoon two of them Mages walked up to Wil and slit his throat. He hadn't done anything. They just did it. Maybe they wanted to keep the rest of us jumping to their orders." He took a long drink. "Then, today, we sighted your ship, and I swear the Mages seemed almost happy, though they didn't look it. Like they'd been waiting for it. They told the captain to take the helm and ordered the rest of us below decks. We spent a long time like that. I was nearest the ladder up, and finally heard one of the Mages say something about the shore. That voice!"

"They sound pretty awful," Jules agreed. "No feeling in the voices at all."

"You've heard them? Well, of course *you* have. Um… the Mage said something and the captain shouted it was death to go closer to shore. But the Mages insisted, I guess. We felt the ship turn and knew we were heading for the rocks."

He hesitated, looking sidelong at Jules. "Those Mages, it was like they knew you and your ship would be there."

"It's not the first time," Jules said. "Why did the Mages want to go closer to shore?"

"I don't know and that's the truth. I had time for a few words with the captain after the ship hit the reef, and he said the Mages just said do it."

Jules shook her head. "If they wanted me dead, they had me right there. Why turn away at that point?"

"I don't know! It was clear enough they'd come to kill you," Daki said. "The captain said once they'd seen you fall they turned away like they didn't care anymore. And I saw them before they left the *Merry*. I don't know Mages, but I know people who've been given a job to do and how they act once it's finished. Like 'all right, that's done with, let's go.' That's how those Mages seemed before they left our ship."

"They think I'm dead?"

"We all thought that," Daki said. "Our captain said he saw the Mage lightning hit you."

"It did hit me," Jules said.

Daki sat staring at her until Jules gave him a dismissive and irritated wave. "It was weak," she said, having decided on that as an explanation. "Maybe Mages secretly use devices like Mechanics do, and there was something ashore they needed to make a strong spell. But they couldn't get it because they ran your ship onto a reef, so they made do with what they could. You can join the rest of your crew. Tell them that we'll put them off in our next port as we would survivors of any wreck."

"Thank you, Captain. We can do work on this ship to pay for our food and berths."

Jules nodded. "We'll take you up on that. Do you have any idea what's in the ship's strongbox?"

"Probably very little. We'd just taken on cargo and hadn't sold it." The former first officer of the *Merry Runner* hesitated. "Captain, I think some of us, at least some of us, would be interested in joining your crew."

"We've got a pretty full crew," Jules said, being sure to sound regretful at the rebuff. "And you'd be signing on to be pirates."

"I can fight, Captain Jules." He held up the hand with a missing thumb. "I served on an Imperial galley until I lost this. Couldn't hold a sword after that. But I learned to use the other hand."

"Well done," Jules said. She knew the Imperials could've kept Daki in service, trained him to fight left-handed, except for the Imperial rule that all legionaries had to fight with the right hand so there'd be no variations or weaknesses in the shield wall.

"I could've still pulled an oar," Daki said, "but they said that wasn't good enough."

"You pulled an oar on an Imperial galley?" Jules asked, surprised. Those on the oars were the lowest level of a galley's crew, worked hard and expected to fight as backups to the galley's legionaries. "But you were first officer on your ship?"

Daki shrugged. "After I left Imperial service I worked hard on more than one ship, and I learned what I had to learn. I earned that berth on the *Merry*," he added, sounding defensive.

"I'm sure you did," Jules said, making another, different, inner appraisal of him. Anyone who could work their way up from the oars to first officer had proven a great deal about themselves. And he'd kept his head after the Mages left, keeping the other survivors busy making a raft. "We've already got a full crew, but we can probably make room for you, at least."

Distress flitted across the sailor's face. "I could not leave the others from the *Merry* unless I knew they'd be all right. The ship is gone, but the captain would expect me to look after those of the crew who remain."

Her opinion of the man rose another notch. "I'll talk to my officers and see what can be done."

"I understand," Daki said, pausing once more, his expression working in the light of the single lantern. "Captain, could you tell me, is it true?"

"Is what true?" Jules said. She knew exactly what Daki was asking about, but annoyance at the question warred with her sense of courtesy.

"The prophecy. Is it true?"

"You'll have to ask that daughter of my line, whenever she shows up," Jules said. "It'll be up to her to make it happen." She waited, tense, to see if Daki would follow up by hitting on her. Daki seemed a decent sort, but she'd been propositioned by enough apparently decent sorts to no longer have any patience with them.

"But you're the first common to ever stand up to the Great Guilds and not be killed," Daki said.

"So far," Jules said, waiting to see what else Daki would say.

He hesitated like a man about to leap across a chasm and looked down at the table between them. "If you are willing…"

One of her hands, beneath the table and unseen by the sailor, slid back to the dagger sheathed at the small of her back.

"I would fight by your side against the Great Guilds," Daki finished in a rush. "I have family in Sandurin. I must think of them as well, but it would be for my children's freedom."

Jules relaxed, nodding, her hand leaving the hilt of the dagger. "I wouldn't ask anyone to ignore the needs of their family. In all honesty, it may be our great-great-grandchildren or even later before that daughter of my line shows up." She paused, hearing running feet that warned of trouble even before a rapid double knock on the cabin's door.

A sailor named Gord stuck his head in. "Cori on lookout is pretty sure she saw a light to the north."

"On the horizon?" Jules asked. "Has it reappeared?"

"Closer than the horizon. Cori thinks the light went out when they spotted our lights."

"Blazes. Pass the word to extinguish all lanterns, and take Daki here to his friends from the *Merry Runner*."

She paused only long enough to blow out the single lantern in the stern cabin before following Gord and Daki out on deck. Racing up to the quarterdeck, having no trouble with the familiar route in the dark, she found Ang still standing near the helm. "Have you taken any breaks today?"

"I ate dinner," Ang said. "Have you?"

She hadn't, so rather than replying Jules looked upward. "Cori! Was the light from an honest lantern, or some of that weird Mechanic light?" Lanterns and candles burned flames that put out a warm, yellowish light which varied in strength. The crew of the *Sun Queen* had seen Mechanic lights, though, which were much more white, much brighter, and never altered.

"It wasn't any of that Mechanic light," Cori called back. "I would've seen it sooner if it was."

"Did you ever see the Mechanics use regular lanterns?" Ang asked Jules.

It was a natural question to ask of her. Jules had been aboard one of the Mechanic ships made of steel, a rare experience for a common. "No. All I saw on their ship were their lights. Too bright to even look at straight on."

"Would they have lanterns, though? Just in case?"

She shook her head, peering over the night-dark waters. "The last time I met with Mechanics they used some small version of their lights that they could put in a pocket. I think Mechanics refuse to use regular lanterns because that's what we use. They always have to show off their special light to make it clear they think they're above us. If Cori saw a regular lantern, that means it's not one of the Mechanic ships."

Ang narrowed his eyes toward the north. "Could be a merchant ship, then. Trying to hide for fear that we're pirates."

"That'd be smart of them, since we are pirates." Jules rubbed her neck as she also gazed north. "Or it's an Imperial ship of war hoping we're pirates and trying to sneak up on us."

"If it's an Imperial galley or sloop, it's only looking for one pirate," Ang said. "We both know who she is. And it may have other Imperial warships nearby."

Jules frowned. "True enough. But we need to take a decent ship. Pickings have been slim lately. I hate to run when there might be a good prize nearby."

"But we don't want to be near when the sun rises if that is an Imperial galley."

"No."

"We don't have to either run or stay in this area," Ang said. "We can head north, get upwind of where Cori thinks that light was. That'll give us the weather gage at dawn." A ship upwind of another ship was said to have the weather gage (though no one knew the origin of the term), meaning that the ship with the gage could quickly turn and run down on the other, or evade any attempt by the other to catch it. "Then if the morning light shows us a ship we want nothing to do with we can run, but we'll be able to swoop down on him if he's a merchant."

"That's a good idea." Jules took a deep breath, angry at herself. "Why didn't I think of it?"

Ang's face wasn't easy to make out in the dark, but his voice sounded amused. "When you lack experience, you tend to think of the two opposite choices. Run or fight. Buy or sell. Win or lose. But with time you start seeing there are a lot of choices in between the two opposites."

"Believe me, I know I need more experience," Jules said, mollified.

"You listen to those who do have it, so perhaps you'll live long enough to learn the lessons for yourself."

"That'd be nice." Jules looked up at the sails, their white shapes ghostly against the night sky. "Let's work out how far to go upwind. Then you and I both need to get some sleep or we'll be useless tomorrow. Who's going to take over the quarterdeck after you?"

"Gord will have the watch, Cap'n."

"Good." Gord had been aboard the *Sun Queen* for years and had plenty of experience before that, though like most of those aboard he spoke little of his earlier life. In any port he was prone to drinking too much and then doing something stupid, but at sea Gord had proven reliable and smart. "If anything happens he can handle the first moments of it while the rest of us get on deck." She turned, wincing as her side flared with pain. "Where's Keli?"

"I'll have him come see you. It hurts?"

"Blazes, yes, it hurts. What do you expect?"

"I didn't know. I've never known anyone to live through being hit by lightning," Ang said. "What would've happened if the lightning had struck on the side where you have the Mechanic weapon?"

Jules paused, looking down at the revolver. "I don't know what would've happened. But I think I'm lucky I didn't find out."

* * *

Jules was up again well before sunrise, the burn down her side making every movement painful as the sky slowly paled in the east and the stars gradually retreated, surrendering their mastery of the sky to the overwhelming brilliance of the sun. She responded to the splendid sky with a sour look, having slept poorly after refusing the sleep draught that Keli had offered because it might make it hard for her to awaken in an emergency. Naturally, no emergency had occurred, since she'd sacrificed any chance of a decent amount of sleep just in case.

It was still morning twilight, the sun not yet risen above the horizon, when the nature of the mysterious light became clear as the dark of night gave way.

"Imperial sloop," Liv said, shaking her head. The Imperial warship was more than a thousand lances south of them, the *Sun Queen* having sailed unseen past it to the north last night. "He was planning on ambushing us come morning. Instead, we've got the advantage of the wind. Let's get out of here."

"Let's do that," Jules agreed. Resting one hand on the rail to support herself against weakness brought on by her injury, she looked up at the sails, studying how well they were drawing. The wind was still coming from just north of east, and while not as strong as yesterday had plenty enough push to let them outrun the Imperial ship.

"He's flying the parley flag!" the lookout called down from high above the deck.

"What?" Jules stared at the other ship, seeing the flag herself as the light of day brightened, the breeze brisk enough to cause it to flap open and provide an unmistakable look at the white field surrounded by a blue border that meant the Imperials wanted to talk.

"It's a trick," Ang said. "They just want us to let them get close enough for their ballista to knock down one of our masts. Liv's right. Let's go."

"Hold on," Jules said. She looked up again. "Are there any more masts in sight?" she yelled to the lookout.

After a pause as the lookout scanned the horizon again, the answer came back. "Just one a ways to the north that has been tracking east since I first spotted it. It hasn't come any closer, just heading east. Looks like a ship from the Sharr Isles on its way to Landfall."

"All right." Jules nodded to Ang. "Last night you reminded me that sometimes there are other choices rather than run or fight. Let's wait and see what this guy does. If he really wants to talk, I want to hear it so I'll know what the Emperor is planning."

"Fair enough," Ang said. "You don't think the Emperor is going to change his mind about you, do you?"

"No." She looked toward the Imperial sloop. "But the more I know about his exact plans, the better I can try to keep the Mages, the Mechanics, and the Imperials busy working against each other. Let's raise our own parley flag in reply and see what they do."

"What if they put on more sail and come this way?"

"Then we put on a lot more sail. They wouldn't be able to catch us before nightfall, and then we could easily lose them in the dark."

"It's still a risk," Ang said. "If the winds shift…"

"We'll out-sail them anyway." Hopefully this decision would be wiser than some of the ones she'd made yesterday.

CHAPTER THREE

As if responding to Ang's concerns, the wind almost immediately dropped a bit and swung slightly more toward the east, causing Jules to fret that she'd made the wrong call. The Imperial ship didn't try to use that opportunity to get closer to the *Sun Queen*, though, and didn't put on more sail. Instead, after sighting the *Queen*'s own parley flag, it put a longboat in the water. The sailors raised a single mast, set the sail, and came coasting over the waves toward Jules' ship. An Imperial officer could be seen in the stern of the boat, resplendent in a dark red uniform and gold insignia that flashed in the light of the sun now peeking over the horizon. Jules couldn't help pausing at the sight. Not long ago she'd worn such a uniform.

"How many of the crew should we arm and have standing by?" Ang asked, jarring her out of a cascade of memories.

Jules looked over the Imperial boat, which held a half dozen sailors in addition to the officer, knowing why Ang felt the need to be alert for treachery. The legionary code of honor took second place to loyalty to the Emperor, meaning they'd do whatever the Emperor ordered them to do. Still, she felt fairly confident making this decision because of her experience as both an Imperial officer and leading these pirates. She knew what both could do. "Ten. Five with crossbows and five with cutlasses. Keep them back unless the sailors on that boat try anything."

"Marta! Gord!" Ang called. "Each of you get four to help you. Marta, your group arm yourselves with crossbows. Gord, your group draw cutlasses. I want you all at the mainmast before that Imperial boat comes alongside."

Liv had come up onto the quarterdeck as well, gazing toward the oncoming boat with a sour expression. "Do you want these goons knowing you're alive?" she asked Jules.

"Maybe," Jules said. "I'm going to wait inside the cabin. When the Imperial representative comes aboard, I'll size him or her up before I decide whether to call out for you to send them in."

"What if you don't want to meet?" Ang asked.

"If I say nothing, tell the Imperial representatives that I'm not aboard, and you know nothing of my whereabouts, and you're all peaceful, loyal subjects of the Emperor, and you're sorry they mistook this ship for Jules' ship."

"And if they rush the deck?" Liv asked.

"There are only seven in that boat. Between Marta's crossbows and Gord's cutlasses we can probably wipe out that boat crew faster than Gord can down a beer."

"And if there's a Mage hidden among them?"

"That's not possible," Jules said. "The Emperor wants me alive. Even if Mages got aboard that Imperial sloop, the crew would know that anything the Mages could do to them would be nothing compared to the Emperor's wrath if they helped Mages harm me."

"That's reassuring, I guess," Liv grumbled.

"Only if I don't think about why the Emperor wants me alive," Jules said. "Ang, if you see anything suspicious when they come alongside, don't wait for me to order the crossbows into action."

Ang nodded with a somber expression. "I understand, Cap'n. You should get into the cabin now before they get close enough to identify you up here."

From that point on, the wait for the Imperial boat to reach them was more annoying than anything else. No one could relax or start other tasks while alert for any sudden move by the Imperial sloop, which might yet put on more sail and try to catch the *Sun Queen* while the pirate crew's attention was on the approaching longboat.

Jules found that waiting was much harder with the burn down her side hurting whether she moved or stayed still. She asked Healer Keli to put more salve on it, glowering at the strange fern pattern of the burn as he did so, then considered taking a slug of rum to help dull the pain but decided that wouldn't be smart with the Imperial boat drawing closer. Alone once more, she sat down for the last period of waiting, trying to get halfway comfortable and wondering what an Imperial representative would think of the sparsely-furnished cabin. Certainly the cabin bore little resemblance to the almost opulent captain's quarters aboard Imperial warships, where polished brass fittings shone in the light of numerous lamps and fine cloths covered both the captain's table and the captain's bunk.

Hearing the calls and commotion that marked the boat coming alongside, Jules got up with a wince and limped to the door, opening it just enough that she could see a portion of the deck while remaining unseen.

Ang stood by the place where the ladder had been dropped, displaying no sign of alarm as he gazed down at the Imperial boat. The sailors in that boat must be behaving themselves.

An Imperial officer gradually came into view as he came up the ladder, his movements strangely familiar.

Jules' hand on the door tightened as she recognized the officer. "I wish to speak to Jules of Landfall," Lieutenant Ian of Marandur told Ang. "Is she aboard this ship?"

Ang didn't reply, waiting to hear from Jules.

She sighed, then called out. "Send in the officer."

Why did it have to be Ian, of all people?

Retreating from the door, Jules took up a position near the stern windows, arms crossed, legs slightly spread as if prepared for a fight. Jules cocked one hip to ensure that the Mechanic weapon was easily visible, settling her expression into what hopefully looked like that of a stern pirate captain rather than that of an injured sailor having trouble keeping on her feet.

Her once-friend and fellow officer in training stepped into the cabin, ducking a little because he was tall and the ceiling low, stopping as he saw her.

Ian didn't seem to have changed, but then it had been only about a year since they'd parted at Jacksport. In Imperial uniform, he looked familiar, the man from her memories, but also strange, because now everyone who wore that uniform served an emperor who sought Jules' capture. The insignia that had marked him as an officer in training was gone, so he'd successfully achieved the status of a regular officer. But then that success had never been in doubt. Even if Ian hadn't been a capable officer—and she knew he was—his family connections would have ensured his promotion.

She noticed he carried a waterproof dispatch case. The sheaths for sword and dagger at his belt were both empty, as they should be for someone arriving under a parley flag.

Jules couldn't be certain of Ian's expression, which seemed a mix of different emotions. Nor could she identify for certain her own feelings, a welter of contradictions that left her bewildered and unhappy. She hardened her face a little more to try to cover her inner turmoil.

Ian looked at her for a long moment, as if waiting for her greeting, before averting his gaze. "You're looking well," he said in a low voice.

"I've been getting a lot of fresh air while out at sea searching for ships to plunder," Jules said. "Plus all the exercise I get running away from Mechanics and Mages who're trying to kill me, and from Imperial servants who want to make me a slave." Anger warred with her affection for Ian and sharpened her voice. "How did the Emperor know my ship would be around here?"

"I was told to find you, and this seemed to be a good place to look."

He knew her that well? Worry about what that could mean if Ian led warships in search of her made Jules' tone harden even more. "Why are you here?"

He hesitated, then raised his eyes to meet her gaze. "I've been worried about you."

"It's a purely personal visit?" Jules asked, letting sarcasm tint every word of her reply. "You're not here with an Imperial warship at the behest of the Emperor?"

Ian stood in the middle of the cabin as if unable to decide which direction to go. "I have a message for you from the Emperor," he finally said, straightening to attention, his voice taking on official tones.

"So it's official business."

Instead of replying directly, Ian took a large envelope out of the waterproof dispatch case. Even from where she stood, Jules could see the heaviness and quality of the paper of the envelope. "This is for you, from the Emperor. I'm glad your captain allowed you use of this cabin. I'm supposed to give it to you in private."

"I am the captain of this ship, Ian."

"Oh." Ian recovered from his surprise pretty quickly. "Congratulations."

"Thanks. So that's a letter from the Emperor for me?"

"Yes." Ian held out the letter, waiting, but Jules didn't move. "Don't you want to look at it?"

She didn't want to limp across the cabin under Ian's gaze. "Put it on the table. I may look at it later."

"Jules…" He made a face. "I'm required to ensure that you read the letter and gave your answer afterwards."

She shrugged, instantly regretting the movement as her burn protested, determined to ensure Ian didn't enjoy a moment of this visit. Not when he'd only come at the behest of the Emperor. "You'd better read it to me, then."

"You're going to make me do that?"

"Blazes, yes, I'm going to make you do that." Jules stayed standing by the stern windows, watching, as Ian, with an angry set to his mouth, ran a thumb under the envelope flap to break the heavy wax seal and drew out the paper inside.

He unfolded the letter, inhaled slowly, then began reading in a formal voice. "To Jules of Landfall, honored by destiny."

Jules couldn't help a scornful cough at that beginning, which caused Ian to pause for a moment.

"Greetings to you, faithful servant of the Empire—"

"Excuse me?" Jules interrupted again.

"Faithful servant of the Empire," Ian repeated stubbornly. "It is my most fervent wish that the future of our people be safeguarded and brought to pass as the prophecy has proclaimed. The overthrow of the Great Guilds will be the greatest event in the history of this world. Even I am humbled to know that the woman whose line will be responsible for this wonder comes from among my subjects, and was protected and raised in the charity of one of the Imperial homes for orphans of the legions."

"He has the nerve to boast about that? Does the Emperor have any idea what conditions are like in those orphanages?"

Ian paused, saying nothing, the light coming through the stern windows on his face shifting as the ship rolled.

"Is that all?" Jules finally prompted.

He began reading again. "The drawings of your... your beauty which have been shown to me surpass my wildest expectations—"

"Drawings of me? Does he mean the ones on the Imperial wanted posters? Oh, stars above," Jules said with a short laugh. "I can always tell when a man is either drunk or wants to get me into bed or both. That's when he starts praising my so-called beauty."

"Those are the only times you've heard that?" Ian asked, his eyes fixed on the letter.

She remembered then, words Ian had spoken. "No. There was another man. I believed *he* meant what he said."

"Thank you," Ian said in a flat voice. "Should I continue?"

"Yes."

"...your beauty which have been shown to me surpass my wildest expectations as does the fire in your eyes. I am certain you would be as fierce a partner and companion to me in—" Ian gritted his teeth. "In bed as you have proven to be in battle."

"Ian—" Jules began, regretting that she had pushed him into reciting those words. Of course a powerful man like the emperor would think a woman would be happy to hear such a thing.

"You asked for this," he replied, biting off the end of each word, before returning to his reading. "It is my understanding that in the course of seeking to protect your legacy you have been accused of violating a number of laws. Rest assured that should you agree to the terms of this proposal, a full pardon will be granted for each and every offense supposedly committed by you."

"How very generous," Jules said.

Ian shot her an angry look before continuing. "Your abilities and accomplishments have been brought to my attention. The Empire would benefit greatly from assigning you a position equal to your skills in command and strategy. Should you agree, you will be promoted to..." He inhaled sharply, staring at the letter.

"Promoted to what?" Jules said.

He looked at her, his eyes wide. "Promoted to General of the Legions, second only to the Emperor in military authority within the Empire."

She stared back for a moment before laughing again. "General of the Legions? Me? Spawn of a legion orphan home? And a pirate. I'm sure the legions would love that! Think of what the centurions would say! How about you, Lieutenant Ian? How'd you like me to be your boss?"

"You're joking about this?"

"Yeah. So what else is there?"

After a heavy breath, Ian continued. "All of this contingent only upon your agreement to accept my promise in full marriage, as First Consort to the Imperial throne. Our children will be first in direct line to the Imperial throne when my reign comes to an end."

"Wow," Jules commented. "First Consort and General of the Legions and a full pardon. And all I have to do is lie there while the Emperor does his business on my body, and then pump out the children when they arrive."

Ian finally cracked under her prodding. "Blazes, Jules! How can you talk like that?"

"How?" She finally took a step away from the stern windows and toward him, her jaw tight with tension, her side aflame from the burn. "Just how many nightmares do you think I've had since that prophecy was spoken to me? How many times do you think I've had to wonder how short my life might be, and what some man like the Emperor might do to me before I died?"

Ian closed his eyes, clearly struggling to regain control. "I'm... sorry."

"Thanks. Give me that."

He handed over the letter. She read through it quickly, seeing the fine script that was surely the work of a court scribe rather than the Emperor himself, feeling her anger rising again. What kind of man sent a profession of avowed love that had been written out by someone else? And how stupid did the people who'd worded this letter think she was? "I wonder what the Mages would think if they knew about this offer?"

"There's no way they should be aware of it. Even I didn't know the contents of that letter," Ian said. "And I was carrying it."

"Oh?" She let the single word hang for a moment. "And what methods do Mages have for learning the secrets we keep? Do you know? Because I sure as blazes don't! They've repeatedly shown the ability to know my movements in advance. What else do they know?" Jules shook the letter at him. "My children, heirs to the Empire? The Mages would love that, wouldn't they?"

"I'm sure the Emperor intends to protect you, and them, from the Mages."

"How?"

Ian hesitated again.

"And what about the Mechanics? Their Guild wants me dead, too, or hasn't word of that reached the Emperor's ears? The Great Guilds want me dead, and my line cut short. They'll kill any child I have to try to ensure that the prophecy never comes to pass. How does the Emperor intend standing up to the Great Guilds?"

"Jules, I don't know the answer to that."

"Yes, you do!" she almost shouted, throwing the letter onto the table. "He can't stand against them! No one can! Which means he'll keep our so-called wedding secret, and any royal heirs I produce secret. Maybe he intends tossing me to the Mages after I've spawned enough royal babies! Or would he just wait until I'd had three or four kids and then finish me off himself to be sure I wouldn't have children with any other man?"

Ian glared at her. "What do you want from me?"

"Stop being a loyal servant of the Emperor!"

He straightened, his hair brushing the wooden planks of the cabin's overhead. "I let you go at Jacksport! I could've won great reward by holding you and turning you in. And if it had been suspected that I'd let you go, the punishment would've been such that death would've been a welcome relief. You know that! Don't accuse me of betraying you when I put my life on the line to give you a chance to escape!"

Jules breathed in and out slowly, remembering that night. Finally, she nodded. "Fair enough. I owe you that. You took a huge risk for me." She ran one hand through her hair. "Doesn't this bother you? Bringing me this offer?"

"I wasn't given an option on whether or not to do it," Ian said, his own voice calmer as well.

"Why'd they pick you?"

His expression grew dark. "Because it was known among our fellow trainees that I was interested in you, and that you might be interested in me. That we were at least friends. You know there were rumors that we were more than that."

"I remember," Jules said. A sudden thought troubled her. "Those rumors said you and I were lovers."

"Yes." He glared at the deck. "I had to swear as convincingly as possible that the two of us had never even kissed. Which I was able to do because it was true. If there had been any evidence that we'd ever slept together, my life would've been cut even shorter than yours might be."

"I saved your life by rejecting your advances?"

"So it seems." Ian studied her. "Jules, you said no one could stand against the Great Guilds. I'd have agreed with you if you'd said that a year ago. But not now. Do you know what people are saying about you? About how you've killed Mages? And battled Mechanics?" He looked at the revolver Jules wore in her holster. "That weapon. You're the first common person to ever have one, to ever use one. Jules, they even say you fought a Mage dragon and lived to tell the tale!"

"Barely," Jules said.

Ian frowned at her in puzzlement. "Barely what?"

"I barely lived to tell the tale," she explained.

His jaw fell open. "You... it's true?"

"There was a dragon, and it was after me, and I did fight it," Jules said. "Not very successfully. But, fortunately, it couldn't swim, so I got away."

"Is a dragon as bad as they say?"

Jules couldn't quite suppress a shudder at her memories of the encounter. "They're pretty bad. I don't want to tangle with one again."

Ian shook his head in admiration that embarrassed her. "Have you really killed Mages?"

"Yes," Jules said, feeling uncomfortable to be telling Ian, as if she were boasting to impress him. "Three for certain. Maybe a couple more."

"What about Mechanics?"

"Have I killed any Mechanics? No. Not yet, anyway."

He gave her another close look. "Some say you're an ally of the Mechanics, helping them."

Jules grinned. "That's what the Mechanics thought. That's how I got this," she added, tapping the revolver with one finger. She let the smile fade. "But then I spoke my mind to some of them, and as a result at the moment the Mechanics want my hide on the wall just as much as the Mages do."

Ian shook his head just as he had when they were trainees together. "How many times did I warn you about speaking your mind?"

"It's who I am. You used to like that."

"I still do."

"Then why did you accept the job of bringing me this offer?"

Ian sighed, rubbing the back of his neck with one hand in a habit she recognized. "I wasn't given the option," he said again.

"There are ways to avoid assignments," Jules said. "You told me some of them."

He looked straight at her. "Not this kind of assignment. The general who gave me the orders took time to ask how my family was. And to express hope that nothing unpleasant would happen to any of them."

Shocked, Jules couldn't speak for a moment, the cabin silent except for the occasional groan of wood as the ship rode the waves and the hull flexed. "They threatened your family?"

He gave her his old, crooked smile. "Oh, nothing so crude and open as a threat. Just an expressed concern for the welfare of my parents and my sister."

Jules rubbed her face, feeling awful. "Because of me. Can they get out of Marandur? Move somewhere else where they aren't so close to the Imperial court?"

"Nowhere in the Empire would be safe, even if they were allowed to move. They know the eyes of the Imperial court are on them."

She stared at Ian. "They know?"

Ian shrugged. "Of course. One of their high-level so-called friends conveyed the concerns of the court for their safety."

"Because of me," Jules repeated. "Your sister already hated me."

"My sister looked down on you," Ian said. "Now she hates you. But she also recognizes the opportunity you present for the family to gain the good graces of the Emperor. If I convinced you to take the offer, the Emperor's gratitude would include my family."

"Blazes." Jules, feeling weak from her injury, managed a couple of normal steps to one of the chairs and sat down carefully, waving Ian to the other. "Take a seat. As bad as I feel about this mess you're in, I hope you understand I can't accept the Emperor's offer."

Ian remained standing, looking troubled. "Jules…"

"Do not offer me a reasonable compromise," she warned him. "You always do that, thinking there's some middle ground that'll make everybody happy."

"But the way things are… All right. I admit no one else could have survived as long as you did. But the only power on Dematr with any chance of protecting your children from the Great Guilds is the Emperor."

"You want me to take this offer?" she asked, not certain that she'd heard right.

"I don't *want* you to!" Ian's face worked with unreadable emotions. "But to keep you alive, to keep your children alive—"

"My children? Wasn't there a time when you hoped they'd be *our* children?"

Ian looked down. "You never had any interest in that happening."

"I didn't say I never would have."

His surprised gaze rested on her. "That's impossible now."

She shook her head, feeling the cold inside that filled her when she had to make a hard choice. "I decide what's possible. I'm the only one who gets to decide who the father of my children will be. No one else does. Not the Emperor. And not you."

"The man has a say in whether he wants to father your children!"

"That's so. But only if I decide the same." Jules drew her dagger and tapped the blade lightly on the table to emphasize her words. "My life was taken from me by that prophecy. I'm taking it back. And part of that is reserving to myself the decision of who will partner with me to begin my line. I will not be coerced into deciding who that is."

Ian gave her a look that mingled anger, frustration, and worry. "The Emperor is giving you a choice."

"When there's only one option given, that's not really a choice." She leaned back in the chair, eyeing him. "I'm truly sorry that your family is in danger because of me. There are places outside the Empire that they could go."

"Outside the Empire?" Ian gusted a small, sarcastic laugh. "My mother and my sister in a place like Jacksport? Mud and raw wooden buildings and rough food? No. They love being near the Imperial court and all the diversions that Marandur has to offer. And…" He spread his hands. "They trust the Emperor."

"After they were threatened," Jules said.

"Not by the Emperor," Ian replied. "By one of his functionaries. Surely, if the Emperor knew, he wouldn't permit such a thing. That's almost word for word what my mother told me. My father served in the legions. He can't even conceive of being disloyal to the Emperor. Meanwhile, my sister dreams of catching the eye of a prince, with the possibility of someday ascending to the role the Emperor has offered you in that letter."

"I'm sorry," Jules said.

He rubbed his forehead in rough, sharp motions. "You're sorry. Thank you for that. But the fact remains that my family faces danger that didn't exist a year ago. As do I. And so do you. Especially you."

"Ian, you could disappear. If the Empire thought you were dead, your family would be safe."

"Disappear to where?"

She took a deep breath, realizing how much she hoped Ian would take this offer. "Here. This ship. Or the ships of some friends of mine. If you use a different name, no one could ever—"

"No, Jules." Ian broke into her words as if it pained him to hear them. "That's not possible. If any hint that I was still alive got back to the Empire, my family would pay a terrible price. I want to protect them by doing my best to carry out the Emperor's wishes."

"The Emperor will throw you away the moment he has no more use for you! I'm giving you an alternative," Jules said, trying not to sound disappointed.

"It wouldn't work. It's too dangerous. The only possible alternative that might ensure the safety of everyone is if you seriously consider the Emperor's offer."

"No," Jules said, feeling defensive. "None of that is my fault. I didn't ask for this."

"If you don't care enough about the fates of yourself or me or my family, then what about the crew of this ship?" Ian waved to encompass the area outside the cabin.

"Are you threatening my crew?" Jules demanded, thinking she must not have heard right. Suddenly, Ian's Imperial uniform seemed not just out of place in this cabin, but menacing.

Ian hesitated, startled. "No. I'm just pointing out what might happen if—"

"Just like that general who expressed concern for your family?" Jules asked, angry again. "Don't play dumb and virtuous. And don't threaten my crew."

He gave her a look of outraged innocence. "I'm not threatening to do anything. But your presence endangers them. You know it."

"I said *don't*."

He glowered at her. "If I know you at all, I know you care about their fates."

She stood up, ignoring the flare of pain down her side, matching Ian's glare with her own. "They voted me captain knowing the risks! They chose to share this fate with me! Unlike some I could name!"

"They—" His initial flare of anger went out as Ian stared at her, confused. "Voted? What's 'voted'?"

"Each of them had a choice of who to back for captain, and they all chose me."

"But… you're the captain!"

"As long as they want me to be captain. They can call another vote and remove me, then vote for someone else."

"That's crazy."

"No," Jules said. "That's freedom."

"You can't run a ship that way!" Ian protested.

"Can't we?" Leaning one hand on the table to steady herself, she used the other to make a wide wave encompassing the sea outside. "There are a lot of pirate ships being run that way. Quite successfully, too. And places like Jacksport and Kelsi's are trying it to run their towns. I think it can work to run cities. A lot of cities. Let the people decide who's in charge and what the laws should be. Let everyone have a voice in that."

"Have you gone insane? Without the firm hand of an emperor or an empress there'd be anarchy! There's always been an emperor or an empress, and nothing else. That's the only form of government that has ever existed."

"Why is that the only type of government in the world?" Jules asked. "And why hasn't anything else been tried? Is it because the Great Guilds haven't permitted it?"

"It's because the people can't decide for themselves what the laws should be!" Ian shook his head like someone trying to wake from a bad dream. "And where would these cities be? Ramshackle settlements like Jacksport? All the land that can support big cities is already part of the Empire."

Jules shook her head as well. "That's not true. Explorers have gone past the Northern Ramparts through a pass and found good lands beyond."

"They must have lied. Those are wastelands."

"And I think," Jules said, "that there are good lands to the west and the south as well."

"What? Like the Bleak Coast?"

"No! Beyond that! Mak believed those lands exist and I mean to prove it!"

"Mak?" Ian paused, looking at her.

Jules felt her face warming, realizing how fervently she'd spoken of Mak. "The former captain of this ship."

"Oh."

"What does that mean?"

"Nothing," Ian said, his face tightening with renewed anger.

She knew what he thought, knew she should explain, and knew she never would explain if someone else demanded it of her and expected the worst of her. And her side hurt like blazes, the burn seeming to draw strength and patience from her with every throb of pain. "Spit it out, Ian."

"Fine! You owe me an explanation, Jules!"

"I don't owe you anything! I don't owe anyone anything!"

"That's nice for you!" Ian said, his voice hot. "I have responsibilities."

"You have responsibilities? *You* have responsibilities?" She waved one hand to indicate everything outside the cabin. "Every time I scratch my stomach the entire world pauses to see if I'm looking any bigger! Do you want to swap *responsibilities*, Ian?"

"You always—" Ian bit off the words, glaring at her. "Is that how you want this to end?"

Jules drew herself up stiffly, one hand on the dagger where it rested on the table, knowing that she'd taken it too far but refusing to back down. "Yes. I think it's time you left, Lieutenant."

The muscles along his jaw stood out as Ian breathed harshly like someone struggling internally. Jules shifted her grip on her dagger, wondering what orders Ian might have been given to carry out if the offer was rejected. Would he try to carry out orders like that? Against her?

She wished she could dismiss her worries. But who could she trust anymore? And Ian had already made it clear that his family's safety rested on him doing what the Emperor demanded. Jules unobtrusively readied her dagger, knowing she couldn't risk trying to disable Ian. If he attacked, she'd have to kill him with her first strike.

Ian slowed his breathing, speaking in an almost calm voice. "The Emperor will want to know your response to his offer."

"That's all?" Jules asked, her voice soft.

He frowned in puzzlement. "I told you my orders. Deliver that message and get your answer."

"Fine." Perhaps the Emperor had been so certain that she'd accept his offer of marriage and royal rank that Ian hadn't been given orders for what to do if she said no. "Tell the Emperor he can…" She stopped to think, realizing that there was no need to set this bridge afire behind her when it might offer advantage at some point. "Tell the Emperor that when you found me I'd been badly injured by a Mage attack, and was too weak to consider his offer at this time."

"You expect me to lie to the Emperor? Knowing what the cost of that lie could be to me and to my family?"

Jules narrowed her eyes at Ian but said nothing. Steadying her balance, she reached with her uninjured arm to roll up the other sleeve as far as it would go, exposing the strange fern-like burn streak along the length of that arm. She held it for Ian to see. "That happened yesterday. And it hurts like blazes today. I *was* injured by a Mage attack."

His anger vanished, replaced by shock. "What did that?"

"Mage lightning."

"You... you were struck by Mage lightning?" Ian's eyes widened again in amazement. "How could you...?"

"I was lucky," Jules said, fighting to control her temper over having to discuss it. "That burn, that pattern, goes all the way down my body and my leg. Do you need to inspect its entire length to satisfy you that I was really attacked by Mages yesterday?"

"No. Jules—"

"You won't be lying if you say I was injured by a Mage attack. Tell your Emperor that I'll think about his offer. It's what he'll want to hear, and it makes you still valuable to him."

Ian gritted his teeth, looking around the cabin. "That's it, then?"

"Does your mission require anything else?" Jules asked, letting her voice go colder, her grip firm on her dagger.

"No." He looked about him one more time, finally settling his gaze on Jules. "There was a time when I would've brought home a woman raised in a legion orphanage, and told my parents and my sister that they either accepted her and loved her as I did, or else they could bid farewell to both me and her. I would've given up everything for that woman."

"Fate has spared you that," Jules said. She wanted to say something else but she wasn't sure what, as the words stayed locked inside her.

"Maybe," Ian said.

He turned and walked out of the cabin before she could ask what he meant.

* * *

Jules waited a short time before following, regaining her composure, seeing when she finally came out on deck that the Imperial longboat was already on its way back to the sloop, the stiff back of Lieutenant Ian still visible in the boat.

"I'm guessing from your expression that things didn't go well?" Liv said.

"He conveyed the Emperor's offer," Jules said, her words clipped. "I said no. He left."

"Seems like you were having a fairly loud discussion about it," Liv said. "You know that guy?"

"I... knew him. An old... friend."

"Friend?"

Jules rounded on her. "I told you what happened! Now lay off, Liv. I lost my mother a long time ago. I don't need a new one." Turning to Ang, she gestured up at the masts. "Let's put on more sail. We'll head east until we lose sight of them, then head north."

"North?" Ang asked.

"Yes, north! The pickings are too slim here, and too many people are looking for me, for us, in the south. We're more likely to find some decent prizes to the north."

But as she looked in that direction, Jules felt something else awaiting her to the north.

"Am I allowed to ask why you're staring that way for so long?" Liv said from nearby.

Jules jerked herself out of her reverie, turning an apologetic look at Liv. "Would it help if I said I'm sorry?"

"Try it."

"I'm sorry."

"Sure you are." Liv looked north. "What's there? What're you spending so much time looking at?"

"I don't know," Jules said. "Just a feeling. There's something there."

"Not more Mages, I hope."

The wind shifted again during the day, so the *Sun Queen* went from a beam reach as she headed north to being close-hauled, the wind off her port bow. But she still made decent progress, the ship's bow cleaving the waters of the Sea of Bakre, her lookouts alert to any sign of sail that might mark a new quarry. There weren't any sightings during the day, but Jules kept her confidence as night fell. "In the morning," she told her crew. "I can feel it. Be ready."

CHAPTER FOUR

The morning dawned clear and bright, the rising sun painting the sails of a merchant ship with a golden tint that hopefully foretold a rich haul aboard. Jules raised her fist in triumph as the *Sun Queen* caught sight of the other ship. "What did I tell you? An easy catch! Let's get him!"

The *Sun Queen*'s crew scrambled to set more sail and swing the ship about into a chase. The merchant ship, as surprised as the pirates, responded slowly, setting more sail gradually as it turned away.

"They're making it easy. It might be another trap," Liv warned.

"There aren't many sailors in the rigging!" the lookout called down.

"Maybe he doesn't have a full crew," Jules said. "But he does have people in his rigging, so it's not like that Mage-haunted ship. Let's get closer and see if there's anything else odd about him."

The chase was short, the *Sun Queen* quickly overhauling the other craft. Jules shouted across for them to haul in their sails, and the other ship slowly complied. This close, it was easy to confirm what the lookout had said. The crew seemed to be about half of what a ship that size should have. Aside from that, nothing else seemed odd or dangerous about this encounter.

Ang brought the *Queen* alongside, pirates throwing grapnels over the railing of the other ship to lock the two ships together.

Jules stood atop one railing, facing the other ship, hoping her still-recent burns wouldn't cause too much trouble. Keli's salves had done a lot to take the sting out of the burns, but he still wasn't happy to see her leading the boarding of another ship so soon. "It's what I'm supposed to do," Jules had reminded him. Her boots polished and her cutlass gleaming, the Mechanic revolver at her hip, she did her best to intimidate the other crew so there wouldn't be any ill-advised resistance.

As the ships touched, Jules jumped across along with a dozen of her sailors.

The jar of her feet landing seemed to roll in a throb of pain up her leg and side, but she clenched her teeth and stood straight, eyeing the frightened sailors on the ship.

One man, dressed in better clothing than the others, including a worn but still serviceable pair of boots, walked slowly toward her, his empty hands held out. "I'm Aravind of Dunlan, captain of the *Prosper*. I yield my ship to you."

"Get your entire crew lined up," Jules directed. "If no one gives us trouble, none of you will be harmed, on my word. What are you carrying?"

"A mixed cargo," Captain Aravind said, his voice and body conveying the resignation of a man who knew he had no choice. "Mostly lumber. I have the manifests in my cabin." He looked around. "Get everyone lined up against that railing!" he called to one of his crew. "Their captain promises no harm to us!"

"Help the captain retrieve his cargo manifests," Jules told Gord. Until the ship had been searched, it would be foolish for her to go inside the cabin or below decks.

Gord smiled and gestured with mock politeness to Captain Aravind, who led the way toward the stern cabin.

Jules waited, impatient, watching the five sailors who apparently made up the entire crew form a nervous line. "Is that all of you?"

The sailors looked at each other. "Ron's not here," one said. "He was up earlier, helping with the sails."

Was the missing man hiding in terror, or up to something else?

"Liv! Take a half-dozen of our people and help a couple of these sailors find Ron."

The captain came back with the cargo manifests as the group went off to search the ship.

Jules only glanced at the manifests. "Why do you have such a small crew, Captain Aravind?"

He looked toward the small group of sailors. "I could only afford to pay this many." His gaze turned bitter as it switched back to Jules. "We were hit by pirates on my last voyage as well. They took a lot. I was able to sell the cargo that remained to me, but that left only enough for purchasing a new cargo."

"You'd have been in trouble if you'd run into rough weather," Jules commented.

"I had no choice," Captain Aravind said.

A commotion at the ladder leading up from the cargo hold drew everyone's attention. Jules saw her sailors hauling along a man who seemed to be fighting for his life.

As they got closer, she recognized him.

The sun seemed to dim, and coldness filled her.

"Stop fighting them, you fool!" Aravind told the captive. "They promised not to harm anyone if we didn't fight!"

"This is a special case," Jules said, her voice low.

Captain Aravind gave her a startled look, his eyes filling with fear as he looked at her.

Jules stepped forward as the captive was hauled to a stop, one of her sailors holding him firmly on each side. He stared back at her, breathing rapidly.

"Not Ron," Jules said. "No. His name is Don. How have things been, Don?"

He didn't answer, staring at her as if seeing death coming for him.

Which, Jules thought, was pretty much true.

"You don't have anything to say, Don? No words for your old ship-mates?" Jules asked. "You left the ship without even saying goodbye, and now you've nothing to say to us? I haven't seen you since just before the ship pulled into Jacksport that time. Remember, Don? I was hiding along the coast and the Imperials came for me, just like they knew exactly where to find me. How do you suppose that happened?"

Don looked about, his panicky gaze flicking from one sailor to another. "I demand trial by the crew! That's my right!"

Liv answered, her voice heavy with contempt. "Trial by crew is the right of members of the crew. You lost that right when you left the ship."

"I did nothing!"

"Nothing?" Gord spat at him. "The last time we saw you, you had a lot of gold for someone who'd done nothing."

"You sold out a shipmate for money!" Kyle shouted.

"I was trying to save you!" Don cried, sweat running down his face. "She's death! You know it! If the Great Guilds don't kill you, the Emperor will! I was trying to get her off the ship so you'd be safe!"

"That'd be the first time you made much of an effort for anyone else in the crew," Liv said. "You were always most concerned for yourself."

"That's right!" Gord yelled. "And the legionaries could've come after us after you told them we were her shipmates! They could've killed us all to make sure no help would come to her." He raised his cutlass. "By rights, any of us could make you pay for that."

"His crime was first against Jules," Liv said. "It's her choice and her right to decide his fate."

Don, his eyes searching everyone else in vain for any sign of support, finally looked back at Jules, his eyes wide with terror.

"Have you got anything else to say, Don?" Jules asked, her voice low and calm. She wasn't feeling anything inside except the cold that filled her.

"Mercy!"

"You know me, Don. I show people the same mercy that they've shown others." Jules drew her dagger, sensing the stillness on deck as all eyes stayed on her, waiting with dread or anticipation for her to render the killing stroke.

But instead of a stab to the heart, she pulled one of Don's arms out from the grip of the sailor holding it. "I'm always fair, Don. I won't kill you straight off, because I was able to get away when you betrayed me and your other shipmates. It was hard, though. Very hard. So I'm going to give you a chance to get away, too. But it won't be easy. The Sharr Islands are west of here, some ways over the horizon. It's a long swim, but a strong enough sailor could make it, I think."

Jules drew the point of her dagger down along Don's arm, drawing a grunt of pain from him, the cut immediately welling blood.

"But, since you also made it easy for the Imperials to find me, I'm going to make it easier for the sharks to find you." Jules cut another long line down Don's other arm. "Have a nice swim."

Don fought furiously as the sailors holding him hauled him to the railing. "No! Please!"

The sailors mercilessly pushed Don onto the top of the rail, pausing as Jules walked up to them. At her gesture, they let go of him. "Goodbye, Don." She jabbed with her dagger, and as Don flinched back he overbalanced, falling with a despairing scream that ended with the sound of a splash.

Jules wiped clean the blade of her dagger and turned back to see Captain Aravind gazing back at her with almost as much fear as Don had shown.

But he stepped toward her despite the warning cutlass that Liv raised. "On your word, none of us were to be harmed."

"On my word if you gave us no trouble. He fought," Jules said.

Aravind glanced at his remaining crew, then back at Jules. "If you mean to do the same for all of us, I beg that you take out your wrath on me, and spare the rest." He had to swallow before being able to say more. "Take… my life… and spare my crew."

Jules shook her head as she looked at the captain, feeling the cold begin to leave her. "Why would I harm any of the rest of you? Have you done me wrong?"

"Not that I know."

"He," Jules said, pointing toward the railing where Don had briefly sat, "betrayed me and the rest of his shipmates. He earned his fate. You, Captain, have just earned my respect. I wish only to know if you were aware of his true name."

"No," Aravind said. "He came aboard as Ron of Centin. He agreed to work for his passage rather than as formally part of the crew because I couldn't pay him. He said he needed to get to Landfall."

"Then you are blameless in this." Jules looked toward Liv. "Anyone else aboard?"

"No," she said, her eyes studying Jules.

"Then let's go over those manifests," Jules told Aravind, leading the way to the stern cabin.

The cabin was sparsely furnished, supporting Aravind's claim of hard times on the badly-named *Prosper*. He brought out the ship's money chest, opened it, and showed the contents to her.

There wasn't much to see. "You have no other money on the ship?"

He reached into a pocket and dropped a single silver coin into the money chest. "Some of the crew might have a little, their own personal funds."

"I see. Why didn't the owner of the ship help you out?"

"I am the owner of this ship," Captain Aravind said, his gaze on her both proud and defiant.

She paused to think about that, looking once more at the meager amount in the money chest. "You'll not be the owner for much longer if this chest is any measure. This isn't enough to pay the bribes the Imperial inspectors at Landfall will demand."

"I... was hoping to make an arrangement with them."

"That's a false hope. Imperial customs officials have small hearts with no room for mercy, and large wallets that need to be filled," Jules said. "Show me your manifests."

The *Prosper*'s cargo was a mixed lot indeed, though mostly lumber as the captain had said. "I'm guessing this is best you could afford to buy."

"That's right. Lumber is cheap in the Sharr Isles as they clear land for new buildings and fields."

"None of this cargo will fetch high returns in Landfall. You'll be lucky to clear expenses even if the customs officers forgo their bribes." Jules tapped the manifests, thinking. Perhaps she could solve more than one problem here. "I know somewhere you can get much greater return for it."

"Where?" Captain Aravind asked, watching her warily.

"Have you heard of the place to the west where Dor is building a new settlement on the south coast?"

"Not much. Just rumors. That's… an illegal settlement, isn't it?"

"In the Emperor's eyes," Jules said. She reached out and closed the money chest. "You still need this to pay your crew."

"I don't understand," he replied, staring at her.

"There are too few decent men in this world," Jules said. "Let me offer you a deal, Captain Aravind. There's not much profit on this ship for my crew, even if we stripped you bare. Lumber from the Sharr Isles is too heavy and too bulky to make good trade for us. But…" She pointed west. "That lumber would be very welcome at Dor's settlement. Here's the deal. You take your ship to Dor's, sell the lumber there along with all else you have, because out there all of these things are needed and are in short supply. When we meet again, you pay this ship two tenths of what you profit from the sale."

"Two tenths?" Aravind shook his head in disbelief. "That would still leave me in much better shape than I am now, if what you say of Dor's settlement is true. You could take everything if you wanted."

"I could. Would you work for me, Captain?"

"For you?" He took a deep breath. "I heard you called Jules."

"That's my name."

"You're…" Aravind saw her tense and wisely changed the subject, shaking his head again. "Lady Pirate, sailing that far west with such a small crew would be very risky."

"I happen to have ten extra sailors aboard," Jules said. "Survivors we rescued off a wreck. They're looking for a new ship. One is an excellent first officer."

"I can't pay them!"

"You can with what this cargo will bring at Dor's." Jules gave him a sharp look. "I'm not a patient woman, Captain Aravind. Will you work for me?"

"Yes." Aravind licked his lips nervously. "What if we run into another pirate between here and Dor's?"

"You tell that pirate this cargo is *mine*," Jules said, slapping the manifests. "If they take from it, they take from me."

Captain Aravind inhaled slowly, his eyes on Jules. "Why?"

She smiled. "I asked a Mage that same question. He told me there's no answer to 'why,' but also too many answers to count."

"A Mage…" Aravind's eyes widened. "You spoke with a Mage?"

"Briefly," she said.

"I don't understand. You ruthlessly killed that man who called himself Ron, but now you're acting in a very… kind manner."

Jules pointed out towards the water. "Don betrayed me to the Imperials in exchange for money. I gave him what he deserved. You stood up bravely for your crew and are trying to make a living as a free merchant. I'm giving you what you deserve. Why is that hard to understand?"

"Perhaps because people getting what they deserve so rarely seems to happen."

She couldn't help giving him a half smile. "Doesn't that make it all the more important that we do that when we can?"

"I suppose it does." He breathed in deeply once more. "I accept your offer, your generous offer, Captain Jules. How do I find Dor's?"

"Sail west along the southern coast. You'll come to a place where the cliffs give way to a large valley with a river running through it. You can't miss it. It's an easy approach and a decent harbor."

"And how do I find you afterwards to pay your share?"

"That'll be harder," Jules said. "I can't set up shop anywhere because that'd attract too much interest from the Great Guilds and the Emperor. You know Kelsi's settlement in the north?"

"I've heard of it," Aravind said. "I can find it."

"There are places there that will hold your payment in credit for the *Sun Queen*," Jules said. "Credit to the ship, not to me personally. Ask around, and you'll be told of them."

"I understand. Consider it done." He offered his hand, and Jules shook it. "Captain, if I can ever do anything else for you, I will."

She nodded solemnly. "Someday I may have need of ships and sailors. When that day comes, remember this day."

"I will. I confess I still don't understand, though. Surely despite the prophecy you don't intend to battle the Great Guilds."

"The prophecy speaks of a daughter of my line, not me. And it would be suicide to battle both of the Great Guilds." Jules waved toward the west. "The common people have to grow stronger. They need to get out from under the heel of the Emperor. We can build free cities out there, or at least as free as the Great Guilds permit. You can help that happen."

Captain Aravind looked toward the west. "I never dreamed of being part of anything greater than trying to make a living. There isn't much room for dreams in this world."

"Yes, there is," Jules said. "To the west."

"But most of the land to the west is a wasteland, behind horrible reefs."

"Everyone says that," Jules said, thinking of Ian yesterday and quickly shoving the thought aside. "But is it a wasteland?"

The question took Aravind aback. "That's what all the charts show."

"Maybe it's time someone checked those charts."

"But ships have gone west, and disappeared! Everyone's heard those stories."

"Everyone has," Jules said. "Big ships, supposedly. With good captains and good crews. What were the names of the ships? Where'd they sail from?"

"They, uh, sailed from Sandurin. "

"In Landfall, everyone knows they sailed from Landfall. When did they disappear? A hundred years ago. Two hundred years ago. Fifty years ago. Did you ever meet anyone related to someone on one of those ships? Someone whose ancestor disappeared in a voyage to the west?"

Aravind's brow furrowed as he thought. "No."

"Odd, isn't it? Wouldn't people talk about that?" Jules nodded to him. "Something to think about. By the way, you're from Dunlan? How'd you end up on the Sea of Bakre?"

His smile held the sadness of long-ago dreams. "I grew up in Dunlan, on the eastern shores of the Empire, the waters of the Great World Ocean before us. The Umbari. You're a sailor. I'm sure you understand the desire to sail beyond the horizon and see what's there."

"Why didn't you?"

"Because the Mechanics Guild forbids the use of ships on the ocean large enough to sail beyond sight of land. All you'll find in the harbor of Dunlan are fishing boats, and not large ones." Aravind looked east, as if seeking sight of that faraway place. "When I was young, a few daring shipwrights tried building new boats, gradually increasing the size in the hopes the Mechanics wouldn't notice. They did. The larger boats and the yards building them were all destroyed. It was quite a fire."

Jules looked east as well. "It makes you wonder what might be out there. What the Mechanics Guild doesn't want us to find."

"They claim there's nothing but endless water all around the world until you finally reach the wastes at the western end of the Sea of Bakre, if anyone could actually sail that far without running out of food and water or being destroyed in the tremendous storms that can roil the ocean. The Mechanics say the ban is to protect us from losing ships that way. But I wonder, as you do."

"Mechanics don't usually spend much time worrying about the fates of commons," Jules said.

"It's said in Dunlan that somewhere out there in the ocean is another great mass of land. A continent like this one," Aravind said. "But that's just a story. I never met anyone who had any proof of it."

"Another continent?" Jules switched her gaze to the west, trying to control her excitement at the idea. "Then we could reach it from the western side of this continent, too, couldn't we?"

"I suppose. No one knows."

Pulling her thoughts back from dreams of another continent, Jules led Aravind back out on deck. "All hands! Gather to listen and vote!"

Once the crew of the *Sun Queen* had gathered so they could hear, Jules laid out her deal with Captain Aravind. "I know as captain I have authority to make such deals on behalf of the ship, but I wanted you all to be aware of it. There's no profit in it today, but we'd get very little from looting this ship. Instead, it's a guarantee of better profit within a few months' time."

"They've got no money?" Kyle asked.

"Just a pittance. They got cleaned out by pirates on their last voyage."

"Pirates?" Marta called in mock outrage. "The scum! They took our money!"

"They did," Jules said. "Anyone who wants to look in the ship's strongbox is welcome to do so."

Daki had been speaking with the other sailors who'd been rescued from the wreck of the *Merry Runner*, and now raised his voice. "Captain Jules, we'd all like to take this offer of employment. It'll keep us together, and offers good prospects for the future."

"Captain," Gord said, "this seems to be the best we can make of this, but we need something better soon, don't we? It's been a while since we landed a good prize."

"We'll get one," Jules promised. "With this ship headed west to Dor's, they won't be telling anyone around here that we're prowling these waters."

"Anyone else?" Liv demanded. "All right. Vote! All in favor!"

Just about every hand went up.

I wish you could see this, Jules thought to Ian. *I wish you could see that people can have a say in their own fates.* "Get your things aboard this ship," she told Daki and the others from the *Merry*. "Fair seas to you."

"Thank you, Captain," Daki said. "What I told you before, it still stands. If you have need of us, call."

A short time later, the grapnels were let go, and the *Prosper* swung about to begin tacking to the west. Captain Aravind, on his own quarterdeck, offered Jules a salute as the two ships separated.

"You made some new friends," Liv commented. "But Gord was right. We need something more substantial than friendship to pay the bills."

"We'll get it," Jules said.

* * *

In the early afternoon of the same day, long before the crew could get restless as the *Sun Queen* slowly trolled the sea lanes for targets, tall masts were sighted coming from the east.

Putting on more sail again, the *Sun Queen* swooped down on her prey.

"Oh, that's a fat one, that is," Marta cried from a spot high in the rigging. "There'll be plenty for us aboard that ship!"

The other ship tried to run, but the *Sun Queen* had the weather gage and could make best use of the wind. She closed the final distance, Jules gathering much of the crew on deck to overawe their prey.

She herself climbed into the lower ratlines, the Mechanic revolver held high. When it came to overawing people, nothing matched that weapon.

On the deck of the other ship, Jules saw crew gathering, armed with crossbows and cutlasses as her pirates were. But the pirates easily outnumbered the defenders, and everything about this encounter felt reassuringly normal. "Strike your sails!" Jules called across the gap remaining between the two ships, brandishing the Mechanic weapon. "Give us no trouble and none will be harmed! On my word!"

The captain of the other ship had seemed ready to fight. But now, staring at Jules, she called out orders. Her crew set down their weapons and hastened up into the rigging to furl the sails.

Once again the grapnels were thrown, and once again Jules led her pirates onto the deck of a prize.

The captain approached Jules, part of a tattoo visible on one arm attesting to her origins on the lower decks. The woman's attitude bespoke the competence of someone who'd spent their life on the waves. But she also displayed a nervousness which Jules thought a natural response to having pirates aboard. "My ship is yours. I hold you to your word to harm none."

Jules gestured to Liv and Gord. "Take two groups and search the ship."

The captain shook her head at Jules, the uneasiness even more apparent. "Not the stern cabins. On your life, not the stern cabins."

Jules looked aft, seeing that on this larger ship the stern cabin had been split into two halves, one to port and one to starboard. "Passengers?" Jules tried to keep her own voice calm.

"On the port side, there's a family of Mechanics."

"Are they armed?"

"Not that I've seen." The captain eyed Jules. "More to your concern is who's in the cabin on the starboard side. It's a Mage, and unless I'm much mistaken you're the woman that any Mage will seek the death of."

"I'm that woman," Jules said. "Just one Mage?"

"Aye. One is more than enough, I'd say."

"Me, too." Jules took a deep breath. "Liv, keep the crew together for now."

"What are you going to do?" Liv asked, her eyes on the door to the starboard cabin.

"Either I wait for the Mage to come out and try to kill me, which he will, or I go in," Jules said, keeping her voice matter of fact. "I'd rather have the initiative."

"Be careful, you fool," Liv muttered.

"I've got this," Jules said, raising the revolver again.

She paused to check the revolver, ensuring that one of the cartridges was in the cylinder ready to rotate into place when she pulled the trigger. Acutely aware that every eye on the ship was on her, Jules began walking toward the starboard cabin. Half expecting the door to fly open and the Mage to leap out at her, Jules was mildly surprised to reach the door without anything happening.

She took a deep breath, letting it out slowly to calm herself, then another breath in. Drawing her dagger, she used the hand holding it to push the door open as Jules sprang inside.

The interior was much dimmer than the light outside, because the curtains on the stern windows were pulled completely closed. Jules barely noticed that, her eyes fixed on the Mage sitting on the deck in the center of the cabin.

The Mage's eyes had been closed, but they opened with a slow deliberation that almost unnerved her. Fixing his gaze on Jules, the Mage studied her with eyes that held no feeling in a face that might have been that of a dead man, so little emotion did it hold.

She centered the Mechanic revolver on the Mage, starting to pull the trigger.

He disappeared.

Jules, one step inside the cabin, paused for just an instant before taking a hasty step backwards to stand in the doorway. Her heart pounding, her dagger before her in a guard position, she searched the apparently empty cabin for any sign of the Mage.

No one else on the ship was speaking, leaving an eerie silence in which the only sounds were the creaking of the ship's wood, the sigh of the wind through the rigging, and the soft murmur of the sea against the hull. Jules strained her ears for any noise that might mark the movement of the Mage, but heard nothing.

A bright beam from the late-afternoon sun lanced through the open doorway and onto the floor of the cabin, dust motes dancing in the light. Jules found herself staring at the movement of the specks of dust.

Something unseen moved through that spot, setting the dust motes swirling.

Jules brought her dagger up just in time to catch the thrust of the Mage's knife aimed at her neck.

She centered the revolver on where he must be, but hesitated, knowing that she couldn't afford to waste a single cartridge.

A glint of light marked the Mage knife swinging at her, Jules shifting her dagger just in time to parry the blow. Breathing heavily, she stared into the empty cabin, wondering if she'd have to shoot the revolver and hope she hit her impossible to see target.

Between one eye blink and the next, the Mage was there, standing to one side of the door where the revolver shot aimed at the center would've missed him. Jules had time to notice sweat streaming down the Mage's face, his muscles quivering with exhaustion, as she shifted her aim. What had exhausted the Mage so quickly? Surely not only two attacks with the knife.

The Mage began another thrust as Jules pulled the trigger and the thunder of the revolver filled the world.

He paused, a blackened hole in the robes over his abdomen, swaying slightly like a man who'd had too much to drink.

Still showing no trace of feeling, the Mage brought his knife up again.

Jules' weapon thundered once more as she pulled the trigger in a spastic yank, so close to the Mage that she couldn't miss.

The Mage jerked, his hand still gripping the long knife but seeming unable to move. After a long moment, he took one halting step back, then his legs collapsed under him. Hitting the deck with a thud, he lay face up, his eyes open.

Jules cautiously approached him, her Mechanic weapon still pointed at the Mage. But he didn't move aside from the rapid, shallow rise and fall of his chest as he breathed.

She stopped, staring at the Mage's face. It was no longer completely impassive and unfeeling. As with the other Mages she'd seen die, some sensation was coming into his expression as his strength failed.

Was the trace of emotion she was seeing something like serenity? Why?

Jules went to one knee beside him and the Mage's eyes shifted to look at her.

"Over... at... last," he said, the celebratory nature of the words sounding odd in the unfeeling tones of a Mage.

"You're dying," Jules said. "Are you happy about that?"

"Ha… ppiness… ill… usion."

"Happiness is an illusion?" It wasn't hard to understand why someone who believed that might welcome death. Jules studied the Mage's face, seeing the traces of old scars that she'd noted on other Mages.

Fighting the revulsion she felt over touching a Mage's clothing, Jules pulled open his robes to expose the Mage's chest.

The ragged holes made by the projectiles from the Mechanic weapon were still spastically spurting gouts of blood as the Mage's heart made its last feeble efforts to serve the needs of his body. Blood had covered much of the chest, but on what was visible Jules could see more old scars that must have been inflicted decades before. She knew of some street gangs in Landfall that used ritual scarring to form hidden marks identifying them as members, but the scars on the Mage showed no sign of any pattern. They showed the randomness of blows rendered by a variety of objects.

Why did every Mage she'd seen close up have such scars?

Jules looked back at the face of the Mage. "How many blows does it take to beat the humanity out of a person and leave only a Mage?" she asked.

But his eyes had closed, and as Jules watched his last breath sighed out, taking his life with it.

She grimaced, bracing herself on her raised knee to stand up.

The one other Mage she'd managed to exchange some words with had seen death coming and feared it. This Mage had apparently welcomed its approach.

Was it too much to ask that the monsters of her world have some consistency?

She frowned down at the body, thinking about that. Mages all lacked any expression on their faces and feeling in their voices. That made them seem identical. Say the word "Mage" and every common would summon up the same image. But the two Mages she'd spoken with had clearly been individuals, different on the inside.

What did it mean?

How could she ever learn the answer?

Jules turned and left the cabin, seeing everyone on deck watching her. "The Mage is dead," she announced, looking away from the awed gazes of everyone watching her.

"What do we do with the body?" The captain of the ship stared from Jules to the open door of the cabin and back again.

"Throw it in the sea," she said, remembering the Mages who'd killed Mak.

Jules looked to the other cabin door, still closed, trying to get herself fully back under control. "I need to talk to the Mechanics."

"Do you mean to kill them, too?" It was hard to tell which answer the captain wanted to hear.

"Not today," Jules said. "Hopefully they won't kill me. But I need to find out what their Guild is up to."

"Don't they want to kill you?"

"They did. Probably still do. But I don't know. Mechanics aren't Mages. There's only one way to find out."

CHAPTER FIVE

S he walked to the closed door, realized she was still holding the weapon in her hand, and placed it back in the holster. Reaching up, she knocked firmly but politely on the door.

"You may enter."

The port cabin was the mirror image of the starboard cabin the Mage had occupied, but where that room now held only death, this one was full of life. The windows were open, letting in light and air. A man and woman sat inside, facing the door, their Mechanics' dark jackets a somber reminder of their status. Behind them stood two children, one a girl who looked to be in her early teens, and the other a boy a few years younger. The children were staring at her with ill-concealed hostility and some fear, while the adults regarded Jules with bland expressions.

"Are you here to try to kill us?" the man asked, as if the question were a normal one.

"No, Sir Mechanic," Jules said, determined to use this meeting to her best advantage. "I wanted to inform you that you need no longer be concerned about the Mage who was aboard."

The woman Mechanic raised her eyebrows at Jules. "You killed him? That's the shots we heard?"

"Yes, Lady Mechanic."

"How many Mages does that make for you?"

"At least four, Lady Mechanic." Jules said it in a flat voice to remove any hint of a boast to the statement.

The woman, though, nodded as if impressed. "What are your intentions regarding this ship?"

"Once my crew is done removing the valuables and cargo that we want, we'll leave and the ship will be allowed to continue on to the Sharr Isles."

The male Mechanic gave her a searching look. "I thought you wanted all Mechanics to die. That was you who said that, wasn't it?"

"Yes, Sir Mechanic." At Jacksport, during her last meeting with Mechanics, when her patience had snapped and she'd spoken her mind to them. It had very nearly gotten her killed instead.

"Why not start here with us?"

Jules studied the Mechanic, trying to judge the intent behind his question. "I'm not a fool, Sir Mechanic. I already have one of the Great Guilds doing all it can to kill me, and the Empire trying to capture me. I don't need any more enemies bending every effort against me. If I killed even one Mechanic, your Guild would be relentless in its pursuit of me, and those around me would suffer. And, to be clear, your Guild and I have the same opponents."

"The 'Great Guilds,'" the female Mechanic said with a sigh. "Why did we allow that term to come into use among the commons? As if the Mages were our equals?"

"We can't control everything," the male Mechanic replied before turning his attention back to Jules. "I saw you look at our children."

"I don't harm children," Jules said. "Never."

"I'm not a child. Neither is my wife here."

"I will never willingly make an orphan of any child."

"Ah. You can display self-control."

Jules nodded. "Contrary to what your Guild believes, common people are not animals."

Instead of taking offense at her words, the man replied in a serious tone. "Not all Mechanics see the commons as animals. There are plenty of us who see them as people. Clearly our inferiors, in need of guidance and control, but still people. And then there's you. We'd wondered if you'd declared war on the Mechanics Guild." He made the idea sound too absurd to be taken seriously.

"I'm not a fool," Jules repeated. "And that's not my destiny."

"Oh, right," the female Mechanic said. "Your daughter will do that."

"A daughter of my line, Lady Mechanic," Jules said.

"A daughter of your line." She gave Jules another close look before speaking to her husband. "Regardless, any sons or daughters of this girl should be tested."

"Yes," the man agreed. "They could well be Guild material."

Jules barely fought down a shudder at the idea of her young children being seized and raised as Mechanics. A memory of Mak's daughter, taken from him as a young girl and turned against him, rose in her mind. She didn't reply to the man's statement, not trusting herself to speak in reply.

If he noticed, the male Mechanic didn't show any sign of it, instead talking in a straightforward way. "It's no secret that there are some changes occurring in this world. Commons escaping the Empire and setting up new towns outside its boundaries. Trying to stop those changes would entail potential major costs, so the Guild is trying to manage them to its benefit. But then we have you. A wild card. What's your name?"

"Jules of Landfall, Sir Mechanic."

"Jules of Landfall." He nodded. "Suppose you had sitting before you some leaders of the Mechanics Guild, and they expressed their concerns to you about your potential to cause problems. What would you say to them?"

She paused to carefully consider her words before speaking. If the free common folk were to survive and grow, they needed the strength of the Mechanics Guild on their side, or at least for it to remain neutral in the fight. "You called me a wild card, Sir Mechanic. I would say that a wise player, no matter the game, knows that a well-played wild card can mean the difference between winning and losing."

The male Mechanic looked impressed, glancing at his wife before addressing Jules again. "That's well argued. Of course, there's no question of whether or not the Guild wins. It's a matter of what winning might cost. You've helped the Guild in two ways prior to this. The Mages have devoted a lot of effort to chasing you, efforts that might have hindered the Mechanics Guild's own work. And the Empire has had its attention diverted from pushing against the rules the Mechanics Guild have laid down for commons to follow. Those Imperial schemes would certainly be fruitless, but potentially expensive for our Guild to put an end to. You were a valuable tool before. Would you be valuable again?"

"It depends on what I'm asked to do, Sir Mechanic."

The woman shook her head at Jules like a teacher reproving a recalcitrant student. "Don't try to bargain."

"I'm not bargaining, Lady Mechanic," Jules said. "I'm being honest that there are things I will not do."

"Such as killing children?"

"Yes, Lady Mechanic."

"A tool with a moral compass of its own isn't necessarily a bad thing," the man observed. "What about countering moves by the Emperor, Jules of Landfall? What about keeping him off-balance?"

"I've been known to do such things," Jules said.

He smiled. "So we've heard. The Guild has an order out for you to be killed if seen, but that might constitute a serious waste. It'd be a shame to destroy a tool that could do some useful work and spare Mechanics from having to get directly involved. All right. Get on with your pillaging and looting of the ship so we can continue on our way to Caer Lyn. We don't want to get there late."

"With the winds as they are, this ship will have no trouble making up the time," Jules said. Not expecting any polite farewell, she backed from the cabin and closed the door. Facing forward along the deck again, she once more saw everyone standing still, watching her. "Is there no task that needs doing?" she yelled. "Get your arms and legs to work! We've spent enough time here already!"

Her crew hastened to transfer some crates, while Liv came up to Jules, eyeing her. "We're bringing off two crates of wine, a crate of vinegar, and some bales of clothing. The ship's strongbox yielded a fair sum and the passengers have contributed a portion of their own wealth. The owner of the ship is a prince, so this will make another friend for you in the Imperial court."

"Good. Let's get it done."

"Is everything all right, Captain?"

"I'm fine," Jules said, feeling emotionally drained and wishing this day was done.

"Why'd you let them live? The Mechanics?"

"I have my reasons."

"This is the perfect chance to get a few," Liv pressed. "Use the Mage's long knife. Everyone can say the Mage killed the Mechanics before you could step in to kill the Mage. The world has a few less Mechanics, it'll make more bad blood between the Great Guilds, and no one can blame you. The Mechanics would probably thank you!"

Jules knew why Liv was urging that action. Every common had experienced bad treatment from Mechanics. Even the captain of this ship would probably be happy with Jules for killing her other passengers as long as the Mage could be blamed. But it went against everything Jules felt. "No."

"But—"

Accumulating tension flared and her temper exploded, but Jules held herself partly in check. "*I do not harm children!*" She stomped away from Liv, everyone in her path hastily making way.

Jules hopped back over the joined railings to the *Sun Queen*, making her way to the quarterdeck through the sailors working to bring aboard loot from the merchant ship. She found Ang standing by the ship's wheel, his expression impassive. "What are you, a Mage?" she asked him, her tones sharp enough to cut through an anchor cable.

"That's not funny, Cap'n," Ang said, a frown forming.

It took her a moment to crawl out of her mood and realize why he was upset. He'd told her once that Mages had killed his mother. Jules felt her face get hot with shame. "I'm sorry, Ang. I'm truly sorry. I didn't think."

"That's all right," Ang said, though his tone of voice still sounded distant.

"It's not all right. I promise you I will never make such a comment again."

He looked at her for a long moment before nodding to accept her apology. "All right," he said, and this time his voice sounded normal.

Angry at herself, Jules ran both hands through her hair. "I think we should head north once we're done with that ship. The moment it reaches the Sharr Isles a whole lot of people will learn that we're in this area."

"And we shouldn't be anywhere nearby when that happens," Ang said. "But I would advise steering in another direction until the other ship loses sight of us so they think we're heading elsewhere."

"Right," Jules said. "Maybe I can help that along." Grateful to be able to do something to take her mind off of her words, Jules went back to the railing and called the captain of the other ship over. "You came from Landfall?" Jules asked her.

"That's so," she replied.

"Did you see many Imperial warships about?"

"Not many," the other captain said. "It's no secret that the Empire's ships of war are scattered across the sea searching for you."

"It's been a while since I've seen Landfall," Jules said, attempting to sound like someone who was wistful and trying not to show it.

The sun was near setting when the transfer of useful cargo was done and the *Sun Queen* cast off. Jules watched the shape of the other ship dwindle in size as the *Sun Queen* headed east of southeast along a line towards Landfall. Hoping they weren't being too obvious, Jules paced the quarterdeck, spotting Liv leaning against the railing, her back to anyone else. It felt wrong, since Liv usually faced inwards so she could talk to anyone else nearby. "Are you all right, Liv?"

"I'm fine," she said, keeping her gaze out over the water.

"You just seem a bit moody," Jules pressed.

Liv, her brow lowered in a scowl, finally looked at Jules. "*I'm* a bit moody? That's the sea calling the river wet, that is. I may be moody at times, but I don't take it out on my friends!"

Jules fought down an initial burst of anger that would only have worsened things. She had to admit that Liv had a point, but... "Liv, you don't—"

"And don't give me that 'I don't know what it's like to be you' bilge! I've been around you enough in all of your moods that I've got a pretty good idea of what it's like, I do!"

Once again feeling defensive anger, Jules felt it fade as she remembered her unforgivable words to Ang. "You've got a point there. I'm sorry, Liv," Jules said. "I've got a mouth on me and a bit of a temper."

"Really?" But Liv finally relaxed as she said it. "More than a bit of both, but that's something we can both lay claim to. What happened to cause that blowup?"

Jules leaned on the railing next to her, looking south. "I'm feeling my way along a dark path, Liv. I never know if the next step will be a wrong one and maybe my last. Did I say the right things to those Mechanics? The whole time I talked to them I had to wonder if they had weapons concealed on them and were just leading me along. If they killed me, what would they do to you guys after that? And I hate having to act subservient around them. Even the nicest Mechanics are arrogant asses. And I was still on edge from confronting and killing that Mage, and having to touch him and his clothes, and confused by his attitude as he was dying, and..." Jules blew out an angry breath. "It can be too much at times."

Liv didn't reply for a moment, gazing up at the sky where the clouds were still lit by the sun. "I admit I can't put myself in your shoes."

"I don't want anyone feeling sorry for me."

"Except yourself?" Liv asked. "Before you answer and speaking of too much, I think we may be in for some bad weather."

Pausing to consider her words, Jules wet one finger and raised it. "The wind's starting to change."

"Yeah. And look up there. Dark clouds moving in from different directions. The lower ones are piling up. The air's not happy. Can you feel it?"

"Now that you mention it, yes." Jules turned to yell across the ship. "All hands prepare for some rough weather! Get everything tied down, check the lines, and check the cargo. Make it an early meal tonight. We may not be able to risk cooking fires later on."

"Do we hold course, Captain?" Kyle, who was on the helm, called to her.

"No. We've opened enough distance from our last prize. Ang! Bring us about on a northern heading, and keep us steady on that as long as we can manage it."

Any hopes that the warning signs might indicate only a brief patch of bad weather were abandoned during the night as a gale came down from the north, whipping the seas to an angry maelstrom and relentlessly beating at the ship and her crew. All through the next day they tried tacking against the storm to continue heading north, but with what Jules thought was little success. The *Sun Queen* breasted each high wave in turn, foam and water breaking across the bow and running along the deck, followed by a plunge into the trough beyond before the bow rose to meet the next storm-driven wave. The wild day gave way to an angry night, followed by another day in which wind and wave battered the *Sun Queen*.

Ang, his clothing dripping with cold water, came down to the cabin where Jules was moodily taking a break. Since the seas were still too rough to risk cooking fires, she tipped some cold coffee into a mug, followed by a slug of rum, and offered it to him. The coffee pitcher rattled in its holder as the *Sun Queen* tossed again under the force of the weather. "Are we making any headway at all?" Jules asked as Ang drank.

He shrugged. "With the sun and stars blocked by the clouds, there's no way to tell. But I'd be surprised if we've made much."

"We could turn and run south."

"There are too many ships looking for us to the south," Ang said.

Jules grimaced. "And heading east would pin us against the coast of the Empire. That leaves west."

"If we turn west, I think we'd be running toward the Sharr Isles, where they'll be looking for us, or if we have made any progress north it might take us along the shipping routes heading to and from Altis," Ang said. "We know the Empire is patrolling that route more lately, and so are the Mechanics."

"Which leaves north." Jules got up wearily. Riding a ship in weather like this was like exercising non-stop the whole time, muscles constantly working even while sitting to maintain balance and avoid dangerous falls or tumbles. Even worse, with so much water breaking over the deck and leaking through the timbers, the crew had to constantly work at bailing out the bilges to keep the ship from slowly sinking. "I'll take the quarterdeck for a while. You rest down here."

"Aye, Cap'n. This storm has to let up soon."

"I think I said that same thing this time yesterday." She went out into the grayish day and the slashing rain, fighting her way up onto the quarterdeck where two sailors instead of the usual one struggled to hold onto the wheel. The sea formed an awesome and powerful sight under the lash of the storm, large swells, dark under the cloudy skies except for crowns of white foam, rolling past in endless ranks. The seas weren't running as high as yesterday, but still an occasional larger wave broke across the main deck, racing along it and tugging at the legs of anyone who had to be on deck, sailors hanging on for their lives to the nearest tether they could grasp. Most of the sails had been taken in so the winds wouldn't break the masts, those sails that were still set reefed to reduce their area. Sailing as close-hauled as she could, the *Sun Queen* struggled to make any way against the storm that seemed to mock the efforts of her and her crew.

Jules looked up at the low clouds scudding past above, displaying an infinite variety of shades of gray, and wondered why the simplest tasks sometimes had to be so difficult.

* * *

With morning, the storm finally slackened. The crew's relief changed to dismay, though, as the wind dropped to nothing and the seas went as flat as the plains around Umburan. The clouds disappeared, leaving a bright sun that fell upon the slack sails hanging from their spars, the waters of the sea forming a mirror. "Blazes," Liv commented. "The sea's angry at someone for sure."

"Thanks," Jules said.

"Oh, not you," Liv said. "Probably that fool Keli again. He said something against her, mark my words, and the sea is having its fun with us because of it."

Keli, walking past not far away, heard. "This isn't my doing. Not everything is my fault, woman!"

Through the rest of the day and the night the *Sun Queen* rested on the eerily peaceful waters while her crew grew ever more restless. As dawn approached on the next morning, though, a breeze finally began to whisper through the rigging. Slowly growing in strength, it teased at the hopes of the sailors until the wind grew strong enough to cause the sails to flap with a noise that seemed thunderous after the quiet of the day and night before.

Normally, rousing the crew during morning twilight would produce a rumbling chorus of complaints, but this time the sailors swarmed happily to the lines. Her canvas finally filling, the *Sun Queen* began slowing gaining way, tacking once more to the north as the sun rose into view to paint the sails with golden highlights.

The moment of glorious relief shattered almost as soon as it began.

"Something coming up from the south!" the lookout called just as Jules began to relax. "A cloud or… I think it's one of them Mechanic ships!"

"Blazes," Jules murmured, looking up to the sails. They were still scarcely filling, the *Sun Queen* barely maintaining steerageway. Out-running a Mechanic ship was nearly impossible at the best of times, requiring strong winds, shallow waters to cut through, islands to hide behind, and bad weather to disappear into. Right now, with the smooth sea offering no hint of shelter and the winds still soft, there wasn't any hope at all. "They're after me."

"We'll fight, Cap'n," Ang said.

"I know you would. All of you. But it's hopeless. You've seen the big Mechanic weapons on the front of their ships. I don't want any of you dying for no reason. Keep us on this course. I'm going to get straightened up. When they get closer, if they make it clear they're in search of us, we'll put the longboat in the water and I'll go see them in person."

"It'll be death this time," Liv said in a despairing voice.

"That's what you thought last time," Jules said. "I made it back that time, and I'll make it back this time." She hoped that she at least sounded confident, because she certainly didn't feel that way.

She went down to her cabin, knowing that the Mechanic ship could close on the *Sun Queen* with amazing swiftness compared to the sailing ships of the common people. Wasting no time, she quickly scrubbed her hair and herself, then put on her best shirt and trousers. Her boots got a quick buffing that couldn't make any impact on the scar down one of them where the Mage lighting had found its path. Jules strapped on the Mechanic revolver, knowing the Mechanics would expect to see it and would take apart the *Sun Queen* if they didn't.

Once back on deck, Jules could see the hull of the oncoming Mechanic ship clearly now, its gray sides gleaming in the light of the morning sun. It had altered course and was clearly heading for an intercept of the *Sun Queen*.

"No bearing drift at all," Ang said in a gloomy voice. "He's coming right for us."

Jules nodded. "Slack the sails and put the longboat in the water."

No one argued, though she could tell they wanted to.

The Mechanic ship was drawing close as Jules stood on the quarterdeck and waved toward it before heading down to the main deck and the ladder down to the longboat. She tried not to look as tense as she felt, waiting each moment to hear the boom of the Mechanic ship's big weapon as it opened fire on the *Sun Queen*. As loud as the Mechanic revolver was, how loud would that much bigger weapon be? And how much damage would it do?

But the roar of thunder she dreaded didn't fill the air. The *Sun Queen* was barely making steerageway with her sails slacked as the Mechanic ship came close, gliding along, the bone in its teeth of a big white bow wave diminishing as the Mechanics effortlessly matched the course and sluggish speed of the pirate ship.

"Let's go," she told the sailors at the oars of the longboat.

"Captain—" Gord began, looking desperate.

"Let's go," Jules repeated. "If you have any faith in me, have it now."

The oars hit the water and the longboat began moving toward the Mechanic vessel. Jules sat in the bow, watching the big ship grow steadily bigger as she got closer to it, its metal sides seeming impossibly strong compared to the wood of common ships.

For a moment her mind wandered, thinking of how easily the Mechanic ship had caught the *Sun Queen*, and how powerful it was. And the Mechanics Guild had more than one such ship. The Mechanics could have easily swept every pirate ship from the sea if they wanted to. For whatever reason, they'd allowed the pirates to not only exist but to grow in number.

But those thoughts only distracted her for a moment. She tried to maintain her poise despite panic that threatened to burst out inside her. She had no way out of this except whatever wit she could bring to bear. If the Mechanics aboard this ship even bothered to speak to her before they killed her.

She saw a rope ladder dropping down the side of the Mechanic ship. They'd let her board the ship, at least.

The longboat came gracefully alongside, Jules feeling a moment of pride for how well her sailors maneuvered the small craft to touch the Mechanic ship as gently as a mother touching her baby.

"Good luck, Captain," Marta called as Jules stood to grasp the ladder.

Jules went up hand over hand, remembering the last time she'd boarded a Mechanic ship. She'd been barefoot then, instead of wearing boots, and part of her wished she was still finding purchase with her feet rather than the slicker soles of her boots. But at least this time she wouldn't feel quite so underdressed compared to the Mechanics.

Reaching the top, she climbed onto the metal deck, the metal sides of the ship's structure rising above her. Several Mechanics waited, three of them pointing the long weapons they called rifles at her. Many other Mechanics stood farther down the deck or higher up, gazing at Jules with curiosity or malice or disdain and sometimes a mix of all three.

One of the Mechanics, a hard-eyed woman, pointed to Jules' holster and gestured soundlessly. Moving slowly and carefully, Jules drew out the revolver and handed it to the woman.

Only when she had a good grip on the revolver did the female Mechanic speak. "Did you come to beg for your life?"

"Not for mine," Jules said. "But the crew of that ship have done no wrong to your Guild. I ask that they be allowed to leave in peace."

"We should make her crawl," one of the Mechanics said, lifting his rifle.

The woman ignored him. "The fate of that crew is up to you. Follow me."

Jules wondered if this was the same Mechanic ship that she'd been on before as she followed her guide through a metal hatch into the housing of the ship. Inside, the passages were as she remembered, walls and decks and overheads of metal, glass-covered light fixtures that glowed with the very bright and very steady radiance which felt unnatural compared to the healthy flames of candles and lanterns, and a low droning sound which seemed to come from everywhere. Maybe all of the Mechanic ships were the same inside, just as they were on the outside.

Jules followed partway down a passage, her guide then taking a turn deeper into the ship, then another that might lead forward. The similar passages and uniform metal fixtures and surroundings made it easy to get disoriented, even though her guide seemed to have no trouble finding her way around. Perhaps some of the numbers and lettering Jules spotted on the walls were addresses or directions.

She glanced back once, seeing the other Mechanics following, those with the weapons holding them more casually but still at the ready.

Had any other common people walked here before her? And what had happened to them after?

They finally stopped before a door that was made of wood. It didn't resemble anything Jules remembered from the other Mechanic ship she'd been on, so either this was a different ship or they'd brought her to a different place inside it. At least the fine-looking door didn't seem like that of a prison.

Her guard opened the door, then stood aside, gesturing for Jules to go in. Nerving herself and trying to calm her heart's urge to race, Jules stepped through the opening.

Inside, the room was lined with wood: paneling on the walls, polished planks on the deck, even light wooden panels in the overhead. Instead of being inside a ship, it might have been a fine room at the home of a wealthy person in Marandur. Although not even the wealthiest there had Mechanic lights glowing inside glass domes. Paintings of landscapes and seascapes were fastened to the walls, and a large, wooden desk was fixed firmly to the floor near one side of the room, heavy wooden chairs with fine upholstery set around it.

Three Mechanics waited in the room, lounging in their chairs on the other side of the large desk like Imperial princes secure in their position and superiority. No, the Mechanics would resent being compared to princes. To the Mechanics, Imperial princes were just as inferior as other commons.

The woman Mechanic who'd guided Jules set the revolver on the desk before leaving the room and closing the door behind her.

Jules recognized the older man in the middle, the "Senior Mechanic" she'd last seen at Caer Lyn in the Sharr Isles. To one side of him was another male Mechanic, younger, but thankfully not the thuggish one who'd accompanied the Senior Mechanic during that last visit.

She barely kept from reacting when she recognized the third Mechanic, a woman of early middle age who gazed at Jules intently.

Mak's daughter. Taken from him when she was a little girl, raised as a Mechanic, somehow turned against her father as well as other commons. Jules had met her briefly in Caer Lyn months ago.

Jules stayed wary as she walked to stand in front of the table. She'd already learned that she couldn't count on any womanly solidarity from female Mechanics, and male Mechanics only seemed to see her in terms of whatever they wanted.

The Mechanics didn't offer her a seat, so Jules kept standing as if unaware of the discourtesy. The younger male Mechanic showed a slightly contemptuous smile as he gazed off to the side, as if Jules wasn't worthy of his attention. The female Mechanic, Mak's daughter, kept her eyes on Jules, but with a guarded expression as if afraid to reveal anything. The older Senior Mechanic, though, sat watching her with a keen gaze, as if he were trying to see her thoughts. But Jules had long experience with hiding her feelings, and kept her expression as unrevealing as possible.

"There are many Mechanics who think you should be killed," the Senior Mechanic finally said. He paused, plainly waiting for her reaction.

Jules knew she could mock them, or play to their egos. Since they apparently weren't going to kill her right away, she decided it might be wiser to try the second approach first. "Why am I still alive, Sir Senior Mechanic?"

"Perhaps because you're smart enough to remember my proper title," he said. "Or perhaps because you represent an intriguing puzzle. By all rights, you should have died long ago. Or been imprisoned. Yet you remain free. Either you're exceptionally lucky, or there's a lot to you that isn't apparent from your status as a common person." The Senior Mechanic paused to gaze at her again. "Most importantly, you recently impressed the right people. That's why you and your ship haven't already been used for target practice."

"The Mages recently rather smugly let us know that they'd killed you," Mak's daughter said. Verona, Jules remembered. That was her name. "Why did they tell us that?"

"Because the Mages thought they had killed me, Lady Mechanic," Jules said.

"Why?"

She hesitated, deciding that the truth would be better than attempting a lie. She had no idea how much Mechanics knew about how Mages behaved. "I was hit by lightning from a Mage. I went down, and they assumed they'd killed me."

The younger male Mechanic laughed. "She doesn't even try to make her lies believable."

"Lightning?" Mechanic Verona asked, her eyes searching Jules. "Where did it supposedly hit you?"

Jules rolled up her shirt sleeve and showed them the scar. "It struck the cutlass I was holding and went down my side and into the deck of the ship. That's what we think happened."

"Come here," the Senior Mechanic ordered, grabbing Jules' arm when she stepped closer. He looked over the scar carefully. "That's not a fake. It's the result of a high-voltage burn."

"But that pattern..." Mechanic Verona said.

"It could be a tattoo," the younger Mechanic objected.

"How would they know what the tattoo should look like?" the Senior Mechanic demanded. "This is consistent with lightning striking a human body." He glared at Jules. "You said it went down your side?"

"Yes, Sir Senior Mechanic," Jules said, trying to sound calm and hold still when she wanted to yank her arm out of the man's grasp. "I was wet on that side. Seawater. That might've had something to do with it."

"Water," Verona said as if Jules had just explained the inexplicable. "The electrical charge ran down the conductor and grounded into the ship and the sea. Talk about dumb luck."

"The lightning must've come from the sky," the senior mechanic said, finally releasing Jules' arm. "The commons superstitiously believed the Mages had done it, and the Mages were happy to encourage that belief in their so-called powers."

Jules stepped back, rolling her sleeve down and trying to commit to memory what Mechanic Verona has said. But she had no idea what it meant. Electial something. Jules knew what it meant to charge an opponent, but how did that relate to what the Mechanic had said? And what was that about the ground, the ship, and the sea?

She didn't bother trying to argue with the Senior Mechanic. Her crew had seen the lightning coming at her from the Mages, not from the sky. But like the other Mechanics Jules had encountered, these also thought the Mages didn't have any real powers. Sometimes it felt like there were three worlds named Dematr. One as seen by the Mechanics, one seen by the Mages, and one experienced by the common people. Unfortunately, the Mechanics and the Mages were really in this world, lording it over the commons. "What does the Mechanics Guild want from me, Sir Senior Mechanic?"

He regarded her again for a moment before replying. "Important people believe that you may once more be of use to the Guild."

Important people? Those Mechanics she'd talked to less than a week ago? What had the male Mechanic said, something about what if she were speaking to the leaders of the Guild? Were he or his wife, or both of them, part of that leadership?

It was a good thing she hadn't killed them.

But what were the Mechanics planning this time? What had that man and woman decided Jules could accomplish for the Mechanics Guild if she wasn't killed? "Exactly how could I be of use to the Guild, Sir Senior Mechanic?"

The Senior Mechanic smiled, his lips a thin line. "The Emperor has decided to establish a new city in the north. West of the Northern Ramparts."

"West of the Ramparts?" Jules asked, startled. "Beyond Kelsi's and Marida's?"

The Senior Mechanic frowned slightly in warning.

"Beyond Kelsi's and Marida's, Sir Senior Mechanic?" Jules said.

"Yes." Satisfied by her belated use of his title, he waved vaguely toward the west. "There's a river that joins the sea. The Emperor is sending ships to build a town at that place even though the Guild has made it clear we do not approve of such actions."

Jules didn't try to hide her surprise. "The Emperor plans to openly defy the Mechanics Guild?"

Mechanic Verona made a disdainful snort. "The Emperor believes his little ambition is secret, that he'll establish this settlement and when the Guild eventually learns of it he'll be able to present it as an accomplished fact that the Guild will let slide rather than make a big deal of it. But of course the Guild knows all about the plan, and isn't happy at all that the Emperor is ignoring the Guild's will in this matter."

Jules nodded in a respectful manner, which this time wasn't entirely feigned. She, like all common folk, believed that the Great Guilds had spies among the commons. For the Mechanics to have a source deep within the Imperial court wasn't surprising, but still impressive given the punishments inflicted on those found to have committed treason, or even sometimes merely suspected of it. But what did the Emperor's plan have to do with her? "What does the Guild want from me, Lady Mechanic?" Maybe repeating the question a third time would get her a straight answer.

"The Guild wants to employ the right tool for the task." Verona smiled unpleasantly before continuing. "That's you."

"It *may* be you," the Senior Mechanic said, his voice growing sharper. "There are plenty of Mechanics who question your ability to serve the Guild in this matter. Your life rides on whether you prove them wrong. The Guild wants the Emperor's effort to fail. But we'd prefer that the Guild not have to flex its might. Directly frustrating the Emperor's efforts could cause him to refuse to back down rather than be embarrassed before his people. That could lead to... escalation. Wasted resources. There are matters beyond your understanding that we must consider."

Jules kept her expression unrevealing, simply nodding as if accepting the casual put-down.

"I still think slapping him down now will stop him from trying anything in the future," the younger male Mechanic complained. "Overwhelming force, to make it clear what'll happen if the commons ignore the will of our Guild."

"You're assuming the commons would react rationally to a display of such force," Verona objected. "We'd be slapping down their little emperor, hurting his pride and theirs."

"If a dog acts up, you let him know the consequences!"

"And if he responds by biting you?"

"Enough," the Senior Mechanic told them. "The founders set things up so the emperor or empress would handle the commons and we wouldn't have to rule them directly. The founders didn't anticipate that those rulers would become strong enough to think they could challenge the Guild. The Guild Masters have decided that we need another tool, something that could counter the Empire without the need for the Guild to constantly monitor its actions."

"Why change things that have worked in the past?" the male Mechanic asked.

"Change is almost always bad," the Senior Mechanic agreed. "But population growth and pressures among the commons have already caused changes in the situation. In the past the commons only looked to one person, the emperor or empress, for leadership. The pirates that have been giving the Emperor trouble were allowed as a means to keep him distracted, but being commons they've never shown any sign of coalescing around a single leader. Now, though, the Guild's leadership believes that thanks to the Mages and their silly prophecy, we've got a chance to try a new tool, someone else the commons will follow, and that's her. End of discussion." As if suddenly remembering that Jules was present, the Senior Mechanic shifted his gaze to her.

But even though listening intently, Jules had kept her outward appearance that of someone listless and inattentive. Common people had figured out that was the safest face to show to Mechanics.

Acting nervous or worried would center the attention of Mechanics on a common and make the Mechanics nervous as well. Whereas acting like a placid, dumb old cow on two legs made Mechanics complacent and more likely to pay little attention to a common. Commons had been employing that defensive aspect for a long time. As Mak had told her, it was always wise to fool people with whatever they expected to see since then they'd be more likely to accept it.

The younger male Mechanic had also checked to see if Jules was paying attention to the debate. "Hey, common!"

Jules pretended to come out of a bored daze. "Yes, Sir Mechanic?"

"What were we talking about?"

"Sir Mechanic?" Mimicking a student suddenly presented with a pop quiz, Jules acted as if she were groping for an answer. "The... effort of the Emperor... must fail."

"Good," the Senior Mechanic said. "You managed to grasp the most important point. As when you killed Mages and the Guild pretended not to be involved, now you will halt the Emperor's work as if acting on your own. The Emperor couldn't ignore a direct action by the Guild, but if a secret project of the Emperor's is stopped by a minor actor, few in the Empire will hear of it. The Emperor can keep his defeat as secret as he did the initial effort, choosing to pretend nothing had happened. That will be far safer for him than moving to counter what took place."

Jules didn't want to seem too sharp, but had to understand what the Mechanics were planning. "Why would the Emperor hesitate to counter something I did, Sir Senior Mechanic?"

"Because responding to an attack on a settlement that far from Imperial territory would require a major military action by his legions, and the Emperor knows the Guild would react to a major military action. We'd destroy the Imperial force, something the Emperor couldn't hope to cover up. He'd be humiliated in the eyes of his people." The Senior Mechanic eyed her. "You offer us a more precise means to adjust the Emperor's behavior."

"You want me to attack the new settlement?" Jules asked, not sure that she'd heard right.

"Wasn't I clear?"

"Sir Senior Mechanic... attack an Imperial town?"

Mechanic Verona gave her a cross look. "Why is that giving you trouble? Haven't you attacked Imperial towns already? The authorities in Sandurin are still flinching at shadows because of what you did there."

"I didn't actually attack Sandurin," Jules said. Although the Imperial authorities might have seen her actions in rescuing some captive laborers and their families as an attack. Especially since she'd killed a few retainers of an Imperial prince in the process.

Could she do what the Guild wanted? Because aside from frustrating the Emperor, that could be a good thing for Jules' own plans. Keeping the west free of the Empire. And attacking an Imperial town was something no common had ever thought of, actually taking armed action against the Empire. One of those cages of the mind that limited actions before they were even thought of. One of those cages that she wanted to break free of to show others it could be done.

She hesitated, thinking. "I'd have to gather other ships and crews to help. Do you know how many legionaries and ships the Emperor is sending to protect this new town, Sir Senior Mechanic?"

"Not many," he replied with a negligent wave, as if such matters were of no concern to his Guild. "He's starting out small in hopes of keeping the Guild from noticing. As for your own efforts, *you* shouldn't have any trouble gathering forces from among those who've fled the Empire. They think you're their... what do they call you?"

Jules tried to keep her angry reaction from showing in her voice. "Captain. They call me captain of my ship. The Imperial authorities call me a pirate."

The other male Mechanic laughed again. "Really? And what do the Mages call you?"

She hesitated again, deciding to tell the truth to see how the Mechanics would react. "One called me a shadow."

"What's that?" The Senior Mechanic sat straighter, surprised, and the gazes of the other two Mechanics sharpened. "A Mage spoke to you? Was it the one who spoke that so-called prophecy?"

"No, Sir Senior Mechanic. It was another. He was dying."

"He called you Shadow?"

"No, Sir Senior Mechanic. He kept calling me *a* shadow. He said everyone was a shadow."

"Maybe that's some kind of weird Mage insult," the younger male Mechanic said.

"Maybe," Mechanic Verona said, "it's a Mage's way of saying everyone not a Mage isn't important. You know, just a trick of the light that can't really do anything."

"That's likely it," the Senior Mechanic said, nodding. "What they've got wrong is that they're Mages, so *they're* not important, and we know everything they claim to do is a trick." His lips quirked in amusement. "You said he was dying, common? At your hands, no doubt. You've rid this world of more than one Mage. That's another of the reasons why the Guild decided to offer you this opportunity to serve it. You might also think of it as a test for you personally."

"A test for me, Sir Senior Mechanic?" Jules asked.

Mechanic Verona answered, her eyes once again fixed on Jules. "The Guild identifies young children with the Mechanic skills and acquires them at that age. It's rare but not unheard of for older candidates to be brought into the Guild if someone of sufficient talent is identified." She waited, watching, to see how Jules reacted to the statement and its implied promise.

Jules wondered whether she was supposed to look thrilled or daunted, but could spare little attention to that in her efforts to avoid shuddering in revulsion at the idea. Did Mechanic Verona really think she'd let the Mechanics Guild do to her what they'd done to her and so many other children of commons? She had no family to be turned against, but no one would turn her against her own people. Horrible enough that the other Mechanics had spoken of her children having to suffer that fate, but Jules herself as well?

Never. Not her children, and not her.

Perhaps Mechanic Verona saw what she was expecting to see in Jules' reaction, though. She smiled slightly. "Handle yourself right, and it could happen."

Stars above, the Mechanics thought they'd just offered the strongest bribe possible. As if certain no common could resist such an opportunity.

Maybe she would've been tempted, Jules thought, but only if she were someone else.

Oblivious to Jules' thoughts, the Senior Mechanic reached into his pack and brought out an object.

Another Mechanic revolver.

"It is necessary," he told Jules, "to make it clear to the Emperor that your actions in this case have the backing of the Guild. We also want to ensure your success." He set the revolver on the table next to the one Jules had brought before reaching into the bag to bring out a leather holster as well. "This weapon has five cartridges in it. You know what cartridges are, correct? Good. Choose someone reliable to use it alongside you. Even the Emperor's vaunted legions can't stop bullets with their shields." The Senior Mechanic grinned as if he'd made a clever joke.

"You're giving me a second weapon?" Jules asked, unable to believe it.

"Like the one you've been carrying, it's a loan, not a gift." His smile turned smug. "The Guild has realized that it doesn't need to dirty its own hands with some necessary tasks. Not if commons can be used instead. The Guild may demand this weapon's return. It would be foolish not to comply if that demand is made. And, of course, you will receive no more cartridges unless you use the weapon in ways that the Guild approves of. Do you understand?"

"Yes, Sir Senior Mechanic," Jules said.

"Gather the necessary forces and destroy the Emperor's ill-advised settlement attempt. Take no more time than is necessary to carry out this task."

"Yes, Sir Senior Mechanic." Jules paused as one of the Mechanic's words went home. "Destroy? Sir Senior Mechanic, is it necessary to destroy the settlement?"

The young male Mechanic glowered at her. "Your instructions are not complicated."

"I understand them, Sir Mechanic," Jules said. "But there's a good chance at least some of those sent to populate that settlement would be willing to live free of the Emperor's control. We could eliminate the Emperor's forces at the settlement and the Imperial leaders there, and leave the settlement to grow as a counter to further attempts by the Emperor to colonize that area."

"Why should we do that?" the Senior Mechanic asked, watching Jules closely.

"It would help establish another means of dealing with the Emperor's power," she said. "Instead of the Emperor using this settlement to expand the area he controls and create a new town or city answering to him, it would be a place populated by people who have escaped his control. A block against the Emperor trying the same thing there again." The Mechanic didn't seem impressed enough by the argument, so she deployed another. "And, of course, if it grew into a city it would be a place where your Guild could build a new Hall, thus expanding *its* power."

"Yes." The Senior Mechanic nodded slowly, an approving gaze on her. "That thought had occurred to us. Can you do it? Can you ensure that settlement remains independent of the Emperor?"

"Independent?"

That question earned her another superior grin. "Not answering to the Emperor. Not subject to his command. Like Altis. And like you. Although naturally you and that settlement will be expected to obey any commands from the Guild."

"Naturally," Jules said.

Independent. A new word. A new idea.

She liked it.

People who could live free of control by the Emperor and his many servants.

She hadn't known how to describe the future she wanted except by using the word *free*. But now she knew another word, another idea. Independent. Freedom from control by the Emperor, and someday from the Mechanics, and from the Mages as well.

She smiled as if agreeing with the Senior Mechanic, but inside Jules was amused by the irony that the Mechanics were helping her forge the weapons that the daughter of her line would someday use to destroy them.

"That's all," the Senior Mechanic said, rising from his seat. "Unless you hear otherwise you can let the town remain after you've captured it as long as sufficient commons there agree to keep it as a bastion against further Imperial actions. You have your orders. Get the job done." He gestured to the other two Mechanics as he headed for the door.

The two male Mechanics rose, the younger speaking in a low voice to the Senior Mechanic as they left the room, but Mechanic Verona paused just short of the door, her eyes fixed on Jules. "How did he die?" she asked in a low voice.

So Mak's daughter did care about his fate. Jules inhaled deeply before she could reply. "Two Mages killed your father."

"He long before that decided to stop being my father," Verona said, her voice growing harsh.

"No, he didn't. He loved you and your mother with his last breath."

Verona scowled and looked away as if refusing to debate the matter. "Two Mages. Maybe someday you'll be able to kill them."

"I already did," Jules said.

The Mechanic's startled gaze went back to Jules. "You're sure it was them?"

"Yes, Lady Mechanic. His blood was still on their knives when I wet my blade with their blood."

Verona bit her lip. "Good." After another pause, as if uncertain whether to say more, she nodded brusquely to Jules and turned to go.

Jules stopped Verona with a question poised in a soft voice. "Lady Mechanic, why does it have to be this way?"

Verona shook her head. "It has to be. You don't understand."

"No, I don't."

"If you haven't yet accepted the way things are, you need to start," Mechanic Verona said. "They're not going to change."

She left before Jules could say anything else. Which was just as well. Jules doubted that the Mechanic would've liked being reminded of the Mage prophecy.

Jules picked up both weapons, deciding to carry both rather than place hers back in the holster. The woman Mechanic and the armed escort were waiting outside the room. They didn't appear happy to see the Mechanic revolvers in her arms, but none objected. Jules followed them out through the passages, trying to see as much as possible of what was around her without the Mechanics realizing she was doing so. At one point, Jules took a quick look at one of the lights, trying to make out the source of its brilliance, but had to just as quickly look away when the intensity stung her eyes.

Out on deck again, Jules couldn't resist taking a deep breath of the fresh sea air that she'd wondered if she'd ever taste again.

Finally placing her revolver back in its holster and gripping the other holster and revolver tightly in one hand, Jules went down the ladder with a series of awkward, one-handed lurches.

Stepping back into the longboat, she saw her sailors staring at her with mingled joy and disbelief. "Let's get back to the ship," Jules prompted them, grinning, and the sailors hastily bent to their oars.

The Mechanic ship began moving away from them faster and faster, the pale smoke rising from a sort of a chimney amidships growing in size and strength. Jules noticed a churning of the water along the stern of the ship. Did that mark the presence of whatever drove it forward? She had no way of knowing.

By the time the longboat once again reached the *Sun Queen*, the Mechanic ship had executed a smooth turn and headed back to the south.

Jules climbed up to the deck, seeing Liv staring at her with amazement. "How did you do it this time?" Liv asked.

"I didn't kill some people I could've killed," Jules said, unable to resist the urge to needle Liv for her earlier advice. She went up to the quarterdeck, watching the Mechanic ship move away. She didn't really breathe freely again until it had disappeared over the horizon.

"Where to, Cap'n?" Ang asked, his eyes on the extra Mechanic weapon that Jules now carried.

"Kelsi's, as planned," Jules said. "I need to talk to some friends, and they're likely to be in that area."

CHAPTER SIX

"**A**re you out of your mind?"

The *Sun Queen* had encountered the *Star Seeker* on open waters. There'd been bad blood between the two ships right after Jules had killed the *Star Seeker*'s former captain, Vlad, for insulting her. But once the *Star Seeker*'s crew discovered that Vlad had been holding out on them and keeping far more than his fair share, relations between the ships had evened out again. Jules hadn't yet met the new captain of the *Star Seeker*, a man named Hachi who seemed to think a dozen thoughts for every word he eventually uttered, but she did convince him to follow her into Kelsi's.

At Kelsi's they found both the *Storm Rider* and the former Imperial war sloop the *Storm Queen*. Both captains, Erin and Lars, had worked with Jules before, and both agreed to a meeting of all four captains, though Erin insisted the meeting be aboard the *Storm Rider*. As much as Jules loved the *Sun Queen*, she had to admit that Erin's cabin was bigger and much better furnished.

At the moment, inside that cabin, the other three captains were staring at Jules as if trying to determine whether she truly had gone insane.

"Are you?" Erin pressed.

Jules leaned back in her chair, deliberately trying to look as casual and unconcerned as possible. "Not yet."

"Attacking an Imperial town," Lars said slowly, as if still trying to absorb what Jules had said. "If the idea is to get us all killed when the Emperor sends everything he's got after us, it's not bad. But I'm not really in favor of it."

Jules shook her head. "The Emperor isn't going to react. Not that way."

"Tell you that, did he?" Erin asked.

"No. The Mechanics Guild told me."

Silence fell, finally broken by Erin. "You're working with them again? I thought they'd decided to put an end to you."

"They had," Jules said. "But I convinced them I could be of use to them alive."

Captain Hachi from the *Star Seeker* finally spoke up. "Why would any of us want to be of use to one of the Great Guilds?"

"Because the Great Guilds offer us the only counterforce that can stop the Emperor from doing whatever he wants." Jules let that sink in for a moment, then unrolled onto the table the chart she'd brought. "None of you asked where this Imperial town is. It's about here," she said, indicating a point nearly due north of the city of Altis.

"There?" Lars said, looking at the chart. "Says who?"

"The Mechanics Guild." Jules tapped one place on the chart. "The Emperor has figured out there're decent lands beyond the Northern Ramparts. The Great Guilds won't let him openly establish towns out there, though, just like they've frustrated the Emperor's attempts to deal with the escapees and bandits in the Ramparts and places like Kelsi's. The Emperor is planning to secretly set up a small settlement at this spot, where there's a big river coming down inland, and get it well established before the Great Guilds know it's there. It's a test, to see how the Great Guilds react. But the Mechanics have already learned of the plan, and don't want it to succeed. They're worried about how much force the Emperor already commands, and don't want him growing any more powerful."

"Why do the Mechanics tell you these things?" Hachi asked.

"They don't tell me," Jules said. "They just talk among themselves in front of me as if I'm not there, because I'm just a stupid common. I stand still, and I listen, and I learn things."

Hachi smiled slightly, inclining his head approvingly toward Jules.

But Erin shook her head, her lips set in a stubborn look. "Why won't the Great Guilds just wipe out this settlement themselves?"

"They don't want to risk the Emperor overreacting," Jules said. "So, instead, the Mechanics Guild asked me to gather a force of free commons and destroy the settlement. They want to use commons to create trouble for the Emperor so the Mechanics Guild won't have to do all the work themselves. They wanted me to destroy the town, but I convinced the Mechanics that if enough of the settlers would be willing to live free of Imperial bondage the settlement should remain and be allowed to grow, so that someday its own people could defend themselves against the Empire."

"We're supposed to die for one of the Great Guilds?" Erin shook her head again. "What's in it for us?"

Jules tapped the chart again. "In the long run, a strong town where free people can grow stronger. In the short run, a new port, farther from the Empire. Far enough to be a lot safer than Kelsi's or Marida's. New markets. New trade routes across the sea. Fat merchants sailing those trade routes. Plus whatever money the Emperor sends along with the settlement. We'll take our shares of that, and maybe some ransoms for whichever Imperial officials are there." She didn't state out loud her personal reason: that once this was done, it would no longer be unthinkable to commons to confront the Empire.

"The Emperor will also send legionaries," Lars said. "And at least one warship, don't you think?"

"I do," Jules said. "We can take them."

"Legionaries?" Erin said. "How do we take them?"

"With this." Jules finally brought out the second Mechanic weapon, laying the revolver on top of the chart.

A longer silence fell, with the eyes of the other captains going to

Jules' hip to confirm that her revolver was still in its holster and then back to the new weapon.

"Who gets that?" Erin finally asked.

"I thought we'd all decide that," Jules said.

"We all get a say?"

"That's right."

Lars leaned closer to study the weapon, moving as cautiously as someone near a dangerous wild animal. "That thing alone would be worth more than any of our ships."

"It's worth more than all four of our ships together," Captain Hachi said.

"We'd have to be able to sell it," Erin said. "And I'm guessing the Mechanics plan on keeping tabs on the thing."

Jules nodded. "They do. They'll probably ask for it back when we're done taking the settlement. Also, it only has five cartridges."

"Cartridges?" Hachi looked over the weapon as if seeking five similar objects.

Moving as nonchalantly as if this was old hat to her, which it was by now, Jules picked up the second weapon again. Removing it from the holster, she opened the thing called a cylinder so she could extract one of the cartridges. "These. Each one is like the bolt from a crossbow, only faster and deadlier. You can shoot them as fast you can pull this trigger."

"Like the trigger on a crossbow?" Hachi asked.

"Yes. Though you don't have to tension the weapon or otherwise prepare it between shots. But each cartridge only works once."

"Those things are what makes the noise when they shoot?" Lars asked. "That thunder?"

"Yes. Don't ask me how. There's something inside the cartridges, inside this brass part. Mak tried to find out more, but no common has any clue as to how it works. What we did learn is that if any common smith or jeweler or druggist starts trying to make something like this, the Mechanics find out. And then they kill the commons involved and destroy their work."

Erin nodded, finally seeming to be partly satisfied. "They don't mind letting us use the thing because they know we can't make another even if we study this one."

"They *think* we can't make another," Jules said. "Maybe someday…" She saw the looks of alarm in the eyes of the others. "Not now. Not tomorrow. Not for a long time, maybe. Based on what Mak learned, I've no intention of trying such a thing on this or any other Mechanic device."

"So you're not insane after all." Erin rubbed her mouth as she thought, her eyes on the chart. "I admit a safe port that far from the Empire would be a good thing. If I ever decide to become respectable, it'd be a nice place to set myself up as a fine, upstanding merchant. How do you think the Emperor found out there was a decent place for it along that coast?"

Captain Hachi leaned forward, pointing to the city of Altis. "Most likely he ordered some ships going to and from Altis to change their courses once out of sight of the island and explore to the north. Ships going from Altis to the Empire could do that without incurring so much delay that the Great Guilds would take notice of it."

Lars nodded, running his finger along the chart from Altis to the Empire. "If anyone got suspicious, the ships could blame any delay on the winds. Jules, do Mechanics know much about sailing?"

"I don't know," Jules said. "They ride sailing ships at times, but I don't know if they pay attention to the work we commons do on them. Those metal ships of theirs don't have any proper masts and no sails, so there's a different art of some sort involved in moving them across the water. Someone told me it might be the same sort of thing that makes the Mechanic trains move across the land."

"What about the Mages?" Erin asked. "Are they going to be a problem?"

"Apparently they still think I'm dead."

"That's good," Lars said. "They won't be looking for you until they realize you're not."

"Haven't you already been seen enough that the Mages would know?" Hachi asked.

Jules made a face. "I've tried to hide my presence when I can. There's something I've noticed about the Great Guilds, though. It's like they only see what they want to see, and only believe what they want to believe. Maybe that's because there's nobody able to tell them they're wrong about anything."

Erin nodded. "That matches what I've seen in Mechanics when I've been forced to deal with them. I won't second-guess your opinion of Mages, as I've always steered well clear of any of them. So you're thinking even if the Mages have heard you're about, they'll ignore those reports?"

To Jules' surprise, it was Hachi who nodded in agreement. "That's how the Imperial bureaucracy works as well. Inconvenient information is simply ignored."

"That's what I saw in the orphan home," Jules said. "Inspectors came by every once in a while, but none of them ever saw anything wrong no matter how clear it was in front of them."

Erin made a face. "I'd still like to know why you *aren't* dead."

"Are you disappointed?" Jules asked.

"Simply curious. If there's a way to protect against Mage lightning, I'd like to know what it is."

Lars and Hachi nodded in agreement, looking expectantly at Jules.

She shrugged. "I don't know. I think the lightning was weak for some reason I can only guess at. The sailors on the ship they'd taken said the Mages insisted on getting as close to shore as possible even though that ran their ship aground. So maybe there was something on the shore the Mages needed to make their lightning stronger."

"What would the Mages need on land?" Hachi wondered.

"I have no idea," Jules said. "But when I described what happened to some Mechanics, they seemed to understand. I couldn't understand them, though. Something about the ground, the sea, and the ship charging them."

"That doesn't make a lot of sense," Erin said. "But... all right. Ground, the Mechanics said, and the Mages wanted to head for shore. Something to do with that, I guess."

"They charged toward the ground?" Lars suggested. "But... that tells us nothing."

"I know," Jules said. "But that's as best I could understand what they said. It was like they knew about how something the Mages did worked, even though the Mechanics say the Mages can't really do anything."

"One more mystery about the Mechanics and the Mages," Lars said. "What's important now is that for the purposes of going after this Imperial town, we can be fairly sure that Mages shouldn't be a problem, the Mechanics want us to do this, and those two Mechanic weapons should allow us to handle any force of legionaries guarding the place. If the Emperor is trying to keep this secret, he couldn't send too many. Just enough to ensure that the laborers sent to do the hardest work don't get any ideas about running away or refusing to follow orders. Aside from that, there isn't any known threat that far west except pirates like us, and we've never threatened a town, so in the eyes of the Empire there wouldn't be any need there for a lot of legionaries."

"No need except for her," Erin said, tilting a thumb toward Jules. "She even invades Imperial cities. But she's never tried to take one over."

"No one has," Hachi said. "Until she proposed it, I never would've considered doing such a thing. It's never been done before."

"Maybe it's time someone did it," Jules said.

"All right, we have the Mechanic weapons to help deal with the legionaries, and Mages shouldn't be a problem there. That still leaves at least one Imperial warship at that town," Lars said. "We can't just make that go away by pretending it's not there."

"Maybe there *is* a way to make any Imperial warship go away," Hachi said, his eyes hooded.

"What are you thinking?" Erin asked.

"The Emperor wants Captain Jules. Wants her badly. If any Imperial warship saw her ship passing by..."

Lars shook his head. "The *Sun Queen* is known to the Emperor's ships, but she looks like a lot of others sailing the sea. The Imperial officers might not recognize it as Jules' ship, and even if they did they might debate what to do, especially if they're not sure she's aboard."

Hachi smiled. "What if I tell them she's aboard?"

Jules raised her eyebrows at him. "It's traditional to avoid warning someone before you betray them."

Erin shook her head admiringly at Hachi before looking at Jules. "This one got elected captain of his ship because he's a plotter. Comes up with sneaky plans."

"I learned that trade in the Imperial bureaucracy," Hachi said. He leaned forward, serious, using his fingers to trace movements on the chart. "So... let's say there's a war galley at the settlement. And let's say the *Star Seeker* just happens to sail by one day, and seeing the settlement the astonished captain, me, puts in to pay his respects to the Imperial commanders."

"Wouldn't they arrest you?" Lars asked. "Or just execute you straight off?"

"Me?" Hachi put an expression of affronted pride on his face. "Why would they arrest me? Everyone knows the captain of the *Star Seeker* is the late and unlamented Vlad. I've ensured the crew keeps mentioning that whenever we encounter other ships. Sometimes people ask them, didn't Jules kill Vlad? It was just a flesh-wound, they reply. The Imperial officers won't have any orders to arrest me. Especially since I'm going to be voluntarily seeking out their permission to ensure it's all right to sail in those waters. After all, I am still, officially, a loyal servant of the Empire on temporary leave from his job in which he ensures that the word of the Emperor is carried out quickly and without error."

Jules couldn't help laughing. "What is it you did in Imperial employ?"

This time Hachi smiled. "Never ask an official of the Imperial bureaucracy what he does. As him or her what their job title is. I assure you my job title is far grander than the actual labors I put into the position."

Apparently Hachi didn't want to provide some details of his past, but that was normal among the free ships. One of the unwritten rules that they followed was that anyone's past was their own, and not required to be shared with others. Since the crew of the *Star Seeker* had been convinced of Hachi's quality, she wasn't in any position to demand more details. "What would you tell the officers at the settlement?"

"I'd ask if the reward for the capture of that renegade Jules of Landfall is still offered," Hachi said, looking virtuous. "And when told that yes, it is, I'd eagerly inform them that Jules herself was planning on coming this same way later in the day, having been delayed by... her crew being drunk or hung-over."

"That's the *Sun Queen*'s crew, all right," Erin said, grinning.

"I'll describe the ship," Hachi said. "And even what the infamous Jules is wearing. Then the Imperial officers will be given time to think, to realize that even if they doubt my story, they can't afford to discount it. If a loyal servant of the Emperor such as myself were to tell others that he'd practically handed Jules over to them but they'd let her slip past, it wouldn't look good, would it? Whereas if it is you, and they capture you, the Emperor's gratitude would make them all rich. Give them half a day to think it over, and when your ship sails past, with someone on the quarterdeck about your size dressed as I described, they will pursue it with every ship they have."

"They'll be bored as well," Lars said, smiling. "Sitting around that town in the middle of nowhere with nothing to do, and the *Star Seeker* probably the first ship they've seen in a while. They'll jump at the chance for action and glory *and* reward."

Jules nodded. "Odds are very much that they would. And what will your ship be doing?" she asked Hachi.

Hachi pursed his lips as he thought. "They probably won't want us to leave, on the chance that I might change my mind and warn Jules. I think *Star Seeker* should ask to remain at the settlement as a sign of good faith as we take on fresh water from the river. Of course the Imperial troops there will watch my ship closely for any signs of trouble."

Captain Erin bared her teeth in a vicious grin. "Meaning they won't be paying as much attention to other places that trouble might be coming from. That'd make it easier for our people to sneak in. Put 'em ashore a little ways from the town once dark falls, then march in and knife any sentries before they sound the alert."

"And when an alert does sound," Captain Hachi added, "my crew would take out any sentries watching my ship and create a second threat for the legionaries to have to deal with."

"You're good," Jules said. "Lars?"

"It sounds like it'd work," Captain Lars said. "We want to hit the settlement at night, as Erin says. I think the *Star Seeker* should show up there around noon, with the *Sun Queen* coming by late in the afternoon or close to sunset."

"Close to sunset," Erin said. "We want that Imperial warship, if there is one, gone as late into the night as possible."

"The *Sun Queen* could tease any pursuer," Jules said. "Let them think they're catching up. Ang and Liv can handle that better than I could. I'll leave enough crew aboard to manage that."

Lars frowned. "You'll be leading the attack on the settlement?"

"Yes," Jules said in a tone that made it clear no one should object. "The Mechanics are right about one thing. Our crews don't entirely trust each other. They can't be counted on to follow any of you except their own captain. But I'm different."

"The girl of the prophecy," Erin said, ignoring the cross look that earned her from Jules. "You're right. You can use that, just as the Mechanics want you to use it."

Jules made a face. "I hope so, but do you really think that matters all that much to commons, to your crews? It's the daughter of my line that will free the world, not me."

"You're right," Lars said, leaning back and waving to the east. "You're just the girl who walked into Sandurin past the legion stationed there and freed a lot of prisoners from under the nose of a prince, and the one who's killed Mages, and the one who's fought a dragon and lived, and the one who convinced the Mechanics to give her one—no, two of their precious weapons. Did I leave out anything? Oh, yeah, also the girl who got hit by Mage lightning and lived. Why would any of that impress anyone?"

"Have the Mechanics offered you any other reward or payment?" Hachi asked. "The question may come up. I'd like to know the answer."

"It's a fair question," Jules conceded. "Aside from not killing me immediately, the only reward that's been hinted at is that they might make me a Mechanic some day. Don't give me those looks! I'd never accept such a deal, even if they're sincere, and I doubt that. There's no way I'd ever become a Mechanic and wear their stupid dark jacket and strut around like I'm an empress."

"But they'd think it was the best bribe they could offer," Erin said.

"That we agree on," Jules said. "They can't imagine anyone wouldn't jump at the chance to become one of them."

"And maybe they're thinking they'd really do it," Erin continued, "for sort of the same reason the Emperor wants you. Make you and your descendants part of their Guild, and what're the odds that daughter would ever rebel against her own Guild?"

"That's possible," Jules said. "I mean, that they're thinking that. But it won't happen. Not me, and not any daughter of my line."

"So you're the one making prophecies now?" Erin leaned closer, her voice growing deadly serious. "Girl, you've survived more than most, but you're carrying the weight of that prophecy on you. You'll always be steering through dangerous waters. Don't decide what path you have to take before you know the way. If you set your mind on how you have to steer, you might miss the signs that you need to change course."

Jules looked back at Erin, who had at least a decade of age and experience on her, feeling frustration and perhaps some fear rise inside her. "Are you saying I should accept an offer like that if the Mechanics make it?"

"I'm saying that neither you, nor me, nor any other man and woman in this world knows how that prophecy will come to pass. If opportunities arise, they may be part of that. Look them over before you cast them away."

"That's good advice," Lars said.

"Good advice?" Jules glared at him. "There are some things I won't do. That also has to be part of the prophecy, right?"

"That's not for us to judge," Erin said. "I simply advise that you not decide such things before you have to. Your heart and your head brought you this far, so I'd be the last to tell you to ignore either one."

"All right," Jules said. "If we can get off the subject of me and that prophecy, there's one more thing we should discuss. Do we try to bring in any other ships on this?"

Lars waved a hand in negation. "Not if I have a say in it. Looking for them would just give the Empire more time to set up their defenses. And of those who might join us, the only ones I'd trust not to betray me are in this room." He glanced at Captain Hachi. "Mind you, I'm not sure I trust him."

"You're wise not to," Hachi said. "However, my crew feels a special debt toward Captain Jules for her discovery that their former captain had been holding out far more than his fair share. Even if they didn't look to her because of the prophecy, they'd be very unhappy if I betrayed her. I doubt that I'd live long enough to walk on land again. For the same reason, I'm confident that my crew will vote to go ahead with this plan since Captain Jules will be the overall leader."

"My crew will be taken aback," Erin said, "but they trust me. I'm sure I can get their approval."

"Same here," Jules said.

Lars hesitated. "To be honest, it might take some work with my crew. The *Storm Queen* has been doing well lately. My crew is likely to look askance at the risk of attacking an Imperial town."

"What if you had that weapon?" Erin asked, pointing to the Mechanic revolver that still rested on the table.

"Me?" Lars looked startled, then worried, then cautious. "That would impress my crew."

"I wouldn't expect you three to entrust me with it," Captain Hachi said. "Nor do I *want* it."

"Worried about using Mechanic devices, eh?" Erin asked with a grin.

"Yes," Hachi said in a way that implied it was the only common-sense response.

"So am I," Lars said. "Is it safe?" He eyed the revolver with mixed skepticism and worry.

"Sure," Jules said. "I mean, it's made to kill things. But if you keep the holster fastened so it can't fall out, and keep your finger off the trigger, it won't shoot on its own. Otherwise it's like a loaded crossbow. Don't point it at anyone you're not ready to kill."

"Just how accurate is that thing?" Erin asked. "Also like a crossbow?"

"Less than that, I think," Jules said. "I haven't been able to practice with mine because the cartridges are too precious. But from what I've learned by using it to shoot at someone, the closer I am to the target the better. Like, only a lance or two away. Maybe I could reliably hit someone from farther off if I could practice a lot, but that's impossible."

"Are you all right with Lars having it?"

"Lars isn't sure he's all right with having it," Lars said.

"You'll be fine," Jules said. "Yes, I'm all right with him having the second weapon."

"It's acceptable to me," Hachi said. "I do have a vote, don't I?"

"You have a vote," Jules said. "You're contributing your ship and your crew. That's it, then. We'll work out remaining details after we get our crews to vote to take part, which we shouldn't do until we're all underway outside the harbor."

Erin nodded. "The last thing we need is some drunk sailors at a bar ashore telling everyone within earshot what we're planning."

"Lars, let me go over this thing with you," Jules said. "I'm sure how it's made is very complicated, but it's pretty simple to use."

"Is it all right if I observe as well?" Hachi asked.

"Sure. I have a feeling if this works the Mechanics are going to be a little freer with making these weapons available to commons who are willing to do what their Guild wants."

"That's an ugly prophecy," Erin said, shaking her head. "Because you're probably right. And because there are plenty of commons who'd work against other commons for their own advantage if the Great Guilds promised them reward."

"That's what the Emperor and prior rulers of the Empire have done, isn't it?" Hachi said. "While also trying to advance their own interests."

"And that's what we're doing," Jules said.

* * *

Walking back to the *Sun Queen* on the next pier over should have been a short, uneventful stroll. But not for her.

A half-dozen big sailors who'd accompanied Jules to the *Storm Runner* surrounded her as they all walked, forming a physical barrier between Jules and anyone outside their group. She hated the sense of being penned in, but realized the need for it. The only way to be sure no Mages saw her was to make it hard for anyone else to see her.

At the head of the pier where the *Sun Queen* was tied up, though, a Mechanic waited, his dark jacket standing out clearly amid the commons around him. Engrossed in conversation with a common woman, he broke off the talk to step over and block the progress of Jules' group when they reached him.

She moved to face the Mechanic, more curious than worried. If the Mechanics Guild had once again changed their minds, they surely would have sent more than one Mechanic to kill her. "Yes, Sir Mechanic?"

He looked closely at her. "You're that one? Yeah, there's the revolver.

I've got a message for you. Fifty legionaries and one sloop. I was told you'd know what that meant."

Jules nodded respectfully, surprised that the Mechanic's tone wasn't contemptuous or superior. "Yes, Sir Mechanic. I understand. Thank you."

He waved off her thanks, leaned close to the woman he'd been talking to in order to say something that brought a smile from her, then walked away.

"I'm sorry a message for me meant you were harassed by a Mechanic," Jules told her.

She smiled again. "He wasn't harassing. He's not like the Mechanics who grab, you know? We've talked before. He's, um, nice."

"A Mechanic?" Gord asked in disbelief.

"Yeah. He's all right."

Gord scratched his head as the woman turned back to her work. "A Mechanic who treats commons like people. Now I've seen it all."

"He treats a common girl he likes as if she's a person," Jules said. "Still, that's something." Maybe that daughter of her line would be able to find a Mechanic or two to help her overthrow the Great Guilds.

Gord and the others began to close in around her again, but not before a call sounded across the pier.

"Lady pirate!"

The voice was familiar enough for Jules to look toward the source, seeing a tall, well-muscled man walking toward her. A broad smile formed as she recognized him. "It's all right," she told her guards. "He's an old friend. How are you, Shin?"

He reached them, smiling. "I'm delivering a message."

"What a coincidence," Jules said. "What is it?"

"It's not for you." He held up a small leather fold for carrying letters. "My commander told me to deliver a message. I didn't find the person I was supposed to give it to, so I kept going, all the way to here. Do you know how far you can get if you just tell everyone who asks that you're delivering a message?"

"You deserted?" Jules asked.

"I guess I have," Shin said. "Maybe I could claim I'm still delivering that message, but I'm not sure my centurion would accept that excuse."

"Centurion?" Gord asked. "You're a legionary?"

"I was," Shin said. "Now I want to work for the lady pirate."

"You can call me Jules like you did before," she said, smiling. "Come on. We have to get back to my ship before any Mages wander along this way."

Ang met them as they came up the boarding plank onto the *Sun Queen*'s deck. He frowned at Shin. "Who is this?"

"Someone who wants to join the crew," Jules said. "He's a deserter from the legions."

"Oh?" Ang didn't hide his skepticism.

"And he's an old friend of mine from the legion orphan home in Landfall," she added.

"Oh." Ang's expression cleared. "You're a brother?" he asked Shin.

Shin nodded. "From Landfall, like Jules. Where were you raised, brother?"

"The home in Sandurin. Welcome aboard."

Jules looked around. "Cori, you're quick. Run to the pier where the *Storm Runner* is and tell them you have a message for Captain Erin. Tell Erin 'fifty legionaries and one sloop.' If Captain Hachi and Captain Lars are still there tell them as well. If not, tell Erin I'm asking her to pass on the message to them. Then get back here as fast as you can so we can cast off."

Cori nodded, her face intent. "For Erin on the *Storm Runner*, fifty legionaries and one sloop, pass on to Lars and Ha…"

"Hachi."

"Got it."

"Go." Jules turned back to Shin. "Do you have any sailing experience?"

"No, Jules," he said. "Only riding on ships, never doing any of the sailor tasks."

"You might as well go below then while we prepare to get underway. Gord, help him find a hammock and a place for it."

"Aye. Come on, you."

"Ang, let's get ready to haul in the gangplank as soon as Cori gets back. I've got a bad feeling about staying here any longer."

He frowned, gazing down the pier at the rough, new town that made up Kelsi's Harbor. "Did you see any Mages?"

"No. But the Mechanics knew I was here." How did they pass messages among themselves so quickly? "They tend to talk around commons without thinking about it, so the commons might be talking about me being here. And I suspect that Mages pay more attention to what commons say than they let on."

As Ang walked across the deck, calling out orders for bringing in lines and readying the sails, Marta stopped by Jules, giving a low whistle as she looked at Shin walking away with Gord. "Look what followed you home. Is he yours, Captain?"

"Shin is just an old friend," Jules said.

"I wish I had an old friend like that. Maybe he'd like to make a new friend."

Jules rubbed her mouth to hide her grin. "He still has to run the gauntlet if he's to be a member of the crew."

"I'm not worried about that," Marta said. "Look at him. Even if we used cutlasses in the gauntlet they'd probably bounce off of all those lovely muscles."

"Marta, Captain Mak used to tell me that you were an example for the younger women aboard."

"That I am! When it comes to our new shipmate, I'm going to show the younger ones exactly how it's done." Marta raised an eyebrow at Jules. "Speaking of younger ones, maybe you should pay attention, too, Captain."

Jules shook her head. "Tips for getting more men interested in me are the last thing I need."

"It's not about getting more men interested," Marta said. "It's about getting the right man interested."

"And just how do I know who's the right man?"

"Trial and error." Marta shrugged. "Most likely a lot of error."

"Sure. Shouldn't you be helping with the sails?"

"Yes, Captain!" Marta ran off with a grin.

Jules, grateful that the conversation had momentarily distracted her from worrying about being in this port, went forward to watch for Cori's return, making sure that the foremast blocked any view of herself from land.

She let out a sigh of relief as Cori came into view among those passing by on the waterfront, but the relief was short lived as Jules noticed how fast Cori was moving. Not simply running, she was sprinting.

Jules did some running herself, back to the quarterdeck. "Ang! Cori's in sight and she looks like someone's chasing her! Is anyone else ashore?"

"No, Cap'n," Ang called back. "We're just waiting on her."

"Start taking in lines!" Spinning, Jules faced the sailors at the boarding plank, her sense of dread spiking. "Haul that in as soon as Cori gets aboard!"

Cori came down the pier, mouth open wide as she sucked in air, dashing to the plank and aboard without pausing. The moment her feet hit the deck the sailors at the plank started bringing it in.

Breathing heavily, Cori bent over, hands on her upper legs. "Cap… tain… saw… Mages… look… ing… at… ships."

"Blazes. Ang! Let's go!"

Ang bellowed orders, sailors up in the rigging moving out along the spars to loose the sails, others hauling on the sheets to let the sails catch the wind. The last lines came aboard, the *Sun Queen* free of the pier, and as the wind caught her sails the gap between the ship and the pier grew at a slowly increasing pace.

"Maybe you should get in your cabin," Keli the healer said from next to Jules.

"I should be on deck until—" Jules grimaced. "Yeah. I should."

She hated turning toward her cabin, hated the sense of running from a foe, but it made no more sense to stand on deck waiting for the

Mages to see her than it would've to stand still waiting for that dragon to catch her outside of Jacksport. That logic didn't make it any easier to walk toward her cabin as the crew, *her* crew, got the ship underway. The captain should be there, should be…

Mak had told her more than once that as captain he had to put the ship and the crew first. "It's never about the captain, Jules. You're their leader, but you're not their master. You serve *them*, so the captain always has to try to think of what they need, not what he or she wants."

"All right, Mak," Jules grumbled as she reached the door to her cabin.

She stepped inside, realizing that Keli was right behind her, blocking any sight of her with the door still open.

"I saw some Mages coming down the pier," he said, as calmly as if discussing seeing some birds fly past. "I just wanted to be sure they didn't catch a glimpse of your backside."

Jules more fell into a chair than sat down, rubbing her forehead. "Thanks, Keli. Though I doubt my backside is all that memorable a sight that the Mages would've recognized it."

"Well, if you're asking my opinion—"

"I'm not. Thanks, Keli," she repeated. "Could you keep an eye on those Mages and let me know when we can't see them anymore?" *If a Mage can see you, a Mage can kill you.* Jules hadn't learned anything to make her doubt that saying.

"Aye, Captain." Keli smiled at her. "Thanks to you as well, for listening to the advice of a healer for once."

"Don't expect it to become a habit." Jules sat in her cabin after Keli left, feeling like a prisoner on her own ship but knowing it would be foolish to go out on deck as long as a Mage might be able to catch sight of her.

Did the Mages already know she was still alive?

Maybe the Mechanics had told them. After all, they liked having her kill Mages, and that was more likely to happen if Mages were seeking her out.

She knew she couldn't trust the Mechanics. Or the word of the Emperor. And the Mages simply wanted her dead.

The only allies she could trust were other commons. And not all of them. Plenty of commons would sell her out for the reward offered by the Emperor. Others, men, saw her mostly as a means for them to stake a claim in whatever was accomplished by that daughter of her line. Her friends, or those commons willing to help her, were among the weakest of the weakest in the world, pawns in the games played by the Great Guilds and the Emperor.

Jules looked over at the drawing that was the sole memento she had of Mak, showing part of Lake Bellad near Severun. *They think you're their pawn. But you're nobody's pawn. You're the Emperor piece.* That's what Mak had said. He must have believed it, too, because Mak had never lied to her.

If pawns were played right, they could dominate the game board.

She'd have to keep playing, and hope she didn't make any wrong moves.

CHAPTER SEVEN

They'd gone far enough from Kelsi's that the harbor had vanished over the horizon, then all four ships had slacked their sails, rolling in the swells within sight of each other while their captains called their crews to vote.

While waiting for the other ships to come out of the port, Jules lined the crew up for the traditional initiation of a new crew member. As they formed two lines with a lane down the middle, some of the crew brandished only their fists, while others held belaying pins or sticks. Shin had grinned and trotted down the gauntlet, occasionally being rocked by a blow but otherwise passing unscathed. Reaching the quarterdeck, he nodded to Jules. "Captain."

She held his arm up, facing the crew. "Is he one of us?"

The crew cheered, and Jules dropped Shin's arm. "I'm glad you're with us," she told him.

"Captain Jules," Shin said, "I am also glad. You ran the gauntlet as well?"

"No," Jules said. "I walked it."

"You walked it." Shin sighed and shook his head at her. "You haven't changed."

"No, I guess I haven't. Join the rest of the crew for the vote."

"Vote?" Shin asked.

"You'll figure it out while the crew discusses it."

Jules stood on the front of the quarterdeck, looking out across the deck and the lower spars where the crew of the *Sun Queen* had gathered to listen. Occupying the only area free of sailors was the chart, unrolled, the corners held down with the weight of belaying pins and cutlasses.

She looked out at the crew, knowing this would be the first time she'd had to try to convince them to do something out of the ordinary without Mak backing her up. If her still somewhat vague plans for the future were to come to pass, it wouldn't be the last time she'd have to do that. Which made doing it right the first time all the more important. Fortunately, she'd heard Mak talk to the crew on such occasions, and knew what had worked for him.

"We have an opportunity," Jules began. "An opportunity for reward that no other pirates have ever had. There's some danger in it, but we'll have some important advantages as well."

She outlined the plan, pointing to the chart and emphasizing that three other ships would be joining them in the effort. The crew stayed mostly silent, leaving her only their expressions to judge their reactions, and those didn't offer any clear picture.

Finishing, Jules put her hands to her hips, trying to look confident and strong. "I call a vote. Should the *Sun Queen* have a part in doing what no one else has ever done?"

"Before we vote," Gord called, "I need some questions answered."

"Speak up then," Jules said.

"Are we doing this for the Mechanics?" His tone of voice made it clear how little Gord thought of that idea.

"The Mechanics," Jules said, "*think* we'll be doing it for them. Because they think we'll only do what they want. That's why they're backing us against the Empire. But you all know how to play the Great Guilds, how to seem like you're being all obedient when you're really doing things your way. That's what we're doing here. Wouldn't you like a fine port far from the Empire where we can relax? Where families could settle? Where we could have families if we wanted? Yes, this'll gain us good short-term profit. But in the long run, it'll give us something even better that we've lacked. That's why we're doing it. I swear before all of you that I wouldn't have agreed to do what the Mechanics want if I hadn't seen the advantages it would bring us."

"Why did the Mechanics agree to it then?" Kyle asked.

"They don't realize we can think that far ahead. They're too smug, too sure of their superiority, to understand that we might not be doing this for them."

"Can we trust the *Star Seeker*?" Marta called.

Jules nodded. "They want a piece of this, and their crew owes me a debt."

"What about that new captain of theirs?"

"I've spoken with him. He's someone we can work with."

Liv looked across the waves toward the *Storm Queen*. "Why'd the second Mechanic weapon go to that ship instead of ours?"

"It's the *Storm Queen*," Kyle said. "They've helped us before. Some of her crew came from here."

"The *Storm Runner* has helped us as well," Ang said. "Captain Erin isn't my favorite person, but she keeps her word."

"Are you comfortable with this?" Liv asked Ang. "It'd be us luring out that Imperial warship and keeping it chasing us."

"We can out-sail any Imperial warship," Ang said with certainty. "Cori can stand in for Cap'n Jules. She's about the same size and her hair matches."

"Hey," Cori said, looking alarmed. "No one said I'd be the decoy!"

"All you have to do is stand on the quarterdeck and look important," Gord said.

"Says you! What if there're more Mages about?"

"Maybe you'll get a special tattoo like Captain Jules did," Marta told her.

"The Mages don't know anything about this," Jules said. "By the time they know there's a town at that spot, the *Sun Queen* and all of us will be well away in search of a good place to spend our earnings."

"If there are any Mages there," Liv said, turning a stern look on

Jules, "they won't be on the Imperial warship. They'll be in the town, where you're going."

"If they are," Jules said. "I'll deal with them." She brought out the Mechanic revolver, raising it above her head. The drama of the gesture bothered her, but it was what the crew needed to see and they cheered it.

"That coast hasn't been charted," Kurt pointed out. The oldest sailor aboard since Ferd had died, he had the caution of someone who'd seen too many others die from not thinking things through.

"The Imperials have seen enough of it to call it safe," Jules said. "It's north of Altis, so it's not farther west than any place that's already been sailed."

Kurt nodded, frowning. "What if there are more legionaries than we can handle? Even with two Mechanic weapons?"

"There're fifty legionaries there," Jules said. "We'll hit them by surprise and knock their numbers down before they can put on armor and grab their swords."

"But, still, if those fifty can prepare…"

She understood his worry. Fifty legionaries forming a shield wall would make a force that even a large group of pirates would have a lot of trouble defeating. "If it comes to that, our ships will be near the harbor. We'll fall back to them and sail off. Legionaries can't march on water."

"I've met some centurions who thought they could," Marta called, raising some laughter from the others.

"May I speak?" Shin asked.

"You're crew," Ang said. "Say what you wish."

"I served in the Emperor's legions for more than a decade. I'm sure that the legionaries in that town will have a first obligation of defending it and making certain the laborers don't cause trouble. They won't chase us if we run, especially at night, because that might be a diversion to lure them out. That's how they'll think."

"That's right," Jules said. "You all know I was in Imperial officer training when… things happened. They beat that into us. Don't think, just follow orders."

Some more questions were raised and answered, but Jules felt the crew shifting to her side of the proposal. She felt confident when the vote was finally held, and wasn't surprised when the great majority of the crew raised their hands in favor. "Raise our flag to the top of the mast," she told Liv.

"How do the other ships look?" Jules called up to the lookout.

"*Storm Runner* and *Star Seeker* have already raised their flags," the lookout shouted down. "*Storm Queen*... hold on. There it is. All three other ships have raised their flags."

Jules felt a moment of exhilaration that faded into a sense of over-reach, as if she'd stretched herself across a chasm to seize a prize and now found herself staring into the peril below.

Ang, standing beside her, inadvertently spoke to her fears. "You have a fleet, Cap'n. This must be the first time in history that a common not in the Imperial service has commanded a fleet."

"Yeah," Jules said, gripping the quarterdeck railing. She'd broken this cage, and even she was a bit scared of what that meant, of the responsibility she now had.

"Are you all right, Cap'n?"

"Yes," she insisted as much to herself as to him. "I just wish... that Mak was in command."

"Mak believed that you would make a good captain," Ang said. "And I know you always seek to do what you think he would. In a way, Mak is still here to offer advice."

That only reassured her for a moment. "Liv's right, though. At some point I have to be making decisions on my own."

"There's no reason you can't keep listening to Mak," Ang said. "Listen to what he tells you, but you decide what to do."

She looked at him, finally smiling. "Thanks." Looking back over the water, she saw the other three ships drifting like the *Sun Queen*, their sails still furled. "What are they waiting for?"

"Your orders, Cap'n."

"Right." Taking a deep breath, she called out across the deck. "All hands make sail! We're putting our mark on history, sirs and ladies!"

* * *

It took a week for the four ships to tack their way west against the winds. By then, the western flanks of the mountains known as the Northern Ramparts were well behind them. Unlike on their eastern side, where the Ramparts reared up like a wall of living stone from the northern plains, on the west the Ramparts had descended more gradually, stepping down to lower heights before becoming hills that merged into a flat expanse of grass.

The crews of the four ships had kept pausing in their work to gaze at that land to their north, where the wild green fields seemed to roll on forever. The coast wasn't entirely welcoming, with stretches where waves dashed against off-shore rocks, but there were also clear areas with beaches that seemed to offer easy access to the land from the sea. Flocks of birds could be seen soaring over the land, and during the late afternoon of the first day after sailing past the Ramparts shouts of excitement rose from the sailors as they sighted a big herd of wild cattle ambling along a little ways inland. The skies above were pristine blue, unmarred by the smoke and dust of human activity.

"This isn't a wasteland," Keli the healer had said to Jules. "It's nothing like what the maps show. I wonder what things are like farther west?"

"Would you like to find out?" Jules asked, grinning.

"Are you serious?" He hesitated, looking again at the fields off the starboard side of the *Sun Queen*. "Maybe. Maybe."

The only difficulties encountered during those days were the winds. Winds always enjoyed making sudden, unpredictable changes, but they could be counted on to have general tendencies in certain areas at certain times of the year. Surely the winds in this region of the Sea of Bakre were the same, but none of the sailors knew the tendencies of the winds here. They could count on an on-shore breeze during the heat of the day when they were close to land, and at night sure enough the winds near the coast came out from the land. In that much, this part of the world followed the same rules sailors had learned elsewhere. But beyond that there seemed to be stronger prevailing winds coming out of the north, though occasionally shifting erratically. The four ships had felt their way through the strange winds, adjusting their sails and their courses as often as necessary to proceed up the coast.

As the sun neared noon on the eighth day since they began heading west, Jules watched worriedly for signs of the Imperial settlement. The Mechanics had said it should be around here, but where? Her crew was already getting nervous to be heading this far west, partly comforted by the pleasant coast but increasingly worried about the deadly reefs which legend and charts said filled the waters of the western sea.

Just before noon the lookout called down to report a sighting of a grayish haze in the sky that told of human fires being used for heating, cooking, and smith work somewhere just beyond the horizon. There could be only one source of such a haze this far beyond the Northern Ramparts.

The *Sun Queen*, the *Storm Runner*, and the *Storm Queen* moved close to the coast to put most of their crews ashore, while the *Star Seeker* sailed on to the west to lay the groundwork for luring the Imperial sloop away from the town it was supposed to protect.

It wasn't until the three ships put their boats in the water and rowed them ashore that any of the sailors set foot on this new land. In the rush ashore through the surf no one had noted who was the first to place their feet on the grass, but no one cared. The Empire could already claim discovery of this land, and had already set people here.

Captain Erin squinted at the sun. "Here's a problem. We need to get close enough to be able to reach the town around the middle watch of the night, but not so close that we're seen."

"We'll send scouts ahead," Jules said. "Three or four sailors who can keep their heads down and their eyes open. When they see the town or any people they can fall back and signal us."

"Three," Lars said. "One from each ship." He wore the second Mechanic revolver in its holster at his belt, and walked with exaggerated care as if fearing a misstep would cause it to kill him or someone else nearby.

Jules had no trouble choosing who to send from her crew. She beckoned to Shin, then waited for the scouts from the *Storm Queen* and the *Storm Runner* to show up. "Everyone keep it down!" she called to the sailors, who were laughing and playing around in the tall grass like kids granted an unexpected recess. "Do you want the Emperor's ears to hear you?"

She knew only the basics of scouting from her training in Imperial service, so Jules began with a question. "Shin, do you have experience as a scout?"

He nodded, solemn and serious now that they were engaged in the approach to the town. "Yes, Captain." Facing the other two selected sailors, Shin spoke with calm certainty. "I will take the center. You two spread out a bit to either side, but not so far you lose sight of me. We need to stay far enough ahead of the main body that they can see just see us if we give warning. But your attention must be aimed ahead of you. Watch for any signs of buildings, watch for sentries, watch for patrols, watch for anybody or anything. Even animals. If we spook some birds or cattle it could tip off sentries watching for trouble that someone might be coming. The moment you see someone or something, stop and signal to me, and I will signal to everyone behind us."

Shin pointed up to the sun. "We will be walking west. As the afternoon wears on, the sun will be in our eyes. That means being extra careful you don't miss anything in the sun's glare, and being careful not to stand up so tall in the grass that you get lit up by the sun like a torch standing high, and so easily seen."

The sailor from Erin's ship nodded, her expression serious. "Just like if we were on a ship heading west as the sun was falling in the sky. Except here we've got grass to hide in."

"Yes. Just like that."

"Should we carry crossbows?" the sailor from the *Storm Queen* asked.

Shin looked to Jules. "I don't think we should. Not as scouts."

"Why not?" Lars asked him.

"If legionaries… my pardon to all present… if scouts carry a distance weapon, they are a little less careful, a little more careless, thinking they can deal with anything they see. Also, the weight and bulk of the crossbow hinders quiet movement. It's best that scouts only have daggers for a close-in fight. That reduces the chance of them trying anything too risky."

Lars nodded. "I get it. Scared sailors are careful sailors. No cutlasses, though?"

"They weigh down the scout, Sir Pirate."

Lars grinned at Shin's use of that title. "Captain Lars is all right. You know your business."

"Are there other questions?" Shin asked the two sailors.

"One for Captain Jules," the sailor from the *Storm Runner* said. "Is there any chance of us running into any Mechanic devices? I heard Mechanics can use some of their devices to see people from a long ways off."

"And kill 'em from a long ways off, too," the sailor from the *Storm Queen* said.

Jules shook her head. "The Mechanics are staying well away from here to maintain the pretense they have no direct involvement in what we're doing. There won't be any Mechanics there, and that means no Mechanic devices."

"Except the ones we've got," Lars said.

"Right," Jules said. "Except the weapons Captain Lars and I have. Go ahead and get a head start on us. We'll start off behind you when you're almost out of sight."

The question did make Jules wonder, though. If the Mechanics kept giving even a few weapons to commons in order to accomplish Guild goals, how long would it be before she might encounter another common person with a weapon like the one given to her? It was something else to worry about for the future.

But not this day. Jules watched as Shin and the two sailors trudged off through the tall, wild grass that sometimes came as high as their shoulders, then turned to look out to sea.

The *Sun Queen*, *Storm Runner*, and *Storm Queen* had all put on just enough sail to hold themselves off the coast while waiting for the afternoon to get late. The masts of the *Star Seeker* were barely visible as that ship headed toward the new Imperial town.

"If Hachi betrays us," Erin said, "and the worst happens to you, I promise I'll track him down and kill him for both of us."

"Same," Jules said.

"In that case, he'd better pray you're the one who dies. I've heard how you handle traitors." Erin turned an amused gaze on Lars. "He's more afraid of that Mechanic weapon than the legionaries will be. Can he use it, do you think?"

"He'll be right beside me," Jules said. "Nothing strengthens a man's resolve more than the desire to look good in front of a woman. And we need to ensure that if any of the legionaries form a line they'll know they're facing two Mechanic weapons." She sighed as two sailors ran past playing an impromptu game of tag. "Blazes. Let's get them walking so they burn off some of their energy."

"And start complaining about the walk," Erin said. "I bet they'll be grumbling before the sun gets there in the sky," she added, pointing.

"I'll take a little longer," Jules said, pointing lower. "How about you, Lars?"

"I'm doubling down with Erin," he said. "Hey! *Storm Queen*! Get your tails over here! There's work to be done!"

"*Storm Runner*!" Erin called. "To me! Let's get to business!"

"*Sun Queen*!" Jules said. Since her ship would be luring the Imperial warship away, she'd had to leave more sailors aboard to handle the sails, so the *Sun Queen*'s contingent was smaller than that of the other two ships. "Follow me."

They set off in three columns that spread out behind their captains to merge into a wide group, trudging through the grass. All told, they were about eighty strong. Far too few to go up against fifty legionaries under normal circumstances. But the two Mechanic weapons, the advantage of surprise, however many sentries they could take out before an alert was sounded, and the sailors from the *Star Seeker* in the harbor, would all hopefully add up to enough to do the job.

Sure enough, the horseplay settled down quickly. Sailors used to walking decks and streets had trouble getting used to marching through high grass that concealed bumps and holes on land that had never been leveled and tamed by humans. The fields that had looked pleasantly flat and regular from the sea proved to be very uneven underfoot. The sun, which had been pleasantly warm when on the water, seemed much hotter here. And as the sailors began to sweat, insects swarmed out to annoy and pester.

"I'm remembering why I chose to go to sea rather than stay on land," Erin commented as she shoved aside a thick shock of grass rising up to nearly her neck.

Jules looked back, seeing that the sailors behind them had begun to straggle, some lagging farther and farther from the front. "We'd better assign some reliable people to bring up the rear and make sure we don't lose anyone."

"Should we make them keep up?" Lars asked, wiping sweat from his face.

"There's no need for that. We should have a long wait for full night once we get close enough to the town. That'll give everyone time to catch up and rest."

Once the task of assigning rear guards was completed, there was nothing else to do but continue to trudge toward the town. "You did this sort of thing during your training with the legions, didn't you?" Lars asked.

"Yes," Jules said. "The initial training. We did all the marching and drilling the ordinary legionaries do."

"Did you like it?" Lars asked.

"Blazes, no. But it was what I'd set my mind on," Jules said. "The proof that I was as good as any of them. That's why I didn't want to quit. How about you?"

"Me?" Lars laughed. "I was apprenticed to a lawyer."

"That sounds easy."

"Blazes, no!" he said, mimicking Jules. "I decided that if my life was going to be that bad, I should at least get to see a little of the world and feel the sun every once in a while. So I ran off to sea. Whenever things got really bad, like one time we got becalmed and ran short on water, I'd just think of being back in that lawyer's office and I'd be happy I'd escaped that fate for a better one."

Jules slapped her cheek to get an insect that had landed there. "The Mechanics told me once they thought maybe if I'd been tested as a little girl they might have taken me. As bad as the orphanage was, I'm happy I escaped that fate."

Erin, trudging along nearby, laughed briefly. "You wouldn't have wanted to be called Lady Mechanic and be able to look down on all of us commons?"

"No," Jules said. "Those people, the Great Guilds, they're no different than the people who run prisons. All they do is control others and tell them what they can't do. If people look up to me, I want it to be because I fought for freedom, for their right to do things and make things and go new places."

"It's hard to believe that freedom will ever happen," Erin said. She looked ahead toward the scouts. "Though you've attracted some fine followers. That big fellow knows his stuff."

"Shin? He was in the legions for, I guess, about ten years before deserting to join me."

"Oh? Lucky you. He's a fine-looking one."

Jules felt her face warming a little more than it already was from the sun. "Shin was like a real brother to me when we were growing up in the orphanage. I can't even think about him any other way. It'd be too weird."

"And folks say pirates have no morals!" Erin gave Jules a look. "What's it like living with the prophecy? Has it gotten any better?"

Jules shrugged, looking down at her feet as they plowed through the grass. "It sucks. I guess maybe I've gotten somewhat used to it. But that girl has messed up my life in all ways, and in romance perhaps most of all."

"'That girl'? The daughter of your line?"

"Yes." Jules managed a smile. "Aren't daughters supposed to be born before they cause so much trouble?"

"That's the usual way of it. Have you thought what you're going to do?" Erin asked.

"Of course I have. But the one idea that seems like it might work… is something I don't want to think about."

Erin nodded, brushing more bugs away from her face. "If you ever want to get drunk and talk about it, I'll listen and keep my mouth shut afterwards."

"Thanks."

They fell silent again for a while, the only noise the swishing sounds of men and women forcing their way through the apparently never-ending grass, the buzz and whisper of bugs and gnats forming an escort for the sweating sailors, and the occasional audible grumble from one of the sailors following their captains. None of the captains had noticed when the grumbling began, so they decided to declare the bet a tie.

As the sun fell low enough to cast painful glare into their eyes, Jules began to worry that she'd miscalculated the distance and the time needed to cover it. How much farther was it to the town? How much longer would they have to walk?

She squinted into the low-hanging sun to be sure she could still see Shin. There he was, his head a darker blot against the grass.

As Jules watched, Shin raised one hand. "Hold it!" she called to everyone with her.

"Did they see something?" Lars asked, breathing a bit heavily and rubbing his sleeve through the sweat on his brow.

"I think so." Jules watched Shin coming back, the two other scouts also coming into view.

Shin reached them, apparently not tired in the least even though like everyone else he had sweat dripping down his body. Jules realized that she found that sight distracting and hastily looked away. "What did you see?"

"One spire, Captain, from a taller building, and masts. Two ships, I think."

One of the sailor scouts joined them. "Two ships for sure. From what I could see of the masts, one's the *Star Seeker* or her twin, and the other's a sloop like the *Storm Runner*."

Jules looked west to where the town lay. "Any sign of sentries or patrols?"

"Not from this far out," Shin said. "I saw no signs in the grass that patrols might have passed recently." He turned and pointed. "There is a… pinnacle. That is the word, right? A pinnacle of rock there. It would make an excellent lookout post, but I have seen no sign of a sentry up on it."

"Could you spot a sentry from this distance?" Lars asked.

"I would see the sun glinting on the sentry's armor," Shin said. "And the only way to pass messages from the top of the spire to the town during the day would be by mirror. I would've seen those flashes as well. I'm confident there is no sentry up there yet, though the legionary commander is doubtless planning to establish one once the town is sufficiently secure."

"Good." Jules shifted her gaze out to sea. The *Storm Runner* and the *Storm Queen* had held back, but the *Sun Queen* had put on more sail and was forging steadily west. She was about even with the sailors on the shore, and would soon pass them. "Ang's timing it right. At that speed they should pass the town just a bit before sunset." She shaded her eyes to see more. "That red shirt we put on Cori really stands out with the sun so low. She makes a great decoy." It had required a fair degree of persuasion to get Cori to wear the flaming red shirt to play the part of the supposedly-flamboyant pirate Captain Jules.

"We can go a little closer," Shin said. "But not beyond that yet. Not until it gets dark."

"Go on ahead and stop where you think it's safe," Jules said. "Come on, everyone. Just a little ways more and then we get to rest until full night."

The straggling group of sailors perked up at the news that the march was almost over. When Shin signaled a halt almost all dropped gratefully to lie in the shade of the grass. Shin himself stayed standing, watching their surroundings, and the other two scouts followed his lead. The bugs were still a problem, but the breeze from off the sea began to freshen as the sun dropped to the horizon, providing some relief.

"There are the masts," one of the sailors who'd been a scout said, pointing. "*Star Seeker's* to the right and just a little farther off, I think, and the sloop a little to the left there."

Jules looked that way, seeing the straight tips of the masts projecting just into view. "Can we see the town from here?"

"We are just a little too far off," Shin said. "There is the spire atop what must be the tallest building."

Which was doubtless where she'd find the Imperial commander of this town, Jules thought. The Emperor might have appointed a mayor to deal with civil issues, but real authority in the town would rest with the senior Imperial military officer. "All right. Relax, everyone."

The sun had dropped so low it was sinking into the surface of the endless sea of grass to the west when Gord called out. "Captain? The sloop's moving."

Jules got up beside him to look. "Any sign of the *Sun Queen's* masts?"

"No. We lost sight of her just a little while back. She's a bit farther off from us, but I think she should be passing by that town about now."

"Yeah. And you're right. The sloop is definitely moving," Jules said as she saw the tops of the sloop's masts slide to the left above the stalks of the tall grass. "He took the bait."

Jules dropped back down to sit and talk to Lars and Erin. "So far, so good."

"Says you," Erin said as she irritably swatted another insect. "I'm surprised the legionaries haven't come to investigate these vast swarms of bugs seeking to feast on us."

"If they've noticed, they probably think something died," Lars said.

"I don't smell that bad." Erin looked upwards where the sky continued to darken, the stars beginning to shine through. "It'll be a little while yet. There'll be sentries posted, some watching the *Star Seeker*, some watching for anything coming from outside the town, and some watching to make sure whatever workers they brought stay in their places and don't try to escape or make mischief."

"With only fifty legionaries, that adds up to a good part of their strength," Jules said. "I'd guess a minimum of ten sentries?"

"Maybe twelve."

"If it isn't ten, it'll be fifteen," Jules said. "The legions always try to break assignments down into groups of five."

"Then we need to count on fifteen," Erin said.

"Can your man Shin take out sentries quietly?" Lars asked.

"He's not my man," Jules said. *My man* was the term a woman used to describe someone in a relationship with her.

"Oh. Sorry. I didn't mean—"

"That's all right. I'll ask."

She wondered how Shin would react to the idea of killing his former legion comrades, but he didn't seem rattled when she asked. "I am not the quietest, though I do have practice. Are there others among the crews who would be good at sneaking up on sentries?"

"Yes," Jules said. "Like Kyle. He worked the streets as a pickpocket when he was a kid. He can move very quietly to get close to someone. Do you think we'll face ten or fifteen sentries?"

"It depends on their centurion," Shin said. "We should assume fifteen." He paused to think. "Five watching the *Star Seeker*. Five patrolling the perimeter of the town, but with more of an eye toward any laborers trying to escape than with any outside danger. And five either watching the laborers or patrolling the inside of the town."

"We can leave the ones watching the *Star Seeker* to Hachi's crew."

Shin nodded slowly. "Do we know how long they have been here?"

"Not too long. A few weeks, at a guess."

"That's good," Shin said. "Long enough to get bored with sentry duty in a place where no one else ever comes and nothing ever happens. They will be… what is the word?"

"Complacent?" Jules guessed.

"Yes. Not as alert as they should be. Give me four good sailors such as Kyle. We'll clear the way into the town."

"Good," Jules said, realizing that Shin, apparently without realizing it, had requested a group of five to lead the way into town: four others and himself. Legionary training instilled habits. "I also need a clear path to wherever the town commander is. If I can take him or her prisoner and make them surrender the town, we won't have to fight the legionaries even if they get alerted in time to form up."

By the time Kyle and three more sailors had been assigned to Shin, the sun had sunk below the horizon. Jules squinted at the moon, a fair ways above the horizon. The "twins" that chased the moon from far behind weren't visible yet. "I think we should advance once the twins rise."

"That feels about right," Lars said.

"Maybe a little early," Captain Erin said. "But rounding up this bunch and getting them ready for the fight will take a bit of work, so it's smart to add in some extra time."

With the sun down, the air grew cooler and the insects diminished. Jules, like the others tired from the long afternoon walk, felt her eyes drooping, but didn't want to risk a nap.

Most of the sailors were lying down in the tall grass and couldn't be seen, but the sound of deep breathing and the occasional snore told of sailors doing what sailors did when they got a chance, catching quick naps.

Even Shin yawned, but jerked to alertness as something small and fast scurried past through the grass. He smiled at Jules. "Remember when you were little, and sometimes we would sit up and look at the stars?"

"That seems like a long time ago," Jules said. "I remember having to drag you outside sometimes. Why did I insist you had to be there?"

"You were scared of Mara. On a night like this," Shin added, pausing to listen to the wind whispering through the grass, "even I am a little unnerved thinking of her."

"Mara?" Jules remembered and laughed. "Mara the Undying. Who was it who told those stories about her?"

"Stev. The staff caught him once and punished him badly." Shin's smile turned rueful. "You know how the Imperial court feels about Mara stories."

"Who's Mara?" Erin asked.

"You never heard of Mara the Undying?" Jules asked in turn.

"Can't say that I have. She sounds like she'd be handy in a fight, though."

"Where'd you grow up?"

"A small town on the coast well north of Sandurin," Erin said. "Halfway to the Ramparts."

"The stories are better known in the south," Shin said. "But lately new legion recruits from the north seem to have heard them, too. When Jules was little, the stories were mostly told by children to other children, but they seem to be more popular with adults these days."

"So who is she?" Erin asked.

Jules pointed in the general direction of Marandur. "Maran was the first emperor, and his consort was Mara, right? Supposedly she was very beautiful, and wanted to stay that way. Shin, was it Maran who approached the first Mages or the Mages who approached him?"

"The stories vary," Shin said.

"Anyway," Jules continued, "a deal was struck to keep Mara eternally young and beautiful, but only if she seduced young men and drank their blood. Some stories say she knew that would be the price, and others say the Mages tricked her and Maran. But she's supposed to still be out there, still looking young and lovely, roaming the nights, finding young men, and luring them to beds they never leave."

"I should have been more afraid of Mara than you were," Shin said to Jules.

"If that Mara was real, you'd have been a victim for sure," Erin said, grinning.

"It's just a ghost story," Shin said. "Something to give people a little thrill when nights are dark. I admit I don't really like the stories. There are enough true dangers in the dark that I've never understood the need to dream up imaginary ones."

Something about his voice caused Jules to look closely at Shin, wondering what dangers he might fear, but he'd already turned and stood up, looking west toward the Imperial town. "Lights are burning," he said.

She stood up as well, seeing the pale glow rising from where the town was. "It's time we started. How much lead do you want, Shin?"

"Wait until you've lost sight of my group, count slowly to fifty after that, then follow."

"All right." As Shin gathered the four sailors who'd help him take out sentries, Jules looked at Erin and Lars. "Let's get our people ready. It's time to take this town out from under the Emperor's thumb."

CHAPTER EIGHT

The silence of the night shrouded the pirates as they moved as quietly as possible through the tall grass. Moonlight glinted on the bare steel of cutlasses carried by many of the pirates. Those with crossbows held them tightly, their cords loose, having been told not to tension and load the bows until ordered. The snap of a crossbow accidentally releasing might alert the defenders, or at the least bring any bored sentries to full alertness before they could be taken out.

Jules walked steadily, her eyes on the glow of light ahead, seeing the town's lights illuminating the masts of the *Star Seeker*. She worried that the sloop would give up chasing the *Sun Queen* and return at any time, but no other masts appeared. The walk took longer than she'd expected, but this time none of the pirates complained. Occasional looks back told Jules that all of the sailors were staying close, their faces set with both nervousness and determination, following their captains.

Who were following her.

The weight of destiny had been riding on her shoulders long enough that sometimes Jules could almost forget it was there. But tonight it redoubled, pressing down like iron bars. If this attack succeeded, it would set the stage for so much more. It would shatter the aura of invincibility, of inevitability, that the Empire had worn for as long as anyone could remember.

But if it failed…

Don't think about that, Jules told herself. *Think only of what you have to do to make this attack succeed.*

But the sound of the tall grass moving as the pirates advanced sounded like a current of barely audible laughter, as if the world itself was laughing at her ambitions and her dreams, and at her.

How long had they been walking? It felt like a very long time, as if the sun would begin to rise at any moment, even though it probably wasn't yet the middle of the night.

Jules came to a sudden halt as she realized the light of the town ahead had changed. It didn't cast as strong a glow into the sky, and as Jules watched the light dimmed yet again.

"They're putting out their lanterns," Gord said from nearby. "Settling down for the night."

"Good," Jules said. She started walking again.

A man shoved through the grass in front of her, drawing a startled gasp from Jules.

"Hold on," he said. "I'm Yuri, off the *Storm Runner*! Shin sent me back to warn you!"

"What is it, Yuri?" Erin lowered the blade that she'd raised when he appeared.

"Ahead, there's a cleared field before the town. Maybe twenty lances deep. And then a wall. A wooden wall."

"They've already got a wall up around the town?" Jules said.

"They probably brought pre-cut lumber," Lars said, his angry gaze turned toward the town. "How do we get through a wall without alerting everyone?"

"Shin thinks the wall isn't finished," Yuri said. "He's moving to the right along it, going inland. When he finds a good spot, or an unguarded gate, he'll go through."

"All right," Jules said, hoping that Shin was right about there being openings in the wall. "When we get to the edge of the cleared area, we'll turn right as well and move around the town until we find where Shin went through."

"And if there's no opening? If the wall's finished?" Erin asked. "By the time we get all the way around that wall it'll be dawn and we'll be in trouble."

"There'll be an opening," Jules said.

Erin looked skeptical and Lars appeared troubled, but neither openly disagreed. Both waved their crews forward as Jules started walking again.

It wasn't much farther on that they reached the end of the grass. All the grass and other vegetation that might allow someone to approach under concealment had been cut short all the way to the wall. The wooden planks of that wall reared up a good two lances, Jules guessed, and since this was Imperial construction those planks were probably thick enough to withstand many blows from swords or knives. It wasn't hard to understand why Shin had gone around the wall in search of a way in rather than trying to force his way through.

Jules turned right and began walking with just a thin remaining screen of grass between her and the wall. She kept looking that way, trying to spot any sentries posted, but saw nothing. To her left lay the open ground before the town, and to her right the crews of the three pirate ships, following Jules around the wall.

She wondered how far they'd follow her if no openings appeared.

They hadn't been walking long, though, when Jules saw another one of the pirate scouts standing right by the wall. She waved to catch his attention, and he waved her toward him.

As she got closer, Jules could see it was Kyle. "What've you got? A way in?"

"Yes, Captain." Kyle pointed to the wall. "There's a sally gate here. That's what Shin called it."

"Yeah," Jules said. "If the town is attacked, the defenders could launch a surprise counterattack by coming out through this gate."

"We *are* attacking the town, aren't we?" Kyle said.

"Yeah, we are. Is the gate locked?"

"No. Shin, and Elli from the *Storm Queen,* stood against the wall so I could climb up over them. I got over the top and down the other side, and opened the gate. Shin and Elli went on to search for sentries but left me here to make sure you knew where the gate was."

Jules peered at the wood, surprised at how hard it was to see the lines where the gate joined the rest of the wall. "Somebody did a very good job on this." She looked back, seeing the other pirates coming her way. "I'll go on through. Send the others as they get here."

"Aye, Captain."

Kyle shoved the unlocked gate open just far enough for Jules to slide through.

She edged inside, listening for any sign of trouble. A street ran inside along the wall, offering an easy way to rapidly shift defenders from one part to another, and for wagons or mules to bring supplies. On the other side of the street, buildings rose into the night, their facades hidden by the darkness. "All ri—"The thump of feet and the rattle of armor provided only a moment of warning before an Imperial patrol turned off a nearby side street and headed their way.

Jules had an instant to decide what to do. Attacking the patrol would raise the alarm for certain. The five legionaries were still moving at a laggardly pace, obviously not alert and obviously not having seen her yet. But squeezing back through the gate would take time and show her against the wood of the wall.

"Patrol! Shut the gate!" Jules hissed at Kyle, then leapt away from the wall, dashing into the night shadows of the nearest street.

She paused in the darkness, listening, while the gate swung closed with an admirable lack of noise. Kyle knew how to be sneaky, all right.

Hearing the patrol stroll closer, Jules retreated up the street away from the wall to avoid any chance of being seen. Like all Imperial towns, the streets had been laid out in a rigid grid, every cross street at right angles to the streets it met. That made it all too easy for someone to see down the street, even in the dark. She moved a good five lances, pausing next to an unfinished building whose wooden bones rose into the night.

The patrol reached the street that Jules had retreated down. And themselves turned toward her.

Her hand tightened on her dagger, but the legionaries were still moving with all of the lack of speed and efficiency of tired, bored soldiers who didn't expect any officers or centurions to show up and witness their lackadaisical patrolling.

But, sloppy as they were, the legionaries would still likely spot her if she stayed where she was or tried moving ahead of them down the street.

Jules stepped through a wall that had only a frame to hold it together. She moved cautiously, watching for anything that if tripped over might create noise, but had to keep up her speed to ensure she wouldn't be in sight when the legionaries reached this building.

She made it through the skeleton of the building and out the other side, trying to control her breathing in case anyone else was nearby.

Blazes! The pirates at the hidden gate would be watching, waiting for the patrol to get well away from the gate before anyone else entered the town. She was already separated from everyone else, with no idea where Shin was or...

Looking about the street she was now on, Jules saw it led to a two story building. Unlike the other structures she could see, which were in various stages of construction, it was completely finished, topped off by the tall spire she had seen earlier. And that told her which building that was.

The Imperial commander's home and headquarters.

If she could take the commander out before an alarm was raised...

It'd be risky, but with that patrol wandering about the alarm might be raised at any time. Shin and the one sailor left with him would have very little chance of taking down five legionaries without a lot of noise.

Maybe it was an opportunity. Maybe it was a temptation.

"Hey," one of the legionaries said, his voice carrying through the frame of the building. "We forgot to check the gate." His comrades grumbled in response. "What if the centurion left a note on it or something else that'll tell him we didn't check it? Come on. It's not that far back."

That settled things. The alarm would be raised as soon as they found the sally gate unlocked. Jules ran toward the commander's home.

She slowed her pace when she reached the steps leading up to the wooden porch, moving carefully to avoid making any betraying sound. The door wasn't locked. Jules opened it and eased through, peering into the deeper dark inside the building and listening, but no sentry was in the reception room beyond the front entry.

There had to be a sentry, though.

Jules tightened her grip on her dagger and went up the indoor stairs as quietly as she could, every moment dreading to hear the sound of the alarm being raised.

Reaching the head of the stairs, she moved her head just enough to see down the upstairs hallway. Moonlight streaming in through an open window provided more light up here than downstairs, giving her a good look at a sentry posted outside one door. Only the town commander would have a sentry specially assigned to his bedroom.

The sentry's head drooped, although she could tell he wasn't asleep, just drowsy. Instead of standing alertly at attention, he'd leaned his back against the wall next to the commander's door, doubtless taking care to ensure he made no sound in doing so.

Jules readied herself.

The sentry yawned mightily, his eyes closed for a long moment. Jules covered the distance from the stairs before those eyes opened again, one of her hands going across the sentry's mouth as her dagger went into his throat. A heart strike would've been surer, but legionary chest armor was good enough to divert a dagger thrust.

The sentry didn't die at once, shuddering and struggling a bit, making enough of a fuss to worry her.

Jules drew her cutlass, tested the door, found it unlocked, and went through in a rush.

Two windows let in enough moonlight to allow Jules to see the gleam of a naked blade as it sliced toward her. She parried the blow with her cutlass, slamming the guard of her sword into the body of her attacker.

He staggered back far enough for the light coming in through a window to show him clearly. Jules' mind registered each important point in turn. Her opponent held an Imperial officer's straight sword which was already being raised for a second strike at her. His feet were shifting to regain his balance, taking on a standard fighting stance. Clearly, this man wasn't someone who'd risen through the ranks as an Imperial bureaucrat, but a veteran of the legions. The noise made by the sentry's death throes hadn't given him enough time to don armor, so he was still in bedclothes. His night clothing looked fine in the moonlight, which together with the officer's sword told her this was indeed the commander of the settlement, whose killing or capture would take more effort, time, and noise than she'd wanted.

Jules closed in, side-stepping a blanket trailing on the floor from the bed, feinting with the dagger in one hand and following up with a slash from the cutlass.

The commander caught the cutlass strike on his own blade, letting it slide off and thrusting his point straight at Jules.

Her dagger knocked the sword tip away as Jules stepped closer and swung the cutlass at his side.

The commander took a hasty step back, standing ready for her next move, sword held at waist height, his breathing harsh in the confines of the room. But he had enough breath to spit out some words. "Traitor. Assassin. I was given this command by the Emperor himself, so whatever gain you hope for will never appear. You and anyone helping you will die."

Jules, side-stepping a little more to come at the commander again from his unguarded side, paused as she heard the man's voice. It sounded shockingly familiar.

The commander shifted his stance, his face becoming visible in the light from the nearest window.

Oh, blazes.

She stood, indecision freezing her muscles and her mind. "Dar'n of Marandur?" Jules said in a low voice.

The commander also stopped moving, peering through the dimness at her. "You came to kill me yet you're surprised to see me?"

"I didn't know you were in command here. I know you because your son and I trained together." Ian's father had visited him a few times, showing obvious if understated pride in his son, and had been rigidly polite when introduced to Jules.

Jules heard a sudden intake of breath, the commander leaning toward her to see better.

"You," he said.

Her mind finally started moving again. "Drop your blade, surrender the garrison, and no one else needs die," Jules said, flexing both of her own weapons slightly to emphasize her words.

He laughed in a way that sounded enough like his son to send a stab of pain through her. "And then what? I was ordered on this mission to prove my loyalty to the Emperor. What do you think will happen to my family if I don't fight you to the death?"

Jules clenched her hand tighter on the hilt of the cutlass. "I don't want to kill the father of Ian."

"How nice of you," Dar'n said, his voice dripping with anger. "And I cannot kill you, because the Emperor insists on having you alive. No matter what you want, I must die or I must capture you."

"No."

"If I live, and you remain free, I will have failed the Emperor. That will mean disgrace and the slow, painful deaths of my wife, my daughter, and my son Ian, who was fool enough to think you a worthy companion. You do not have honor, but I do. I will not buy my life with theirs."

"*I won't kill you,*" Jules hissed at him. "Nor will I let you destroy me! Wake up! The Emperor sees you as a useful slave. Why serve a man who'd kill your family if you fail here? Why die for him?"

"If you do not understand honor, I cannot teach you," Dar'n said, now contemptuous. "But even though I can't harm you, the same isn't true of whoever you came with. Somebody must have brought you here and gotten you inside this town. They will all die." He turned toward the window, his mouth widening to shout a warning.

Jules lunged forward, slamming the cutlass guard into Dar'n's face before the surprised commander could react.

He parried her next blow, trying a move to disarm her which Jules easily countered. Her next move nearly tore the sword from his hand, but he managed to maintain his grip.

In every fight that lasted beyond the first few clashes of blades, there always came a point where one of the combatants realized the other was better and their own chances growing less with every moment. Jules wasn't the best sword fighter in the world, but she knew a lot of tricks, and could handle both her cutlass and the dagger in ways someone trained in Imperial sword drill had trouble countering.

She saw the look come into the commander's eyes as he realized that she was going to win, saw his posture shift from offense to defense, and knew it was time to end this.

Ducking under his blade as her dagger diverted it upwards, Jules punched the guard of the cutlass into Dar'n's gut.

As the commander fell to the floor, his sword came up point-first in the only countermove available to him, but stopped in mid-motion as he remembered that he couldn't kill Jules.

She stepped inside the blade's reach, setting her feet for another blow to knock him out.

Dar'n's eyes met hers, a strange mix of fatalism and resolve in them. "I can't win, but I will not lose." His free hand came up suddenly, grabbing her dagger hand. Her training and experience told her that he'd try to push aside the blade or twist it out of her grip, so Jules braced herself to resist those moves, and was unprepared for what the commander did next.

Instead of trying to counter the threat of the dagger, the commander abruptly pulled her hand straight toward him.

As Jules stared in horror, the dagger she held went deep into his chest.

"Why?" she whispered, realizing the blade had pierced the commander's heart.

Dar'n's smile was twisted into a grimace by pain. "For... for..." He blinked as if trying to stay awake, then his face went slack and his last breath sighed upward.

Jules staggered back, her dagger coming free from the body of the commander, blood forming a dark sheen on its blade.

She'd just killed Ian's father.

His hand had done the work, but it had been her dagger, held in her hand.

A sudden noise jerked Jules out of her shock. She spun to face the door, both blades at the ready.

"Captain?" Kyle, out of breath and worried. "Captain Erin sent me here to look for you. We had to fight a patrol to keep them from locking that gate again. It made a lot of noise. We think—"

The rapid clanging of someone ringing an alarm bell resounded through the night.

"Blazes." Jules tried to shake herself out of her shock. She had work to do, and people counting on her. Wiping the dagger's blade clean on the bedding, Jules ran out of the room.

The town still felt ghostly in the night, but now the ghost was loud and angry, the alarm echoing off of any structure walls that had been completed. Jules saw a large group nearby, their cutlasses visible, and ran to them. "Who's here?"

"Lars," he called back, running to meet her, followed by the pirates with him. "Erin headed toward the legionary tents to see how many she could take out before they armed and armored themselves."

"Where are the tents?" Jules asked.

"Over there, we think."

"Let's go help Erin kill legionaries."

They ran down otherwise empty streets. "Where are the citizens?" Lars panted as he ran beside her.

"You know the rule when alarms sound in Imperial towns," Jules said. "Everybody stays where they are and waits for orders. Unless they panic and start fleeing, which can happen. These citizens are staying in their tents. If the legionaries watching the laborer encampment leave their posts, some of the laborers might try to bolt, but they won't be a threat to us."

Dashing into a plaza facing the waterfront, Jules saw half-armored and armored legionaries forming into a line under the bellowed orders of a centurion.

"There's about thirty," Jules guessed. "A few less."

A rattle of swords and the twang of crossbows sounded from where the *Star Seeker* sat moored as Hachi's pirates attacked the legionary sentries watching their ship.

The centurion let out a couple of impressive obscenities, ordering some of his legionaries to run to help the sentries fighting the *Star Seeker*.

"There's about twenty left facing us," Erin said, joining them.

"That's better," Jules said. "It'll still be tough."

She felt a surge of relief as Shin's voice sounded nearby.

"Get into a line!" Shin shouted, gesturing with his sword. Under his direction, the pirates formed into a ragged line facing the now sharp, rigid line of legionaries.

For a moment, motion paused as the Imperial line faced the mob of pirates.

Jules, walking to the front center of the pirate group, felt a moment of strange displacement as she came to a halt facing the Imperial soldiers.

It hadn't been all that long ago that she'd been one of those soldiers. She'd stood in such a line, calling out orders. For a weird instant it felt as if she were both here facing the legionaries and there as part of their line, two possible versions of herself facing off against each other, the Jules that *was* preparing to fight the Jules that might have been.

She shook herself out of the odd sensation. The situation didn't allow any time for such nonsense. There were more than three times as many pirates as there were Imperial soldiers, but it didn't take a military expert to know the pirates wouldn't hold against an advance by the armored, disciplined legionaries.

Not without some help.

"Lars!" Jules called, reaching back to sheath her dagger. "Get up here with me!"

She brought out the Mechanic revolver, looking it over as its metal glinted dully in the light of moon, trying to control her breathing.

"Is it time?" Lars asked. His eyes seemed huge in his face as he gazed at her. "We need to use these things?"

"Yes," Jules said. "You and me together. You have no practice with aiming yours, so wait until they're close, point it at the center of a legionary, and pull that trigger slowly to shoot the weapon. Don't jerk it, or the shot will go wild."

"Wait until they're close," Lars repeated. "Don't jerk the trigger."

"Stand beside me, in the center of our line," Jules said. She took up position, seeing how her presence cheered the nervous pirates on either side of her. About ten lances away, the legionary line faced her, a wall of shields lined up side by side. As long as the legionaries held their formation, their shields would protect them from crossbow bolts. Without the Mechanic weapons, this fight would have had to be resolved the hard way, hand to hand, a type of fight the pirates couldn't hope to win against armored legionaries. In the center of the Imperial line stood the centurion, shield and sword in hand, ready to lead them and glaring at the pirates in a way that promised no mercy.

In the night, that centurion seemed to resemble one of those who'd given extra attention to Jules during her initial training, trying to force a girl from an orphan home to give up her chance at an officer's commission.

She raised the Mechanic weapon over her head, brandishing it. "Legionaries! You can't fight this! The man to my left has one as well! There is no shame in yielding!"

No answer came, but then she hadn't expected one. Jules looked over at Lars to be sure he had his revolver out. Lars was holding his with both hands, the front still pointed toward the ground. "Steady," she told him. "Like a crossbow. Stay steady, keep it pointed at the center of the target, and pull the trigger with a smooth motion. Got it?"

"Got it," Lars said, licking his lips.

The pirates, heartened by Jules' display of the Mechanic weapon, were yelling insults at the legionaries. The Imperial troops stood silently, maintaining their discipline.

"Advance!" the centurion called out, his voice booming through the night.

He sure sounded like that one centurion she'd hated because of his treatment of her.

Regardless, Jules decided, he'd do as a stand-in even if he wasn't the same man.

The legionaries began advancing with a slow, steady gait, the wall of shields seeming to move like a fortress given legs to propel it.

"Hold on!" Jules shouted to her nervous pirates. "We'll take them!"

"Hold our line!" Shin called out as well. He raised his sword, shaking it. "For freedom!"

Jules brought up her own revolver, steadying it with both hands as she aimed at the center of the centurion's body.

The legionaries would charge when they got within three lances. Enough distance to build up speed for the impact with the imposing line, but not so far that they would tire themselves charging a long distance. That was how they trained. That was how they would fight. To change the routine was unthinkable.

When Jules estimated the legionary line was four lances distant, she began slowly squeezing the trigger of her weapon.

As always, the boom of the weapon surprised her, the jolt of it jerking her arms back.

The legionary on the centurion's right staggered one step, then fell, his neighbor closing the gap in the shield wall. But the advance halted, even the Emperor's soldiers momentarily unnerved by the crash of the Mechanic weapon.

The centurion had continued forward another step, scowling as he realized his soldiers had stopped. Turning, he yelled at them. "Advance!"

"Hey!" Jules shouted, her voice harsher and louder than even that of the centurion. "Look at me while I kill you!"

The centurion turned back to face her as her finger tightened again and the revolver boomed once more, the noise echoing from the buildings.

He jolted back, staring at her, then down at the hole in his chest armor.

Another boom startled everyone as Lars' weapon shot. Probably more through luck than skill, another legionary in the line fell.

Jules aimed at the legionary wall and pulled the trigger again as the centurion swayed and dropped like a tree whose roots had given way.

She stepped forward as another legionary was hit and shouted with pain. Lars stayed beside her as Jules walked toward the legionary line, her Mechanic weapon aimed at them.

The legionaries could fight swords and daggers and spears. They could withstand a hail of crossbow fire. But they'd never faced weapons which seemed able to slay easily despite their shields and armor. There were no better troops in the world than the Emperor's legionaries, but even if there had been, those troops would've been shaken as well.

Lars's weapon thundered once more. Jules didn't see if he hit anything, instead swinging her weapon slowly across the front of the Imperial line. "You're next!" she cried, knowing that every legionary facing her would think that her weapon was aimed at him or her.

The legionaries broke, scrambling backwards as the pirates roared and charged. The shield wall fell apart, some soldiers dropping their shields in panic, and legionaries trained to fight with comrades standing steady beside them found themselves facing enemies alone.

Shin led a large group of pirates toward the *Star Seeker* to hit the legionaries there in the rear.

Jules let the other pirates stream past her as they swamped the isolated, individual Imperial soldiers. "Give them quarter if they try to surrender!" she shouted.

Walking steadily, the sounds of fighting already fading as the last legionaries either died or threw down their swords and held out empty hands, Jules reached the spot where the fallen centurion lay. She knelt next to him, using the flat of her cutlass blade to turn his head so she could see his face clearly.

Oh, yes. She knew him.

He was still alive, but clearly not for much longer, glaring at her with the last remnants of his strength. Remembering the humiliations he'd heaped upon her, Jules leaned closer and smiled at him. "Remember me, Centurion Rasel? You failed then, and you failed tonight. Take that with you into the dark."

She stood up as the centurion's face went soft with death, seeing Lars watching her.

"Blazes, Jules, you're a cold one," he said.

"The world made me this way," Jules said. "People like him made me this way. I don't waste mercy on those who never gave it to others."

Lars grimaced, nodding. "It's not my place to say you're wrong. There'll be a healer in the town, right?"

"Right," Jules said. "We need to find that healer. Did you or Erin bring the healers from your ships?"

"We both did. Gabral! Where's Chati? Tell her to get to work on these injured." Lars grimaced as he looked at the blood pooling on the ground. "The fights are exciting, but I've never liked what comes after. What about the commander of the settlement, Jules? Were you able to capture him?"

Her momentary satisfaction vanished into a dark pit inside her. Jules looked toward the building where Dar'n's body still lay. "He's dead," she said, wondering why the taste of victory felt like ashes in her mouth.

Erin, also nearby, turn to some of her sailors. "Take a couple lanterns to the end of the pier and signal to let the *Storm Runner* and the *Storm Queen* know it's safe to come into port. They should be close enough by now to see the lights."

"Speaking of ships," Lars said. "We've still got an Imperial sloop to worry about."

Jules spotted one of her sailors. "Gord! Get to the *Star Seeker* and make sure Captain Hachi has a lookout watching for the return of that Imperial sloop!" She rubbed her face, trying to shake the renewed sick feeling inside at knowing her hand had killed Ian's father. "We need to get this town nailed down. Get any legionaries who surrendered under guard somewhere they can't make trouble. Make sure the citizens don't try anything and that the laborers know to stay in their tents."

"And do all that before that sloop returns," Erin said. She raised her head slightly and bellowed loudly enough to be heard clearly streets away. "Listen up! We will loot this town properly! No free-lancing! If any sailor attacks, assaults, or steals from a citizen or laborer, or destroys any property, I will personally slice your neck so deep your head'll flop back as you die!"

"The same goes for me!" Jules shouted.

"And for the sailors from the *Storm Queen!*" Lars added.

"We should have thought of all that before we took the town," Jules grumbled.

"It's not like any of us have done this before," Lars said.

"We need to divide it up," Captain Erin said. "I'll take care of making sure the citizens and property are locked down."

"I'll handle the legionary prisoners," Jules said.

"That leaves making sure the laborers stay quiet to me," Lars said. "What should we tell Hachi to do?"

"Make sure he's got control of the waterfront," Erin said. "Let's move. We've only got until that sloop comes back, and we've no idea how long that might be."

Jules told off a group of sailors from her ship to haul the bodies of dead legionaries somewhere out of sight, strip them of their armor and weapons, and then guard the weapons and armor. That done, she went in search of the legionary prisoners, hoping that no one had done anything stupid or needlessly cruel to them.

Taking over a town, she realized, was a lot more complicated than seizing a ship for a brief period. Neither she nor any of the other pirate captains had really thought beyond gaining control, or even past defeating the legionaries. And, assuming they maintained control, who would run this town once the four pirate ships and their captains departed?

It couldn't be her, Jules knew as she walked rapidly among the half-built structures. Even if she didn't lack experience at such things, even if her temperament was suited to such a job, her presence in one town for an extended period would be like casting bread crumbs onto the water to draw a lot of fish, only in her case it would be drawing Mages with murder on their minds.

She passed by the finished home of the former town commander, seeing a sailor already posted at the door to prevent looting.

Among her other priorities, she'd have to ensure that Colonel Dar'n's body was prepared properly for a respectful burial.

Ian would hate her for what had happened this night. He had every right to.

Jules spotted the tall shape of Shin and headed toward him. "Do you know where the legionary prisoners are?"

"They've been taken care of, Captain," he said, saluting her. Shin gestured toward the partially-completed building next to them. "The lower walls are finished here. I have some sailors blocking the stairs up to the unfinished second story and partially blocking the window openings. With your permission, I was going to set up a guard schedule."

"You have my permission," Jules said, relieved. "How are the prisoners? Do they seem likely to cause trouble?"

"I do not think so," Shin said, his brow furrowed as he considered the question. "The defeat has shocked them. They have lost their weapons and armor, and their leaders. They know we greatly outnumber them. And they know they're alone. Any help for them is far off to the east."

"Not yet," Jules said. "We still have to deal with that sloop which is hopefully still chasing the *Sun Queen*. It'll come back eventually, though. Maybe pretty soon." She heard hammering and saw another window opening being blocked by boards. "You did a great job setting this up. Are you sure all you did in the legions was stand in the line of battle?"

"A veteran learns many skills," Shin said. "I'm not exceptional."

"You look exceptional from where I stand," Jules said. "Do any of these captured legionaries seem interested in joining with us? We can tell the Empire that any who join us were killed in the fight so they wouldn't have to worry about retaliation against their families."

"I can speak with them," Shin said.

"Do that later." Jules pointed toward the waterfront. "We may well need you when that sloop gets back."

Leaving Shin to oversee the work on the impromptu prison, Jules went in search of problems that no one might have dealt with yet. She soon came across Erin at the rows of tents where Imperial citizens were still living.

A group of citizens was listening as a man in an Imperial suit that bore signs of being hastily donned spoke to Erin. "What are you saying?"

Erin, looking and sounding as if her last thread of patience was about to snap, spoke in the manner of someone addressing a toddler. "The Empire no longer owns or controls this town. We have taken it. You will take orders from us."

"That's… inconceivable," the Imperial official said. "I must speak with Colonel Dar'n. He is in charge here, by order of the Emperor."

Understanding why Erin was about to explode at the man, Jules stepped in. "This town is now independent."

The official blinked at her in confusion. "In… da…?"

"Independent. It means this town is no longer part of the Empire."

"What? You can't just make up a word that means… something ridiculous! Every town is part of the Empire. Every person in the world is a citizen of the Empire. Except the Great Guilds, of course."

"Not any more," Jules said. "This town is now free. Which means you do as you're told." She no sooner said it than she realized how absurd the two statements were together, but the Imperial citizens didn't notice. The Empire might not encourage imagination, but it taught its citizens to do what they were told to do. Faced with confident authority, the officials and citizens backed down.

After posting some more pirates to make sure no citizens thought things through and tried doing anything, Jules and Erin headed back toward the town's sole pier, where the *Star Seeker* was tied up.

"Is that a real word?" Erin asked her.

"Independent? Yes," Jules said. "That's what we pirates are. We don't answer to anyone unless we want to. We're independent."

"I never realized it," Erin said. "So it's just a word for what we already are?"

"And for what this town will be, and what places like Marida's and Jacksport already are."

"We didn't have a word for it, did we?" Erin looked about her in surprise. "We didn't have a way to describe a place that wasn't part of the Empire unless it was part of one of the Great Guilds. Is it strange that things seem to have changed just because we now have a word?"

"Words help us form ideas," Jules said. "And this idea is bigger than most, isn't it?"

"Where'd you get it from?"

"Some Mechanics used it. I don't think they realized how important that idea is in a world that's never had it before."

"Where'd the Mechanics get, though?"

"Where'd they get any of their ideas and devices?" Jules asked. She looked out over the water as they reached the pier. The night had almost run its course, the sky brightening with morning twilight. The *Star Seeker* was still tied up, but both the *Storm Queen* and the *Storm Runner* had anchored in the river away from the pier. "Do you think that Imperial sloop is still chasing the *Sun Queen*?"

Her answer came not from Erin, but from a lookout high on the *Star Seeker*'s mast.

"Masts in sight! It looks like that Imperial sloop coming back!"

CHAPTER NINE

"A re you certain?" Captain Hachi called up loudly enough to be heard along the waterfront.

"Aye, Captain!"

Erin ran one hand down her face, glaring out to sea. "If that sloop is close enough to see then it's too close for my ship and the *Storm Queen* to get underway without being seen."

"Maybe we can catch him just outside the harbor," Captain Lars said as he ran up.

"That's not good odds if he's at all alert. A lucky shot from that ballista of his and it'd be the remaining ship one on one against a crew of angry legionaries."

"We still have the Mechanic weapons," Jules said. "And surprise."

"Yes, but—"

Captain Hachi came striding up, looking thoughtful. "I was just looking at the *Storm Queen* at anchor and thinking how it was a twin to the Imperial sloop," he said.

"She *was* an Imperial sloop," Lars said. "Until the *Sun Queen* and *Storm Runner* captured her."

"Do you think she could still pass as an Imperial warship?"

Lars hesitated, thinking. "As long as the crew stays out of sight. We haven't changed any parts of her, and we keep a neat ship."

Hachi smiled. "There may be a way to capture that Imperial ship without a sea fight. Without any fight at all."

"What're you thinking, trickster?" Erin asked.

"I am thinking that if we can get a dozen or so sailors into that captured legionary armor, we might be able to fool that Imperial sloop's officers and crew into doing just what we want." Hachi paused, pursing his lips in thought. "It would require me to expose myself as a pirate, but I wasn't really planning on going back to my job in the Imperial bureaucracy anyway."

Jules turned to search the surrounding area, spotting one of her sailors. "Marta! Get Shin! He's over that way! I need him to get into that dead centurion's armor! And get a dozen more good men and women into armor as well! We need a force of fake legionaries and we need them fast."

* * *

The light of the rising sun shone on the sails of the Imperial sloop as it glided up to the pier on the other side from the *Star Seeker*, lines going across to those waiting on the shore. Laborers from the town, told by Jules that they were volunteering to help and interspersed with pirates to keep them quiet, caught the lines and tied up the sloop.

Jules, watching from a building just off the waterfront that offered good cover, watched the sloop's crew furling their sails. Their movements were those of tired sailors with no trace of worry or alarm in their actions. "Go," she told Shin.

Shin gave her a proper legionary salute. With one hand casually resting on his breastplate in a way that covered the hole in it made by the Mechanic revolver, Shin led his group of disguised pirates out onto the waterfront.

Jules winced as she watched how sloppily the pirates marched, but hopefully the sloop's officers wouldn't notice.

Shin halted his group with a barked command, then walked to the foot of the brow, which the sloop's crew had just set onto the pier. "I have orders for the captain," he said, his voice carrying just the right note of authority.

An Imperial officer appeared, her dark red uniform bearing signs it had been worn all night. "What is it, Centurion?"

"Colonel Dar'n wishes to see the captain immediately."

Even from a distance, Jules could see resignation in the slump of the captain's shoulders. She'd be expecting to get chewed out for not capturing the ship carrying Jules. But instead of immediately coming down the brow, the captain frowned at Shin. "I haven't seen you before, Centurion."

"No, Captain," Shin said without hesitating. "I came with the reinforcements on the *Raptor's Strike*."

The captain looked over at the *Storm Runner* where it rode peacefully at anchor. "Why was the *Raptor's Strike* sent here?"

Shin shook his head. "I don't know the reasons, Captain. The captain of the *Raptor's Strike* is with Colonel Dar'n."

"Of course you wouldn't know the reasons," the captain grumbled, only the otherwise quiet of the waterfront letting her voice carry far enough for Jules to hear. "We thought we heard noises earlier from this direction, Centurion, while we were out waiting for the off-shore breeze to subside. Like the sound of Mechanic weapons. Did Mechanics come on that other ship anchored out there?"

"No Mechanics came on that ship, Captain. What you heard was thunder," Shin said, calmly reciting the explanation that Jules had suggested if the sound of the Mechanic weapons had carried.

"From a clear sky?"

"Yes, Captain. The weather is odd out here, I think." As the captain frowned, Shin spoke in deferential tones. "Colonel Dar'n expressed his wish that you come right away."

The captain turned to another officer to give some orders, then walked down the brow and past Shin. Shin barked some more commands and led his "legionaries" in her wake, staying close behind the captain.

Jules sized the captain up as she walked closer. Imperial dagger at her belt, of course, as well as a regulation straight Imperial officer's sword. Nothing that couldn't be handled.

Fading back down the street as the captain and Shin's escort approached, Jules stepped into an empty doorway past the point where the captain could be seen from the ship. She watched the captain stride past, eyes forward, looking tired but determined.

Stepping out directly behind the captain, Jules placed the edge of her dagger across the captain's throat. "Don't—"

Tired and surprised though she was, the captain reacted with impressive speed, dropping limply through Jules' grasp and drawing her own dagger.

Jules slashed at the captain, but her blow only cut a line down the side of the Imperial officer's face.

As the captain opened her mouth to shout a warning to her ship, Shin stepped behind her and swung the hilt of his legionary sword against the back of her head. Jules, her dagger aimed at the captain's heart this time, shifted her blow as the captain dropped, instead stabbing her in one arm.

"She's a tough one," Marta commented from where she stood among the rank of false legionaries.

"Did anyone on the ship notice?" Jules asked Shin.

Shin, looking back that way, shook his head. "I don't see any signs of alarm."

"Good. Let's get her gagged and bound." Jules stepped back as her sailors did what sailors did well, knotting and tying ropes.

As the task was completed, Captain Hachi strode up, wearing the suit of an Imperial bureaucrat. Jules raised her eyebrows at him as she took in the suit. Imperial rules dictated the garb worn by different levels of officials. She'd only occasionally glimpsed, from a distance, a suit like this one. "You didn't tell us you were that high ranking an official," she said to Hachi.

He smiled. "I didn't think you'd be all that impressed. I rose high enough in the ranks of the Imperial bureaucracy to be able to see that the path ahead would just be a more refined, politer, version of the cut-throat competition at lower levels. Being tired of that, I thought I'd try piracy as a more civilized alternative."

"You won't be able to go back to that Imperial job once the crew of that sloop sees you," Jules said.

Hachi shrugged. "It's not as if I liked the job. And in any event, I'd already decided I like this life better. You are Shin?" he asked.

Shin nodded respectfully. "Yes, Captain."

"Excellency," Hachi said. "I'm His Excellency again."

"Of course, Your Excellency," Shin said.

"We'll wait a short time longer, long enough for the captain… where is the captain?"

"We shoved her in there," Gord said, pointing to the partly completed building next to them.

"She can't get loose?"

"Blazes, no. Them knots are tight, and so's the gag on her mouth. Even if she wakes up soon, all she'll be able to do is think curses at us."

"Good." Hachi looked over the fake legionaries. "You all look impressively dangerous. If we do this right, there shouldn't be any fighting. Shin, you understand your role?"

"I do, Your Excellency."

"I'll be watching," Jules said. "Erin and Lars are ready with a big force of pirates, out of sight of the pier but close."

"Then we are ready. Follow me," Hachi said to Shin, and began walking with exaggerated dignity toward the pier.

Shin led his fake legionaries behind Hachi, Jules following as well until she had to stop in concealment as the others marched on toward the Imperial sloop.

As the group approached the sloop, the ship's centurion met them. "How many I assist Your Excellency?"

"Are you in charge?" Hachi asked, his voice having taken on the air of someone who knew his own status was superior to anyone else in the area.

"No, Your Excellency. Captain Kathrin is ashore to meet with—"

"I *know* that. Who is in charge in her absence?" Hachi said, sounding peeved at having to ask again.

The Imperial officer who the captain had spoken with before leaving the ship walked quickly onto the pier. "I'm the second in command, sir. Lieutenant Martine."

"Lieutenant Martine." Hachi looked him over skeptically. "All right. I have orders for you."

"From Colonel Dar'n?"

"From the Emperor." Hachi gave the nervous lieutenant a little time to absorb that information before he pointed toward the *Storm Runner*. "Do you see that ship? It brought me. Why do suppose someone of my rank was sent here?"

"I... I do not know, Your Excellency."

Hachi sighed loudly, as if explaining was both tedious and annoying. "There is a spy among your crew."

"A... a spy?" the increasingly rattled lieutenant asked as the ship's centurion stared in shock.

"A spy for the Mechanics. Reporting to them what the Emperor's loyal servants are doing. You were unaware of this," Hachi added, making the simple statement sound menacing.

The lieutenant looked at the ship's centurion, who had taken on the look of someone who no longer wanted to be noticed and only shook his head at his officer. "We had no idea, Your Excellency. Of course not."

"You had no idea." Hachi shook his head, his entire bearing that of someone carrying out a grim task. "Perhaps that can be overlooked, *if* the spy is captured quickly and smoothly enough. Get your entire crew onto the pier. I want them all here, lined up. Ensure none of them have weapons, not even those odd knives that sailors carry. And no armor. Your centurion will have to remove his, and you can leave your sword and dagger on the ship while telling your crew to get lined up here."

"The entire crew, your Excellency? Regulations say we have to leave a small watch team aboard at all times."

Hachi paused. "What was that? I was expecting to hear *yes, Your Excellency, at once, Your Excellency*, but instead there was something else. Must I repeat myself? Get your entire crew on the pier now, lined up for my inspection. No weapons, no armor. Your ship won't go anywhere while you're all standing right here, will it?"

"No, Your Excellency," the lieutenant said. "I mean, yes, Your Excellency. At once." He turned to the ship's centurion. "Pass the orders. Get the entire crew lined up without delay."

"Yes, Lieutenant Martine!"

The lieutenant and the centurion ran onto the Imperial sloop, calling out orders.

Hachi waited on the pier with outward signs of growing impatience of the sort only a real Imperial official would display as unarmed sailors and legionaries came tumbling off the sloop, hastily forming into three lines facing him.

Lieutenant Martine came running down the brow again, his sword scabbard and dagger sheath empty. The centurion, having just finished a head count, saluted.

"This is the entire crew, your Excellency," Martine said. "Except for the captain, of course."

Hachi looked over the lines of sailors and legionaries with a cold glance that caused every member of the crew to stiffen with worry, then turned and gestured to Shin. "Centurion, take your detachment and search the ship. Ensure that no one is hiding."

Lieutenant Martine jerked with surprise. "But, Your Excellency—"

"Are you questioning the Emperor's orders? Again?"

"No, sir!"

Shin led his force of fake legionaries around the ranks of the crew. Jules saw the ship's centurion take note of the sloppy marching, frowning in disapproval, but cowed by Hachi's persona he said nothing.

Once at the brow, instead of leading the fake legionaries aboard, Shin lined them up to block access to the ship, shields ready, facing the backs of the ranks of the crew.

"What are they doing, Your Excellency?" Lieutenant Martine asked Hachi, bewildered.

"You ask a lot of questions," Hachi said.

As the lieutenant quailed at the tone of Hachi's voice, Captain Erin's call echoed across the waterfront. "Forward!"

Jules walked out of concealment and toward the pier as pirates erupted from nearby buildings and streets, their weapons gleaming. She joined them as they faced off against the shocked crew of the Imperial sloop. "Thank you," Jules said to Hachi. "Your Excellency," she added.

"What... what...?" Lieutenant Martine asked, staring at the pirates and Hachi.

"Surrender your crew and none will be harmed, on my word," Jules told him.

"I can't—" Martine's denial choked off as he realized what had happened, his unarmed crew blocked from getting back on the ship, and faced with large numbers of pirates brandishing weapons. His gaze went to the town as if expecting help to appear from there.

"We've already defeated the Imperial soldiers here," Captain Lars said. "They're dead or prisoners."

"You and your crew can be dead," Captain Erin said, "or prisoners. Your choice."

"Captain Kathrin—" Lieutenant Martine began to say.

"Is already our prisoner," Jules said.

Lieutenant Martine stared at her, his eyes changing in an instant that told her what he'd do. Like Colonel Dar'n, he knew the price that would be paid for such a failure.

An instant later, Martine hurled himself at her.

Jules, having had that instant to prepare herself, twisted aside rather than meet the lieutenant's charge head on. Her dagger caught his near arm, digging in and forcing it away, while Jules swung the guard of her cutlass against the side of Martine's head. The crunch of the side of his skull breaking sounded unusually loud across the otherwise quiet waterfront, the blow knocking the lieutenant aside to fall limply onto the wooden planks of the pier. "Not this time," Jules whispered.

But Lieutenant Martine's attack had bought a few moments for the rest of the Imperial crew to think, and now the ship's centurion raised his voice. "You all know the price we'd pay at home if we surrender our ship without a fight or even a scratch on us! Follow me and die with honor!"

With a roar mingling defiance and despair, most of the unarmed sailors and legionaries from the sloop followed their centurion in a charge back toward their ship. Shin's false legionaries locked shields to meet the impact, holding the mass of bodies long enough for the pirates facing the ship to themselves charge the crew.

But one large group from the sloop, perhaps following the lead of their lieutenant, charged toward Jules and the pirates around her.

Jules knew what bare hands could do in a fight, especially when they belonged to desperate men and women. She brought her cutlass and dagger up, catching the first Imperial woman sailor to reach her on the blade and twisting it to force her aside. She yanked the dagger free as a second sailor pushed close enough to grab Jules' arm holding the cutlass. She took a step back, stabbing with the dagger and plunging it into his side, but the sailor hung on and punched her with his free hand.

Jules slashed the dagger at the man's eyes, causing him to flinch back, following up with another stab into his chest.

The press of bodies forced her back another step as another Imperial sailor lunged at her, but a moment later the group of attackers was swamped by pirates hitting them from both sides.

Jules pulled herself away from the struggle, looking across the pier. A normal fight was marked by the loud clanging of blade on blade and the thuds of impacts against armor. Not this fight, though. The unarmed Imperials fought only with their hands, so the noise of the struggle was marked by the screams and cries of those fighting and injured, and over all that the sickening crunching sound as bones broke under the merciless blows of the pirates.

The ship's centurion went down under Shin's blade as he strove to break the shield wall blocking access to the ship. Around him, the rest of the frantic Imperials fell like wheat before a harvest scythe as the pirates pressed in from all sides.

Pressed together too tightly to fight, those of the Imperial crew that were still standing fell one by one as the pirates continued to rain blows on them.

"That's enough!" Captain Lars bellowed. "They're done! Stop this!"

"Aye!" Captain Erin shouted. "It's over! Break it off, you louts!"

Jules, wondering why she hadn't shouted the same command, watched the surviving Imperials give up as their desperation gave way to hopelessness. Something finally clicked inside of her, though, as she took in the dead and wounded Imperials lying on the pier. "They'd have a healer on that ship. See if their healer is still alive! Someone get the healers from the ships, and you, Kyle, find the town healer and get her here."

"Blazes, that was ugly," Erin muttered as she came up to Jules. "Are you all right?"

"I'm fine," Jules said, not feeling anything inside as she stooped to wipe blood off of her dagger and cutlass.

She straightened to find Captain Hachi, his suit somehow still unmarked, looking soberly at the remnants of the fight. "My plan wasn't as successful as I hoped," he said. "See how little I still know of people, even after all these years of learning how to manipulate them."

"You know why they fought," Jules said. "It couldn't be helped. And we might've lost a lot of our own trying to fight them any other way."

"Pirates have their virtues," Hachi said. "But they're not soldiers. If you mean for towns like this to stand on their own, they'll need soldiers to defend them and fight their battles."

"Then we'll get soldiers," Jules said, willing coldness to fill her as she gazed at the dead and injured. She'd known that the path she'd set for herself would likely take her through such things, but seeing the reality in the light of the morning sun still tore at her.

"We?" Erin asked as she walked up. "Are you thinking the rest of us will be at your beck and call? I'm a pirate. If I wanted to fight wars, I'd have joined the legions and gotten myself a shiny set of armor."

"No one's expecting you to serve my dreams," Jules said. Not wanting to discuss it any longer, she turned to face toward the town. "We need to have a talk with the captain of this ship."

"I'll get Lars," Erin said.

The four captains walked away from the waterfront and the remnants of the one-sided battle, down a new street with the skeletons of new buildings rising on the soil of a new land. But Jules's thoughts stayed on the waterfront until they reached the place where the Imperial captain had been left.

And found it empty.

Jules was still trying to tamp down her emotions and not yell with anger when Kyle came running up to them. "I was looking for you, Captain. We took that Imperial officer to the big building where we could guard her better."

Inhaling slowly, Jules nodded. "Is she still tied up?"

"Sure thing, Captain! Gord's knots—I tell you, the man ties a knot like no other sailor I've ever met."

Afraid that she still might snap at Kyle, Jules forced a smile and nodded to him before leading Erin, Lars, and Hachi to the completed building where Colonel Dar'n's body still lay upstairs. As they were about to reach the building, though, Jules stopped. "Hold on."

"What is it?" Lars asked.

"I was thinking of something we were talking about earlier," Jules said. "About the rest of you." She bit her lip, looking toward the building where the Imperial captain was held prisoner. "I'm the only one of us that officer has seen. If we all four go in to talk to her, she'll see you three and know the parts you played here."

"You're thinking you should talk to the captain alone?" Erin said.

"Yes. You can be close enough to listen, unseen. But you and your ships and your crews will become targets of the Emperor if it's known you were equals in taking this town."

"And your ship and crew?" Hachi asked.

"We were already targets of the Emperor," Jules said. "I'm not trying to claim credit for this in anyone's eyes except his."

"You are trying to claim the blame," Lars said. "I'm not sure I'm comfortable with you taking a dagger thrust that should be aimed at all of us."

"She's right, though," Hachi said. "It would be better for the rest of us if the Emperor's eyes were fixed on her."

"I may not be a legionary obsessed with honor," Lars said, "but it still bothers me."

"You're not asking it of me," Jules said. "I'm making a free choice here. That's important to me, that I can decide such things instead of being only a plaything for destiny."

Erin looked her over before nodding. "All right, then. I admit the wisdom of what you say, and it's your right to decide it."

"I will also agree," Hachi said.

Lars grimaced, looking away, before finally nodding once as well. "All right."

Jules let out a sigh of relief. "Give me your Mechanic weapon," she told Lars. "I'll need to show that officer who was backing us."

Holding Lars' revolver, her own in its holster, Jules walked the rest of the way to the front door. Opening it and looking inside at the reception area, she saw a couple of pirates lounging on a comfortable couch while they watched the Imperial captain, who was tied to a substantial chair. "You two take a break outside," she told the pirates. "I need to have a private chat with this lady."

Gesturing to Erin, Lars, and Hachi to stand outside by the door-way out of sight of the Imperial captain, Jules left the door open after the guards left. Dragging a chair to face the one where the captain was tied, Jules sat down, resting Lars's revolver on one broad arm of the chair.

Then, annoyed with herself, she got up again, using her dagger to cut free the gag over the captain's mouth.

The once perfect uniform of the captain of the newly-captured sloop now bore scuffs and slashes. Her dagger sheath and sword scab-bard were empty, not that the woman could have reached either with her arms and hands tightly bound. A rough bandage soaked with blood covered one side of her face where Jules's dagger had slashed it.

Another bandage was wrapped tightly around her arm, where blood barely showed against the dark red Imperial uniform to mark the place where Jules's second thrust had gone instead of into the captain's heart.

The Imperial officer studied Jules with a look that promised slow and painful death. "You may have won this day," she said in a voice rendered hoarse by her injuries and the pain of the gag, "but I will hunt you all down and make you pay for this with blood."

"The Emperor wouldn't be happy to hear you threatening injury to me," Jules said, leaning back in her chair in a deliberate show of casual disregard for the threat.

"Why—?" The officer stared at Jules, her face hardening even more. "You."

"Me," Jules said.

"That supposed Mage prophecy won't protect you forever!"

"Oh, the prophecy was real," Jules said. "And so far it hasn't really protected me from anything. In fact, it's been the source of a lot of trouble for me. What's your name?"

The Imperial officer glared for a moment before answering. "Captain Kathrin of Law."

"Law? Where's that?"

"A small town east of Emdin," Kathrin spat in reply. "I bear its name with pride."

"Wait." Jules looked closer at the officer. "Captain Kathrin? No-Quarter Kathrin?"

"I don't know what you're talking about."

"You don't know your reputation among other Imperial officers and sailors? I heard that you're a hard-ass who never learned the meaning of mercy. Every officer trainee I knew was scared of being assigned to a ship you commanded."

Captain Kathrin smiled. "I admit such a reputation would suit me. I do my job."

"If I wasn't smart," Jules said. "I'd kill someone like you. But it happens that I need you."

"If you think I'll serve your purposes, you're not only treasonous but also stupid."

Jules smiled at her. "But you do your job, don't you? And that means delivering a report to the Emperor of what happened here. A candid, truthful report. That's what you'll do, right? Because your reputation is also that you're as hard on yourself as you are on others. You won't try to minimize or conceal anything to make herself look better."

After a long pause, the Imperial officer nodded. "Why you think that will help you, I don't know. But I will tell the Emperor everything that I can. Where is Colonel Dar'n? Where is the commander of this town?"

Jules outwardly stayed relaxed, but she took a moment to steady her voice before replying. "He's dead. He died fighting in defense of this town."

"How do I know that's true?"

"Because I told you that's what happened," Jules said, her voice growing cold.

If Kathrin noticed Jules' warning reaction, she gave no sign of it. "How does a town with a garrison of fifty legionaries fall to a band of pirates?"

"How does an Imperial sloop get captured by pirates?"

"You're lying!"

Jules shook her head. "You'll see soon enough. Your crew did fight, but they lost."

"Lies! What happened here? Did Dar'n surrender the town and the garrison?"

Jules came up out of her chair in a swift movement, reaching out and grabbing Captain Kathrin's throat. "Colonel Dar'n died defending this town," she said, each word coming out slowly and forcefully. "He refused to surrender. That's what you will tell the Emperor. It is truth. If I hear that you have reported something different, that you have dishonored the memory of Colonel Dar'n, you won't have to come looking for me for revenge. I'll find you. And you will beg for death a thousand times before I finally grant your plea. Do you understand me?"

Despite the pressure on her throat, Kathrin kept her eyes fixed defiantly on Jules. "I understand you," she said, her voice rendered even more raspy by Jules' grip on her throat. "I'll tell the Emperor exactly what happened. And his wrath will shake the world."

"Will it?" Jules said, seeing that her smile startled the Imperial officer. Letting go of Kathrin's throat and stepping back, she sat down again and tapped Lars' revolver with one finger. "Do you know what this is? Where it came from?"

"Everyone knows you have that. And that the Mechanics also want you dead now. It won't save you."

"Perhaps this one will, then," Jules said, bringing her own revolver out of its holster and holding it next to the other. "The Mechanics and I have… an understanding."

Even Captain Kathrin had trouble dealing with that revelation. After a long pause, she narrowed her eyes at Jules. "The Mechanics dare to attack the Empire?"

"The Mechanics believe the Empire should do as they direct," Jules replied. "The Great Guilds run this world, don't they?"

"Not forever," Kathrin said. "And I'm not speaking of that prophecy."

"You're thinking that the Emperor is powerful enough to challenge the Great Guilds?" Jules asked. "You've seen their ships, haven't you? All metal, moving so fast in any direction, those very big weapons on them. Have you seen them up close? Have you been inside one? I have. Your ship, my ship, any ship of the common people, wouldn't last more than a few breaths against a Mechanic ship. And their Guild, so I've heard, has four such ships."

Kathrin frowned as if seeking a forceful reply, but stayed silent.

"And," Jules said, "many weapons like this." She raised her own revolver slightly to emphasize her words. "I've heard them speak of even worse weapons, weapons that could destroy vast numbers in one blow. The Emperor is surely wise enough to know that war with the

Great Guilds would be a mistake. If any of his advisors are urging such action, they are not serving the best interests of the Empire."

"There are also the Mages," Kathrin said, eyeing Jules to watch her reaction.

"The Mages are no friend to anyone," Jules said. "They'll kill me if they can, to keep from having their Guild overthrown someday. How do you think they'll react if the Empire and the Mechanics Guild go to war? I'll tell you what I think. I think they'll let both sides bloody themselves and then move in to take complete control of everything. Also not a good thing for the Emperor and the Empire."

"What do you care about the welfare of the Empire, traitor?"

"I care about the people of the Empire," Jules said, sitting forward. "Not the princes and the officials, but the people."

Captain Kathrin's smile held more scorn than that of any society matron viewing a newly-rich rival. "A pirate? Do you consider yourself compassionate? How many people have you personally killed?"

"I don't keep count," Jules said. "I only kill if I have to, or if someone deserves it," she added with a meaningful look at the Imperial officer. "No one said the Mechanics were involved here. Did I say such a thing? No. But we have these weapons, and the means to shoot them. We may gain access to more of them. Those who make such weapons may decide to take other actions if they decide it's necessary. I couldn't say, of course. I only speak for myself. But the Emperor will want to know everything before he decides what to do, weighing the welfare of the Empire in the balance. Remember that this town is a secret project. Few knew it was here, few knew the Empire reached this far. And that means few will know of any defeat here. Perhaps the Emperor will prefer to keep things that way."

"You're hiding behind the Mechanics," Kathrin said, looking contemptuously at Jules. "Serving *them*. The girl whose line will supposedly free the world, but you sold yourself out faster than a cheap courtesan on Marandur's streets."

"I never sought the cheap pleasures of Marandur's streets," Jules said, stung despite her pretended indifference to the insult. "You seem to know a lot about them, though. Maybe you'll live to see them again, if the Emperor is more merciful than you are." Pointing east, Jules spoke again before the Imperial officer could reply. "You, your crew, and the captured legionaries will be taken back to the Empire and set ashore on an empty coast. Because I'm merciful."

"I demand to speak with Centurion Rasel," Captain Kathrin said.

Jules shook her head. "One, you aren't in any position to make demands, and two, Centurion Rasel who commanded the legionaries here is dead and won't be speaking with anyone. I regret to inform you that the centurion from your ship also died fighting. His actions should be remembered with honor."

"What of Lieutenant Martine?"

"Injured during the fight. If he recovers, you'll see him. He also refused to surrender."

Kathrin looked at Jules, then slowly shook her head. "How much blood do you have on your hands?"

Tired, stressed, and feeling the cold inside her, Jules drew her dagger. Standing up, she rested the point of the dagger just beneath Captain Kathrin's chin, pressing just enough to sting. "There'll probably be a lot more blood before all is done," she said. "I didn't ask for this, but I'm going to see it through. And anyone who fights me will pay a price. If you don't want your blood on my blade, you'll steer clear of me from now on."

The Imperial captain didn't answer, her eyes still bearing their promise of vengeance someday.

Sheathing her dagger and picking up Lars's revolver, Jules went outside. "Back on duty," she called to the guards, hooking a thumb toward the inside.

Walking away from the building, she waited until Lars, Erin, and Hachi joined her at a safe distance. "Well?" Jules said, once she knew Captain Kathrin could no longer hear them.

Erin shrugged. "It was as you said. You took it all on yourself."

Lars, accepting his revolver back from Jules, said nothing.

Captain Hachi looked up at the sky. "I've decided that I won't be fighting you, Captain Jules. I value my existence in this world too highly."

Haunted by the memory of Dar'n's body still in the building, Jules spotted Marta walking past and called to her.

"Yes, Captain?" Marta asked.

"I need a favor," Jules said. "I know you help Keli lay out bodies when someone dies. Upstairs in that building is the body of Colonel Dar'n, the Imperial commander of this town. Could you lay it out properly for burial?"

"All formal and everything, in uniform, Captain?" Marta said.

"Yes. He... deserves that."

"Consider it done, Captain. I'll get some others to help and see it through."

As Marta went in search of help, Jules noticed the other captains watching her.

"Did you know this Dar'n?" Erin asked.

"That's none of your business," Jules said, not wanting to discuss the matter with anyone.

"If you say so, but I've another question." Erin raised one hand and touched Jules lightly on the chest. "Is it lonely in there where you keep everything locked down tight?"

"Knock it off," Jules said. "None of you have to live my life."

She walked away, knowing what Ian would think when he heard what had happened here, visions of the ugly, one-sided fight against the unarmed Imperial crew filling her memory. The sun overhead beamed down on the town, but Jules didn't feel any warmth from it.

CHAPTER TEN

T

he former Imperial town, now independent—though few people other than Jules understood even a little what that meant—had been built alongside a mighty river flowing down from the north. As Shin had noted last night, not far outside the town a rocky hill patched with dirt and brush rose steeply, like a tower of stone more than ten lances high. On top of the natural landmark was a flat area on which Imperial workers had already begun a watch tower to crown the hill. By the standards of the mountains of the Northern Ramparts, the mount was minuscule, but out here surrounded by otherwise nearly flat land along both sides of the river, it dominated the landscape.

Jules, restless, wanting to be alone and wondering when the *Sun Queen* would return, decided to climb up for the view. A rough path had already been worn to the top, making the journey a tiring but not too difficult climb. Remembering the refugees she'd rescued from Sandurin fleeing west through a pass in the Northern Ramparts near Kelsi, she couldn't help wondering if the settlement they'd founded had been set up somewhere to the north on the banks of this same river.

But as she pulled herself onto the top of the natural spire, she bit back disappointment at seeing someone else already seated on a convenient stone.

Captain Hachi, who'd been gazing to the east, nodded in wordless greeting.

Feeling awkward, Jules gestured in the same direction. "Thinking of home?"

Hachi shrugged. "Home can mean many things."

"What's it mean to you?" Jules asked, walking to the north side of the hilltop and looking in that direction.

He took so long to answer that she looked back at him. Hachi wore a thoughtful expression as he considered the question.

"Somewhere you belong," he finally said. "And feel safe." Hachi turned his head to look down at the settlement. "I've been thinking that this place might be a good home for the *Star Seeker*."

"I think it could use someone like you," she said.

"Was that a compliment?" Hachi asked, as if dubious it could really be such a thing.

"Yes," Jules said. "And this town would certainly be a safer home port than places closer to the Empire. Safer for you and your crew, anyway."

"But not safe for you."

"Mages tend to show up if I stay anywhere for any length of time. As well as Imperials eager to win favor with their Emperor by bringing me back in chains to warm his bed."

"I admit I've never had to face either problem myself." Hachi tilted his head slightly as he studied her. "Where do you belong, Captain Jules?"

"If you're asking where I feel safe," Jules said, "that'd be aboard the *Sun Queen*."

"At sea." Hachi nodded slowly. "That's your empire."

"That's a strange way to say it." Feeling uncomfortable to be asked about her feelings, Jules nodded to the east. "Where was your home before?"

"Centin." Hachi smiled in a thin, humorless manner. "Where I worked as one of the Emperor's many hands and eyes and ears."

"A pretty high-ranking hand, judging from that suit of yours," Jules said.

"That's true. I was expected to continue seeking promotion, but even if I never got another I was set for life. If I played the game right."

"Why did you come out here? Did you make a mistake?" Jules asked.

"No." Hachi grimaced. "I stopped caring. The game gets more and more complicated the higher you rise in the Imperial bureaucracy. Did you know that? But the stakes, how much the results matter, keep getting smaller. I saw men and women whose talents and intelligence couldn't be denied, whose responsibilities were vast, and they were bending their efforts to complex plots aimed at getting an office with a better view of a garden, or obtaining funds to add a new bath fixture that their rivals would envy."

Jules frowned at him. "How does important stuff get done?"

"By people who aren't playing the game, who aren't concerned with the trappings of high office, who just do their job." Hachi shrugged again. "And no one knows their names, and the rewards go to those who spend their efforts playing games. I decided I didn't like either choice."

"Why not?"

"I wanted to do things that mattered, and I wanted people to notice." Hachi's smile turned rueful. "I'm not very virtuous. I just wanted something better for me."

"At least you're honest," Jules said, returning her gaze to the north.

"Am I? How do you know I'm telling you the truth?"

"Maybe I don't care whether or not you're telling the truth," she said. "It doesn't matter to me."

He laughed. "You're as hard as they say. What are you looking for?"

Jules pointed along the river. "I knew a group of people who went west through a pass in the Northern Ramparts. They'd been told of wide plains beyond. I'm wondering if this river comes from there, whether whatever town they've built is along its banks and if someday they'll come downriver and meet the people here."

"Were those the slaves you rescued from Sandurin?" Hachi asked.

"I helped get them out of Sandurin," Jules said.

"So that town that may be somewhere up this river owes itself to you, and so does this town. Didn't you say the Mechanics wanted to simply destroy it?"

"They did."

Hachi sighed. "You make new homes for others, but can never have a home for yourself."

"My home is the sea," Jules said.

"Then why are you looking inland?"

"Because I want to."

He didn't answer for a moment. "Part of me thinks you'd have been very good at the bureaucratic games," Hachi finally said. "But most of me thinks you'd have lost your temper and started killing people who were in your way."

"Only if they deserved it," Jules said. She turned to look south and felt a moment of happiness as she spotted masts. "That's probably the *Sun Queen*. I'll have to cut this conversation short."

"I have a feeling you were about done with it anyway," Hachi said as Jules started back down toward the town.

* * *

The *Sun Queen* had just enough room to tie up at the end of the pier. Jules went aboard, forcing a smile. If the crew who'd lured out the Imperial ship saw her mood, they might think she was unhappy with them. "You guys did a perfect job. By the time that sloop came back we were ready for it."

"You captured it." Ang nodded his approval. "Was it hard?"

"Harder on the Imperials than on us." Seeing Keli, Jules called to him. "Keli, there's need of your skills ashore. The town healers and those from the other ships would be glad for you to join them."

"That much work, is it?" Keli made a face. "I'll get my bag and see what I can do to help."

Liv smiled at her. "So you did it. And lived to tell the tale."

"That's right," Jules said.

"What's the matter?"

"Nothing."

"Jules, or Captain Jules if I must, if there's anything—"

"There's nothing," Jules said. "I did what I had to do. That's all."

Liv eyed her, finally nodding in reluctant acceptance. "All right. Cori will be happy to know she's no longer a decoy. What's the name of this place, anyway?"

"The name?" Jules realized she and the others had simply been referring to it as *the town.* "I need to find out."

She found Lars and Erin talking near one of the buildings under construction. Some of the laborers brought along to build the town were at work on the outside. "There didn't seem to be any reason not to let them keep doing their jobs," Lars said. "I don't think most of them have figured out their bosses will be changing."

"Did any of those laborers mention the name of this town?"

"The name?" Erin yelled to the workers. "What's the name of the town?"

They paused in their labors, looking at each other. "It doesn't have a name," one of them finally said as the others nodded in agreement. "There was supposed to be a ceremony and the name given. I guess that would've happened when we got enough of the buildings done."

"You must call it something," Lars said.

"The Western Port," another of the workers said. "That's what everyone says."

"Western Port has the advantage of being a correct description." Lars grinned at Erin and Jules. "It's a port, and it's farther west than any place except maybe Altis."

"And it celebrates none of us," Erin said. "Putting one of our names on this place would be an insult on top of injury to the Empire."

"This isn't Julesport," Jules said.

"Julesport?"

"I'm going to found that city someday. But this isn't it."

"Oh, good," Erin said in the tone of someone humoring a friend. "Because calling this place by that name might provoke the Emperor into doing something a lot of people would end up regretting."

"I'm fine with Western Port," Jules said. "If the people who live here ever want to change it, they can do that."

As they spoke, Hachi walked up with a large metal ring holding several keys. "I located this in the commander's residence," he said. "Perhaps it's time we found out what's in that stronghouse."

"Hold on," Erin said. "You," she called to a passing laborer, "lend me that axe." Hefting the tool, she grinned at the other captains. "Just in case one of the locks is sticking."

The stronghouse they'd discovered was attached to the commander's residence, but mostly buried and accessible only via the residence basement through a heavy door reinforced with metal straps. The door and its lock had been impressive enough that they'd decided to wait until they found the key rather than try to force it.

Picking up and lighting two lanterns in the residence, Jules, Erin, Lars, and Hachi went down to the basement where the door was set into one wall. Hachi examined the keys, finally selecting the largest and putting it in the lock.

The key didn't turn when he first tried it, but Hachi bent to apply more force and it slowly rotated until a loud click sounded from the lock. Lars helped him push open the door, revealing a room large enough to hold all of them, the walls made up of heavy timbers. Two shelves ran across the back, the lower one holding a single moderately-sized money chest. One the floor another, larger chest rested.

"Let's start small," Hachi suggested, applying different keys to the lock on the lesser chest until he found the right one. As he opened it, Erin raised a lantern to illuminate the contents.

"Not bad!" Lars cried. "That's a good amount of silver, and some gold eagles as well."

"Not bad," Erin agreed. "Let's see what's in the big one."

But none of the keys Hachi tried fit that chest.

"Could the right key still be hidden?" Jules asked him.

Hachi shook his head, frowning down at the larger chest. "I checked everywhere I could get to. I found these keys in a hidden compartment. If there's another compartment, we might have to tear the building down to find it."

"There's an easier way," Erin said. She put down the lantern she'd been holding and gripped the axe with both hands. "Stand back or bear the consequences."

A half-dozen powerful blows of the axe produced splinters but little else. "That's a good chest," Hachi said.

"Let's take it in turns until we break it," Lars suggested.

Somewhere around the twentieth blow of the axe it bit through. Several more blows were required until the wood around the lock broke. Using the axe blade as a wedge and its handle as a lever, they pried the chest open, the lid finally popping up and slamming back.

Jules raised her lantern to see inside, her breath catching.

No one said anything for several moments until the silence was broken by a low whistle from Lars.

"That's nice, that is," Erin said.

Hachi bent down to reach into the piles of Imperial gold coins, the eagles stamped on them gleaming in the lantern light. "Yes. Very nice."

"Why would they have that much money here?" Lars wondered.

"Bribes?" Erin guessed. "Maybe they planned to pay off the Mechanics if they showed up?"

"That's possible," Hachi said, "but I don't think so." He pointed to the smaller chest. "That's probably the money sent with the commander. The smaller coins, and the fact that Colonel Dar'n had a key to it, means it was probably meant for pay for the legionaries and other expenses of the town. But this…" He smiled at the trove of gold coins. "No key. I think that's our answer."

"How?" Jules asked.

"Imperial princes, and high-level officials, have been known to acquire substantial wealth through means contrary to the laws of the Empire," Hachi said. "I wouldn't know anything about that, of course."

"Of course," Erin said.

"But that creates a problem if the Emperor decides someone is stealing from *him* and starts looking for the loot. The best way for the prince or official to protect themselves at that point is to hide their ill-gotten gains."

Lars nodded. "Like in a town that most people in the Empire don't even know exists."

"Yes." Hachi let some of the gold trickle through his fingers, the coins making tiny sweet chiming sounds as they fell back into the chest. "Order an upstanding officer like the late colonel to take this chest along, say it's all authorized and proper, and plan to collect it back when the investigators have moved on."

Jules looked at the coins, realizing she'd been worried that Ian's father had been part of something illegal. "You don't think Colonel Dar'n knew what was in the chest or where it came from?"

Hachi shook his head. "No. Keeping him ignorant of the contents would allow the colonel to deny with all sincerity that he knew anything and prevent him from potentially passing information to other hands of the Emperor." He looked at Jules. "Unless you think he was the sort to be bribed."

"No," Jules said, relieved by Hachi's explanation. "I think you're right."

Erin leaned closer to look at the coins shining in the light of the lanterns. "Splitting that four ways will make a mighty sum for each of our ships."

"What about splitting it five ways?" Jules asked.

"Five ways?" Erin eyed her, suspicious. "Did you promise something to another without telling the rest of us?"

"No." Jules pointed upwards. "I'm thinking of the town. If they have this in their treasury, they'll be able to buy the goods and materials they need to expand, and that'll bring merchants here."

Lars frowned unhappily. "It's not like the town played any role in defeating the legionaries."

"Shouldn't the pay go to those who earned it?" Erin added.

But Hachi gave Jules an approving look. "I agree with Captain Jules.

A fifth share of this money would be a big investment in this town, an investment that could pay substantial reward to us in the future."

"It could pay us substantial reward *now*," Lars said.

"It will," Hachi said. "We need to count this, but a fifth share for each of our ships is going to be impressive. We could take it all, but then we'd be like a farmer selling not just his crop but all of his seed for next year. He'd gain a bigger reward today, but tomorrow he'd have nothing."

Silence fell again as Erin and Lars thought.

"They'd owe us," Erin finally said. "I want them to know that. I want preferential treatment here from this point forward."

"That's fair," Hachi said.

"I agree," Jules said.

"And that also means," Erin said, "that we need someone in charge here when we leave that we can trust with this. Someone who won't take it and head back to the Empire to have themselves the party of a lifetime."

"That'd be some party," Jules said. "But you're right about that."

"If the rest of you agree," Lars said, frowning again, "I can't justify holding out. But my agreement for a five-way split is only if we find someone to take over here that all four of us think can be trusted."

That was a high hurdle to cross, Jules thought, but she couldn't argue with the reasoning behind it. "All right. We need to move ahead with getting this town organized for after we leave, anyway."

* * *

That afternoon, a meeting was called in the square near the former home of Colonel Dar'n. Imperial citizens and officials were in one group, the laborers who were indentured servants in another. Sailors from the four pirate ships were gathered on the outside of the square to both listen in and keep an eye on the citizens and laborers.

Hachi had been chosen to present the radical new ideas to everyone, since he was most accustomed to thinking in political terms.

"Anyone who wishes to return to the Empire will be taken there and put ashore on the coast. But anyone who wants to be free can stay. You have a choice. To remain servants of the Emperor, or become men and women who decide your own destinies. From this day onward, Western Port will be a free town. And all who stay here will be free," he added, looking at the indentured laborers.

The laborers stared back at him, some gap-mouthed with surprise or disbelief.

"You are speaking nonsense," the surviving senior Imperial official cried. "There are no towns that do not answer to the Emperor's command!"

"What of Altis?" Hachi asked. He let the resulting silence last for a few moments before continuing. "Yes. A free city has been in existence for as long as the Empire. You've been taught not to think of it. But it exists. If Altis can rule itself, why can't this town? Why can't you have a voice in the decisions made by your leaders?"

Jules watched, unhappy and uneasy as the Imperial citizens and even a few of the laborers reacted with confusion and reluctance to the choices they were being given.

"You have to remember," Hachi told her once the meeting was over and everyone had been given time to make up their minds, "that those sent here would have been carefully chosen. The Empire ruled out those with minds of their own, or laborers who might be natural leaders and foster revolt or escape. We have a singularly placid herd of people here. That so many have reacted positively is surprising."

"So many of the indentured laborers, you mean," Jules said. "Do you think any of the citizens will stay?"

"I think," Hachi said, "that even those citizens inclined to stay were smart enough not to make their choice known in public, where loyal servants of the Empire could make note of it. Give them a few days, and let them make their choices in private, and even some of our legionary prisoners might decide to stay and start new lives."

"How would we protect their families back in the Empire from retaliation?" Erin asked.

"We can provide them cover for their decisions. Perhaps those who return can be told those who remained died while attempting escape. Or we can announce anyone remaining has been enslaved to serve the awful pirates."

"I didn't see any good candidates to lead this town stepping forward," Lars said. "None I'd entrust with gold."

"I didn't either," Hachi said. "But we have a few days to see if any of the citizens prove capable of that and willing to take the role. Captain Jules and I will keep working toward that end."

Jules shrugged. "Hopefully. There are times when the immense nature of my dreams collides with the overwhelming force of how things are. I need to get used to that."

* * *

Night had fallen. Jules, restless, had checked on the prisoners and their guards before heading back toward the pier.

A burst of sound from inside a partially-finished building caught her attention.

Jules pushed open the door to find about a dozen pirates sprawled about. The smell of wine filled the air, and several empty bottles lay on their sides. A wooden case holding more unopened bottles sat in the center of the room, a candle burning next to it. With only that light to illuminate the room she couldn't make out faces well, but thought she recognized all of the pirates as being off the *Storm Runner* and the *Storm Queen.*

And they were all clearly drunk.

Silence had fallen when Jules entered, but the partiers quickly recovered from their surprise.

One of the pirates hoisted a bottle. "Have a drink!"

Jules shook her head. "That case of wine is loot. It hasn't been shared out among the ships and their crews. You're stealing from your shipmates."

"Those are hard words," a male pirate said, his voice slightly slurred from drinking. "We're only taking our share early, that's all."

"Lay off the drinking and get back to your ships," Jules said.

"You ain't our captain," a woman said, grinning. "We don't have to take orders from you."

"Then I'll tell your captains what you're up to and they can deal with you," Jules said, beginning to turn back to the door.

"Blazes, you're stuck up!" another drunk called. "You need a man, you do!" A chorus of loud laughter followed the statement.

Jules clenched her fist, her movement paused, but decided to let it pass rather than let things get worse. She took a step back toward the door.

"How about him?" a female pirate called, shoving at a tall pirate. "He's a looker! And not bad, if you know what I mean!"

"How would she know what you mean?" another yelled, setting off more laughter.

The male pirate wavered to his feet, grinning, partially blocking Jules' path to the door. "Yeah. How about it?"

"No," Jules said. "Get out of my way."

"She's shy!" a pirate at the back of the room called.

The pirate in front of her kept smiling, the wine on his breath easy to smell as he spoke again. "Come on! I can be gentle, I can! Unless you like it rough!"

Fighting her temper, Jules felt her face hardening into an expression that anyone not drunk would've been intimidated by. "I said no." She used one arm to push him partly aside and took a step past him toward the door.

"Stuck-up bitch!" the man cried.

She felt a large hand grab her backside.

Jules' eyes hazed red. When her vision cleared, she found herself facing the pirate again. Her dagger was in her hand, and the point of the dagger was in the man's chest perhaps a thumb's width. Had it gone in any deeper, the man's heart would've been pierced.

His eyes huge with shock, the pirate stumbled back, tripping over another pirate and falling, blood staining his shirt.

The room had once again fallen silent. "Get back to your ships,"

Jules said between her teeth, pointing her dagger toward the pirates. "NOW!"

They edged past her, eyes wide, momentarily intimidated.

Jules followed, her dagger still out, worried that some of the drunks would regain foolish courage and try to attack her in the street. But they were all headed for the waterfront, grumbling and complaining.

Going back inside, Jules hoisted the half-empty case of wine and hauled it to the commander's house, where a pirate was stationed to prevent looting. "All of these remaining bottles had better still be full in the morning," Jules warned him.

Tired and angry, she went back to the *Sun Queen*.

* * *

"Captain Jules? Captain Erin is here to see you."

"Send her in."

Erin came into Jules' cabin, her expression somber.

"It's pretty late for a social call," Jules said.

"You know why I'm here," Erin said.

"Because some drunks from your ship complained that I was mean to them?"

"Not just that."

"Have a seat," Jules said, waiting until Erin sat. "What is it, then?"

"One of my crew was injured, he says by your knife. The others back him up."

"And you're here to render judgment on me?" Jules asked.

"No," Erin said, her words short. "I came to hear your side of things before making any decisions. Did you cut that man?"

"Yes."

"Was there a reason, besides him not following orders from you?"

Jules didn't answer for a moment, resisting the urge to refuse to defend her actions since they didn't need any defense. "There was reason."

Erin rubbed her eyes as if weary. "Will you share it with me?"

"The man propositioned me. I told him no. Twice. Then he assaulted me."

Her hand came down and Erin glared at Jules. "You told him no two times and still he laid hands on you?"

"That's right."

"That was not told me. But I don't doubt your word, even if I'd be wary of the claims of drunken sailors anyway. You had every right to cut the man." Erin paused to study Jules. "Why didn't you kill him? That's your reputation."

"I honestly don't know," Jules said. "Something stayed my hand."

"Well, I'm glad you didn't. It could've made for bad blood between our ships."

"There's been enough blood spilled in this town."

Erin nodded. "Aye." She stood up. "Captain Jules, I apologize on behalf of my ship for the insult and the attack rendered against you. The man responsible will have his punishment, and if he balks I'll put him off the ship."

"Thank you, Captain Erin." Jules waved inland. "I put what was left of the wine in the commander's house under guard. Those other drunks from your ship and the *Storm Queen* stole what they drank from their shipmates."

"I'll ensure my crew, and Captain Lars, know that as well." Erin nodded in farewell. "I'll see you tomorrow."

After Erin left, Jules still sat with a single lantern burning, gazing morosely out the cabin's stern windows.

Another knock on the door made Jules flinch. Angry, she spoke sharply. "What? Who's there?"

"Shin, Captain Jules. May I speak with you?"

Gritting her teeth in upset at having talked to Shin like that, Jules schooled her voice to be nicer. "Of course you can. Come in. Please."

She stood up as Shin entered. He looked tired from his day's work, but Jules thought she saw something else, some other problem, riding beneath the outer weariness. "Please sit down."

"Thank you." Shin sat, facing her, waiting while Jules also sat down.

"Is something wrong?" Jules asked, worried for him.

"It may be," Shin said. He looked at her with an intense gaze. "I heard there was some trouble ashore tonight."

"I handled it," Jules said.

"So we heard. From Captain Erin."

"I don't have to explain every detail of my life to everyone around me," Jules said, irritated again.

"You were an Imperial officer, Jules. You know an incident such as that should be reported."

"All right," Jules said, looking away. "I should have told Ang when I got back to the ship. It's not like I killed that sailor." She paused. "I almost did. I don't know why I didn't."

"That bothers you," Shin said. "That you don't know why you *didn't* kill him."

"Maybe. I'm under a lot of pressure."

He nodded in understanding. "Your friends worry for you."

Jules had to fight down a surge of annoyance. "My friends should realize that their friends sometimes need to deal with things on their own."

"There is a darkness in you, Jules. It has grown even in the time I have been with you. Something hard and cold looks out from your eyes at times."

She was momentarily unable to answer, shocked by what he had said. When at last she found words, she shook her head at him. "There's probably no one else but you that I'd let say that to me."

"That is a problem," Shin said. "You do not want even those closest to you speaking their concerns for you."

"Shin, you're not just a brother because we were both raised in an Imperial orphanage. You're as much a brother to me as a man born of my mother would have been. But even you can push me too far."

He nodded again, but there was no sense of agreement in the gesture. Looking at the deck between them, he spoke in a lower voice. "Jules, there is something I must tell you. Something I have never spoken of to anyone else."

Her irritation vanished again, washed away by a wave of worry for her oldest friend. "What is it?" Jules said, surprised by the way he sounded and starting to dread what Shin might be preparing to say, though she had no idea what it might be.

"One of the things I remember most about the orphan home," Shin began, surprising her again by speaking of that, "was the dreams of you and many others. Do you remember those dreams?"

"I had a lot of dreams," Jules said. "None of them came true."

Shin looked up and frowned at her. "That is not true. You earned the right to become an Imperial officer. Didn't you tell me how much you dreamed of being able to prove that you were as good as anyone else, even though you had been raised in an orphanage and were looked down upon?"

"I'll concede that dream almost came true," Jules said.

"But there were other dreams. Do you remember? You'd imagine that your mother was still alive, and that one day she would miraculously show up at the orphanage to take you home and take care of you once more."

He paused, and Jules nodded, memories of old despair filling her. She rested one elbow on the table, her hand to her forehead. "Yes. How could I forget that? I cried myself to sleep more than once when I was a little girl because I'd convinced myself that would happen and it didn't. But I accepted the truth eventually. We all had to do that."

Shin stayed silent for a moment, then spoke in an even lower voice. "I was different. Your dream was my nightmare."

"Nightmare? I don't understand."

"I feared that my mother might someday come, that she wasn't dead, and that she might take me home."

Jules stared at him, questions tumbling through her brain. But all she could get out was one word. "Why?"

"Not all women succeed at the task of mothers," Shin said, his eyes still on the floor, his words coming out slowly in that very quiet voice. "I remember nothing of my father. He died when I was so young that there are no memories of him. Because of that, I also have no memories of what my mother was like when he was alive. She must have been different then, I think. But my father died serving in the legions. And my mother... in the time I knew her, something was broken inside. Something was wrong. My memories of her... are of pain and of fear."

Jules' breath caught. "Shin..."

"It is hard for you to understand, I am certain," he said. "She would be fine at some times, but other times would suddenly become angry over the smallest of things. Enraged and striking at us. I was so small, but I tried to protect myself and I tried to protect my sister."

"Sister?" Jules stared at him. "You have a blood sister?"

"I had a blood sister," Shin said, his voice growing so faint she could barely hear it. "A year younger than me. We were so small, but when the night was dark and quiet, and our mother asleep, we would plot in whispers of the day we would escape. We would go to school one day, perhaps, and never come home. We would walk in another direction, until we found a safe place."

"What happened?" Jules asked, her own voice faint, dreading to hear the answer.

Shin sighed. In anyone else, it would have sounded theatrical. But his sigh carried the weight of too much hidden pain to be anything but real. "I had begun my first year of schooling, relieved to be away from home for part of each day, but my sister, a year younger, would not start for another year. I went each day, fearing for my sister while I was gone. One day..." He paused once more, breathing deeply. "I came home from school and... the memories are vague. I have never been able to remember much of that day. There was blood. I think I ran to the house of one of our neighbors, screaming for help. Somehow I ended up there. They took me inside, and one went to get the Emperor's police. I sat in a corner of their home for a long time, listening to shouting outside."

Shin paused again. "The shouting stopped. It grew dark. Finally, two officers of the police came to me. A man and a woman. I do remember that the man wouldn't look at me, but the woman did, and she seemed very sad. She said they would take me to my new home, where I would live from then on. I asked about my sister. They… said nothing. I asked about my mother. They said my mother could no longer care for me. They took me to the orphanage, and there I remained. But ever after I worried that someday my mother would appear at the orphanage and tell me I must come with her. I didn't know for certain if she was dead, you see."

"Was she?" Jules whispered.

"Yes. Some time after I joined the legions, I went back, because I wanted to learn where my sister had been buried. The police report said only that there had been a fight and my mother had died as a result. She and my sister had both been burnt as the bodies of the poor often are, their ashes scattered in the Park of Memory."

Jules felt tears coming. "Why didn't you ever tell me?"

He shook his head as if its weight was hard to bear. "You could not have understood back then. You, and the others, could not have understood that your dreams of happiness were the same as my nightmare."

"Why are you telling me now?"

Shin raised his head to meet her eyes, his voice a little louder. "For two reasons. I know you carry a burden, but I don't think you realize the burdens that others carry as well. Burdens inside them that no one else may know of, that they alone must carry, even though no one else can see them."

"It's not the same," Jules said, then instantly regretted her words. "I'm sorry. I have no right to say that. I have no idea how I would have… I'm sorry. Are you telling me I should stop feeling like the burden is crushing me?"

"No," Shin said. "Only you can feel that weight. But others can help you bear it, if you let them."

"That's easier said than done." Jules wiped at her face angrily. "This doesn't make sense. You were a brother to every orphan who needed help or protection. You protected me. You've always been kind and strong. You've never shown your past in your actions."

"I have shown my past," Shin said. "Just not in the way that people expect. I made a choice, Jules, and that is the second reason I told you of my past. I had suffered. I had failed to protect my sister. I had seen what could happen to those who could not protect themselves, and I had felt what it was like when others lost control of themselves. I made a vow to myself, those first nights in the orphanage. I would not stand by and let others suffer. I would do what I could to help others who needed help. I would not hurt without cause, no matter how angry I became."

"Why are you telling me this now?"

"Because of what I said earlier. I, and your other friends, have seen a deeper darkness growing inside you, my sister. There has always been a hard center to you, a place inside where you would never yield, no matter what happened. That hard center has served you well. But you've grown even harder inside, as if you seek to seal off your heart and show only anger to the world."

Her emotions torn because of Shin's revelations, Jules waved an irate hand in dismissal of his words. "I have every right to be harder inside."

"The choice is yours," Shin said. "But it is a choice. This is also why I told you my secret. No one can control what the world does to us. No one can prevent pain and suffering and injustice. What we can control is who we choose to be in the face of such things. I choose to be, I have tried to remain, the man you call brother."

Jules squeezed her eyes shut, a storm raging inside her. "And you don't like the choices I've made?"

"Your choices are yours to make. I cannot make you change them. I only wished to tell you my concern."

"Why?" Jules demanded, rubbing her eyes. "Why come in here and dump this on me?"

"Because I am still your brother of the heart, and I still want to protect you. My shield and my sword cannot defend you against the darkness. That is why I told you of my past."

"You never told anyone else?"

"No. It was too hard."

"But you told me." She covered her face with both hands, trying to regain her emotional balance. "Blazes, Shin. I never realized you'd been carrying that around inside you all this time."

"Yes." He sighed again. "It is strange. There is another reason I haven't told anyone before this. I don't want people to think ill of my mother."

"What? But she—"

"She was broken." Shin looked earnestly at Jules. "I cannot believe if she had been whole that she would have done such things. She was hurt. I cannot forget the ill she did, but I do not want others to hate her. I do not want to hate her, even though it is very hard. My sister... I failed her. I do not want to fail you."

"Shin..." Jules got up, going to the stern windows to stare out into the darkness. Without really willing it, she turned her head to look at the drawing that was her sole memento of Mak, remembering how he'd felt about the wife and daughter he'd lost, and how he kept that from showing except on rare occasions. "There's so much I have to do. I don't know how to do it. It seems impossible, an endless road to endless failure. I don't know why I'm not already dead several times over. Maybe tomorrow the Mages will finally finish me, or the Emperor's agents will get me, or the Mechanics will once again decide I'm too much trouble. And..."

He waited, saying nothing.

"I have to do it alone. I've never been the easiest person to know," Jules said. "I'm not exactly a romantic dream. But before, I could imagine finding someone. A partner in life. Having a family. Now... I could've killed that man tonight. Not for the insult. For laughing at me because I can't look at any man without thinking of that prophecy."

Shin spoke in the same quiet voice. "You are not alone. You have friends. You have allies. They did not have to help you. They want to. You made that happen."

"Sure. I'm so warm and fuzzy. Everybody wants to cuddle with me." Jules turned to look at him again. "Yes, I feel the dark inside me. I guess I've been scared of that, too. Where do I find the light, Shin? How did you do it?"

"I found that when I reached out to others, they brought light with them. Do you remember the times we would laugh? You would make a very silly joke, and we would laugh, and I would feel stronger and happier. If you seal yourself inside, the darkness grows. If you open yourself to others, the light can come in."

"The darkness is very strong, Shin."

"I know. Sometimes others are not enough. In such times, I am told, healers can help."

"I need to be able to stand on my own," Jules said.

"That doesn't mean you *always* have to stand alone," Shin said. "And when you succeed, you should try to feel that success. You have always looked for what you didn't do well so you could beat that challenge. That's given you strength. But you need to let yourself be happy with what you did do."

"Maybe." Jules went back to the chair facing Shin and sat down. "Thank you. I will take your words to heart."

He smiled. "I can ask for nothing more."

A sudden thought came to her. Startled, she weighed it, not happy with the idea. But... "Shin, one of the things I'm worried about is the future of Western Port. They don't have any leaders except for the Imperials we're sending home. I can't stay, because my presence would be such a danger to the town. But they need someone who can give them confidence and leadership. Someone who won't demand absolute power, but will help them rule this town the way pirate ships are governed. By voting."

"It is difficult to find such a leader," Shin said.

"I think I have found one," Jules said, looking at him. "The problem is, I don't want to ask him to leave my ship. I'm happy to have him around. But I think the people here, this town, need someone like him."

Shin gazed at her in surprise. "Me? Jules, I have only been a simple legionary."

"I've been watching you, especially since we took this town. You jumped in and got things done before I even thought of some of them. Why weren't you a centurion?"

He shook his head. "As a centurion I would've been responsible for enforcing Imperial discipline."

"And you didn't want that. I don't want Imperial discipline here, either," Jules said. "But we still need rules and laws. As was emphasized to me in person tonight."

"You want me to leave the ship and undertake this task?" Shin asked.

"No! I don't want you to." Jules smiled at him. "I've really liked having you around. But… I need someone to do this. Someone the other captains would also trust. And I think you could that be person." Should she mention the fifth share of the gold that could make Shin's job much easier? No. Not yet. She didn't think Shin could be swayed by greed, but it might sound too much like an offered bribe.

Shin sat quiet for a while, clearly thinking. Finally, he made an uncertain gesture with one hand. "I must consider this for a while. That is all right?"

"Of course it is," Jules said.

He nodded again. "I must also speak with Marta."

"Marta? Why?" She read the answer on his face before he could speak. "Really? You're that serious about her?"

"We have enjoyed each other's company," Shin said.

"Shin, as your sister, I think you should know that Marta is one of those women who got her heart burned badly when she was young, and has kept it locked tight ever since. I don't doubt that you're enjoying your time with her, but—"

"I know of Marta's past," Shin said. "And I was a legionary for some time. I know all about those who seek to exploit men for their own amusement or profit. I do not think Marta is such a woman."

"That's your call to make," Jules said, resolving to have her own private talk with Marta. "And if you decide to stay here for a while, and Marta wants to stay with you, I won't try to hold her to the ship."

"For a while?" Shin looked startled. "So you do not want me to stay the leader here for a long time?"

"No! Just long enough for them to get their legs under them. They lack other leaders now, but there'll be more men and women coming here. People who can take on such responsibilities. And Captain Hachi says he plans to make this his ship's homeport. He knows all about administrative things, so even though he won't be here all the time, he can help get that set up." Jules smiled at him. "And when you're comfortable that you've done what you should, I want you back with me."

* * *

Two days later, Captain Erin and the *Storm Runner* departed, carrying extra "passengers" in the form of Imperials who wanted to go home. "I'll drop them off north of Sandurin," she'd told Jules. "What with the time it'll take us to get there, and the time it'll take them to walk to the nearest town, it'll be a little while yet before the Emperor finds out what's happened here."

"Fair winds," Jules wished her.

"You, too. That Shin is a good choice to keep an eye on things here. It must've been hard to lose him, but no one else would've been accepted by Lars." Erin had eyed Jules before she left. "Your seas seem a bit calmer the last couple of days, if you don't mind my saying so."

"After listening to some good advice, I had to decide what course I'd steer," Jules told her.

"Good. I'll scour Marida's and Kelsi's for some sailors in search of berths and bring them back to help crew our new sloop gifted us by the Emperor. Make sure Hachi doesn't run off with it before then." Erin ran her eyes over the new ship. "I'm thinking of making that little beauty into a new *Storm Runner*, and turning my current ship into an honest trading vessel and occasional smuggler. A girl has to cover all the angles, doesn't she?"

"I'll keep an eye on Hachi to make sure he doesn't steal the sloop before you can. You keep an eye on that Imperial captain."

"Kathrin? Aye. She's a scary one. She'll stay in irons until we off-load her on the Imperial coast."

Hachi stood beside Jules on the pier as the masts of the *Storm Runner* slowly vanished to the east. "*Star Seeker* will leave tomorrow."

"You're not planning on taking that sloop with you, are you?"

He pretended to be affronted. "How could you ask such a thing?"

"I notice you're not saying no." Jules shook her head at him. "Whatever happens with that sloop has to be negotiated between you and Erin. Lars doesn't want it since he's already got one, and I can't spare the people to crew it."

"Oh, all right." Hachi glanced sidelong at her. "I spoke with Shin earlier. For what my opinion is worth, I think you've made a good choice in him. He has ability, and humility. That combination is too rarely found."

Jules nodded. "I've more commonly found people whose lack of ability is paired with lack of humility."

"That is often the case." Hachi frowned out to sea. "Is that a low-lying cloud?"

Jules looked, feeling tension rise inside. "Maybe. Or maybe it's one of the Mechanic ships."

It didn't take long for the answer to become obvious as the gray shape of a Mechanic ship rose over the horizon, the cloud issuing from its chimney growing in size as the ship drew closer. "We've got visitors!" Jules called. "Everyone get ready!"

CHAPTER ELEVEN

"I'll meet them," Jules told Hachi, Lars, and Shin. "Whatever their reason for coming, it must be about our seizing control of this town."

"If they're unhappy," Lars said, "you don't have to fall on your sword for us. We all participated in the decisions that brought us to this point, though maybe Mechanics won't understand that any more than Imperial citizens do."

"I've gained the impression that there's some kind of voting in their Guild," Jules said. "Though there also seems to be a rigid hierarchy of some kind. I'm not sure how it works."

"Another mysterious Mechanic device," Hachi said. He paused. "That was a joke."

The Mechanic ship approached steadily, far faster than a sailing ship could have tacked north with the winds as they were. It slowed as it neared the area where the wide river met the sea, approaching cautiously closer until a large metal anchor on its bow rattled down into the water with an impressive splash. The chain attached to the anchor paid out with a smoothness that impressed Jules.

After a while, perhaps to ensure the anchor was holding, the ship lowered a boat. Mechanics went down a ladder into the boat, but no oars came out. Instead, the boat began moving steadily toward the pier.

"What the blazes?" Lars wondered. "How are they moving that?"

"There isn't any smoke as there is from the ship," Hachi said. "One Mechanic in the back is steering. The others don't seem to be doing anything."

"I'll go to the top of the ladder to greet them," Jules said. "You guys wait here."

"Hold on," Lars said. "They'll want this." He held out the Mechanic revolver in its holster.

"Yeah, they probably will," Jules said. She stuffed both revolver and holster into the back of her pants inside her shirt. "But if they don't, there's no need to remind them of it. If they ask for it, I'll bring it out."

As the boat neared the pier, Jules could see turbulent water at its stern. Something down there was driving the boat, perhaps related to the oddly large, boxy seat occupied by the Mechanic at the tiller. He had some other device on a stand before him that had at least one lever on it.

Jules switched her attention to the Mechanics getting out of the boat. In the lead was a female Mechanic whose gaze searched her surroundings as she climbed the short ladder to the pier but ignored Jules and the other commons. Other Mechanics got out of the boat behind her, also climbing up to the pier. The woman who had gotten out first turned to speak with the others in a low voice, the resulting conversation seeming more like her giving orders than requesting information.

Jules waited, trying to keep her temper in check. This was, after all, how Mechanics usually treated common people.

The female Mechanic finally took notice of Jules, frowning in her direction and beckoning with one imperious hand gesture.

Taking long, slow breaths to maintain her composure, Jules walked up to her. Her unadorned black jacket, the same one every Mechanic wore, gave no hint of rank or seniority, but Jules thought she had begun to recognize certain behaviors. "Yes, Lady Senior Mechanic?"

The Mechanic began to speak, then paused to give Jules an appraising look. "Have we met?"

"No, Lady Senior Mechanic."

"How do you know I'm a Senior Mechanic?"

Jules wanted to say it was because she was acting like an even bigger jerk than other Mechanics, but remembering the consequences the last time she spoke her mind, instead gave a polite answer. "You have the air of greater authority, Lady Senior Mechanic."

"Unusually insightful," the Senior Mechanic replied, eyeing Jules the way someone would look at a horse that had suddenly spoken. She didn't bother with greetings, though. "Here are your orders. We're going to lay out a location for a future Guild Hall and the plaza around it. The location will be marked. Nothing is to be constructed in that area and nothing is to be built that will impair access to it. It doesn't matter how long it is before the Guild returns to build that hall. Is that clear?"

"Yes, Lady Senior Mechanic," Jules said.

"They're already building on the riverside," one of the other Mechanics complained.

"They need piers on the river," a third Mechanic said.

The female Mechanic ignored them, too, concentrating a glare on the newly-constructed wall that went around the town and was anchored at both ends on the river itself. "Are you planning any defenses in or on the river?"

"No, Lady Senior Mechanic," Jules said.

"Good. Make sure any future walls don't hinder access to our site, either," she told Jules. "Nothing is to be built upstream of the location we choose that would pollute the water. That includes any discharge of sewage or animal waste or industrial chemicals into the water, no matter how small. Is that clear?"

Jules hesitated. Simply saying yes was the safest course, but she had to know what she was agreeing to. "Indus-trial chem…?"

"Oh." The Senior Mechanic turned to her companions. "What do the commons call them?"

"Agents," another Mechanic said. "Tanning agents, smelting agents, dying agents. They just use that one word."

"Of course." She frowned at Jules. "No agents used in any produc-tion of anything. Hides, metal, clothing. Anything."

"Yes, Lady Senior Mechanic," Jules said, having difficulty hiding her resentment.

"Are there any other settlements upriver?"

Jules tried to sound like she was being as cooperative as possible. "We don't know, Lady Senior Mechanic. None that are close. There may be an earlier settlement much farther up the river, established last year by people who came overland through a pass in the Northern Ramparts."

The Mechanic sighed as if Jules had singled her out for aggravation. "Typical. Brad! Can we get a recon flight?"

"All three Guild Masters would have to agree," a male Mechanic responded. "There hasn't been an approved flight for decades. Reliability problems with aging equipment, and worries about the commons seeing."

The female Mechanic turned her annoyance back onto Jules. "I want an expedition up that river. All the way to its origin. Fully mapped, all human settlements identified."

Jules glanced quickly at the other Mechanics, who had the look of people who were used to casually being given difficult tasks and somehow trying to deal with them. Instead of trying to negotiate a compromise, Jules simply nodded. "Yes, Lady Senior Mechanic."

"Get to work," the female Senior Mechanic told her minions, turning away from Jules as if she no longer existed. "Somewhere up there," she said with a wave up the river. "I'll be on the ship."

The Mechanics all went back down the ladder into their boat. Jules saw the Mechanic in the stern move a lever on the stand before him, and the boat moved away from the pier, a slight humming noise barely apparent over the sound of the water and the wind.

Jules watched the boat drop off the Senior Mechanic at the ship, then proceed up the river, passing the anchored *Storm Queen* and the current boundaries of the town. Walking back to Hachi, Lars, and Shin, Jules shrugged. "I guess they're planning on setting up shop here someday."

Hachi nodded as if unsurprised. "Nothing else would so surely warn off the Emperor from trying to retake this town. Simply making clear their intentions will serve as a strong deterrent."

"Will we really send an expedition all the way up the river?" Shin asked.

"Someday." Jules smiled. "Remember, we're just commons. Stupid, inferior commons."

"You're an unusually insightful common," Hachi said.

"Yeah, you could see how impressed she was," Jules said in a dry voice. "We need to follow their demands when it comes to that area for their Hall. And we do want them here, as you said, to keep the Emperor from thinking he can move in again. But she neglected to say *when* we should send that expedition upriver. Which means there's no rush."

"It will take a long while to prepare properly," Shin agreed. "But what if she returns soon to demand our findings?"

"I don't think she will. You heard her. Giving orders and not worrying about how hard they are. People like that rarely remember to follow up, because they don't really care that much about the tasks they toss off for other people to do."

Hachi sighed. "Like Imperial princes. Do this, no matter how difficult, because it's my whim. And most likely he never cares once it's done."

"Someone should go up the river when it can be arranged," Lars said. "If that other settlement is there, we need to know, and they'd be happy to find out they have a connection to the sea and trade with other places."

"That's so," Hachi said.

"Here's your weapon back," Jules said to Lars, reaching back to pull the revolver and holster out from under her shirt.

"No," Lars said. "That will attract too much attention to me. Since we've done our work here, and I don't have Mages singling me out to kill, maybe I should let you keep it."

"It's incredibly valuable," Jules said.

"And incredibly high-visibility," Lars said. "Besides, when the

Mechanics do come looking for it, they'll come to the person they gave that weapon to. Which is you. Better for you if you have it to give to them."

"I guess you're right about that. You shot it three times? So it only has two cartridges left anyway." She looked down at the weapon, remembering something else. "Did you hear what she said about a flight? Can Mechanics fly? Do they have devices that can do that?"

"I've heard some stories," Lars said. "But old ones. No one believes them, and I've never heard of anyone seeing such a thing."

"Like the Mara the Undying stories," Shin suggested. "Something fantastic to entertain others."

"Mages can fly," Hachi said. "I saw one near Centin. I think it is something they recently learned to do, because no stories mention it."

"They can fly?" Jules asked, alarmed. "Mages can fly? How can they fly?"

"It was a giant bird. Huge. A Mage rode on its back. I saw it," Hachi added as he saw the skepticism on the faces of the others.

"Where could you hide a huge bird?" Lars said. "Wouldn't people have seen them before now?"

Jules wanted to dismiss the story for her own comfort, but shook her head. "How many people have seen dragons except when they attack? Somehow the Mages hide them. You saw the one that chased me. They can't keep something like that in their Guild Halls. If anyone saw a herd of those dragons strolling across the land they'd make note of it. But I've never heard of such a sighting."

"That's true," Lars said, looking worried. "And now giant birds. Do you think they'd be dangerous? I mean, aside from the Mage riding one?"

"A mouse thinks a hawk is dangerous," Hachi said. "Would we be mice to such birds? That's not a far-off comparison to the size of the Mage bird I saw."

"And that daughter of my line is supposed to beat people who can handle such creatures," Jules said. "I hope she's smarter than I am, because I don't have a clue how that would be done."

"Are Mages people?" Shin asked. "They often seem not human."

"Yes, they're people," Jules said. "Somehow they get turned into Mages. It seems to require a lot of punishment, but that's just a guess. And, speaking of Mages, if the Mechanics know we've captured this town, the Mages might soon be learning of it as well. The *Sun Queen* should probably sail soon."

"Can you wait until the day after tomorrow?" Shin said. "That will give us more time to ready the Imperial servants the *Sun Queen* will carry home."

"Maybe." Jules smiled at a sudden thought. "I want some of that last batch of prisoners to be put to work doing something that'll let them see the Mechanic ship anchored there. Then get them inside again before that ship leaves."

"So they'll report back that a Mechanic ship guards the town?" Shin smiled as well. "I will see to it."

The Mechanics took the rest of the day to select their site and survey it, putting in metal spikes to mark the boundaries. None of them bothered to talk with anyone in the town again before they returned to their ship. The anchor was lifted, the chain rising with a low rumbling roar, then the ship left the river and headed south.

Jules watched Captain Hachi and the *Star Seeker* depart the next day. Lars took out the *Storm Queen* soon afterwards.

It felt odd being the only ship in port, the local population having shrunk considerably with the departures of three of the ships and their crews, as well as the Imperial citizens and legionaries who'd chosen to return home. The town, which had seemed crowded at times, felt almost abandoned. But nearly every indentured laborer had leapt at the chance to be free, and knowing they'd now have a chance to own what they had been laboring on had been continuing to work on the town buildings or on the fields outside the town where crops would soon be planted. The former Imperial citizens and legionaries who'd cautiously let Shin know they wanted to stay had been publicly declared prisoners who'd remain at the town because of their skills. But when the last of those returning to the Empire had departed, the so-called prisoners would be as free to move about as any of the other inhabitants of the town.

"Are you going to be all right?" Jules asked Shin the next morning as the *Sun Queen* readied to leave.

"Yes," Shin said. "Captain Hachi helped me find some capable assistants. We will be fine. And relieved that the last prisoners we must watch are gone. Good luck on your trip east."

She didn't tell him that she'd decided not to take the *Sun Queen* east to drop the prisoners off on Imperial shores.

While the final preparations were underway, Jules went outside the town walls a little ways to a newly marked off plot of land where temporary stones indicated rows of graves. She stood looking for a while at the stones, thinking of those who had died defending the town, and the few pirates who'd died fighting them. Going to one fresh grave with a particularly large rock at its head, Jules saluted. "I'm sorry," she told the spirit of Colonel Dar'n. "We both did what we had to do. You won't have to worry about your son ever being interested in me again, if that's any comfort. I packed up your personal items, and will send them to Ian when I can. May your rest be long and filled with peace."

She walked back into the town, leaving the new graveyard behind her, wondering how many more graves might fill it in years to come.

Back aboard the *Sun Queen* as the lines were being taken in, Jules saw Marta pausing to wave at Shin on the pier. "I thought maybe you'd stay with him," Jules said.

"Maybe someday," Marta said. "It was too soon. He's a nice one, though."

"Don't hurt him."

"You warned me before and I took heed. If I go back to him and tell him it's to last, I'll mean it. But for now," Marta said, bending to grab another line, "my home is still here."

Once outside the harbor, Jules stood on the quarterdeck, breathing in the air of the open sea with relief. "Too long on land and I feel like I'm in a prison," she told Ang. "Take us east until the town is out of sight, then bear south for Altis."

"Altis?"

"Yes. After the *Storm Queen*, the *Storm Runner*, and the *Star Seeker* have all dropped off people on the coast, I have a feeling the Imperials are going to expect this ship to be next. They'll have a lot of warships laying for us along the coasts near Sandurin."

"That's likely right," Liv said, walking up to them. "But there may be an Imperial warship in the harbor at Altis as well."

"If so, we'll figure out a way around that," Jules said.

"And then?"

"On south and then west to Dor's." Jules looked up, seeing the shape of a bird flying past. Was it flying low, or was it high up and much larger than it should be? "The waters around here are likely to see a lot of unfriendly traffic soon if the Mages have figured out that I'm still alive."

"Those Mechanics should keep their mouths shut when others can hear," Liv grumbled.

"Those Mechanics probably told the Mages directly," Jules said. "I've done what they wanted at Western Port, and they want the Mages to keep their attention on me instead of causing problems for the Mechanics Guild."

"Never count on the gratitude of emperors or the Great Guilds," Ang said.

"I don't. I have friends that I count on."

Liv tilted her head slightly at Jules. "That's a new attitude."

"You got a problem with it?" Jules asked.

Liv stared at her, then laughed.

* * *

The *Sun Queen* reached Altis late in the evening, gliding into the impressive harbor ringed by hills. A few lanterns marked the town high above the harbor, as did the brighter, steadier lights that marked a Mechanics Guild Hall. Substantially more lanterns showed along the waterfront, where sailors would still be drowning their sorrows and doing things that would create new sorrows for them in the morning. "Beautiful harbor," Liv commented. "How come the town isn't bigger?"

"There's nothing inland but rocks," Ang said. "That's what I've heard."

"So why's the town here?"

"It's got a beautiful harbor."

"I'm more interested in why there's a full-size Mechanics Guild Hall up there," Jules said. "Why'd they build that here? But we're not going to get any answers to that. I don't see any Imperial warships tied up," she added, peering toward the waterfront. "Are there any at anchor?"

"No," Liv said. "Maybe you were right about the Empire gathering ships along the coast near Sandurin. They left Altis open because they don't expect us to show up here."

"Let's get close to the docks, put the boat in the water, and send our reluctant passengers ashore," Jules said.

There were only a couple of ships anchored in the harbor, one flying the flag of the Mechanics Guild. But it was a regular merchant ship, made of wood and propelled by sails, doubtless used to transport cargo for the Mechanics. Jules gazed at it, wondering what might be in whatever crates that ship held.

But no pirate was crazy enough to attack a ship flying the flag of the Mechanics Guild. No amount of treasure or strange Mechanic devices would be of use to the dead, which anyone who tried that surely would soon be.

The *Sun Queen* eased her way through the harbor until she was not far from the waterfront. The harbor waters were placid, so the *Queen* slacked her sails while the longboat was put in the water and those who wanted to return to the Empire were sent down into it.

"You promised to return us to the Empire's shores," one of the prisoners protested to Jules.

"That'd be hazardous to our health at the moment. You'll have no trouble finding a ship here to take you there," Jules said. "Don't you trust your Emperor to help you out?"

Jules and the others waited out the longboat's journey to the waterfront and back again, oars flashing as the *Sun Queen*'s sailors wasted no time. "Any problems?" Jules asked Gord, who'd been in charge of the boat, as the rest of the crew quickly hoisted it in.

"An officer on the pier wanted to know what we were doing and why we hadn't anchored. I told him we were on a special mission for the Emperor and got the longboat out of there while our former passengers were all yelling at him to arrest us."

"Let's go," Jules told Ang.

"To the sheets!" Ang yelled.

There was some sort of guard post under construction near the mouth of the harbor, but no one hailed them or pursued them as the *Sun Queen* cleared the harbor of Altis and swung south.

* * *

Ships heading toward Dor's settlement never aimed straight for it. Instead, they tried to reach the southern coast of the Sea of Bakre well east of the settlement before turning west. Sailors feared the idea of overshooting Dor's, ending up west of it, and blundering further west into the deadly waters that every chart and legend promised.

The morning that the *Sun Queen* reached the southern coast and turned west, Jules stood on the quarterdeck trying not to scowl at the sun, the lively waters of the sea, and the gray walls of the cliffs that lined the southern coast. Occasional cracks in the cliffs allowed small, rocky beaches to exist, but none big enough to hold more than a small group of people. The waves rolling in endless array produced sheets of spray as they battered at the unyielding rock, rainbows appearing and vanishing as the sun's rays met the mist formed from the spray.

"Anything wrong?" Liv asked as she came to stand by Jules.

Jules let the scowl finally show. "Rough night."

"I thought things were quiet. Gentle seas and fair winds."

"It was rough here," Jules said, using one finger to tap the side of her head. "I kept dreaming about Mak." She hesitated, reluctant to share, but thinking of Shin's advice she pushed the words out. "I was on deck, and the Mages were there, and I was trying to reach Mak in time to save him, but I never could. My arms and legs moved so slowly, and every time Mak died and I couldn't stop it."

"Blazes," Liv muttered. "That's hard. You know no one could've saved Mak."

"I know that here," Jules said, touching her head again. "Knowing it here," she touched her chest, "is another thing. I don't know why I kept having that nightmare, though. Do you think Mak is mad at me?"

"Mak? You think he'd send nightmares your way?" Liv shook her head. "That wasn't like him. You know that. It seems like that nightmare was about not doing something you needed to do. Is there something you feel guilty about? Something you should've done?"

"Yes," Jules said. She turned her head to look west. "Maybe it's time I did it."

Sailing west some distance off the coast, they spotted a few landmarks that told them the *Sun Queen* wasn't far from Dor's. Just after noon, the cliffs suddenly opened, a tremendous gap revealing a valley open to the sea and a river flowing through that valley to spill its fresh water into the Sea of Bakre.

A natural line of rocks extending into the sea formed a breakwater for the harbor, where another pier had been built since the *Queen's* last stop here. Jules saw a lot of new buildings inland as well, as the *Sun Queen* made her way to the pier and tied up.

Dor, a short, broad man with a ready smile, met Jules as she walked onto the pier. "Always a welcome visitor," he said. "I owe you for sending us that lumber."

"The *Prosper* delivered?" Jules said.

"It did! Captain Aravind kept singing your praises for directing him to a new market. He was headed back to the Sharr Isles to pick up more wood there for us."

Jules looked over the town as they walked toward it. "You've already used that lumber."

"Sure have." Dor pointed proudly at different buildings. "That one, and there. And some in that new pier you tied up to. What'd you bring?"

"Not much in the way of cargo," Jules said. "My crew has money to spend, though."

"Oh?" Dor gave her an appraising look. "Why sell your cargo in one place and spend the profits in another?"

"We picked up the money directly," Jules said, remembering the glee with which her crew had welcomed the sharing out of the loot from the gold chest. She glanced toward the north. "From the treasury of an Imperial town."

Dor stopped as if he'd suddenly run into an invisible wall. "You looted an Imperial town?" He sounded more worried than impressed. "The Empire won't stand for that."

"It was a special case," Jules said. "I'll explain it all." She looked about again. "Have any Mechanics paid you a visit?"

"Not directly," Dor said, eying her. "Every once in a while one of their metal ships will sail past and slow down to take a look at us, but they've yet to set foot here. Are you telling me the Mechanics had something to do with you pillaging an Imperial town?" He gave a meaningful glance at the Mechanic revolver at Jules' hip.

"Capturing an Imperial town," Jules said with a grin. "And, yes, the Mechanics had their reasons for supporting the deal."

"Is that why you came here?" Dor asked, still serious. "I started this town to offer a refuge for those seeking freedom and opportunity outside the Emperor's grasp. And everyone who comes here has to assist in building defenses, because everyone knows that someday the Emperor will try to add this place to his holdings. But I'd prefer not to provoke such an attack."

Jules made an apologetic and calming gesture. "It's all right. The Empire thinks I'm somewhere else. And you know I can't stay any-where for long, because the Mages would come for me long before the Emperor sent his minions."

"That's so," Dor agreed. "We had a couple of Mages wander about last month. They came on a ship, went through the town without showing any interest in anything, and then left in another ship. People were thinking they hadn't realized the ship they were on was coming here and left as soon as they could."

"That's possible," Jules said. "How long have they been gone?"

"Um... three weeks, going on four."

"Good. They probably weren't looking for me, then. I was sure you'd have warned me right off if there were Mages about."

They came to a place where a broad road, still mostly dirt, ran straight south alongside the river, up the valley until sight of it was lost in mist. A good ways up that valley a wall was being constructed across a narrower part of the valley from one side to the other. "You're not going to try to defend the town itself?" Jules asked him.

"We can't manage that," Dor said. "The wall would have to be a lot longer if it was closer to the harbor, and a lot taller. Even if we could get it done, there aren't enough people here yet to defend such a wall. If the Empire shows up, we'll retreat upriver and hold that position as long as we have to." He looked back toward the water. "Someday we'll build a wall right on the harbor. Someday when this is a city. Maybe more walls, too. I took a vow on my wife's grave that I'd never let the people here suffer under the bondage of the Empire." He gave her a glance. "I know I can't keep out the Great Guilds if they want to set up shop here, but someday that daughter of your line will take care of that part of things, eh?"

Jules, seeking to change the subject off of the prophecy, nodded to the south. "What's making that mist?"

"Oh, that?" Dor waved toward the south. "The river comes down a series of falls. Short ones, but we'll have to do a lot of work there if we're to make the river navigable down to the sea."

"How about beyond the falls? Do you know what's there?"

"We haven't been able to spend resources exploring, but beyond those falls the land looks to be fairly level, and it spreads out as far as can be seen," Dor told Jules. "They're rich lands. I can feel it. Someday we're going to follow that river to its source. People keep telling me the grassy field will give way to desert, and the river's source will be in some sort of rocky, inhospitable mountains. But they told me I'd never find any place along the south coast where I could build a city!"

Reaching one of the older buildings, meaning part of it had been thrown together a couple of years ago, Dor beckoned Jules inside. "Baba's Bar is one of the oldest businesses in town. I sense there's a lot you need to tell me, and Baba's has a private room at the back where we can talk."

The private room was just large enough to not feel cramped, dominated by a table in the center with chairs set around it. There were no windows, and the walls had a comforting feel of solidity to them. A lit lantern on a shelf provided more than enough light for the room. Baba herself brought in a bottle and glasses, shutting the door firmly behind her as she left as a sign that they wouldn't be disturbed.

"To old friends," Dor said, pouring wine into the two glasses, "and to those who we love who're no longer with us."

Jules nodded, picking up her glass to drink the toast.

"I'm sorry about Mak," Dor continued after drinking as well.

"Thanks," Jules said. "I'm sorry about your wife. What happened?"

"The usual. Death in childbirth." Dor sighed, looking down at his glass.

"That's what happened to my mother," Jules said.

"They say that the Mechanics never lose a mother that way. That they have devices that can save someone even in the most difficult of births."

"I've heard that," Jules said.

Dor leaned back, gazing toward the east-facing wall. "How could someone have such a thing and not share it with those in need? We'd pay. We'd gladly pay."

"There's a lot I don't understand about the Mechanics," Jules said. "But they don't really see our problems as their problems."

"That's nice for them," Dor said. "Now, what's this about you looting an Imperial town and living to tell of it?"

"There's a new town on the coast north of Altis," Jules told him.

"North of Altis?" Dor rubbed his chin, startled. "What's it like there? The maps show a waste."

"It's good land," Jules said. "The Northern Ramparts give way to plains that seem to run forever." She explained what had happened, at least those parts she wanted to tell, while Dor listened intently.

"Blazes," Dor said when Jules was done. "So the Mechanics wanted the Emperor to get a bloody nose, but didn't want to do the dirty work themselves."

"Pretty much," Jules agreed. "But now there's another free town, and room beyond it to expand."

"And you came from there. It'll be another trade route opening up, I think." Dor picked up the wine bottle and reached to refill Jules' mug. "To the future."

Jules nodded, though she barely sipped, her eyes on Dor. Even before the prophecy she'd learned to be wary of getting drunk around men who might be getting drunk themselves.

"Do you think she'll do it?" Dor asked after taking a drink.

"She?"

"That daughter of your line. Is it possible?"

Jules shrugged. "It must be possible someday. Right now I can't imagine how anyone could overthrow the Great Guilds. Mak thought it'd be sometime a long while from now, when the Great Guilds had gotten weaker and the free people had gotten a lot stronger. Like when this town of yours has become that city you talk of."

"I never thought of it that way." Dor's eyes went distant. "How... I'm sorry. I think of deciding on my wife, who was all I could've wanted. And then I think of being in your shoes instead, and trying to make such a choice of a partner knowing the consequences it would have for everyone's future."

"I really don't like talking about it," Jules said.

"And, uh," Dor continued, "any man who was interested in you would have to phrase his offer carefully, to make it clear he valued you and not the prophecy."

"If you're looking for a new wife to look after your daughters, I assure you that there are many, many better choices than me," Jules said.

"You have many fine qualities," Dor said.

Which she knew he meant sincerely, but she was still getting annoyed by his persistence. "Any man who is seen as being close to me would be marked for death by the Mages, and by the Emperor."

"That's so, but... I know I'm not the greatest prize, but if you ever—"

He stopped speaking as Jules brought out her dagger from under the table. Words hadn't discouraged Dor, so perhaps this would. Resting the tip on the surface of the wood, she pivoted the dagger as if admiring the play of lantern light on the blade. "What was that you were saying?"

"Um, ah... well... strangest thing," Dor said. "It went right out of my head. I have no idea what I was going to say next."

"Good." Jules looked up, meeting his eyes. "You're a decent man, Dor, and you're doing good work here. I'd hate to have to kill you."

Dor nodded, then unexpectedly grinned. "You know, Jules, it's probably not necessary to kill every man who expresses an interest in you."

"I haven't killed all of them, but if it comes to that I'll take the risk," Jules said. "Better safe than sorry."

He leaned forward, arms on the table, still smiling. "Your dating life must be a little bleak."

"It was never all that great," Jules said.

"And now every man in the world wants you."

"Every man in the world wants to get me with child," she said. "I doubt they're enthusiastic about me as a life partner."

Dor shrugged, leaning back again. "Being your partner would be an interesting life. Likely a short one as well."

"Like mine," Jules said, picking up her glass for another drink. "There isn't a man in the world I can trust to be interested in me rather than in the prophecy." But even as she said those words she knew they weren't true, that there had been one man who'd wanted her before the prophecy. How could he possibly want her now, though? Thoughts of Ian went straight to the memory of her dagger going into the chest of his father, darkening her mood.

"Not one?" Dor asked, unaware of her thoughts. "Jules, I've got two daughters. Their mother didn't survive the birth of the second, so I can only hope her spirit is in some place that brings joy. I've sometimes imagined her or my daughters facing your situation and… feeling grateful they didn't and they won't. No innuendo or double meaning intended here. Can I do *anything*?"

Jules offered him a small, wry smile. Without knowing it, he'd said the right thing. "You're a decent man, Dor," she said again. "Make this a strong city. One that can stand against anyone who attacks."

"I'm already preparing for the day the Empire tries to take it."

"I don't mean only the Empire. Someday… that daughter of my line might need a city like this."

He nodded to her, absolutely serious. "Done. For the sake of the city I hope to start here, for the sake of my descendents who the prophecy says will someday be free, and for the sake of a woman given a burden no one else has to carry." He raised his glass again in a toast.

Jules returned the toast, smiling wider. "Here's to Dor's Castle."

"Castle? Ha! I do like that name, though. It speaks of strength and resolve, a place that can stand off any enemy." Dor set down his glass. "Dor's Castle. Yeah. I'm going to start using that. Are you headed back east after this?"

"No," Jules said. "The east is still far too dangerous for me, I think."

"Back north then? To… uh… Western Port?"

"No."

"You said you're not staying here, and you can't sail south, Jules. There's a lot of land in the way." His eyes grew alarmed. "You don't mean to go farther west than here?"

"The idea had crossed my mind," she said.

"Jules…" Dor gestured outside. "My ship only ended up here because we were too far west to begin with and then got hit by a storm that drove us even farther. We were very low on water, so I took the risk of creeping along the shore looking for any inlet, and found this valley letting onto the sea. If we hadn't found it when we did, I doubt my crew would've gone much more west. They had no wish to die, and thirst can be survived better than jagged reefs and poisoned land beyond them."

"I promised Mak I'd see what was in the west," Jules said.

Dor shook his head. "The promise is all very well, and I'm sure you meant it, but there's not a sailor in the world who wants to risk those waters. Have you ever met anyone who sailed to the western edge of the Sea of Bakre?"

"No one's ever tried," Jules said.

"Or no one's ever come back from trying," Dor said. "Which do you think your crew believes? Mak was a fine man, the finest I ever met, but he knew his dream wasn't practical. That's why he never went west."

"I made a promise," Jules said.

Dor spread his hands in the old gesture of helplessness. "I can't talk you out of it, I see. But you'll have to talk your crew into it. And, since I'm an honest man, I hope you won't be able to. I'd hate to see you lost in those waters. A lot of people would."

Jules snorted. "You and they just want me to have a baby or two before I get myself killed."

"I'm not going near that subject again," Dor said. "Especially not while you still have that dagger out."

"Smart man. Don't tell anyone else about my plans, all right?"

He nodded, raising his glass in salute to her. "Done. It'll be easier for you to change your mind if no one else knows you wanted to do it."

"I won't change my mind."

CHAPTER TWELVE

The *Sun Queen* spent a week at Dor's. Even though the town lacked anything on the scale of the diversions a city like Land-fall or Sandurin offered to sailors eager to spend their earnings, it had its share of businesses and individuals willing to offer what those sailors wanted as long as those sailors had money. By the end of the week, the pirates of the *Sun Queen* were both considerably poorer and considerably happier than when they arrived, and a lot more gold eagles were circulating in the local economy.

But whereas bad times seem to last forever, good times always end well before anyone wants them to. On a bright morning with a fresh-ening wind and some high clouds that foretold possible rough weather coming in, the *Sun Queen* stood out of the harbor at Dor's, clearing the natural breakwater and heading north with just enough sail set to maintain steerageway.

When they were well clear of land, Jules called a meeting of the crew. She stood on the quarterdeck looking down onto the main deck and into the lowest spars, where the men and women had gathered. Ang and Liv also stood on the quarterdeck, and Kyle was on the helm, having little to do with the seas and the wind so accommodating this morning. Everyone looked reasonably content, except for those whose reddened eyes and pained reactions to noise and sunlight spoke to the price they were still paying for their celebrations the night before.

Jules looked them over, knowing that she'd have trouble convincing these sailors to do as she wished.

Wanting to start on a high note that emphasized how well things had gone recently, Jules called to them. "Did we all have a good time at Dor's?"

A roar of approval answered her question.

"And my last proposal, to capture that Imperial town to make it free, did that work to our profit?"

Another roar of approval. "We never earned so much at one haul before!" Gord called.

Jules smiled at them. "It was risky, but it paid off, didn't it? No one else had ever done such a thing, but we did it, didn't we?"

She paused again, waiting for applause that rose and slowly died down.

Hopefully they were ready for her next words. Over the last week she'd gone over them again and again, trying to imagine every question that might be raised, and finding an answer for each. Whether they'd accept her answers could only be learned by trying them.

"I'm hoping that you'll trust me again," Jules said. "I'm hoping that together we can once again do something no one else has done, and put our mark on history."

This time her words didn't bring applause, just curious, expectant looks.

Jules pointed west. "You all know that Mak wanted to see what lay there, beyond where others have gone. Yes, I know what the charts show. And you all know what the charts showed of the land west of the Northern Ramparts! Wastelands and treacherous waters! That's what the charts say! But you've been there, and you saw a good harbor and fair fields. You walked through the grass on what the charts say should be desert like that of the Bleak Coast.

"What if it's the same here in the south?"

She paused to judge their mood, seeing worry settling over her crew. "What if it is? Why not go and look? Find out for ourselves? Who knows what treasure might lie out there? Someone made those charts and someone put lies on them. We know that from what we've seen in the north.

"Would you like to be the first to set eyes on whatever might lie to the west? That's where I want to go. Will you go with me?"

Silence, then a low murmuring as sailors spoke with each other. Jules waited, trying to look calm and confident and unworried.

Old Kurt spoke up first, his voice carrying easily. "And if the charts are right about what lies to our west? What becomes of us?"

"If we encounter those reefs, if we see that wasteland," Jules said, "then we'll turn about. Why would I push forward if that happened?"

"Where's the profit in it?" Gord wanted to know.

Jules waved to the west. "If we find something new out there, what do you think that'll be worth? Another harbor like the one Dor is building in? Good waters? Whoever charts those things can sell that knowledge to those who need it. That's if we don't find things valuable in themselves. You've all heard of Carlos of Emdin! How he explored the flanks of the Southern Mountains, braving the wastes there, and found the crater of diamonds? Diamonds lying on the ground waiting to be picked up! Who's to say something like that isn't west of here?"

That gave them pause, a few smiling at the idea though most still looked more fearful than hopeful.

"I've looked at those charts," Kurt said. "They warn of reefs that can't be seen until you're in among them and have no room left to turn about. How do we deal with that?"

Jules shook her head. "Reefs that can't be seen until you're in among them? Do any of you know of such reefs anywhere? You've all done lookout duty. From up there," she pointed up to the tops of the masts, "you can see the color of the water change as it shallows, and you can see submerged rocks and the rough water over them. Isn't that so? If we keep a close watch, we'll spot any reefs before we get among them."

"What if the rocks are too deep to be seen?" Cori asked.

"If they're that deep," Gord said reluctantly, "we can't hit them. But what if the water isn't clear? What if it's muddied, hard to see through?"

"If we see water that's muddied or that turbulent," Jules said, "we'll know it's a sign of danger. Just as we would anywhere else! That's so, isn't it?"

More nods, even old Kurt agreeing with her words.

"We can't see well at night," Marta called. "How do we spot danger ahead at night? We should anchor when it starts to get dark, and only proceed in the morning when we can see well enough."

"I'll agree to that," Jules said.

"What if it's too deep to anchor?" another pirate called.

"We hold our position through the night, setting just enough sail to keep us from wandering," Jules replied.

"How long would we head west? How far?" Kyle called from the helm behind her.

Ang answered, also from behind her. "If the charts speak the truth, even with contrary winds we'd be in bad waters within a week."

"If we go two weeks without seeing anything," Liv said, "we'll know the charts are wrong in that much."

Jules turned enough to give them both a grateful glance, but in doing so saw the reluctance in Ang and Liv as well. They were backing her, but they weren't happy. Facing the rest of the crew again, Jules spread her arms. "You know me. You knew Mak, who also wanted to see what lay to the west. We're not going to go charging ahead blindly. We'll keep our eyes open and our knowledge of the sea at the ready. And we may find things that your grandchildren will be boasting of a hundred years from now."

A sailor named Imari, wearing a stubborn expression on her face, called out. "I'll say it since no one else will, and because you brought up grandchildren, Captain! Should you be running this risk? Given what has not yet transpired?"

A rumble of agreement followed Imari's question.

Jules, tamping down the anger the question brought, took time to form her words before replying. She'd have to play her strongest card. "I'm going to tell you what Mak told me. Mak said that the prophecy says nothing about what I'll do beyond someday having at least one child. But, he said if that child, if the line from me, is to overthrow the Great Guilds, then when that daughter comes she will need strength at her back. The Emperor or Empress of that time won't help free the world. That daughter's strength must come from the free people who stand with her. And where are those free people to come from? Some will come from Dor's, some from Western Port, but that won't be enough. We need to find new places where new cities can flourish, and free people can grow and rally to her someday when that daughter calls. This is part of that. Help me find the land we will need to become strong. Strong enough to someday free this world!"

She waited, breathing hard after the speech, hoping she'd convinced them.

"Let's go!" Kyle cried from the helm.

A chorus of shouts in agreement followed, though not from everyone.

"I call the vote," Ang shouted. "All in favor of Captain Jules's proposal raise a hand."

It was a majority, Jules saw. About two-thirds of the crew. Less than she'd hoped for. But enough.

* * *

And so the *Sun Queen* ventured west, into waters that (as far as anyone aboard knew) no one had ever before sailed.

That didn't make for a happy ship. Jules noticed the sailors who were not at work tended to congregate near the bow or the port side, watching anxiously for any sign of danger. She'd ordered extra lookouts posted, two on the foremast top and one on the mainmast top, but still the crew worried that they'd miss something.

Keli the healer came to stand by Jules as she stood on the quarterdeck, gazing south and west. The line of cliffs on the shore continued on, seemingly forever, with no signs of another break such as the one where Dor was building his town. To the west nothing could be seen but waves and a low bank of clouds.

"Why are they so worried?" Jules asked him. "They trust me, don't they?"

"Not as much as they trusted Mak, but well enough," Keli said. He leaned on the railing, gazing at the cliffs. "What they fear is what they don't know."

"Then the way to conquer that fear is to learn what we need to know," Jules said.

"That'd be logic, but you're dealing with people. And not just any people, but with sailors." Keli nodded his head toward the west. "Do you know what lies out there? The monsters and the dangers of our imaginations. That's what fills the west. And when it comes to monsters and other dangers, our imaginations can create far worse trolls or dragons than any Mages have ever had at their call."

"Are you afraid of going west?"

"Of course I am. I've seen how the sea can tear a ship apart with little warning, or none at all." Keli tapped the railing for emphasis. "We can't console ourselves with our knowledge and our experience, because our knowledge and our experience tell us the sea is full of danger, and unforgiving to those who don't pay her proper respect. You've got a good crew here, but it's because they're a good crew that they're unhappy with going west into waters that legend tells them are devourers of ships and sailors."

Jules ended up dropping anchor a bit before the sun reached the horizon because they reached a place well suited for it. The weighted line used to find the bottom beneath the ship showed enough depth of water to be comfortable, but shallow enough that the anchor cable wouldn't have to be paid out too far. The anchor quickly snagged on something and held well.

"There are probably a lot of rocks on the bottom here," Ang said, his expression unusually glum even for him. "Fallen from the cliffs."

"What's the problem, Ang?" Jules asked him. "We stopped while we could still see well. Isn't that what everyone wanted?"

"Yes," he said. "But, you see, that gives everyone more time to worry about what will happen tomorrow."

"There's no way to keep the crew happy, is there?" Jules said, exasperated.

"There is a way," Ang said. "Turn back east."

"The crew voted to go west," Jules said. "They approved doing this."

Instead of answering her, Ang looked to the west. "That bad weather we've been fearing is finally moving in. It should reach us tonight."

Jules spared an angry glance at the clouds before going to the rail and looking down at the water. "I'm sure you're all hoping it blows us east."

Ang didn't say anything.

She ate alone in her cabin, picking at the fish. Dor's might have lacked in some things, but they had a lot of fish. Jules was already tired of it.

About midnight Jules was awoken by the sound of rain pattering on the quarterdeck over her head. A few rumbles of thunder rolled through the sky, but the winds stayed moderate and the sea didn't get rougher. She finally fell asleep, exhausted.

When she blinked awake the next morning, it was still raining. Jules went on deck and found the crew was still below. From the look of the clouds it was well past dawn. She walked to the bow, where the anchor watch sat huddled against the rain. "Any problems?"

"No, Captain."

Jules squinted ahead through the rain. Visibility was reduced, but she could still see three or four hundred lances ahead.

Going below decks, she found the crew sitting about or lying in their hammocks. "Ang, Liv, let's get going."

Ang stood up, stooping in the limited headroom on the second deck. "How much sail, Cap'n?"

"We'll need to limit our speed because of the lower visibility. Get us going and we'll see if we need to add on."

"Aye, Cap'n."

The crew moved more slowly than normally, Jules fighting herself to keep from yelling at them. It bothered her that neither Ang nor Liv had roused the crew earlier. Had that ever happened before?

Some of the crew went up the masts. As furled sails dropped to fill with wind, other crew members pulled on the sheets to adjust the angle of the spars. Everyone else went to the windlass and began winding in the anchor, a slow and backbreaking job that couldn't be hastened.

Jules waited, thinking that the windlass was being turned slower than usual, but that might be just her mood.

The crew was dragging its feet, though.

What would Mak advise her to do? Get tough? No, this wasn't the time for that. Go among them, reassure them, let them know she wasn't being reckless and their fears were being listened to.

It proved hard, though. Jules felt as if she were trying to push a rope, the rain dampening spirits as well as the outside of the ship and her crew. As she made the rounds, trying to cheer everyone up, Jules noticed that the *Sun Queen* was barely making way toward the west. She went up onto the quarterdeck, finding Liv there, and Kurt at the helm. "Why don't we have more sail on?"

Liv looked up at the sails rather than over at Jules. "You said put on enough for the visibility."

"We can see a good four hundred lances, Liv. At this speed that's about how far we'll get over the entire day."

"I'm not sure how much else to put on," Liv said.

Jules, by what she considered a heroic effort, managed not to yell at her. "Set the topsail."

"Yes, Captain."

Lunch and dinner were sodden affairs as the rain continued, working its way into every crevice of the ship and every opening in clothing. It wasn't particularly cold or hot, nor particularly windy or rough, just an apparently unending drizzle that offered monotony and misery in equal measure.

The bottom seemed deep here, with the sounding line not finding the bottom anywhere they tried, so as the grayish light grew darker the sails were reduced to just enough to allow the *Sun Queen* to slowly head north.

They spent the rest of the night tacking first north and then south in equal measure, trying to hold their position until daylight. The crew had to be called up repeatedly to work the sails, which didn't help anyone's mood.

"It's still raining," Jules said as she went out on deck the next morning, as tired as everyone else from the labors of the night. "What do you say the visibility is?"

Ang stared off the bow, frowning. "Three hundred lances. Maybe less."

She thought it was farther than that, but didn't want to get into a battle of wills with the crew sinking deeper and deeper into gloom. "Let's see how it goes today. Ang, can I count on you?"

He gave her a surprised look, then nodded. "I will do my job as well as I can, Cap'n."

"Thank you."

In her cabin, Jules gazed morosely at the chart that claimed to show these waters. She'd called in Liv and Gord for their impressions. "The coast came out along our course yesterday, didn't it? Farther to the north."

"That's what I thought," Gord said.

"But first thing this morning we seemed to round a headland and angled back south a little," Jules continued.

Liv nodded, her eyes on the chart. "It's not a lot. The coast is still running mostly east/west as far as we can tell with the weather like this."

"That matches the chart, I guess." Jules tapped the coastline. "But this shows reefs along this coast. Have you seen any?"

"No," Gord said as if reluctant to admit to it.

"Have the lookouts report sighting reefs to the south?"

Liv hesitated, then shook her head. "No. Not that it means all that much with the rain and the clouds making it hard to see far."

"If the reefs were coming out as far as this chart shows," Jules said, "we should be seeing them."

"Unless they're fully submerged," Liv said in a low voice.

Jules closed her eyes for a moment, trying to imagine what else she could do. "We haven't seen any signs of danger ahead. Tell me truthfully, you two, why isn't that making anyone feel better?"

Gord made a face. "Captain, it's the weather. That's part of it. Like the sea herself doesn't want us going this way and is trying to discourage us."

"I realize I'm not nearly as experienced as you, Gord, but from what I've seen, when the sea wants to make a point she's neither subtle nor gentle."

"That's so as far as it goes," Liv said. "But the sea follows her own rules. Maybe she expects us to be smart enough not to keep going in the face of her hints."

"Thank you for your advice," Jules said, hearing the edge in her voice.

Going up on deck again, she unhappily gauged the speed of the ship, then once more ordered another sail set.

She went up to the bow, one foot on the bowsprit as she stared out into the rain. Nothing but water, as far as the eye could see, which today like yesterday wasn't nearly far enough.

As light began fading and her crew began searching about them with growing anxiety, Jules gave in to the unspoken demand and began trying to find a place to anchor. Fortunately this night the bottom was shallower, enough so that the ship could drop anchor and let the crew rest well. Or as well as they could with rain dripping down over everything.

They had sighted the occasional beach on shore, usually narrow but sometimes with a little rough terrain inland of it. That should have been cheering, to see some yielding of the southern cliffs, but each beach soon came to an end.

After eating a cold meal, Jules went forward again, as far west as she could on the ship. She found Marta there as well, eyeing the waters gloomily.

"The waters are getting choppy," Marta said.

Jules looked down, noticing the chop had increased a bit. "You're right."

"That can be a sign of shoals or reefs ahead," Marta added, emphasizing her words.

"We'll stay at anchor here until the light is good enough to continue on in the morning," Jules said. "We'll keep on nice and slow and careful," she added to reassure Marta.

"Captain..." Marta looked about as if trying to avoid looking directly at Jules. "Maybe we should turn back."

"We haven't run into anything yet," Jules said.

"Yeah, but..." Marta, frowning, headed below.

As Jules went to her cabin, she saw Keli out on deck as well, the healer looking south to where cliffs still faced the waters of the sea. "Everyone will get a decent night's sleep," she told Keli.

Keli twisted his mouth before replying. "That's not always a good thing."

"Why not?"

"Because men and women who're working constantly have little time or energy to think. Give them time to think, time to lie in their hammocks and get rested, and they have time to think of those monsters their imaginations tell them are just ahead in this muck."

"Keli, what else should I do?"

"You're pushing them west," Kelli said. "They're going to be more and more discontented with every lance west we go from here."

"You're telling me to turn around?" Jules asked. Herself tired and sick of the rain and sick of trying to raise the spirits of the crew, she felt the inner cold that wouldn't yield to anyone or anything. "When we haven't seen one danger?"

"Haven't *seen* is the word," Keli said.

"No! The crew voted to go west! We're going west!"

"You asked me for my advice," Keli said, his gaze on the water. "I gave it."

"Thanks," Jules said, walking to her cabin and barely stopping herself from slamming the door shut.

* * *

When Jules woke the next morning as the watch changed on the quarterdeck above her head, she noticed both that the rain had stopped and that the view out of her stern windows was of a whitish-gray mist. Uncertain whether to be relieved or upset at the change in weather, and worried by the silence that seemed to enshroud the ship even more closely than the fog, Jules went out on deck and barely avoided shouting an obscenity.

The *Sun Queen* was wreathed in fog so heavy that from the quarterdeck the view of the mainmast and anyone near it was partly obscured. The water in the fog condensed on anything it touched. The wood of the ship and the yardarms. The lines of rigging. The faces of the men and women gazing into the fog with what seemed even more worry than they'd shown the night before.

At least they were up on deck this morning, though their abnormal silence was unnerving. Jules kept her voice soft as she greeted those sailors nearest her, receiving only nods in response.

No one looked directly at her. No one was working. In the midst of the thick fog the world seemed to be suspended in a moment, like someone standing on a cliff almost ready to jump but still hesitating.

Disturbed by the fog and the behavior of the crew, Jules went up onto the quarterdeck, relieved to find Ang there. "How's it look?"

"You can see," he said, gesturing around. "We can't move in this."

"No, we can't," Jules said, walking toward the port side in a vain attempt to spot any sign of the land in that direction. "We'll have to wait until it lifts a little."

"Perhaps it won't lift until we head east."

She stopped, her last step coming down so heavily it seemed the thud carried like a shout through the fog. Biting her lip, Jules got a grip on her upset before turning to look at Ang. "Why would that make a difference?"

He shook his head at her. "Cap'n, I urge you to turn back."

"Why? Because of fog? Because it rained?"

"The signs are ominous. This voyage does not have the sea's approval."

"You want to give up?" Jules looked across the ship, raising her voice. "Who else wants to give up?"

No one answered.

Walking to the front of the quarterdeck, Jules called again. "You voted to go west with me! Who has changed their minds?"

Marta called back from near the mainmast. "Do you mean to go on?"

"Blazes, yes!"

A long pause followed, while Jules wondered what to say next.

The silence was broken as another voice called out from on deck, starting out low and gaining in volume. "I call for a vote of the crew!"

Startled, Jules looked to see Cori walking aft, appearing out of the fog to stand by the mainmast. Other sailors came out of the mist from where they'd been out of view farther forward. In what seemed a few moment's time, the entire crew was standing on the deck, looking up at the quarterdeck. To Jules' dismay, none of them appeared to be surprised by Cori's call for a vote.

She looked back, seeing both Ang and Liv on the quarterdeck now. Both were watching her with downcast faces.

Cori continued, speaking in tones that combined reluctance and resolve. "I call for a vote of the crew," she repeated. "A vote to cancel the last vote. A vote to turn the ship about, head east, and return to the safe waters we have always sailed, and the trades of piracy and smuggling that we know."

Jules had seen the warning signs, had been troubled by them, but still hadn't expected this. "Haven't I earned your trust?" she called to the crew.

But nearly all of them kept their eyes and faces averted from her.

Only Marta answered. "You still have our trust as captain. But that doesn't mean we'll blindly follow you to our deaths."

"I gave you my reasons! I explained why we can do this, why we have to do this!"

Silence.

"Has there been any danger sighted? Have any of you seen or heard danger before us?"

Kurt replied. "The charts all show danger. Clear warning signs. If a sign warns of a pit ahead, do you keep walking until you fall into it?"

"You know the charts lied about conditions in the north!"

Silence again.

They didn't want to debate it, Jules realized. They'd decided, and they wouldn't listen to anything she said. Despair filled her, the weight of the world and the prophecy and her many responsibilities bearing down hard.

And she couldn't fight anymore.

Jules lowered her head. "Call the vote, Ang," she said.

Hearing nothing, she looked back at him.

Ang shook his head, his expression stubborn and sad.

Swallowing before speaking to keep her voice steady, Jules spoke louder. "Cori, you asked for the vote. Call the vote."

Startled, Cori looked about her at the rest of the crew. "All right. I... I call the vote. All those who wish to head back east, raise your fist, and say aye!" She raised her own clenched right hand. "Aye."

Jules, her heart sinking, watched as the crew raised their hands singly and in small groups. "Aye." "Aye." "Aye." Even old Keli the healer finally, reluctantly, raised his hand. "Aye."

She looked about, momentarily voiceless with disappointment and despair, to see that Ang and Liv still had their hands down. Aside from them, only Gord hadn't raised his arm, his face set in angry lines.

"The... the vote passes," Cori said. "The crew has spoken."

Jules didn't trust herself to speak. She breathed in and out slowly as the crew waited. Taking another deep breath, Jules gripped the quarterdeck rail with both hands so no one could see the way they trembled. "The vote carries," she said. "This is a free ship, and I will not change that. The ship will return to the east."

At least they didn't cheer, Jules thought. The crew didn't display any happiness at their victory.

What could she do? There was only one course left, because her heart told her she could not turn away as the ship now would.

Jules tried to keep her voice even as she spoke again. "The *Sun Queen* will need a new captain."

A murmur broke out on deck.

Gord called over the noise. "That's not so! The vote was over a course of action! Not over you as Captain!"

Shaking her head, Jules swallowed and tried to speak calmly. "No. I cannot remain with you. I must find what lies to the west. Mak calls to me to find that, and…" Her voice almost broke. "My heart tells me my fate lies there. I must leave the ship and wish you all the best for your future. You must vote a new captain. I strongly support Ang for that role and hope you will vote him captain. He is honest, and capable, and a good seafarer."

The growing murmur of voices on the deck went silent.

Everyone stared at her. They were finally looking at her, in surprise and dismay.

Jules swallowed again before speaking. "I ask only one thing, in recognition of the good fortune I have been able to bring the ship, and that is that the small boat be lowered, and provisioned with fresh water and some hardtack. I do not know how much farther my journey to the west will take me, and the small boat will make that task easier."

Not a sound answered her. Even the drops of water suspended from the rigging and yardarms seemed unable to fall.

She fought down another wave of disappointment at the lack of response. "I understand that replacing the small boat will cost the ship. My share of the plunder we've acquired is in my cabin. My former cabin. I've spent very little. You can have it all to cover the cost of the small boat."

Still not a word, everyone gazing at her in utter silence, the mist swirling to form brief curtains hiding and then revealing the faces of those who watched her.

Blazes. How had it come to this?

Mak, what should I do?

Jules closed her eyes, nerving herself, then looked out at the crew again. "All right. I see that is too much to ask. So I ask that instead the small boat be lowered to take me ashore. I can swim the distance if needed, but I expect a long walk to the west ahead this day, and for days after, and would much prefer dry boots for that."

Still no response.

"Even that is too much, then?" Jules looked across the deck, trying to keep her voice steady and failing. "Will you at least put a line over the side? Have I not earned that much from you? Put a line over the side so I can climb down to the water instead of having to dive from the deck."

No one moved or said anything.

Jules stood on the quarterdeck, momentarily unable in her distress to say anything else.

"Captain Jules," Keli said, his voice finally breaking the unnatural silence that had once again enveloped the ship. "Why is your heart so set on this? Can you tell us that?"

"I made a promise," Jules said, hearing her voice crack on the last word. "I made a promise to Captain Mak." Did she finally see a reaction then? The members of the crew looking at each other? "You know why we came west. I told you. To find new lands, to build new cities as homes for commons like us where we can live as free as the Great Guilds permit. To help the commons grow strong, strong enough to stand against the Empire, and strong enough to overthrow the Great Guilds when the daughter of my line comes to lead them."

Jules had to pause, steadying herself. "With his last breaths… Captain Mak… asked me to promise to make that happen. He asked me to promise to make that happen for all of you, for all the common folk. I promised Captain Mak that I would do it, and that I would do it for him. And I will, to my last breath. That is why I must keep on west. For us, for all who will come after us, and for Captain Mak. Even for that daughter of my line who has made a wreck of my life.

Even for her I have to do this. I made a promise. And I keep my promises."

Silence again answered her. Shaking her head, her heart feeling as heavy as a stone, Jules managed to speak again. "Will you not at the least put a line over the side for me? No? Then I'll do it myself."

She walked toward the ladder down to the deck, the sound of her boots on the wooden deck loud in the silence that once again engulfed the ship.

But as she reached the head of the ladder another voice rang out. "I call for a vote of the crew!"

Startled, Jules stopped walking, looking to where Cori still stood near the mainmast. "I call for a vote," Cori repeated, her voice carrying clearly, emotion trembling along each word. "I call for a vote of the crew, to follow Captain Jules into the *west*, and to the ends of the world and beyond if she asks it of us! Because she would brave those waters for us, and we should brave them for her!"

"I call the vote!" Ang shouted, not waiting for any questions or debate.

Jules stood, stunned, as Cori shoved her fist into the air. "Aye!"

Ang, Liv, Gord and Keli also raised their fists. "Aye!"

And as if that had been a great wind to fill a sail, suddenly every hand of every other sailor in the crew shot upwards and their voices rang out loudly enough to roll to the unseen land to the south and echo back to the ship as if a giant called to them through the mist. "AYE!"

Jules had to grab onto the quarterdeck railing for support again. She realized the wetness on her face was no longer only that of the mist, but also of tears. She wiped the tears away, trying to find her composure. "A fine crew you are," Jules finally managed to say, her voice shaking. "You get me all worked up, and then you go and change your minds. You're a terrible lot. Each and every one of you. And I've never been prouder to be your captain. We'll wait here until the fog lifts enough to see a safe distance ahead. Until then, get on with your work, and... and..." She shook her head at them. "Thank you."

Jules turned to see Ang and Liv smiling at her, and went down on deck as Cori ran to the foot of the quarterdeck and stopped before her. "Captain—" Cori began, looking as if she'd begun crying as well. "I'm... I..."

Jules extended her open hand toward Cori. "Peace, girl. You spoke your heart. Both times. Nothing lies between us."

"Thank you, Captain!" Cori said. With a grin, she ran back forward.

Jules realized that Keli was standing beside her. "What is it you want, you old shark?"

Keli smiled. "I was thinking what a shame it was. Perhaps the best moment you'll ever have, and so few to witness it."

"I meant every word," Jules said.

"We knew that. We could feel the truth in your words. You weren't telling us what we wanted to hear. You were speaking from your heart, and offering all you are in service to our future even after we'd rejected you." Keli looked upward at the swirling mist. "I hope that, wherever he is, Captain Mak was able to see and hear you just then. Because he'd be that proud of you right now."

Her vision blurred as her eyes filled with tears again. "What kind of healer are you?" Jules demanded, blinking furiously. "You're supposed to make people feel better but here you have me crying like a baby. Isn't there some work you should be doing somewhere else?"

Keli just grinned and strolled off along the deck.

Jules looked ahead, pretending to watch the activity on deck and in the rigging, but her thoughts were elsewhere, wondering if Captain Mak somehow could still know what was happening in this world. *I hope I am making you proud, father of my heart. I will never stop trying.*

As if in answer to her words, a slight breeze came up and the waves began murmuring along the hull as if calling to the *Sun Queen*. The fog began thinning as the wind freshened, the bowsprit coming into sight from the quarterdeck.

Ang called from near the helm. "The wind's coming out of the northeast! It'll push us west easily!"

And the crew cheered while Jules felt the wind on her face and marveled at how the world could change so quickly.

Liv came up to her, wearing a shame-faced smile. "That weather wasn't a warning. It was a test. The sea wanted to know if we deserved to learn her secrets. You had the right of it all along. I won't question you again."

Jules laughed. "Don't you dare promise that! Don't you dare, Liv! I need you second-guessing me, and making me rethink what I'm sure of. Keep doing that."

"Is that an order, Captain?"

"Yes, that's an order, my friend."

The fog didn't dissipate, but it continued to lift until they could see for a few hundred lances all around. The crew went to the windlass to lift the anchor, and up into the rigging to set the mainsail. The *Sun Queen* caught the wind and began moving west again, and if any of the crew still harbored fears they gave no sign of it.

Jules stood on the quarterdeck, wondering what they would see when the fog finally lifted, and whether the crew's mood would last if the weather turned against them again.

CHAPTER THIRTEEN

The *Sun Queen* continued west through the rest of the day, occasional rain showers punctuating the mists that seemed to be a permanent aspect of this area of the Sea of Bakre. Sometimes the mists would lift enough for the ship to put on more sail, other times they'd close in again and sail would have to be taken in. Jules guessed that the crew in their current mood would've let her go faster at times, but she resolved not to take advantage of that. Sometimes it was necessary to dive right into something, but there were also times when caution made sense. Not knowing what was ahead made this a time when wisdom called for care.

The wind also played games through the day, veering a bit, now more from the north, then more from the east, suddenly gusting slightly or suddenly dropping off, but overall remained congenial. The crew took that as a good sign and worked the sails with a cheer that had been lacking since they left Dor's.

As the fading light warned of sunset occurring somewhere beyond the clouds and fog, Jules sought for a decent place to drop anchor. The land occasionally visible when the fog lifted enough showed that the cliffline had turned a bit to the north again. Not much, still mostly trending to the west, but a bit. Were they nearing the western end of the sea? The depth of the water as measured by the sounding line had stayed fairly steady, so there wasn't any trouble locating a good anchorage.

Jules went to the bow, looking into the mist as the light faded, listening intently for any sounds beyond the rippling of the water around the hull.

"Nothing," Marta said from nearby, her mood very different from the night before. "I don't know if the fog is thickening again or if we're just losing visibility as the sun goes down, but right now you can't see what's ahead much past the bowsprit."

"Have you heard any surf?" Jules asked. "Any sounds of breaking water?"

"No. Lots of seagulls out there yelling at each other. There must be a lot of fish in these waters. But when the gulls shut up it's just quiet. That's odd, isn't it? Aren't those reefs supposed to be just ahead? Yet the swells roll on with no sign they're hitting anything."

Jules leaned out a little further, knowing that wouldn't help but still straining her eyes. "If our chart was right, we'd already be a ways into those reefs. We'd have hit them yesterday."

"If the map was right," Ang said, coming up to stand with them, "I think we'd be anchored in that wasteland instead of riding on water. I can't be sure because we can't get a decent position with the sun and stars hidden, but that's what I think."

Jules looked to port, where the nearest land once again was hidden by mist. "Do you have any feel for what the land is doing? Do you think it's going to turn north on us soon?"

"It's hard to judge, Cap'n," Ang said. "But if you ask what my gut feels, it says the waters ahead are clear for a ways at least. It feels... open," he said, waving vaguely forward.

"Let's try something," Marta said, holding up a piece of scrap wood. She tossed it out into the water just to starboard where they could see it.

Jules spotted the small splash, watching the wood. "It's... moving east."

"Pretty fast," Ang said as the piece of wood disappeared into the fog. "There's a strong current on the surface."

Marta nodded, looking down at the water. "There's a strong current running from the southwest, I think. I noticed we didn't seem to making as much headway, and look how the anchor cable is tending."

"The ship is being pushed east," Jules said. "A strong current from the west. Where's a strong current from the west coming from?"

"Fisherfolk find deep currents sometimes," Ang said. "Well beneath the water. They lower their nets deep and find their boat being tugged along. Maybe that's what's happening here. A strong, deep current from the east, hitting a shore ahead and rising to the surface to be pushed back from the west."

"Maybe." Jules shook her head. "But wouldn't even a strong current lose a lot of force when it hit the coast and rose to the surface?" She stared around into the mist. "You know what it puts me in mind of? A great river reaching the sea, like where the Ospren River lets out in the Sea of Bakre."

"It's sort of like that at Western Port," Marta said. "And at Dor's. But not this strong this far from land."

"What comes from a river is fresh water," Ang said. "If it's that, could we tell the waters here weren't as salty?"

"We'll give it a taste in the morning," Jules said. "Could we have entered a river without knowing it? One so wide we couldn't see the other side in this muck?"

"Those are ocean swells marching past," Marta said. "I never seen the like of that on a river."

"True." Jules shook her head. "That chart is worthless. Can we agree on that now? I wonder if those reefs even exist?"

"We'll still go carefully in the morning, won't we?" Ang said.

"Of course we will. We didn't come this far to blunder into trouble."

* * *

Fog still billowed around the *Sun Queen* as she got underway the next morning, finding her way ahead slowly in the limited visibility.

A taste of the water that morning produced quick agreement that the salt was as strong as ever. Whatever was producing that current from the west, it wasn't a source of lots of fresh water.

The fog thinned some more, the ship putting on more sail, surging ahead as if eager to find what lay ahead. Winged shapes would flash briefly into sight as seagulls flew past close enough to be seen. The rest of the time the raucous cries of the gulls formed a constant background. Jules wished the birds would shut up so that any sounds of surf could be heard.

The fog shredded away to the south and the land in that direction came into view, producing startled reactions from everyone. "We've rounded a cape!" Liv said. "Look at the land heading south!"

"It might be one side of a large bay," Ang cautioned. "South beyond it a little ways the shore could curve back quickly."

"Take us a little closer to shore," Jules ordered. "Keep us at least a thousand lances clear of it."

"Aye, Cap'n."

But as midmorning approached the coastline to port kept dropping off to the south. "If we're going to keep it in sight, we'll need to come farther to port," Ang said.

"Keep on this course a little longer," Jules said. Visibility in every direction but south was still limited by the fog. The wind, becoming more lively as the sun rose beyond the fog, was still coming from north of east. "Hey, Liv, how far inland are we now, according to that chart?" Jules asked.

"Thousands and thousands of lances," Liv said. "Only it doesn't show the land dropping off to the south like that. It should've long since come hard to the north and formed a barrier that way. You know that skull on the chart? The one on the land that warns of no water?"

"Yeah," Jules said. "What about it?"

"It's just a guess," Liv said, "but I think we're about where that skull is on the chart."

"There seems to be a lot of water about," Ang said.

"Yeah," Jules repeated. "Someone forgot to tell all of those seagulls that there isn't any water here." She stepped up onto the rail, holding onto a shroud line, gazing to the west. "Come on then," Jules called into the fog. "You've had your fun, but we've had enough of you! Go trouble some other waters and let us see what lies about us!"

As if responding to her words, the breeze immediately began to freshen, and the fog began shredding.

"You're a scary one, sometimes," Liv said to Jules.

"I didn't actually make that happen," Jules said. She stared to the west as the fog blew away, scattered scraps of white mist fleeing to the northeast. "There's land. Running about north/south, isn't it?"

"That's no wasteland," Liv said. "You can see the green on it from here."

Jules looked to the south, seeing open water ahead. "Bring us to port, Ang. Stay even with the coast to port. Let's see how far south this runs."

The crew were gathered on deck, some climbing into the rigging to look to the west where hills reared up above the sea. "Trees!" old Kurt called from the maintop. "Lots of trees! There must be good soil there as well as water!"

Keli walked up, gazing across the water. "So, you were right it seems."

"I spent my time imagining good things ahead," Jules said. "Instead of monsters."

The wind grew in strength again, the *Sun Queen* leaping forward. Even though a little fog still lingered, Jules had all sails set, her heart bounding the way the ship did across the waves. "How does it feel, Ang? To know we're the first ship to sail these waters? To see this land?"

Ang didn't usually smile much, but a broad grin creased his face. "It feels very good, Cap'n."

"The land to port comes a bit west up ahead!" Kurt called down.

"Steady on," Jules told Ang. "Stay even with the coast until we see something off of our bow."

But though the land on both sides gradually closed in, a substantial gap remained ahead where only water could be seen.

As the sun neared noon, the *Sun Queen* ran between a headland to the west and another to the east, and suddenly the land fell off on both sides.

The ship had been filled with the buzz of excited conversation for most of the morning, but now a silence borne of awe fell across the deck.

Jules stared ahead. Stared at an endless body of water running off to the horizon to the west and the south and the north. Looking back, she could clearly see now that the *Sun Queen* had come through a strait separating two bodies of water. The strait, and the Sea of Bakre, were behind them. Ahead lay…

"It's another sea," Liv said, her voice hushed.

"Another sea," Jules said. "The Sea of Bakre isn't locked inside land. It opens into another sea. We're not trapped. There's an endless sea before us, a whole world beyond the Sea of Bakre, and *we've found it!*"

She turned at the sound of laughter, seeing Ang pointing around. "Look, you pirates!" he called to the crew. "The far west, the new sea, and we're the first to lay eyes on it because of Captain Jules!"

"We should name it for her!" Cori yelled back. "She brought us here!"

"Aye," Ang said. "The Jules Sea! What say you all?"

"Have I no voice in this?" Jules cried, embarrassed.

"I call for a vote!" Cori said. "All in favor of the Jules Sea raise your hand and say aye!"

The hands went up and the crew shouted aye and Jules had to look away for a moment as her chest filled with a happiness it had rarely known. "I can't ignore a vote of the crew. If you lot insist on it, I guess we must call it the Jules Sea."

"We'll see how the Great Guilds like that name on their charts!" Gord yelled.

Jules looked toward the north, where the land ended in a cape, a feeling coming over her. "Liv, that headland to the north. Where would you say it is on that chart?"

Liv squinted at the headland, then at the sun. "At a wild guess, about here I think," she said, folding the chart so Jules could see.

"That's about... look!" Jules pointed at the chart, and then at the headland to the north. "If we're about there, then what we're seeing might be that, right?"

"Might be," Liv said cautiously.

"It's not Cap Astra like the chart says. It's *Cape* Astra." She jumped up onto the starboard rail, hanging onto the lower shrouds, staring to the north. *We found it, Mak. There it is. Are you with me? Do you see it? We found Cape Astra.*

"That means somebody was here a long time ago," Ang said, scratching his head. "Somebody named that cape."

"If so," Jules said, looking back at him, "their chart lied about everything else. Whoever they were, their own name deserves to be lost. Change the chart! Make it Cape Astra!"

But Ang still hesitated. "Cap'n, if that place meant so much to Mak, should we rename it? Call it Cape Mak?"

Jules paused, her eyes going back to the cape, remembering how Mak spoke of it. "No," she finally said. "To Mak it was Cap Astra. That was the place that called to him. I'll give it the proper name of Cape, but if we renamed it, it wouldn't be the place Mak longed to see. In memory of his dreams, I think it should remain Cape Astra."

Liv nodded firmly. "If his spirit is still seeking the place, it'll be seeking that name. I agree with Jules."

"We should write these things down," Ang said

"I'll get something," Liv said, running down the ladder.

She was back almost immediately, carrying both a pen and ink, as well as the small table from Jules' cabin. Gord hastened to help her carry the table up to the quarterdeck and place it to one side of the helm.

"Now, what is it we need?" Liv said, squinting at the chart. "We need to fill in the coasts along both sides here. And this would be Cape Astra, so I'll add that 'e.' What about that strait we came through?"

"With all the gulls?" Gord said. "Gull Strait, I'd call it."

"Either that or the Strait of Fog and Mist and Gloom," Liv replied.

"Gull Strait sounds better," Ang said.

"Yeah, but it also sounds too informal," Liv replied. "How about Strait of Gulls? That's fancy."

"Do it," Jules said, smiling.

"And the Jules Sea... and that's it for now?"

"Yes," Ang said. "Captain, we have our choice of courses. Do we go north to see more of what lies there? Orn south along this coast? Or west?"

Jules hesitated, thinking of how much there was to see and learn and discover. "Let me take a look around before I decide," Jules said. She went down on deck, past sailors who were staring at the new world before them, and reached the main mast. Going to the rail, she swung onto the shrouds, climbing up to the maintop where Lana had joined Kurt on lookout. "What've we got?"

"Land to north and south," Kurt said. "Nothing certain to the west but water. There might be some mountains way off that way. Do you see?"

Jules nodded, shading her eyes to look to the west. "Might be mountains, or just haze. Whatever it is isn't attached to the mainland."

"Another island like Altis, maybe?" Lana said.

"Maybe. But bigger, if all of that haze marks mountains. It stretches quite a ways. Have either of you seen any sails or anything ashore that would speak to people living here?"

Both shook their heads. "There's no sign man or woman has ever laid hand to these lands," Kurt said.

"No sails," Lana added. "Not a one."

Jules looked west again, where the haze that might be the tops of mountains beckoned. She felt those western waters drawing at her. But what if this was another side of the Umbari Ocean? She'd been taught the world was a globe, so sailing west into that ocean should eventually bring them back around the eastern side of the Empire. But how long would such a voyage take? With possibly no other land between here and there where water and food could be found? And even if they could make it, why would she want to end up on the eastern side of the Empire?

To the north, her view of Cape Astra showed it rising from the water with walls of rock facing the waves on three sides. The coastline running north on either side of the cape was interrupted by what might be a harbor on the eastern side. Inland, the terrain to the north appeared to be fairly low and tree covered, rising gradually as it went.

A beautiful sight, but nothing drew her to it.

Jules hung on to a shroud as she pivoted on the maintop to look east. They'd cleared the strait, but almost abeam of the *Sun Queen* the waters let into a partial natural harbor. Hills rose well inland, leaving a broad plain running down to the water. It would make a decent site for a town someday.

Then south. The land was curving out a bit to the west, but gently. Little more could be seen from here.

Satisfied that she'd seen all there was to see for the moment, Jules prepared to go back down to the deck. "Kurt, Lana, keep a good lookout. If you don't know whether to tell us of something you've sighted, go ahead and tell us. I'd rather hear too much from you than too little."

Going back down the shrouds, she passed members of the crew climbing higher in the rigging to see more for themselves. Resisting the urge to shout "I was right," Jules went down to the deck and then back to the quarterdeck.

Gord was pointing aft. "That weather we met coming this way. That's the reason, I'll bet. The waters of the two seas meet in that strait. We all marked how choppy it was. That's for the same reason, I'd bet."

"Would fish like that?" Jules asked.

"Those who work the fishing trade have told me that anywhere two types of water meet you tend to see more fish. And those currents there, what must those be like? They probably bring lots of fish near the surface."

"That'd explain the gulls," Liv said.

"Which course?" Ang asked again.

"I'm feeling like we should continue on south. That's the same land that Dor's is located on. But I'm not sure." Jules reached into a pocket and brought out one of the Imperial gold coins. "Shall we see what fortune says?"

"It wouldn't hurt to ask," Gord said.

"All right. Emperor we go north, eagle we go south."

She tossed the coin into the air, flashing in the sun as it flipped about, and caught it as it fell. "Eagle. Fortune is telling us to go where my feelings suggested. It's afternoon, though, and we don't know what might lie ahead. I don't want to be sailing down this coast in the night. Should we anchor in that harbor we can see to the east? Tomorrow we can get an early start and make a full day of exploring to the south."

"It wouldn't hurt to test the harbor waters and the lay of the land," Ang said.

"Bring us about and take her in. Let's see what this land holds for us."

The harbor was a decent one, with a line of hills on a promontory that blocked winds off the sea and would stop any storm coming off that expanse of water to the west. The harbor bottom proved to be sand, with pristine beaches lining the water. Ashore, fields of grass led down to the water, patches of trees dotting them. The dusty colored shapes of deer could be seen among the trees, their heads raised to gaze toward the *Sun Queen*. "Marta!" Jules called. "Get together some good shooters, arm yourselves with crossbows, and we'll get you ashore to see if you can get us some fresh meat for dinner tonight!"

* * *

They ate on the beach, spits holding chunks of fresh venison set near roaring bonfires built from driftwood and fallen branches. "Nobody's been here before us," Marta told Jules. "I'm certain of it. The deer were curious, not worried, as if they'd never been hunted by people. I felt a little bad about shooting them. Not enough bad to pass up a chance at fresh meat, but a little bad. And we saw no sign of habitation."

"You didn't go in that far," Liv said.

"No, but anybody around here would've gone to the beach, right? If there're no roads—and we saw no trace of roads, old or new—they'd need to use boats. And there's none here."

"No sign of them," Jules agreed. She looked out into the darkness beyond the fires, where eyes glittered in the night as inquisitive animals watched the sailors. "Tomorrow we'll see what's farther south."

The night would've been perfect, except that as she lay on the beach looking up at the stars, Jules kept wishing that Mak were here, and that kept leading to thoughts of Ian, and that led to remembering the moment when her dagger went into his father's chest. It would've been a great time to be able to talk to Shin, but she'd chosen to have him stay at Western Port. And there wasn't anyone else who could understand why she'd feel melancholy on the day of her greatest triumph.

* * *

The next morning they continued sailing south, or rather southwest, as the shore continued to run in that direction. As sunset approached the land began curving back to the south and then east, so they anchored off the westernmost point for the night.

"It's eerie, isn't it?" Keli the healer commented to Jules as they stood on deck, looking at the dark mass of the land to the east. "No lights, no fires, no sound of human labor and trouble."

"Or sounds of human joy," Jules said. She leaned on the quarter-deck rail, looking across the water. Somewhere on the darkened shore a large animal coughed or barked, the sound carrying through the night. "No one's there, though. Or if they are, they're hiding really well. Why do you suppose that chart, everyone's charts, of the western part of the Sea of Bakre were so inaccurate?"

"Someone didn't want us coming here," Keli said. "That seems clear enough."

"But how do you convince everyone that the west is a trap for ships? Why was everyone so certain that it was death to brave those waters?"

"I guess the Empire might've been behind it," Keli said. "Trying to keep everyone under the Emperor's, or an Empresses', thumb."

"Maybe," Jules said. "Or maybe it was the Great Guilds, and even the Emperors and Empresses didn't know they were being scammed to keep them from breaking out of the box the Great Guilds have made to confine everyone who isn't a Mechanic or a Mage. Do you know what I heard some Mechanics say? They were talking about the Empire, and they said things had been set up that way."

"Set up?" Keli asked.

"Yeah. Like it wasn't Maran, the first Emperor, who organized things, but someone else who put the Empire in charge of all the commons."

"The Mechanics? How could they have done that?"

"I don't know." Jules looked up at the stars parading brilliantly overhead. "But if the Mechanics did make the world like this, they made some mistakes. I think they're trying to fix those mistakes."

Keli rubbed his neck, frowning in thought. "How does that help us? Should we be trying to prevent them from fixing things?"

"I think," Jules said, "that if we can convince the Mechanics that something good for us will fix their problems, we can get them to stand back and let it happen. Maybe even help, like they did when we captured Western Port."

"I've had enough experience with Mechanics, all of it bad," Keli said, "that I can't imagine they'd do anything that would benefit us."

"In the short term they have to see it as benefitting them," Jules said. "It's in the long run that we win."

"The long run." Keli laughed softly, the sound almost like that of the wind soughing through the trees on the shore. "Not many people think in terms of the long run. Ask any healer. But you do."

"Only because Mak taught me to," Jules said. "And, to be honest, whenever I think of what's happening now or is likely to happen soon, it gets kind of depressing. As much as I hate that prophecy, at least it gives me something to hope for in the future, though I won't be around to see it."

* * *

As they continued southwest the next day, the view ashore seemed to grow greener and lovelier with every lance the ship traveled. Even the waters they rode were pleasant, the *Sun Queen* rolling gently as low waves of brilliant blue paraded past. Jules begrudged every moment not spent on the quarterdeck or up a mast, watching as a new world slowly revealed itself.

And then, in the late afternoon, she saw it.

"There it is!" Jules grabbed Ang's arm in her excitement, pointing. "See it?"

"Looks like a good natural harbor," Ang said.

"Yes. I'll have to build up the rocks across the west side into a good breakwater, but get that done and that harbor will be proof against any storm!" Jules grinned, pointing farther inland. "Hills back there, a good plain leading down to the harbor, a river coming in there. It's perfect, Ang!"

"For what?"

"For my city," Jules said. She leaned on the railing, gazing at the spot. "Julesport. My city. Which will never be a respectable place. A harbor where pirates can always find an out-of-the-way berth for their ship and their business. A place where merit matters and not where you grew up or how grand your family is. Julesport, Ang. I'm going to see it built there. And every time the Great Guilds look at a map, they'll see that name. And they'll know who founded that city, and that a daughter of her line will someday sweep them away."

She turned to look back, seeing Ang bent over the chart. "What are you doing?"

"Writing in the name," Ang said.

Jules came to look, seeing the shape of the bay and the hills behind it already inked in, and beside it the name Julesport. "Blazes, I wish Mak was here to see this."

They anchored in the harbor that night, in *her* harbor. And despite all the worries riding her, Jules slept peacefully that evening, happy to have found a place that would be hers even if she could never make a home there.

* * *

Each evening Jules reluctantly decided they'd gone far enough, and each morning she looked south and decided on just one more day of exploration. There were plentiful streams coming down to join the sea, so they had no trouble getting more fresh water while stopped for the night, and the game ashore continued to act if it had never been human prey, making it easy even for pirates not accustomed to hunting on land to bag fresh meat each night.

A few days after they headed south from the future site of Julesport, the waters changed.

Jules realized that she had been standing on the quarterdeck gazing to the west for some time. Ang, beside her, was doing the same. "Something's different about the waters," she said. "Do you feel that, too?"

Ang nodded, pointing to the sea. "Look at the swells. They're bigger, broader."

"Yes." She looked west again. "It feels like there's nothing there. For a while after we left the Sea of Bakre it felt like there was land to the west, and we could spot the haze of what might be mountaintops in that direction. But now the waters to the west feel... empty."

"I feel that, too." Ang rubbed his chin, watching the swells roll in, the *Sun Queen* riding each in turn with ponderous grace. "We may have reached the ocean."

"The same ocean that's off the eastern end of the Empire?" Jules asked. "The, um, Umbari?" It had taken a moment to recall the name of the ocean she had never seen and no one had ever been allowed to explore.

"It's possible," Ang said. "I don't know."

Other sailors who'd spent a lot of time on the water confirmed the same feelings, so Jules had the chart marked to show the waters they now sailed might be part of the Umbari or another ocean.

After a few more days of sailing south, they saw a big river letting out onto the sea. The mountains were long since behind them, only rolling hills visible as far as could be seen from the coast. The day after they reached the large river, the coastline began swinging back to the east. The ship went east for days, the coast actually bending to the northwest for a while, before the land began tending south again.

"I'm seeing a lot more marshland," Liv commented. "And is it just me, or is it growing warmer during the days and the nights?"

"A bit warmer," Jules agreed.

"How much farther are we going to go? Mind you, it's a pleasant trip. Nicest voyage I've been on."

"One more day south," Jules said. "Then we'll head back to share the news of our discoveries."

"You've been saying 'one more day' for a while now."

"I mean it this time," Jules said.

* * *

Little new was seen during the morning of what was to be the last day of exploration in this direction. Jules glimpsed occasional coastal marshes, some vying for the grander title of swamps. Aside from them, fields of grass stretched to the east as far as the eye could see, interrupted by groves of trees that looked to be of different kinds from those around the Sea of Bakre.

The coastline had been trending nearly straight south this day when the *Sun Queen* rounded a small, swamp-ridden headland and found itself steering toward a town.

"What the blazes?" Liv demanded as the crew rushed on deck and up into the rigging to gaze ahead. "What's a town doing here, all by itself?"

"Why didn't we see any of their boats before now?" Ang asked.

"No ships in sight!" the lookout called down. "Just a few small fishing boats!"

"Small fishing boats." Jules, fighting disappointment that someone else had found this place before she had, shaded her eyes against the sun as she looked ahead. "Can you see their waterfront?" she called up to the lookout.

"Aye. Not much there, Captain. A pier. Looks plenty big enough for us to tie up there."

"A town on the ocean with nothing larger than small boats?" Liv said. "That's strange, that is."

"It reminds me of what Captain Aravind said about Dunlan," Jules said. "Let's go see what these people can tell us."

The mystery only deepened as the *Sun Queen* drew nearer to the town. A substantial stone wall encircled it, the near end extending into the water a little ways before ending in a tower. The town itself wasn't newly constructed, with buildings of raw wood. The structures that could be seen weren't wood at all, but seemed all to be made of stone and brick.

"They've been here a long time," Keli commented as he walked onto the quarterdeck. "Some of those buildings put me in mind of Landfall."

"They do," Jules said, looking over the appearance of the buildings. "Almost as if the same people built them. Is this an old outpost of the Empire?"

Keli shook his head. "The Empire couldn't have kept such a secret for so long. And it wouldn't have kept a secret like that. Every citizen would've been told about the glorious achievement, and how far the hand of the Emperor or Empress stretched."

"They don't seem to be flying any flags over the town," Liv added.

"Why the wall?" Jules said. "They're ready to defend themselves against a big attack. But we haven't seen anyone else out here until now."

The *Sun Queen* came into port slowly, as a crew on one of the small fishing boats stared at the ship like people who'd never seen such a craft before. "Can we tie up, do you think?" Jules asked Ang.

"The pier is for certain long enough to hold us," he said. "But if all that ties up there are boats such as that one, the water may be too shallow."

"That's a real chance, isn't it? Let's anchor out and take the longboat in." Jules paused, eyeing the crowd beginning to form on the waterfront. A small crowd, less than fifty, with no sign of uniforms among them. Instead, it looked like a normal mix of adult men and women as well as children of various ages. "They must be hiding whatever soldiers or police they have. That's not a good sign. Let's make sure our boarding army is armed."

By the time the *Sun Queen* had anchored in the small harbor next to the town, and the long boat lowered, the afternoon was well along. A reception group had been formed on the waterfront of the town, the remainder of the town citizens standing a little ways off to make room for those who awaited the longboat.

Jules carried her cutlass, her dagger, and had the Mechanic weapon in its holster on her hip. It seemed like a good idea to impress these people.

Liv and Ang had stayed on the ship, ready to get her underway quickly if needed. In the longboat with Jules were Keli and Gord, as well as the sailors wielding the oars.

As they rowed closer to the pier, Keli squinted toward the town. "Either the entire rest of the population is in hiding, or this is just about everyone they've got. Maybe two hundred all told."

"That's an awfully big town for that few people," Gord said.

The town officials stood back as the longboat came alongside the pier, not moving as a couple of Jules' crew jumped onto the pier to tie lines to stone bollards that looked worn about the middle from many years of use. That reminded her of the older piers at Landfall as well.

Jules climbed onto the pier, trying to look dignified. Her shirt and pants were clean, her boots shined, though of course the scorch caused by Mage lightning couldn't be buffed out. She walked over to the group waiting to greet her, none of whom were wearing anything like the suit of an Imperial bureaucrat. Even though their clothing was the same as that of the other commons, the way they stood and watched her made Jules certain that these were officials of the town. Stopping before the men and women, Jules belatedly realized that she hadn't rehearsed what to say to them. A polite introduction seemed like a good start. "Good afternoon," Jules began. "I'm Captain Jules of Landfall."

The officials exchanged troubled glances, before one man finally replied. "I am Kahya."

To her surprise, he had about the same accent as that of many of the Mechanics she'd encountered. Jules waited, and when nothing else followed prompted the man. "Kahya of…?"

"Of?"

"Where you're from," Keli said, having followed Jules. "I'm Keli of Alfarin."

"And I'm Gord of Sandurin," Gord said, joining them.

Jules saw no trace of recognition in the eyes of the officials as everyone named their cities of origin. "You've heard of those places, haven't you? Landfall is one of the biggest cities in the world, and the oldest city in the Empire."

"The Empire?" a woman asked.

"You—" Jules had to take a moment to recover from her surprise, gazing around at the old buildings. "You haven't heard of the Empire?"

"No," Kahya said. "And you should leave."

"Why?" Keli asked.

"That is forbidden," Kahya said, pointing towards the *Sun Queen*.

"Like at Dunlan?" Jules said. "Do Mechanics rule here?"

"Of course Mechanics rule here," the woman said, "though it has been long since…" She stared at Jules. Or rather, Jules realized, at the holster on her hip. "Lady! Forgive us! You weren't wearing your jacket so we didn't realize!"

The other officials gazed at their companion in confusion, so she pointed. "Look! She bears one of the weapons!"

Kahya's attitude instantly changed. "My apologies, Lady Mechanic. It's been so long since a Mechanic paid us the honor of a visit that we didn't realize who you were."

Jules glanced at Keli, who wordlessly indicated he thought Jules should play along with the mistake of the townsfolk. "That's all right," she said, wondering if it had been right to accept the apology. If she was supposed to be a Mechanic, shouldn't she act rude and superior? Give orders? "How about the proper greeting I should have received when arriving here?"

"Welcome to Pacta Servanda, Lady," Kahya said, he and the others standing straight while he spoke.

"That's better," Jules said. She noticed Keli and Gord eyeing her and gave both a surreptitious wink before facing the officials again. "So... ships are forbidden here."

"Yes, Lady. Ships like that. We only know of them from paintings. We haven't violated the rules given us. The only ships that have ever docked here have been those of the Mechanics Guild."

Mechanics Guild ships. Jules tried not to show any reaction as she nodded. "Of course. The metal ships of the Mechanics Guild. You said it's been a while since any Mechanics visited?"

"Yes, Lady," the woman said. "Thirty years. No, thirty-one years. I was just a child when the last Mechanics left."

Jules realized she needed to learn a lot more about this place, but needed an excuse for asking questions that a Mechanic should already know the answer to. The officials facing her were all of early or late middle age. How much would they know of or remember about Mechanics who'd left thirty-one years ago? "I've been sent to check on this town, to ensure that you remember your history."

"If you seek history," Kahya said, "you should speak with our former mayor. He's old enough to remember when there were many Mechanics living here. We will take you to him if you will permit us to show you the way. I am Kahya," he repeated, "the current mayor, and this is Corda, the assistant mayor."

"I will permit you to show me the way," Jules said, thinking she sounded like a stupid Imperial court functionary when she tried to speak as arrogantly as the Mechanics with whom she'd dealt.

And she thought that perhaps she glimpsed some well-hidden resentment in the eyes of some of the town officials, the same as that evinced by common folk everywhere. At least, you could see it if you knew how to look for it, and you only knew how to look for it if you felt that same resentment of Mechanics, and also hid it as well as you could when faced with them.

"None of these buildings seem to be new," Keli commented as they walked along a broad street away from the waterfront. "Many appear to be empty."

"Yes," Corda said.

After a pause to see if she'd elaborate, Keli continued. "Has there been disease here? A plague?"

"Nothing beyond the usual illnesses. Most of these homes and offices were used by Mechanics, or by the common people who served their households."

"Most of the population was Mechanics?" Jules asked, looking at another apparently empty dwelling as they walked past it, the long-closed door and windows somehow seeming sad.

"Not most, but at one time it wasn't unusual for a few hundred to be here," Corda said. "Our former mayor can tell you of those days."

They reached a larger building, fairly imposing compared to the rest of the town. As the group entered, Jules could tell this was the town hall. Walking down otherwise deserted hallways where their footsteps echoed on the marble floors, they reached a large office with an open door.

Kahya looked inside. "A Mechanic has arrived, Terrance. She doesn't wear the jacket but she has a weapon."

Jules walked into the office, seeing an old man rising from his chair and bowing his head to her. "Lady Mechanic. Welcome back to Pacta Servanda."

"Thank you," Jules said, looking about the office. It held an inde-finable aura of age. On two of the walls were paintings, both bearing signs of age, one showing a ship like the *Sun Queen* sailing in a stormy sea, and the other a range of impressive mountains with an unusual sort of castle in the foreground. "I'm here to see how well you remember your history."

Terrance paused, eyeing her, before smiling. "Yes. I may tell her things the Mechanics Guild would not want widely known," he said to Kahya, Corda, and the other town officials. "Could you give us privacy?"

"Yes. Certainly." The others backed out, retreating down the hallway, the sound of their footsteps seeming unnaturally loud in the mostly empty building.

Terrance waited until the sound of a closing door told of the others leaving, then gave Jules a keen look that included Keli and Gord. "You are not a Mechanic, Lady. Why are you here?"

CHAPTER FOURTEEN

Jules tried to frown like a Mechanic. "Why would you say that?"

"Because you thanked me for greeting you, and explained to me what you were doing," Terrance said. "Mechanics never express thanks, and never explain to common folk. They simply demand what they want."

"Yes," Jules said. "I'm not used to doing that."

"Where did you get the weapon?" Terrance asked, his voice carrying no hostility, just curiosity.

"I've been working with the Mechanics to do a few things. They gave me the weapon to kill Mages with."

"Mages?"

Keli started with surprise. "You've never heard of Mages?"

"No. What are they?"

"Strange people who always wear robes. You've never seen one?"

"No," Terrance said. "We know nothing about the world beyond our town wall. Well, that is, we're allowed to travel up to ten thousand lances beyond the wall to hunt or farm, but that's the extent of it. Please sit down."

Jules took one of the chairs, which was clearly old but still sturdy. "What is this place?"

Terrance shook his head. "If you mean to ask why a good number of Mechanics once lived here, I can't answer that. I'm old enough to remember when the town was full of Mechanics. Hundreds of them. About fifty years ago most of them left, leaving only a small group. And then about thirty years ago that small group also departed, with instructions that everything be kept as it was and all rules abided by." His eyes grew distant with memory. "I was the mayor then. They gave their orders in a way that made it sound like they'd be back soon. Maybe they did expect to return soon. One Mechanic told me to look after his garden in the manner of someone planning to see it again before long. But it's been thirty years. And not a Mechanic to be seen during that time."

"You still follow the Mechanic rules or orders?" Keli said.

"Yes." Terrance looked about him. "As I said, we're not supposed to go more than ten thousand lances from the walls. Any buildings marked for Mechanics should be entered only to clean and repair, and any locked doors in those buildings must be left locked. No new buildings inside the walls. No building outside the walls. No digging up of roads or digging deep outside the walls. Things like that."

"And no ships," Jules said.

"And no ships," Terrance repeated, his old face creased by a smile. "Is that how you came here? On a ship?"

"Yes," Jules said. "Like the one in that painting."

"Ah. I'd like to see it. I've never seen a real ship with sails, just the Mechanic ships that used to come now and then."

"What did the Mechanics do here?" Jules asked. "Hundreds of them?"

"I don't know," Terrance said. "None of us do. None of the common folk who took care of the town ever knew. I told you that Mechanics never explain. We did what we were told, and didn't try to learn what was forbidden."

"Didn't anyone ever try to escape?" Gord asked.

"Now and then," Terrance said. "Some young hot head would take off. The Mechanics usually found them quickly and... killed them. As punishment and as an example to the rest. I don't know what happened to the few who managed to not be found."

"Is that why you have that wall?" Gord asked. "Not to keep attackers out, but to keep you in?"

"Maybe," Terrance said. "To be honest, my memories as a boy were that the Mechanics simply liked that wall. They liked seeing it and walking on it. It seems a strange reason to put so much effort into building a wall, but that was done when the town was built so no one remembers anything about it. It does serve as a physical form of the rule that we must stay here."

"When was the town built?" Jules asked. "How old is it?"

"About two centuries," Terrance said.

Keli frowned. "The town is as old as the Empire, then. But you know nothing of the Empire?"

Terrance shook his head. "We know nothing of the rest of the world. Supposedly there are vast deserts inland beyond our horizon, but no one has ever gone to see and returned."

"Deserts?" Jules said. "At least the Mechanics were consistent in their lies. We're from the lands around the Sea of Bakre."

Terrance shook his head once more. "I have no idea where that is."

"It's north of here. The eastern part is ruled by the Empire. No one lived in the areas west of the Empire until recently. According to our charts, and legend, the western part of the sea was a deadly maze of reefs backed by desert wastelands."

"But you came anyway?" Terrance smiled again. "You break rules?"

"I break rules," Jules said. "I break cages. And now I am certain that the Mechanics were the ones to create those false charts, to keep common people penned in the eastern side of the Sea of Bakre, just as they kept your people penned in this town."

"Were there more of you?" Keli asked. "You don't seem enough to have served that many Mechanics."

"There were a lot more commons in those days," Terrance said. "Most were taken away with the Mechanics when they left. We've never known what happened to them."

"And that first group left fifty years ago?" Keli said. "Altis was once even smaller. Just a few hundred people and that big Mechanics Guild

Hall. But I met someone who told me that suddenly a lot more common folk showed up and Altis grew quickly into a more substantial place. None of the new people would say where they'd come from. I think he said that was about fifty years ago."

"Altis?" Terrance said. "That's another town?" He sighed, sadness in his eyes. "There's so much I've never been allowed to see."

"Why didn't you build a ship and leave that way?" Jules asked. "Once the Mechanics left?"

"Because we didn't know when the Mechanics would come back, which might be any day, and because we have no idea how to build such ships aside from what we see in paintings like that, and because we had no idea if there was any place else to go."

"Such a pretty town," Keli said. "But it's a prison, isn't it?"

"It was obviously something else," Jules said, "if all those Mechanics lived here. Whatever it was, the Mechanics stopped needing it. Or decided they didn't need it. But they left the rules in place. Do you think something might be hidden here?" she asked Terrance.

Terrance shrugged. "That's possible. Maybe likely. Only a fool would go looking, though. All of us know the Mechanics have means of knowing when someone goes somewhere they're not supposed to be. Speaking of which, why did you come here if the Mechanics wanted everyone to stay on the eastern side of that sea? Everyone except those of us here in Pacta Servanda, of course."

Keli answered. "For as long as anyone can tell, everyone lived in the Empire under its rules, and if anyone tried to escape, the Empire's legions and ships would hunt them down and bring them back. Oh, there were some small groups in the Northern Ramparts, that's a big chain of mountains, but otherwise everyone stayed in the Empire. Then, oh, fifteen years ago or so, something changed. For some reason or other, the Empire stopped hunting down and returning everyone who escaped."

"I think the Mechanics told the Empire to stop doing that," Jules said.

"Maybe," Keli said. "But towns started popping up in areas a little west of the Empire. Things are changing a bit. No one knows why."

"Some Mechanics said in my hearing that the Emperor was too powerful and thought he could challenge their Guild," Jules said. "I think the Mechanics, some of them anyway, want other places now, other cities that can keep the Empire from getting any stronger."

"Why do people want to escape this Empire?" Terrance asked. "It sounds as if it is much bigger than this town."

"Vastly larger," Keli said. "Many cities with many thousands of people in each of them. But the cities can't hold everyone. There are more people than the Empire can handle, so many want to go somewhere... um, less crowded. And some, like those of us here, want more freedom. We want to have a say in how things are done. Emperors and Empresses aren't very big on people deciding things for themselves."

"Nor are Mechanics," Terrance said. "Yet they are permitting this? It must be for reasons of their own, not out of regard for what the common people want."

"You obviously do know Mechanics," Jules said. "A lot more people should be coming to this region once we get back with our chart. What are the rules here for when new people show up?"

Terrance frowned in thought, the moment growing longer as the others waited. "There is no rule," he finally said. "I'm certain of it. The Mechanics must not have expected anyone like you to ever get here."

"So people could settle here if they wanted?"

"There's no rule against it, and we do have empty homes."

Jules looked toward one wall, thinking of what they'd seen. "I'm going to be honest with you. There's a small harbor here, and nothing special about the land outside the town that we can see. We've passed a number of places that look far better suited for towns and eventually cities. A lot of people will choose those places. But I'm sure some will want to come here."

"New people," Terrance murmured. "How strange to think of such a thing. Have you noticed people staring at you? They've never seen new faces, except when a child is born."

"What do you want us to do?" Jules asked.

"Not to sound rude, but it would be best if you left. Everyone in town is going to be worried that some Mechanic device will be reporting that your ship is here, and that we're violating the rules." Terrance spread his hands. "And, to be honest, there's not much here you'd be interested in. We're not set up for visitors."

"Do you have a bar?" Gord asked. "A tavern?" he added as Terrance shook his head. "An inn?"

"We're not set up for visitors," Terrance repeated.

"Do you have anything you'd want traded up north?" Jules asked. "Any goods you create?"

Terrance considered the question, looking toward the picture of the odd castle as he thought. "We have some preserved fruits. We can spare a little, but not much. And there's wood." He touched his desk.

Jules took her first good luck at the wood and inhaled in sudden surprise. "That's beautiful. It has an amazing grain to it. I've never seen anything like it."

"Nor have I," Keli said. "The trees it comes from must not grow in the lands around the Sea of Bakre."

"We have planks in a warehouse," Terrance said. "In case they're needed for repairs. We could part with some of those."

"Would you like to be paid for them?" Jules asked. "We have Imperial eagles," she added, wondering how she'd estimate how much that wood would be worth.

"Those are coins?" Terrance shook his head. "Why not sell it for what you can get, and bring back whatever goods you think we might want. I have no idea what you have and we don't."

"Do you have weapons?" Gord asked.

"In storage," Terrance said, his eyes saddening. "We're going to need them with more people coming this way, aren't we?"

"You might," Jules said. "Are you going to tell everyone else I'm not a Mechanic?"

"Not yet. Maybe once you're gone." Terrance smiled, looking around the office.

For the first time, Jules did as well, seeing well-crafted furniture including cabinets for filing documents, walls of white plaster, and at the back a window giving a view of the outside. The office held the comforting feel of a place that had existed for a long time and would be here for a long time yet.

"I've lived a long life," Terrance said. "If the Mechanics do have devices that tell them you were here, and they wish to blame and punish someone, better it be me than someone younger. If the others don't know you weren't a Mechanic, they can sincerely be held blameless."

"You wouldn't go very far in the Imperial bureaucracy with attitudes like that," Jules said. "Thank you."

"You see? You pretend to be a Mechanic and then you say thank you again to a common!" Terrance laughed. "You really need to practice being unpleasant to your inferiors."

"I guess that's a compliment," Jules said. "We should get back to our ship so I can let everyone know we're all right."

"I'll have Kahya and Corda escort you back while I arrange for some families to contribute preserved fruit," Terrance said. "Look after my town, will you?"

"I'll do my best," Jules said.

As they walked back to the ship through the nearly empty streets of Pacta Servanda, Jules found her spirits sagging.

Keli noticed. "What's eating at you?"

Jules shrugged, looking ahead at Kahya and Corda, who were far enough in the lead that a low-voiced conversation probably wouldn't be overheard. "I hate to admit to it, but I was proud of us having found these places. Of us being the ones who'd first seen them. But now I know that's not so. The Mechanics have always known about these waters and these lands."

"That's what's bothering you?" Keli laughed. "And how many knew of all this before? Except for Mechanics, and maybe not many of them?

Everywhere we've been west of Dor's and south of the Sea of Bakre is new to every common person on this world, from the lowest beggar in the gutters of Landfall to the Emperor himself on his throne in Marandur. As far as they're all concerned, you did discover all of this. Maybe you could say all you'd done is discover a secret the Mechanics had kept for a long, long time. But that is a mighty discovery in itself, and something to be proud of."

"*I* didn't do it," Jules said. "*We* did."

"Oh, nonsense. Tell her, Gord. We'd have never put a toe west of Dor's if not for her, and we'd resolved to turn back short of that strait despite her, until she shamed us into following her all the way here."

"That's what happened," Gord agreed. "We found all of this because of you."

"I don't like taking credit for things other people have done," Jules said. "Or sole credit for things others helped me with."

Keli laughed again, the sound of amusement bouncing off the walls of the old, unused buildings they were passing. "At times I've wondered what would make that daughter of your line so special she could free the world," he said. "But then you say something like that, and I think if this girl passes such things on to her daughters, perhaps that prophecy could be real." He rubbed his chin, looking about again. "Speaking of that prophecy—"

"I'd rather not."

"Speaking of that prophecy," Keli continued as if he hadn't been cut off, "the people here have never seen a Mage. They don't know what Mages are. Clearly, the Mages have no more idea this place exists than anyone else living around the Sea of Bakre. If someone had a special reason to avoid Mages, this could be a fine place for that person to stay a while."

Jules looked about as well, at the old buildings that put her in mind of Landfall where she'd grown up. "There'd be worse places. I guess every other place there is would be worse."

"The Empire doesn't know it exists, either," Gord said. "The Emperor's hand could never find you."

"Others will learn about this town eventually," Jules said. "But you two have made your point. I was already thinking that perhaps we should leave this town off the chart. These people may have a wall around their town, and the fear of the Mechanics Guild to keep others in check, but I'm still worried about the world suddenly showing up at their doorstep."

"As you say, that'll happen sooner or later," Keli said.

"Then why not try to make it later?" Jules said. "For their sake as well as mine."

"I'd keep quiet about this town if asked," Gord said. "If anybody else in the crew talks about the place, the rest of us could laugh and say they were making it up."

"Sailors telling stories that are a bit exaggerated and perhaps not entirely truthful?" Keli said. "I guess folks might believe that could happen."

* * *

The longboat crew didn't bother to hide their relief when Jules and the others returned, or their disappointment at learning that a port town could exist without bars, taverns, and inns.

Once back on the ship, Jules asked Keli and Gord to tell the crew about the town while she spoke with Ang and Liv. "I'm thinking this is a sign of sorts," she said when done. "That we should head back north from here."

"I agree," Ang said. "If there is a chance at encountering a Mechanic ship, it would go ill for us if we were seen. They've kept all of this secret, and will want to keep it that way."

"Which would mean silencing us," Liv said, "and destroying that chart. We should get it to Dor's, as a start, and get copies made, and get it sent around to as many places as we can."

"We'll sail in the morning, after Terrance of... of Pacta Servanda visits the ship."

* * *

The former mayor of Pacta Servanda came out to the ship the next morning on one of the fishing boats hauling planks of wood. As the crew hoisted the wood aboard, Terrance stood on the deck of the *Sun Queen*, gazing around with delight. "So many new things. So many new people. It's a little unnerving, but also wonderful." He shook his head, smiling, then reached into a pocket to pull out a small, polished fragment of wood. "Here. Our carpenters thought you would want this. It's a finished piece of the wood, showing how it looks when sanded and finished."

"That's lovely!" Liv said, eyeing the wood with amazement. "Jules said it looked nice, but I had no idea."

"Will this help you get a good price for the wood?" Terrance said.

"It will," Jules said. "I'm going to store this in the ship's money chest," she told Liv and Ang. "And now, I think we owe our friend here a look at the world."

She led them into her cabin, where the chart already lay open upon the table.

Terrance hunched over the chart for a long time, muttering to himself, sometimes shaking his head. Finally, he straightened with a sigh. "The world is much bigger than we knew. Pacta Servanda is certainly a very long ways from everywhere else people are found."

"There must have been a reason why the Mechanics put this town here," Jules said. "So far from anywhere else."

"There must have been," Terrance said. "I have no idea what that reason was, or if that reason still exists. The Mechanics left, after all."

"You never saw anything that might offer a clue?" Liv said.

Terrance hesitated, his eyes looking into the past. "Once… I was a little boy. I heard a sound in the sky. I was about to look up when my father told me not to. Never look at the sky when you hear that noise, he said. The Mechanics forbid it. My father said he'd only heard the sound a few times, and never in the last several years before that moment."

"A noise in the sky?" Jules said.

"Yes. Nothing like anything natural would make. You know, not like an animal or a bird." Terrance paused again. "I can't remember any details of that sound after all these years, but I do remember something odd. Have you heard Mechanic devices as they work? They always sound... rhythmic. Is that the right word? As if many things are moving together in the right way. But that noise in the sky, it made me think of an animal gasping for breath. It didn't sound like an animal gasping for breath, but there were hesitations and... I don't know how to describe it anymore. It sounded like whatever was making it was hurt somehow. Or old and straining with effort. That was just how a boy felt hearing it. And I've never heard such a sound again."

"I've heard loud noises bounce off of low clouds," Liv said. "Maybe that's what it was."

Jules didn't say anything, her eyes on the chart but her mind elsewhere. Remembering the Mechanics at Western Port saying something about a flight, and there not having been any in decades. And remembering Mak suggesting that over time the Mechanics Guild would weaken, that its jealous control of Mechanic devices would cause them to lose important knowledge, and that the Mechanic devices would gradually wear out and be lost. Maybe what Terrance had heard had been such a thing. And maybe when it was lost, the Mechanics had left here.

But even if that was true, had it been the only reason why this town was so far from other places? That implied not just secrecy but security. And that inexplicable wall about the town. Perhaps even now it protected some important Mechanic secrets?

There was no way to know.

Terrance was moving one finger down farther south on the chart, beyond Pacta Servanda. "I see you have nothing drawn in here south of our town. We rarely speak of this lest it somehow get back to Mechanics, but about twenty years ago a few daring souls took one of our boats a little beyond the horizon to, um, search for new fishing grounds along the coast. They said the coast ran fairly smoothly for a long ways before turning west abruptly. Just beyond that turn a mighty river met the sea. Worried that the further they went the more likely the Mechanics would learn of it, they turned back at the river. That's the extent of what we know of the world beyond our town, and, as I said, you didn't hear any of it from me or anyone else in this place."

"You must have been a good politician," Liv said.

"I hope that's a compliment." He looked around the cabin, smiling. "Part of me wants to come with you. To see places I've only dreamed of, and places I didn't dream of because I couldn't imagine they existed. But that might doom those in this town. So I'll stay."

"You're a fine man," Jules said. "One last question. The name of your town is unusual. Does it mean something?"

"I assume the Mechanics named it," Terrance said. "We didn't realize the name was in any way unusual because it was the only name of a town that we knew. As to what it means, your guess is as good as mine. You don't know the words pacta or servanda?"

"Never heard them," Liv said. "They must be Mechanic words."

"We'll be back," Jules promised Terrance as he prepared to climb down into one of the fishing boats.

The morning wasn't far along when the *Sun Queen* stood out of the small harbor and sailed north on a beam reach.

The voyage back felt unexpectedly tense, everyone now alert for any sight of a Mechanic ship or one of the low-lying clouds that might mark the presence of one just beneath the horizon. "There hadn't been a Mechanic in that town for thirty years," Keli reminded Jules. "The Mechanics obviously aren't making regular trips through these waters."

"Let's hope they don't have a device that would've let them know we were there," Jules said.

They'd passed the big river joining the sea, heading north-northwest toward the future site of Julesport and looking forward to the waters changing to mark their passage into the Jules Sea, when a storm came charging out of the west as if the ocean was angered at their leaving.

Massive waves rolling in from the west and high winds tried to drive them onto the shore, every bit of their skills needed to avoid that fate as sails ripped and rigging parted. Sails reefed to minimize strain on the masts, the crew exhausted from frequent calls to adjust the sheets, they finally clawed their way north far enough to escape the brunt of the storm.

"We're in the lee of something!" Ang called to Jules over the still-driving rain as they stood on the quarterdeck in soaked clothing. "Something's helping to block the storm."

"Maybe those were mountains we saw to the west. Large islands, something like that," Jules called back, grabbing the rail to steady herself as the *Sun Queen* corkscrewed over a swell. She blinked away rain, looking to the east. "We couldn't have stayed off the coast much longer with that storm trying to push us onto it. We'll put into Jules-sport when we get there to repair the rigging and sails, and get some fresh water."

That stop cost them another two days, but at the end of that time, with the weather turning placid again, the *Sun Queen* turned north-northeast toward the Strait of Gulls. As they passed south of Cape Astra, Jules went up in the rigging to gaze to the north, thinking of Mak, happy to know that she'd fulfilled his dream. Part of that dream, anyway.

The weather closed in again as they headed northeast through the strait, but this time they knew what to expect. Rounding the coast at the mouth of the strait, the ship headed east for Dor's, everyone looking forward to being in familiar waters again and relieved that they hadn't encountered any Mechanic ships before reentering the Sea of Bakre.

"We're back in the Sea of Bakre," Liv said to Jules. "I never expected to say that, because I never expected to leave it."

"You're welcome," Jules said, leaning on the railing and raising her face to the sun as it broke through the clouds. "Two more days to Dor's, do you think?"

"That's just a guess. That rotten weather made it hard to spot landmarks on our way west, or get a good feel for the distance we covered each day."

It turned out to be a good two and half days more, the sun setting as they neared the valley opening onto the sea. Since Dor's still lacked the lighthouses and buoys that Imperial ports maintained to ensure safe navigation, Jules decided to wait until morning to enter port rather than risk trying to reach Dor's piers in the dark.

The sun rose the next morning through a rosy sky that the crew eyed with concern. Red sky at morning, sailors take warning, the old saying went. With storm clouds threatening to the north and east, the *Sun Queen* sailed back into the harbor at Dor's.

As they tied up, other sailors on the pier called up to the crew. "Where'd you come from? Kelsi's? Jacksport?"

"We came from Julesport," Liv called down at them. "Buy me a drink tonight and I'll tell you all about it!"

Dor himself showed up soon, walking aboard as the final lines were tied off and the boarding plank set on the pier. "It's always good to see the *Sun Queen*. What've you got for us?"

"Not much," Jules said. "Some exotic wood that'll probably be worth its weight in gold when Imperial princes get a look at it."

"Exotic wood? Where'd you find that? Western Port? I'm glad you gave up that crazy idea of sailing west," Dor said. "I've been worried since you left."

"Yeah," Jules said. "About that. Come to my cabin so I can show you where we found the wood."

She had Ang and Liv lay out the chart on the table, standing behind it while Dor looked at it with first a casual glance and then growing amazement.

He finally looked up at her again, followed by searching looks at Ang and Liv. "Are you saying you went west and found this? You've actually laid eyes on everything on this chart?"

"We have," Ang said.

"This isn't a joke? Because it doesn't seem possible."

"It happened," Liv said. "We went there and we saw all that. Mind you, it's not a perfect chart, just the best we could do."

Dor ran one finger just above the chart, following the coast west and then south. "Strait of Gulls, Cape Astra, Julesport... on the Jules Sea." He grinned at Jules. "I'm not saying you didn't earn the right to name those places, but..."

"The name of the port is my doing," Jules said. "The name of the sea was forced upon me."

"That's so," Liv said. "You've never met a more humble person than Captain Jules."

"You saw trees here?" Dor said, pointing to the land north of the strait. "Big ones?"

"Yes," Jules said. "Tall enough for masts. The forest ran as far north as we could see." She tapped the strait. "And here, those members of my crew experienced in fishing say these look like very rich fishing waters."

"The gulls attest to that," Liv said. "Thousands of them. Only plenty of food would draw so many."

"You've got some other harbors marked here," Dor said, pointing to two places.

"That's right," Jules said. "One north of the strait and one at the south end. The northern one is the better of the two, but both can shelter ships."

"And decent land around them?"

"Some mountains behind the northern one, but room for fields as well."

"And no one there? No sign of people?"

"Not between here and that river," Jules said, deliberately pointing out the river well north of the town of Pacta Servanda. The chart itself stopped a little north of the town, showing the marshy coasts that wouldn't look attractive to anyone seeking to settle in the new lands, that having seemed the best way to protect knowledge of the town's existence for a while.

Dor rubbed his eyes before looking at the chart again. "Jules, do you know what the Emperor would do if he got his hands on this chart? He'd burn it."

"I was thinking the Mechanics would. Why the Emperor?"

"Because what's been holding people back from escaping the Empire's grasp is worry about where they'd end up. Sure, some are happy to find homes in the Northern Ramparts, but it's rough in those mountains. Others want good harbors and good fishing and things like lumber so they can build new lives in a place where they can grow and raise families. And that's what you've found!" Dor shook his head. "When this gets out, the trickle of people sneaking out of the Empire will turn into a flood. The Emperor won't be able to stop it."

"You've been to places like Landfall," Jules said. "'Crowded' is a mild way of describing them. The Empire has more people than it can sustain. This gives them a chance to get rid of a bunch of those people."

"But the Emperor will want to control them wherever they go," Dor said. "The Empire will see these new lands as a place to expand into, but only on the Empire's terms. Which means the Emperor will want to control this information. Or make sure no one else ever sees it."

"The Mechanics don't want the Empire to expand," Jules said. "They think the Emperor has too much power already."

"Who told you that?"

"Mechanics."

"Really?"

"Yes," Jules said, "really. I told you that the Mechanics Guild made possible our capture of Western Port up north. That was to keep the Empire from expanding past its current borders."

Dor looked at the chart. "What do you think the Mechanics will do when people start flooding west?"

"I don't know," Jules said. "My impressions are that the Mechanics are trying to figure out what to do, and that they've got a lot of internal debate going on about that. Which increases the chance that they'll take so long to decide that, by the time they make up their minds, there'll be too many people in the west to go back to the way things have always been before."

"Huh." Dor frowned, scratching his head. "Any idea what Mages think about it?"

"They want me dead," Jules said. "As soon as possible. That's what Mages think about it." She realized abruptly that she hadn't worried about Mages for a while, not since learning that the town of Pacta had never even heard of Mages. But she was back where the danger from Mages was real and ever-present, and needed to keep that in mind.

"Don't you think they'd be interested in these new lands?" Dor said.

"Mages? No," Jules said. "They're not interested in the lands people already occupy."

"I don't know," Dor said, frowning down at the chart.

"Why this sudden interest in what Mages think?" Jules asked him.

"Um…" Dor looked at her with a guilty side glance. "There were a couple of Mages here again. But they left two days ago," he added hastily as Jules glared at him.

"Maybe you should have mentioned that Mages were around right at the start," Jules said angrily.

"They're not around anymore!" Dor protested. "They left. Just like the earlier ones I told you about."

"They came and left on a ship?" Liv asked.

"Um… no."

"They walked?" Jules said, incredulous. "Across the waste and the Southern Mountains?"

"I don't know," Dor said. "I mean it! No ship had arrived for several days, but suddenly these Mages came walking through the town. Of course we were scared and stayed out of their way. They walked just about everywhere. That's why I think they might be interested in these places."

"They were looking for me," Jules said.

"If they were, they didn't find you and they left!"

"How do you know that they left?" Ang asked Dor. "No one saw them arrive? Were they seen leaving?"

"No," Dor admitted. "But no one's seen any sign of them for the last couple of days. One thing I know about Mages is that they don't take enough notice of common people to bother with hiding from us."

"There's truth to that," Liv said with reluctance.

"They do conceal themselves when they see good reason," Jules said. "Like the way they can make themselves invisible to sight. Don't tell me that's just a story! I've seen it."

"Those Mages expected you to be here," Ang said. "Two days ago. If the ocean storm hadn't delayed us, and if we hadn't stopped at Jule-sport to repair the ship, we'd have arrived while they were here."

"That storm was a gift after all," Liv said. "Something unpredictable that messed up the Mages' knowledge of where you'd be."

Dor stared at Liv and Ang, then back at Jules, looking miserable. "I'm sorry, Jules. I thought the threat was past."

She shook her head at him. "For me, the threat is never past. Ang, those Mages might still be here. We need to get some fresh water and provisions aboard and get out of port fast."

"I'll get what you need here as fast as possible," Dor said. "Blazes, Jules, I'm sorry. What you've discovered is a huge gift to everyone who wants to escape the Empire's grasp, and I've repaid you by putting in you in danger."

"That's all right," Jules said, strapping the holster for the Mechanic revolver to her belt and checking the weapon. "I know you didn't mean it. But you do owe me. Liv, give Dor one of the copies."

Liv brought out a copy of the chart that had been painstakingly drawn during the voyage back, handing it to Dor, who stared at it in renewed disbelief. "Jules, what's on this chart is worth a fortune. And you're giving it to me?"

"I don't want that chart only being seen by people who can afford to pay a fortune," Jules said. "Make more copies. Give them to any ship that calls here."

The crew wasn't happy, deprived of a chance at the entertainments that Dor's offered and the chance to boast to all of those ashore about what they'd seen and done. But Jules paid for a few cases of wine and beer to be delivered to the ship and promised some free days underway to enjoy them.

The last of the provisions came aboard about noon, Jules standing on the quarterdeck gazing inland for any sign of approaching Mages. She noticed that Dor had formed a line of men and women, arms linked to bar passage to even someone unseen, across the landward side of the pier. The boarding plank was drawn in, the last lines came off, and the *Sun Queen* got underway again.

She cleared the harbor, sailing under the push of a strong wind as if the sea was trying to help them escape. Jules looked about, seeing that the storms threatening that morning had reached them. Rain fell from numerous patches of low clouds dotting the sky, . In other areas the sky was clear and the sun bright. "I wish the weather would make up its mind," she commented to Ang.

"I've seen this before," he said. "It'll likely last all day."

"Ship in sight off the starboard bow!" the lookout called down. "Looks like a sloop."

Jules ran to the quarterdeck railing, staring at the shape of the ship that had emerged from a bank of rain thousands of lances away. Probably more by chance than design, the ship had been able to get fairly close before being seen because of being concealed by the storm. "Can you tell if it's the *Storm Queen*?" she shouted back to the lookout.

"No, Captain! I can't tell."

"Likely Imperials, then," Liv said, her expression grim.

"Get us into cover," Jules told Ang.

A strange noise made her look up, seeing a bird flap by close over her head.

No, the bird wasn't close overhead. It was much higher up.

And it was huge.

The bird swung about, bringing into view a Mage seated behind its neck.

"Hachi was right. He did see that," Jules said, amazed that her voice sounded so calm.

"There's another!" Liv yelled, pointing.

Jules spun to see, watching another immense bird wing into sight and head for the *Sun Queen*.

It didn't take a master sailor to see that the birds were moving so fast they'd be all over the *Sun Queen* well before she could reach the shelter of one of the patches of rain.

One of the huge birds swung close, its massive claws striking the foremast, the entire ship rocking to the blow.

CHAPTER FIFTEEN

"They mean to knock our masts down," Ang yelled. "They're so fast the ship can't dodge them."

"Head for one of the stormy areas," Jules called back to him. She couldn't give in to the fear roiling her guts at this new and horrifying danger, not when the crew was depending on her to get them through this. Concentrating on her job helped keep her calm enough to think and call out orders. "If we get inside one of those, they won't be able to see us as well, and maybe they won't even fly into them. Birds don't normally fly in storms, do they?"

"Those aren't normal birds!" Liv said.

"I can see that!" Jules went to the forward rail and yelled down to the deck. "Crossbows! Grab every crossbow we've got and use them!"

"I don't think crossbows will stop those things," Ang said.

"Probably not," Jules said, remembering that she had one more thing to do. "I'm going to get the other Mechanic weapon." She ran down onto the main deck, filled with half-panicky sailors rushing to arm themselves. "Steady!" Jules called to them. "We can fight this!"

Inside her cabin, she pulled out the second Mechanic revolver. After the events at Western Port, she had only five cartridges left in her weapon. The revolver Lars had used held three .

Jules switched one cartridge from the second revolver into her own weapon, filling the cylinder. That made six shots. Against two monster birds and the two Mages riding them.

Out on deck again, Jules dashed back to the quarterdeck. "Where are they?"

Ang pointed. "One there, another there."

"Take this and use it if you need to," Jules said, thrusting the second Mechanic revolver at him. "It has two shots. Don't waste them."

Looking as if he was putting hand to a poisonous snake, Ang took the weapon.

The nearer of the birds veered in close to the *Sun Queen*, one massive claw grabbing at the mainmast for a moment that caused the entire ship to shudder. A few crossbow bolts chased the creature as it flew onward. Jules thought she saw one bolt hit but glance off the side of the bird. "Those feathers are so big they're like armor."

"What're your chances of hitting them with that Mechanic weapon?" Liv asked, her anxious eyes trying to follow both birds at once.

"From here or anywhere else on deck I have no chance at all." Jules looked up, knowing only one thing would give her a decent shot at the creatures. "I need to go up in the rigging."

"That's too risky, Cap'n," Ang protested. "They're here after you. If you present yourself as a target like that—"

"They'll come at me, and get close enough that I can hit them with a shot," Jules said. "We have to stop them before they knock any of our masts down." She tapped the revolver in its holster, trying to feign the confidence she didn't really have. "This thing can kill Mages. It can kill their creatures, too."

Ang and Liv exchanged a look, their helpless expressions revealing that they had no better ideas.

"I'd say be careful," Liv said, "but that'd sound stupid given what you're doing. Try not to get killed."

Jules nodded to her. "I'll do my best." Turning, she ran down the ladder to the main deck again, rushing to the shrouds leading up to the main top.

She swung onto the shrouds and climbed quickly, trying to keep an eye on where the huge Mage birds were. One swept close to the ship, causing Jules to pause and grip the shrouds tightly, her body pressed against the rigging. The bird snapped at the top of the mainmast with a beak large enough to hold half a cow. Whatever made up that part of the Mage creature glinted in the sun more like polished metal than the usual sheen of a raptor's beak.

Jules had to force herself back into motion as the bird swept past, climbing the shrouds as fast as she could until she reached the maintop with a sign of relief that she realized made little sense. She was now high up on the mast, a clear target for the attacks of the immense birds.

The lookout, Kyle, was still at his post, though flat on his stomach and clinging to the mast.

"Get down on deck," Jules told him.

Kyle looked up, his face drawn with fear. "I should stay and help you."

"You'll just be in the way. You've shown your courage by sticking with your post. Now get down on deck and fight from there!"

He nodded quickly, darted some glances at where the birds were as they swooped around the ship, then almost dove off the maintop. Grabbing onto the rigging, Kyle went down so fast it was more of a controlled fall than a climb down to the main deck.

Jules, alone on the maintop as it swayed with the motion of the ship, couldn't move for a moment as what she was doing hit home. This was crazy. She was going to die this time. But it was also her and the ship's only chance.

The approach of one of the birds drove her back into motion. Jules wrapped her arm about the mast where it rose through the center of the main top, putting the mast between her and the oncoming monster. Her other hand brought out the Mechanic revolver, holding it so tightly it hurt.

She leveled the weapon as the bird bored in toward her. Maybe if she could hit the Mage riding it, kill him or her, the bird would lose its guidance and fly away.

But as the bird closed the final distance, it went into a stoop to strike at her, extending its huge claws forward, the wings curving out to either side, the chest rising to block Jules' view of the Mage on the monster bird's back.

Hachi had said a person might be to one of the Mage birds as a mouse was to a hawk. It certainly felt that way now, Jules thought, with a sudden sympathy for mice.

At least the bird's enormous chest made for a target that would be very hard to miss, even with the maintop swaying beneath Jules' feet.

Rattled by the approach of the monstrous bird, Jules shot her weapon before she'd intended. But the shot went home, the bird flinching and uttering a scream that seemed to tear the sky in two. One tremendous claw clenched at her as the bird veered off.

Jules watched, her heart pounding, hoping to see the bird fall, but it curved around in a graceful sweep of wings. She might've hurt it, but it was far from out of the fight.

Five shots left.

Holding on tightly to the mast, Jules pivoted to look around for the other bird.

And saw it coming in from behind her, claws already extended.

Jules swung around the mast to put it between her and the massive raptor, bringing her revolver up and firing as soon as it was aimed at the creature.

Another sky-ripping scream sounded as the top of the mast rocked from the strike of the bird. Jules clung to the mast as it jolted, acutely aware of how far down it was to the deck if she fell. As the bird winged away, Jules looked at where the claw had struck, seeing a deep gash in the wood just above where her arm had been clinging to the mast.

The first bird swooped past the side of the ship at about mast height, banking its wings so that the Mage on its back was shielded from the flurry of crossbow bolts fired by the crew from the main deck. Jules thought she saw bolts bouncing off the creature's chest, and others flying harmlessly through the ends of wing feathers.

The huge bird flapped its wings, rising higher at an amazing pace, the Mage on its back looking down toward Jules.

If a Mage can see you, a Mage can kill you.

Why wasn't she already dead?

Jules searched the sky for the second bird, seeing it flying past the bow, the Mage riding it also looking at her.

Why weren't the Mages using spells on her?

Why were they depending on their monster birds to kill her?

Was it too hard to think or do spells when moving at the incredible speed of a bird in flight? How could the Mages even breathe when the air was moving past them so quickly?

More mysteries, more questions with no answers she could ever hope to learn.

The bird that had come around the bow had angled to sweep along the port side. Its wings and chest protected its Mage from being hit by any of the crossbow bolts fired at it, but from where Jules was high on the mainmast she had a clean shot at the Mage.

She'd never tried using the Mechanic weapon to hit a target moving past her so quickly. Her Imperial training on the crossbow had included shooting at targets racing by at the speeds horses could achieve, so she knew she had to lead her target. But the rate at which a horse could gallop was nothing compared to the pace with which the immense birds flew past.

Still, the revolver hadn't done enough damage to the birds. She'd have to risk a shot at the Mage.

Jules' thoughts had taken only a moment of time. She raised the Mechanic revolver, her hand swinging through the air to try to match the movement of the bird as she tried to aim at the right place ahead of the bird despite having no good idea how far ahead that might be.

Her finger tightened on the trigger, the boom of the weapon filling the air.

The bird and the Mage riding it flew on past the stern.

She'd missed. Maybe she hadn't led the target enough. Maybe her aim had been off and the shot had gone over the Mage's head. Jules had no way of knowing.

She had three shots left.

Realizing that she hadn't kept track of where the first bird was, Jules spun about, seeing it stooping in for another strike at her. She jerked herself around the mast again to put it between her and the attack, raising the weapon and shooting just before the bird reached her.

The boom of the weapon and the deafening screech of the huge bird and the crunch of wood as the bird's claws dug into the maintop all seemed to happen at the same time. Instead of striking and flying off, the massive bird clung to its perch, one set of claws digging into and through the wood of the maintop, the other wrapped about the mainmast higher up. Its beak, looking sharp enough and hard enough to shear through the side of one of the metal Mechanic ships, stabbed around the mast at Jules, while its flapping wings buffeted her with the strength of a powerful storm.

The beak closed with a snap so close to her arm that Jules thought she felt the force of it. Terrified as she shifted her grip on the mast, she missed a hold as the wind from the wings tore at her. Grabbing on with both hands to keep from being knocked off the maintop, her grip on the Mechanic revolver slipped. A frantic effort to snag it failed, the weapon dropping from her grasp. Sick inside, Jules watched the weapon fall all the way to the deck, where it landed with a loud thump on the wooden planks.

Despite her fears, the weapon didn't shatter and the two remaining cartridges didn't both shoot at once. Perhaps it still worked, and one of her crew could use it.

She had no time to rejoice in that slim chance though. The huge bird still clung to the mainmast, its wings beating at her, its deadly beak coming around the mast to make another try at her. With nowhere to dodge that beak this time, Jules had no choice but to swing off the maintop, holding onto the shrouds nearest it.

Under the weight and force of the Mage bird perched on the mainmast, the *Sun Queen* heeled far over, the main deck almost awash on the port side as the entire ship tilted. The mainmast groaned under the strain, and shouts of alarm from the sailors on deck came to Jules as they slid to the port rail and clung to it to keep from going overboard.

Jules at the top of the mainmast found herself dangling not over the deck, but way out over the water. The grasp of her boots on the ratlines failed, her feet going out from under her, so that she hung by both hands from the shrouds, the sea far beneath her.

Out of the corner of her eye, she spotted something, turning to look.

The second enormous Mage bird was already stooping for another strike, its claws extended, aiming straight for her to pluck Jules from her precarious hold the way a hawk might yank a squirrel from a tree.

She looked despairingly from one Mage bird to the other, realizing she had only one chance to avoid being caught and killed by one or the other of the huge raptors.

Jules let go her grip on the rigging.

She fell, the second bird uttering an ear-splitting, disappointed squawk as its strike missed.

Jules saw a blur of masts and sails and rigging fly by her gaze, then a momentary view of the side of the *Sun Queen* before her booted feet hit the water hard enough to partly stun her. She went deep from the force of the fall, seeing the water darken around her as a rush of bubbles fled upward. Jules stroked her arms and kicked her legs frantically, trying to follow the bubbles back toward the surface.

She burst back out into the sunlight and air, gasping for breath.

Blinking salt water from her eyes, Jules looked around for the *Sun Queen*, seeing the ship already hundreds of lances from her and moving farther away by the moment. She'd stopped being moved along with the ship as soon as she let go of the rigging, but with all sails set the *Sun Queen* was still moving at the best speed she could manage.

Had the crew seen her fall? Why hadn't they come about already to pick her up? The bird perched on the top of the mainmast had let go, but both creatures were still flying around the ship, making stabs at the rigging and the masts, as if they thought she was still aboard.

How could the birds have missed her fall?

The Mages riding those birds might've missed it, though. Both had been unable to see Jules, their views blocked because of the bulks of their flying mounts. If the birds were responding to orders from the Mages, they might be getting told to keep attacking the ship.

Jules, her thoughts running fast, had just started to think about how to signal the *Sun Queen* when the rush of water behind her and a small wave that lifted her warned of nearer company. She twisted in the water, staring at the looming wooden hull of the sloop they had sighted earlier and forgotten until now. A look up at the deck gave Jules a view of sailors and legionaries in Imperial uniforms looking down at her. Twisting back to swim away, Jules was suddenly surrounded by splashes as men and women with ropes tied around their waists dropped into the water around her.

She groped for her dagger, finding the sheath empty. She'd lost that weapon, too, while fighting the Mages and their birds. Jules struck out with her bare hands at the men and women swarming her in the water, using every skill and dirty trick she knew, including clawing faces, tearing at nostrils, and thumbing eyes. But for every attacker who fell back, another surged forward, grabbing her arms and body until several of them had her tightly pinioned.

Those still on the sloop began hauling in the ropes tied to the swimmers. They rose out of the water in an entwined mass, sliding upward along the side of the ship, Jules struggling vainly to get an arm free and break their grips.

The heap of Jules and her captors tumbled over the railing and onto the deck, giving her a momentary chance to break free, but several of those waiting on deck piled on Jules, pinning her down, their weight driving the breath from her.

"Get her below before those things see her!" a voice ordered.

A voice that sounded a bit familiar.

Despite Jules's struggles, she was hauled to a ladder, the whole group more falling down to the next deck than taking the ladder. Once there, Jules was held tightly by a half dozen burly sailors, unable to move.

"Get us into the cover of one of those storms!" Jules heard a woman order.

Oh, blazes. It was her.

A moment later Captain Kathrin of Law came down the ladder. She paused before Jules, smiling, the scar made by Jules' dagger at Western Port a clear line down the side of her face. "The shoe is on the other foot, isn't it?"

Jules, exhausted from her struggles, just looked back at the Imperial officer.

"I'd love to stay around here and capture that ship of yours," Kathrin said. "But I can't risk any damage to the *Hawk's Mantle*. My orders are very clear, that as soon as anyone gains control of you, they are to proceed as quickly as possible to an Imperial port and hand you over."

Jules finally got enough breath back to speak. "The Mages will know you have me. They'll come through you and your ship and your crew to get at me."

Captain Kathrin shook her head. "You'll have to do better than that. Those Mages didn't see us bringing you aboard, and I got you below decks fast. The Mages have no idea that we have you."

"Fool!" Jules spat. "Do you think Mages are normal people? They don't need to see me to know where I am or where I'm going! If you keep me, they will find this ship and they will destroy it."

"You're unexpectedly boring," Kathrin said, crossing her arms as she looked at Jules. "The Mages will never know the Emperor has you. Let me give you something else to think about. Once we've turned you over to the proper people at Landfall, I'm going to come back out here. I'm going to find that ship of yours, make it my prize, and see every one of your crew hanged. They'll dangle from their nooses along the waterfront at Landfall like ornaments to delight the Emperor."

Jules glared at her. "You're worse than a Mage."

"Why, thank you. A good professional reputation takes a lot of work to maintain, right? Oh, you wouldn't know anything about that, would you?" The captain gestured to those holding Jules. "Get her down to the brig."

The grips on her were so tight that Jules couldn't even try to break free as she was hauled along the deck and down another ladder, then brought aft to where a flickering storm lantern was mounted to a strong bulkhead. Next to the storm lantern a sturdy door held closed by a stout beam marked the entrance to the ship's brig. The door's heavy hinges were on this side, a clear sign that the door was meant not to keep people out, but to keep people in. About eye level on the door was a small window, a grid of iron bars letting through a little light and air but not anything else.

The door was opened and Jules was yanked inside the small compartment, her arms held as manacles fastened to the rear bulkhead were clamped on her wrists.

"Careful there," Captain Kathrin warned her legionaries. "The Emperor doesn't want her damaged. Make them tight enough to hold her but not so tight they cause her harm."

"I was wrong," Jules told her, having to sit on the deck because of where the manacles were chained to the after bulkhead. "You're a humanitarian."

"That hurts." Kathrin inspected the manacles after her crew was done, nodding in approval. "Nice tattoo," she said sarcastically, seeing part of Jules' burn mark visible on her wrist and lower arm.

"That's not a tattoo," Jules said. "It's a scar, from Mage lightning. You should be hoping that you'll be as good at surviving Mage lightning as I am, because you'll be facing that when they come to get me."

That set even Captain Kathrin back for a moment. Finally, she shrugged. "I can deal with anything the likes of you could survive. I'll see you at Landfall."

Jules glared at the captain's back as she left, then paused outside the brig as someone wearing boots approached.

"We're under concealment of the storm?" Kathrin said. "Good. Did those Mages come after us before we lost sight of them? No? You seem to have done acceptable work, Lieutenant. You know we have a visitor. You'll be in charge of her guards. Keep a minimum of two guards on duty at this door at all times. They're not to interact with the prisoner at all, not even a yes or a no. If she gets free, harms herself, or harms anyone else, you will be held accountable. Understood?"

"Yes, Captain."

Jules felt her heart stutter as she heard that second voice. It couldn't be him.

But a moment later the lieutenant stepped into view, looking at Jules with a face that might have been carved from stone. He said nothing before turning away.

Captain Kathrin must have told him how his father had died, fighting Jules.

"Ian! Listen to me, please! Ian!"

The door slammed shut, the beam dropped into place, and she was alone.

Jules gazed in despair at the door to her prison. Captured by the Emperor's minions, no way to escape her potential fate at his hands, her crew possibly not even knowing what had happened to her during the fight with the Mages, herself a sitting duck chained here if the Mages came for her again, and Ian not only one of her captors but believing she'd killed his father on purpose.

As far as worst nightmares went, this had to be about as bad as it got.

* * *

The only means she had of passing the time inside the brig was by noting when the guards outside her door changed. But even that was an uncertain measure, because as time went on sometimes she dozed or lapsed into a daze, unaware of whether the guards had changed. The two meals she was fed might mark the passing of days, but Jules knew that one Imperial technique for disorienting prisoners was to alter the schedule of meals, leaving the prisoner uncertain of how many days had gone by.

The tiny brig remained unchanged, the lantern light ever providing feeble illumination through the bars of the small window in the door. The movement of the ship changed as the sea altered or as the ship tacked, but even that had a relentless monotony to it.

As the captain had ordered, no one spoke to her. During her meals, the door would open and two extra guards would give her bread and a wooden flask of water. They'd watch until she finished, apparently worried that she might try to choke herself to death on the bread. The chamber pot that was the cell's only fixture would be emptied, the extra guards would take back the wooden flask and leave. The door would shut and Jules would be alone again.

She could hear noises on the ship, sometimes the thump of especially loud feet somewhere or shouts, but not enough to learn anything.

Alone in the dark with her thoughts, Jules fought against despair. At least a thousand times the words *I'm sorry, Mak* went through her mind. How could she get out of this? Fate wouldn't care how her line was established, whether it was by a man of her choice or by an Emperor forcing himself on her while she was chained to a bed. Maybe that daughter of her line would wear Imperial dark red and lead the legions against the Great Guilds. But how could that be? The prophecy had said that daughter would free the world. A world controlled by the Empire wouldn't be free. And so she sought consolation in the feeble hope that the prophecy might still point to her escaping what now seemed an inevitable fate.

But maybe she'd done everything the prophecy needed except have a child. And she knew she'd deliberately avoided any encounters that might have produced a child. Not that there should have been any rush—she was still young—but Jules admitted to herself that the prophecy had made it doubly hard to decide on having a child because it was no longer a choice but an obligation.

What if that meant she'd avoid ever having a child if left to herself? What if because of that the prophecy demanded she be forced into having a child to ensure her line was established? The ugly thought kept surfacing, laying responsibility for her current woes on herself.

Jules knew she was blaming herself for something that wasn't her fault, blaming herself for being faced with this, but she couldn't entirely banish the self-accusations that gnawed at her. She knew that

Mak had always felt guilty that his daughter had been taken by the Mechanics and that his wife had died, even though nothing he could have done would've prevented either event. This was the same thing, wasn't it? Thinking something bad happening to her was her fault.

It wasn't true. She didn't deserve this. No one deserved this. She'd fight it.

But in the dark, alone, it was hard to come up with ways of fighting that were anything but fantasies at this point.

Jules tried to imagine ways of killing herself even if chained and unable to reach any weapon. Or ways of killing the Emperor, perhaps locking her teeth in his throat as he lay on her. Those thoughts would bring momentary satisfaction, but after a very short time were both dark and uncomforting, because her odds of success seemed so small.

She'd long since vowed to herself, while enduring life in the Imperial orphanage, that if she ever had children she would love them and protect them no matter what it took. But could she love them if the children were forced on her by the Emperor? Jules sat in the dark, tormented not just by what might happen to her but also by what might happen to the children she didn't yet have.

There finally came a time when the motion of the ship changed from rolling across swells to the mild, gentle rocking of a craft sailing across smooth waters. They must have reached the grand harbor at Landfall. What would they do? Sail the ship up the mighty Ospren river all the way to Marandur? No, that was unlikely. The winds might stall such a journey, and the ship would have to fight the current of the Ospren the whole way, slowing it even if the winds were good. The Emperor wouldn't want to risk any delay in getting her into his hands. The fastest way to Marandur from Landfall would be riding on the Mechanic "train" that ran between the two cities, but there was no way the Imperials would try bundling her unnoticed onto that. They'd be too worried about the Mechanics discovering her and taking her. No, she'd probably be hauled into an armored wagon pulled by teams of strong horses that could bring her to Marandur as quickly as possible.

The thoughts of how she'd reach an awful fate distracted her briefly from the agony of waiting for the ship to come alongside a pier.

She felt the ship slowing. Or was that her imagination? No, the sloop must be taking in sail. After a long wait, she felt a jar and heard the groan of wood from the ship as it settled against a pier. The faint sound of shouted orders carried to her as lines were put across and the sloop securely tied to the bollards on the pier.

Jules gazed at the door to her cell, wishing for a moment that the Mages would still somehow come to kill her and end everything.

She waited for the guards to open the door, wondering what time of day it was. Would she have a chance to see the sunlight before she was confined again? Or was it night?

Shouts came to her, probably on the sloop's deck but loud enough to carry into the brig.

Screams.

The ship lurched suddenly, as if a great weight had been placed on it.

She heard the guards outside the door exchanging worried murmurs.

More calls, shouts, alarms.

Then came a sound she'd never heard before, a discordant roar as if a hundred people were shouting at once in anger but were unable to form any words. Jules felt the hairs on her skin prickling as she stared at the door.

Mages. It had to be Mages attacking.

As the noise outside rose to the din of battle, booted feet came rushing to the brig. "All hands on deck! Now!" Ian's voice ordered.

"But—" one of the guards began.

"Captain's orders, all hands on deck, now!"

The guards took off at a run.

Jules heard the bar across the door being lifted. The door swung open.

Ian stood there, his face still a mask of stone as he looked at her.

Had he come to kill her?

But, after a moment, he pulled out a ring of keys and bent to insert one in the shackle holding one of her hands.

As the shackle fell open, Ian stepped back, tossing the keys at her. "Save yourself."

He'd turned and nearly gone out the door before Jules found her voice. "Ian! Please! I didn't kill him!"

Ian paused in the doorway, his back to her.

"Your father used one of my blades to kill himself, to ensure no dishonor would come to his name and so you and the rest of his family would be safe! I swear that's the truth! I'd never have killed your father, Ian!"

Another moment of hesitation, then Ian bolted away. She heard his boots running across the deck and up the ladder.

Flexing her hand stiffened by being in the shackle for so long, Jules fumbled with the keys, trying to get her other hand free, cursing as her shaking hand had trouble inserting the key into the shackle. But finally it fell free and Jules got to unsteady feet as the ship lurched once more.

She staggered out of the brig, one hand against the nearest bulkhead, moving as fast as she could toward the ladder up to the next deck. This deck was deserted, everyone in the crew probably on deck taking part in the fighting that could be clearly heard. Her legs regained steadiness as she moved, but it was still hard to get up the ladder.

On the next level, just beneath the main deck, the noise of fighting resounded much louder. Light showed through the hatch leading out onto the main deck, but it wasn't sunlight. Instead it flickered with the orange unsteadiness of flame.

Bracing herself at the foot of the ladder, Jules went up onto the deck as fast as she could.

It was night, but there was plenty of light to see by because the bow of the ship was on fire, the flames having already reached the foremast, dancing their way up the mast and racing up along the rigging.

The light silhouetted a massive, horrible sight near the mainmast. Taller than any man or woman, and perhaps three times as broad across, raged a creature with unnaturally long arms ending in massive, malformed hands.

A Mage troll.

As Jules reached the deck and caught sight of it, the troll roared again, the awful noise almost as unnerving as the sight of the creature.

Jules faced the backs of a double row of legionaries and sailors who were facing the creature, Captain Kathrin behind them ordering them into renewed attack. As she watched, the troll swung its long arms at the Imperials, scattering legionaries and sailors as if they were dolls, some striking their captain as they fell so that she went down as well.

That removed one obstacle for a moment, but the monster still stood between her and the pier.

Ian came running from one side, his sword poised, driving the point into the troll's skin. But the sword barely seemed to scratch the beast, which swung a backhand that hurled Ian away.

It was powerful beyond belief, but it was sluggish in its movements.

The troll's eyes rested on Jules as she sprinted forward, breathing fast, terrified.

It reached toward her as she got close, but at the last moment she dropped, sliding across the deck between the legs of the creature that reacted too slowly to grasp her. As Jules scrambled to her feet behind the troll, it pivoted, swinging one huge fist that met the mainmast before it reached her. Splinters flew as the mast shattered. Jules darted toward the pier as the mainmast fell, the snapping of stay lines echoing over the sound of fighting like smaller versions of the noise made by Mechanic weapons.

She leaped over the ship's rail onto the pier, finding herself in the midst of at least a dozen small fights between Mages and legionaries or sailors. As Jules' feet landed on the pier, a small group of nearby legionaries flew in all directions as the wooden planks at their feet exploded in a shower of heat and splinters. One of the legionaries came to rest next to Jules, already dead, one side of her body scorched black with extreme heat. Jules knelt by the body, pulling the legionary's dagger out of its sheath.

Straightening, she found herself facing a Mage who swung his knife at her, his eyes resting on Jules without any visible feeling as he tried to kill her. She managed to parry the knife, then slammed the palm of her hand against the Mage's head hard enough to stagger him.

Backing a step, Jules looked around frantically for a way through the mass of individual fights.

Her eyes met those of a legionary.

"It's her!" he shouted.

Instantly, the many individual melees turned into a single battle, centered on her.

Jules hesitated, seeing no way out, as legionaries and Mages charged toward her from all sides.

Impossibly, a large hole in the formerly solid pier suddenly gaped below the feet of some of the legionaries. They fell through it with cries of shock.

With no other option, Jules dove through the hole after them.

She hit the water, coming up again gasping for air, stunned to see that the hole in the deck of the pier had disappeared as mysteriously and quickly as it had appeared. Legionaries were all about her, but none of them spared a thought for Jules as they all splashed desperately to shed their armor before it dragged them down and drowned them.

Jules lunged toward the side of the pier away from the Imperial sloop that had been her prison. She'd almost reached one of the piles supporting the pier, a thick pillar of wood worn by years of exposure, when Jules saw one of the legionaries who'd fallen through going down for probably the last time. Angry with herself, Jules halted long enough to reach into the water, grab the woman's arm, and pull them both to the pile. Shoving the legionary's hands to the wood, Jules snarled at her. "Hold on to this!"

As the nearly-drowned legionary looked at Jules with dazed eyes, Jules felt around the legionary's belt, finding her dagger and pulling it out to add to the one she already had. Pushing off from the pile, Jules stroked desperately for shore, reaching the sea wall which was a steeply sloping fortification of rocks ranging from big to very large. Pulling herself up onto the rocks, Jules breathed deeply a couple of times, then launched herself up the slope, which fortunately was only about a lance in height between the water and its top.

Rolling onto the waterfront, Jules paused on one knee to stare back at the pier, momentarily paralyzed by the sight. The fire on the sloop had spread along the deck, reaching the fallen mainmast, which was blazing furiously. The foremast formed a pillar of flame rising into the night sky, clearly showing that the troll had fallen through the main deck. It had smashed through the near side of the ship and was now plowing into the side of the pier, massive fists shattering wood and anyone unfortunate enough to be in their way, trying to reach the spot where Jules had dived through the hole that wasn't there. Mages, Imperial legionaries, and sailors were battling on the pier, or trying to escape the flailing of the troll, most of them apparently unaware as of yet that Jules had escaped the melee.

Run, you idiot, Jules told herself as she realized she was staring at the fight instead of getting away.

She came to her feet just in time to see a Mage's long knife coming at her in a thrust, the woman's impassive eyes a strange contrast to the deadly intent of her actions. Jules managed to dodge the thrust, hurling one of her daggers at the Mage. The dagger hit the Mage's throat, though whether it penetrated or got stopped by the Mage's robes Jules couldn't tell. The impact knocked the Mage back and down, though, and Jules vaulted over her and dashed to join the merchant sailors from other ships on the waterfront who were fleeing the area of the fighting.

She wended through the sailors, trying to blend in, as the battle continued to rage behind her. Alarm bells were ringing in the city, calling both firefighters and Imperial police to the site.

Another inhuman bellow from the troll echoed off of nearby buildings. Jules glanced back, seeing that the entire sloop was now engulfed in flames. The troll stood amid the ruins of the pier, still striking out at anything within reach, though the number of Mages on the pier seemed to have dropped dramatically.

If Ian hadn't given her the means to escape her shackles, she'd have still been chained in the brig of the sloop when the troll finished smashing its way through the ship to reach her. Or she'd have been chained in there when the fire got far enough aft to consume the brig.

Had Ian survived? Had he made it off the sloop? Would Imperial commanders blame him for her escape even though it had been the only thing that had prevented her from dying inside that brig?

And he'd done that, run that risk, even while believing that she'd chosen to kill his father.

Which led to a thought of Captain Kathrin, who'd probably told Ian that Jules had boasted of killing his father. If she was alive, was she bitterly remembering Jules' warning that the Mages would destroy her ship to get at Jules? The thought of that was almost enough for Jules to wish Kathrin had survived the attack.

Shoving those thoughts aside to concentrate on escaping, Jules followed a stream of refugees from the fighting onto a side road leading away from the waterfront. She hadn't gone very far down that road when she saw Imperial police ahead, arriving and forming a line to seal off the area. That's what they did in such cases, she knew, forming a tight perimeter and then arresting everyone inside it on the theory that they must all be guilty of something.

Which meant she couldn't be found inside the police lines.

Frantic sailors fleeing the troll and the Mages were coming up against the line of police, battering at them and making a mess of their line. Jules went for what seemed to be the biggest gap, and had almost made it through when a heavy hand fell on one of her shoulders. She pivoted, looking at a large police officer whose eyes widened as he stared at her. There were far too many Imperial wanted posters with drawings of her on them, Jules thought as she slammed the dagger she still held into the police officer's chest. The force of her thrust and the blade of the dagger easily penetrated the leather chest armor of the officer, piercing his heart. She pulled out the dagger as the officer unsuccessfully tried to yell, staggering and falling. Jules squirmed through the mess of sailors, trying to avoid being seen, as more shouts arose where the police officers were now wielding their hardwood clubs with abandon on the sailors trying to get past them.

Another street, the fleeing crowds bigger now as citizens who lived in this part of the city also fled as word and rumor spread of a battle involving Mages and one of their monsters. Spotting a woman wearing a cloak with a hood, Jules worked her way through the mob until she was next to the woman. Tripping her, Jules went down along with the woman as if they were falling together, but really aiming to ensure that her head hit the cobblestones hard enough to stun. Using the threat of her dagger to create a small, momentary gap in the panicky crowd, Jules yanked off the woman's cloak and pulled it on. Grabbing the still-stunned woman's arm, Jules pulled her to the side of the street where she wouldn't be trampled, then rejoined the mass of people running away from the water.

She was alone, in an Imperial city, surrounded by who knew how many hundreds or thousands of legionaries and Imperial sailors, all of whom would be looking for her. Of the thousands and thousands of citizens in Landfall, many would turn her in immediately if they recognized her, either in hopes of reward or out of loyalty to the Emperor. Any citizens who sympathized with her would be too scared to help her. And the Mages knew she was here, and would quickly learn that neither the troll nor any of the other Mages at the waterfront had managed to kill her.

But she'd escaped another cage. She was alive, she was free, and she had a dagger.

That would have to be enough.

She would escape this city, she would make it back to the sea, or die trying.

ABOUT THE AUTHOR

"Jack Campbell" is the pseudonym for John G. Hemry, a retired Naval officer who graduated from the U.S. Naval Academy in Annapolis before serving with the surface fleet and in a variety of other assignments. He is the author of The Lost Fleet military science fiction series, as well as the Stark's War series, and the Paul Sinclair series. His short fiction appears frequently in *Analog* magazine, and many have been collected in ebook anthologies *Ad Astra, Borrowed Time,* and *Swords and Sadwdles.* He lives with his indomitable wife and three children in Maryland.

Don't miss the adventure that started
it all...

THE DRAGONS
OF DORCASTLE

PILLARS OF REALITY ✹ BOOK 1

JACK
CAMPBELL

NEW YORK TIMES BESTSELLING AUTHOR

FOR NEWS ABOUT JABBERWOCKY BOOKS AND AUTHORS

Sign up for our newsletter*: http://eepurl.com/b84tDz
visit our website: awfulagent.com/ebooks
or follow us on twitter: @awfulagent

THANKS FOR READING!